WEDLOCK

By

JACOB WASSERMANN

Translated by LUDWIG LEWISOHN

BONI & LIVERIGHT

NEW YORK · MCMXXVI

WEDLOCK

WEDLOCK

PART I

I

THE young man came for the second time that evening. He requested the maid to give his card to Mrs. Laudin and to ask her whether he might wait for the doctor. The card was not a very clean one; the words printed on it were: Konrad Lanz, Student of Chemistry.

Pia Laudin was just crossing the hall. She threw a casual glance at the card and an equally casual one at the poorly dressed man of about twenty-four who stood before her in his muddy boots and wet trousers and raincoat.

"My husband will probably be late," she said, and added with an overtone of distrust, "Do you want to consult him in his professional capacity?"

"Yes, in his professional capacity, Mrs. Laudin," was the hesitating answer, supported by a beseeching look.

"Then you had better go to his office. My husband is so intensely occupied all day that it is impossible for him to receive clients at home in the evening."

"Mrs. Laudin," the caller stammered, "I, too, alas, am free only in the evening. I give private lessons . . . I would lose pupils. . . . The matter is so very pressing. . . . Moreover, I have known Dr. Laudin for a long time. . . . In the office they might not let me see him personally. . . . And to explain this affair to one of the other gentlemen . . . I have no confidence in any one but him. Do let me wait, Mrs. Laudin."

[7]

Pia Laudin reflected. She felt very sorry for the young man. She turned to the maid who, full of curiosity, had remained standing in the kitchen door and said, "Take the gentleman into the library."

She herself went into the living room where her daughters Marlene and Relly, fifteen and thirteen years old respectively, were sitting at a table working at their lessons. If Pia did not look after them occasionally they lost themselves in endless conversations and could not keep their father company during his belated meal. And he set store by that.

"Fancy, children, the apples have come," she called out to the girls. "A great sack full of red-cheeked apples. Tomorrow you can store them in the pantry."

"That will be jolly," said Relly, and threw down her penholder. "Can't we do it this evening? I need some relief from this stupid geometry. Where is the bag? In the hall?"

"You stay where you are," Pia answered, and controlled an impulse to laugh. All of Relly's expressions were of an explosive suddenness; often one could hardly understand what she was saying, her tongue ran on so swiftly. "I don't want you girls to be running up and down when father comes home and he may be here any moment now. He doesn't like it. By the way, have you been upstairs to see grandmother? You must keep her company for half an hour. But one of you at a time. Together you are too much for her."

Marlene looked up from her copy book. "This Cato, mother, is the most disgusting creature in the whole world," she said. "I can't endure his pretentious virtue. Austere? I consider him a hypocrite. Such people have always existed apparently for the purpose of bringing decency into disrepute."

"I can't understand such talk," Relly broke in with an injured and belligerent air. "Why, he's a historical personage and surely one must respect historical personages."

"Why?" Marlene asked. "Why must one? That's mere prejudice. All these obligations are prejudices."

[8]

Relly was about to be indignant, but her mother told her to be quiet. "Don't fight about Cato now," she said; "see to it that you get through with your lessons. And Marlene, you had better keep such revolutionary sayings to yourself."

Far away, beyond several doors, was heard the crying of a baby. "Ah, ha, the dwarf Uistiti is making himself unpleasantly noticeable," said Marlene, wrinkling her nose. This was the name by which, among themselves, half in tenderness and half in contempt, the sisters called their little fourteen-months-old brother Hubert.

Pia looked at her wrist watch. "It's eight o'clock," she murmured. "I must see that he gets his bath. Now no more about Cato, please, and don't forget grandmother, either."

"Mother can hardly stand, she's so worn out," Relly said, when Pia had left the room. "I should hate to run a house. And I could never be as heroic about it as mother is. Other women sigh and are as cross as two sticks. They always want you to be astonished at what they accomplish; they want you to say: poor woman, how she has to plague herself. But mother is serene from early until late and never takes it out on any one when things go wrong, and if ever she has a headache she locks herself up in her room and doesn't even tell father. I think that's truly heroic. Don't you?"

Thoughtfully Marlene moved her head from side to side. "Yes," she answered, "but if you go on chattering you will never get done."

Relly, however, who was passionately attached to her mother, would not permit herself to be interrupted. With dancing eyes and red cheeks she leaned far over the table and continued: "It starts early in the morning. The cook comes to ask what is to be the menu of the day. Next comes the grocer with his bills. Then the telephone rings. Then the linen must be counted. Then the electrician comes. Then the telephone rings again. Then the dwarf roars. Then the chauffeur turns up and wants information. Then she has to see whether the silver has been polished. Next the nurse comes and asks whether the dwarf is to be taken out. Long conferences. Then comes the dressmaker because our frocks have to be attended to. Then grandmother sends word that mother is to play a game of dominoes with her. The telephone again, the ladies from the charity association, the——"

"For heaven's sake, shut up," Marlene cried, laughing, and put her fingers in her ears.

But when Relly was once well started it was not so easy to stop the flow of her discourse. With astonishing agility of speech, she continued, "And so it goes on day after day and year after year. Cooking, baking, washing, roasting, mending, sweeping, dusting—she has to superintend everything and think of everything. And when father opens the door of the house everything must be as fresh as new paint. There must be friendly faces and no speck of dust. The table must be set and the food exquisite and the fires going and everything in its right place and he doesn't dream of the trouble it has all cost. I can't imagine how mother stands it. And she stands it so well, too! After all, she is thirty-six and when you look at her you could quite believe her to be no more than twenty-three. She doesn't have to bedizen herself like Mrs. Arndt or put on rouge like Mrs. Kadelka. Mother is just beautiful."

Relly drew herself up and her face was proud.

"Yes, she is a beautiful woman," Marlene agreed, somewhat reservedly.

2

When Pia came from the room of her youngest she heard resounding laughter from the lower floor. She was almost immediately enlightened as to its cause. Relly had not been able to deny herself the pleasure of examining the bag of apples. The apples were the gift of friends who lived in the country; Relly had spent many pleasant days with those friends and the fruit was like a message to her. She carefully undid the loosened rope and the bag opened and collapsed; it was too late to do anything and dozens of apples rolled out on the floor. She cried out and Marlene joined her and the maid rushed from the kitchen and all three, kneeling on the floor, started merrily hunting the apples.

The confusion was at its height when the hall door opened and Dr. Laudin appeared. "Well, well," he murmured in good-natured surprise, "what are you doing there?"

The excited merriment grew calm. Pia greeted her husband, accompanied him to the bathroom, rang for the maid, told her to serve, brought forth her husband's silk dressing-gown, gave him a casual report of the events of the day— Laudin had not been home since morning—and did her best to emphasize the agreeable and minimize the annoying. What she said was not significant but merely the objective summing up of the mother and the housewife.

She had a gentle and at the same time careful voice which began each sentence in a somewhat deep key and then melodiously rose higher. She used exclusively the commonest words in the simplest order. But her face had an expression of the most winning sweetness which was further intensified by the peculiar radiance of the large, gray eyes and the unclouded smoothness of the brow.

She sat down at table with him while he was taking his meal. She herself had already dined with the children; that was the rule of the house, since no one ever knew when Laudin would come home. Sometimes it was ten o'clock, sometimes even later. She sat as quietly as she spoke, almost modestly, and as though she had been idle all day and had spent the evening merely waiting for her husband. Her hands were folded in her lap, her head gently inclined toward the left; her wheat blond hair was fastened in a simple knot in the back. It was unusually abundant.

Marlene sat at her mother's right, Relly at her left. Both

regarded their father silently, the younger girl with a sincere and trustful expression behind which there was a gleam of the cunning of a gamine; the older with clear and attentive eyes which nothing escaped. She followed a certain movement of the folds and lines upon his vast arched protruding forehead, which she had often noticed and which seemed to employ her thoughts more than ordinarily. Everything in this face was familiar to her: the veiled eyes that seemed, out of a kind of shame, to avoid looking at any one for more than a moment, the broad fleshy nose, the mouth shadowed by a thick mustache, the round good-natured chin and the thick brown hair in which there was as yet no thread of gray. It was in every respect a generously modeled face, pale with work, stamped by the labor of thought, the parts flowing together in a captivating harmony.

There was a twitching upon Marlene's lips as though she wanted to say: if only I knew what goes on inside of you; I would give a great deal to know what you are keeping from us. She had had this expression for weeks, but no one had observed it.

Laudin said: "Fraundorfer wants to dine with us on Sunday. He seemed to be very anxious about it and so of course I invited him. I hope you don't mind, Pia. He intends, moreover, to ask you by telephone."

"He hasn't called up yet," Pia answered. She smiled and nodded toward Marlene. "I'm perfectly willing, but Marlene doesn't seem to be very well pleased."

"But father knows that I don't like Dr. Fraundorfer very well," Marlene hastened to declare, and blushed. "He's frightfully clever and cultivated, I know, but nothing in the world is sacred to him. And then it's horrible, too, the way he drinks. The other day on Hallowe'en when he was dining with us, he emptied a whole bottle of wine by himself, and as if that weren't enough he asked for cognac."

Relly's eyes were amazed. But whether she admired her

sister's temerity or rather deprecated it one could not well say.

"Ah, you children," Laudin answered. "You are so ready to pass judgment. What do you know about a man like Egyd Fraundorfer. He has his reserves; you can't reach his ultimate I. And as for things sacred—precisely what is 'sacred'? Does one carry it about for show? But consider for a moment his relation to Nicolas, his son. Think of all the love behind that, the shy and secret love, the almost romantic love. You must go beyond mere words."

Marlene hung her head. Relly smiled in triumph.

Laudin, too, smiled now. "To be sure, if I brought Nicolas to you, you'd like that a great deal better, Marlene," he said, teasing her.

Marlene nodded so that her braids danced and looked at her father with radiant eyes. "I do like him, that's true," she said. And Relly seemed to share this taste, for she, too, blushed.

"Not too much, I hope," Laudin answered. "I'm afraid, too, that the competition is too strong for you. The boy lives wholly for his music. I saw in the paper yesterday, that next week he is going to conduct at the choral society for the first time. Quite a respectable career at eighteen."

He had finished his meal, laid down his knife and fork and, smiling, drew from his coat pocket a little donkey made of rubber. "This is for Hubert," he said. "I bought it for him to-day to have the pleasure of seeing him play with it." He put the toy on the table.

"Again," Pia cried with affectionate reproof. "But you just brought him the chimes. Look, Frederick, you're spoiling him thoroughly."

"Spoiling him?" asked Laudin, and shook his mighty head. "On account of this little toy? Dear God! Consider, Pia, by the time the boy is fifteen and we are able to have an insight into the results of his bringing up, I shall be sixty-three. Or we had better say would be sixty-three. For it is, of course, uncertain whether I live that long. So drop the little rubber donkey into the scale of our evil possibilities, my dear." He kissed her hand.

The words were jesting, but there was a darkness in their depth which all seemed to feel. "I didn't mean it that way," Pia said soothingly. Then she added, "I have a disagreeable surprise for you. A young man has been waiting for you in the library since half past seven. His name is Konrad Lanz. He would not be put off, and insisted on seeing you at any cost. You know I haven't the heart to turn people away; it's a fault, and I see from your expression that I should have done so. Forgive me."

"Yes, Pia, one must have a refuge somewhere," Laudin answered with perceptible reproachfulness. "But since the thing has happened I had better attend to the man at once." He arose, nodded to Pia and the girls and went out.

Konrad Lanz sat crouching in a corner of the great library which was illuminated by the light of a single bulb. When Laudin entered he arose hastily and went up to him and said: "I beg you to forgive my boldness, Doctor. I know how precious your time is in every sense. But I didn't know to whom else to turn——"

"I don't see, however, Mr. Lanz, why you didn't take the usual way," Laudin interrupted him, dryly; "like every worker, I am entitled to my hours of rest."

The young man bowed shyly. "I have tried to explain to Mrs. Laudin and to offer her my excuses," he said. "I can continue my studies only by giving private lessons. From seven in the morning until seven in the evening I cannot freely dispose of my time without suffering severely as a result. I am wholly without means, wholly; my sister Caroline, whom I must now support, too, is equally destitute. So I thought that if I were to appear in the office of so well-known an advocate as yourself I should be sailing under the false colors of a client who can pay a fee. And to confess my poverty there seemed to me a more impudent procedure than to present myself privately as a suppliant. I considered this the more honest way. Then, too, I was afraid that I would not get to you personally. And for all these reasons and also because I have known you for a long time and have confidence in no one but you, I—I ventured——"

"Really? You say we've known each other for a long time? How?" Laudin once more interrupted the nervous flow of the student's words. He pointed to a chair. But Lanz did not see that gesture; he drew a deep breath and continued somewhat more calmly. "Eleven years ago I lived with my parents in Wasa Street in the same house with you, Doctor. I saw you almost daily when I started for school in the morning. You came down the stairs with a brief-case and this brief-case inspired me with the highest respect, with something like awe. To me it was the symbol of everything mysterious. It would often happen that I would wait for you at the door, at the risk of being late to school, only that I might have a glance at your brief-case. But that isn't everything, that isn't the main thing. . . ." He hesitated.

Suddenly Laudin observed him more sharply. "I remember," he said, and laid his index finger diagonally across his chin. "Lanz . . . Lanz. . . . Wasn't your father a book-keeper? Wasn't he employed by a firm in St. Margaret's? The firm failed. . . . Your father had invested his savings in the business. . . . It was a fraudulent bankruptcy. . . ."

"It is most kind of you to remember all that," said Konrad Lanz. "You stood by my father at that time in the most magnanimous way, and succeeded in forcing the creditors to repay him a great part of his money. My father's gratitude was boundless and without your help I could not have continued at college. You helped my sister, too, and got her a position. She was almost twenty at that time. My parents, to be sure, fared worse and worse and two years later died at almost the same time."

Laudin's features had lost their cool reserve. "Sit down,"

he said to Konrad Lanz, "and tell me exactly what brings you to me now."

3

"It concerns my sister Caroline," Lanz began, "but I must tell things in their proper order and so I had better begin with the farm of Hartmannshof and with Hartmann and his wife.

"Out there near Kottingbrunn, not in the village itself, but on the road that leads to the mountain, there is an estate, a country house with farm lands, which belong to a certain Hartmann and is therefore called Hartmannshof. It was the ancestral estate of Hartmann's parents. During the political collapse and the period of inflation, he succeeded, by some lucky strokes of business, in saving a moderate fortune. Before the war he had been a builder in the country; he had repaired houses and built new roofs. But he had given up this occupation and now served in several communal offices. For instance, he was fire inspector and an expert on assessments. For years his health had been poor.

"He had never lived very harmoniously with his wife, whose name is Brigitte, but it had come to no open conflict. She was a city woman; before her marriage she had been a governess. She had always considered herself above the other women on the farms. Yet she seems to have been a capable manager, one of those who attend thoroughly to their affairs and in whose household there is no waste. Hartmann had already passed his fortieth year, had lived with the woman for nine years and had two boys of six and eight, when a dull dissatisfaction, if you want to call it that, became increasingly more intense. He would wander aimlessly about the neighborhood; he would neglect his obligations, and was unable to apply himself steadily to any task. He avoided ever being alone with his wife and it appeared gradually that during all this time he nursed a single thought which slowly ripened into a plan of action. He went to his wife one day and proposed to her that they should part forever.

"The woman could not understand what was going on within him. He was a simple-hearted person in her opinion. And indeed he was that, but not in the manner in which she thought. In addition she considered him secretive; she ascribed a certain furtiveness to him and, from all descriptions, I cannot help thinking that he must have been afflicted with a very special kind of sensitiveness which made him seem, as it were, to be lying in ambush, especially in Brigitte's eyes. She was profoundly convinced that he must have a definite motive for demanding the divorce and zealously took to spying on him in order to catch him in that infidelity which, according to her way of thinking, she was bound to assume. But her trouble was in vain. Finally, in fact, she was forced to give up this hope and the man became accordingly ever more mysterious to her, so that she finally declared he was crazy. In the meantime no day passed in which he did not speak of their separation; he said his present life was unendurable to him; it must be changed; he must have his freedom.

"The woman wanted to restore a semblance of peace and because she thought that he would not consent to her conditions, she said finally: very well, I shall get a divorce, but first you must make Hartmannshof over to me. He was taken aback; he did not know what to answer. Next day he said: I will think about it. He thought about it for a week and came to her and tried to make her moderate her demand or consent to a sharing of the estate. But she was not even satisfied to have the transfer of the property included, as is customary, in the decree of divorce; no, she declared that first she must have the house. Afterwards, one could discuss other things. So Hartmann went with her to a notary and together they went to the record office and had the house inscribed in her name.

"When this had been done, she journeyed to the city and took counsel with a lawyer. Hartmann thought that everything was on the way to being solved now. But he was greatly in error. With the help of the lawyer the woman began a long intrigue of mere delay and false promises. At last she came with a new demand. She wanted two hundred millions * for herself and her children. She said that she could not live and support her children on the property alone; she had to have the cash, too. It was a clear case of blackmail and Hartmann did not know what to reply. Horror overcame him. The woman's greed destroyed whatever bond there may ever have been between them—so he himself expressed it later—and left her nothing but his contempt. His only wish was to break that chain. Possessions and property were indifferent to him, if he could only get back his own life again, and so he did not take the trouble to engage in contradiction or conflict but once more did the woman's will. During the time that followed, Brigitte, precisely as she had done after the house had been turned over to her, made hypocritical preparations toward fulfilling her promise. And it was in this interval that Hartmann made the acquaintance of my sister Caroline. We have an aunt living out there, the widow of a tax collector who lives on her pension as best she can. My sister spent the winter with this aunt. Her health was impaired; she had worked in a dressmaker's establishment for several years and her lungs had become affected. I won't praise Caroline; she isn't exactly pretty and the years have made her fade a little, but she is good and compassionate and has brains, too. Not a week had passed since they had first seen each other before they became inseparable. Hartmann had a deep trust in Caroline. She had the strength or the gift of making his oppressed soul feel erect once more,

* The time of the story is that of the monetary inflation in Central Europe. The two hundred millions were in paper crowns and equaled twenty thousand Austrian schillings of the present stabilized currency or (about) two thousand eight hundred dollars.

and of filling him with a new confidence. But, as was natural, his constitution had been deeply shaken. Now came these new and strong emotions. It was a cold, moist winter. Hartmann fell seriously ill and, as fate would have it, on a day when Brigitte had journeyed to the city once more in order to consult her attorney. She had taken the boys with her. On the same day the maid-servant had run away; the woman had had a quarrel with her. Hartmann was alone and his fever rose. With difficulty he communicated with a neighbor and begged him to send word to Miss Lanz, who was living in such-and-such a place. Caroline came. She called in a physician. She nursed him. For four days she did not leave his bedside more than ten minutes. It was pneumonia. One may well say that she snatched him from the claws of death. The crisis was passed and the fever subsiding, when Brigitte appeared. She saw the situation at a glance. First of all she ordered Caroline to leave the house. She said: This is my house. Then she covered Hartmann with jeers. Ah, ha, liar that you are, and play-actor, she cried out, at last I have you; at last I have tracked you down. She talked herself into a greater and greater rage, partly because it was pleasant to her to be able for once to vent all the rancor that was in her. Up to now, she cried, she had let him lead her around by the nose and for the children's. sake she had good-naturedly borne with his wicked goings on. Why, at times she had been stupid enough to believe in his innocence. Now, however, that the whole fraudulent business had come to the light of day, there could, of course, be no further question of a divorce and she intended to inform her attorney of that decision at once.

"She stuck to that. Hartmann knew that he had nothing to hope for. He knew her. He knew, too, now, that her intention had always been the same. She had simply cheated him. A week later, since he felt well on the road to recovery, he got up by night, sat down at a table and wrote a will in which he left all the money which he still possessed and which was deposited in securities in a bank in the city to his friend, Caroline Lanz. After the necessary deductions in favor of his children there would still have remained one hundred and fifty million crowns. This was the sum he named to Caroline before his death. Very well. He signed the document, put it in the drawer of his old desk, locked the drawer and had the feeling that he had provided for Caroline. Obviously there exist states of mind which are satisfied by the existence of a mere document. Three or four days later he packed his belongings into a valise, waited till evening came, and went away. At the railroad station Caroline met him and they journeyed on together. . . .

"They settled down in Styria. Hartmann had old friends there. He found a position in a cabinetmaker's establishment. He kept the books and made out the bills. He became so popular among the workingmen that they chose him as their spokesman. He earned as much as he and Caroline needed. They lived in a little apartment on the edge of the city. At the end of the year a child was born to them. He was happier than he had been on any other day of his life; but you could tell that only from his eyes and gestures, for he had grown more silent than ever. He did all his work with the greatest ease. I happened to see him at this time. He would often look at Caroline as though he wanted to thank her for having met him. I believe that no breath of turbidness would have clouded his soul had he been able wholly to forget the years spent with his first wife. But he could not do that. When I was visiting them, he and I took a walk together and he said to me: I used often to think of death and sometimes wish that death would come to me; now my whole desire is to live and each day seems too short. That, you see, was unluckily the reason why the will which he had left at Hartmannshof slipped so entirely from his mind. It didn't even occur to him to renew it; he could easily have secured the position of Caroline and their child by means of a second draft. Her position would be very different now.

"But I mustn't become too diffuse. He came home one evening from the factory with a violent chill; he went to bed and lost consciousness at once. It was not until the middle of the night that he regained it for some minutes. During that brief space a terror overcame him that he would not have time enough to explain to Caroline about the will. Hitherto he had not been able to bring himself to do so and had put it off from day to day. Every evocation of his former condition had become repulsive to him and his disinclination to think of death and of the end of his happiness was great. But he had this last chance to tell her everything, to state the sum in question with exactness and to give her the key to his desk. Then he sank back among the pillows and twelve hours later he was dead.

"It is useless to describe my sister's state of mind. It is easy to imagine. Brigitte was, of course, informed of Hartmann's decease; she arrived in great haste, snatched all the possessions of the dead man, his clothes, linen, shoes, watch, ring, and departed in equal haste. Caroline, in her grief, had no thought of resistance and the woman did not even stay for the funeral. Caroline and her child came to the city to me—luckily I could give them a little garret room—and when she had recovered from her first despair I said to her: You must go out to Kottingbrunn and fetch the will. So on a Sunday two weeks ago, she took the child on her arm and went out there. I wanted to accompany her but she said, no. I must go alone, she said. Well, she reached the place and asked to speak to the woman of the house. The two boys were standing by the door and staring at her. After a while Brigitte appeared. My sister stated her business. The woman looked at her up and down, looked at the child asleep in Caroline's arms and said coldly: If you please, there's nothing in the way of it; go right up and fetch the rag your-self; if ever it was in the drawer it will be there now. Caro-line mounted the stairs and heard the woman's coughing behind her. They came into the room, Caroline laid the child on a bed, took out the key and wanted to unlock the drawer. But she saw at once that the drawer was not locked at all. In it there lay a little pile of papers; Caroline took the papers out and examined each one. There were receipts, a few letters, a few sketches for buildings, but no will. The other drawers were empty and had no locks at all.

"Caroline looked at the woman; the woman looked at Caroline. Neither said a word. Caroline's limbs began to tremble and she had to lean against the old desk; all the blood flowed to her heart because she knew, now, that she and her child were doomed to misery and want. Brigitte had folded her naked arms; she had been kneading dough and her skin was white with flour. About her thin-lipped mouth hovered a repressed smile as though she wanted to say: What proof have you? What can you lay at my door?

"And so Caroline went away again. And that is all that took place. And now I ask you, Doctor, is there no way of forcing the woman to give up the will? Consider the situa-tion of my sister. She is utterly helpless with her little child. She is but a shadow of her former self. She cannot think of working. And as far as I am concerned, the best I can do is to pay the rent and buy some bread and a little milk for the baby. What is one to do? On the one hand, Doctor, there is clear justice; on the other hand, there is a wrong that cries to heaven. What can one do?"

4

Laudin reflected for many minutes. Then he said: "First of all, I must warn you not to harbor any illusions. The woman has unquestionably destroyed the will; hence she cannot give it up."

"But she cannot deny its having existed," the young man cried.

"Why should she not deny it?" Laudin answered, shrugging his shoulders. "Since she did not shrink from suppressing it, why should she now hesitate to deny its existence? How are you going to prove that the will ever existed, that it was, in fact, ever drawn up? But even if that can be proved, how will you bring the additional proof of her having had knowledge of it? One statement would be confronted by another and your sister had no witnesses who were present when Hartmann made his last dispositions."

Konrad Lanz looked at the lawyer as though he had expected a miracle and was now being fed on the harsh disillusion of facts. Laudin smiled at the young man's depression. "I am a lawyer and must stick to the facts," he said. "Were I an unerring searcher out of the truth or but a little more gifted in that respect, I would not have to point out those wearisome paths which soon discourage all, or at least most of those who seek a road to justice. Nevertheless, your case interests me. Not only on your account personally, but for impersonal reasons, too. I will see what can be done." He took a notebook out of his pocket and wrote a few words in it. "To-day is Thursday. Could you get off for two or three hours on Saturday morning? Good! I think your presence is important. Be in my office at ten o'clock. The car will be waiting and we will drive out to Kottingbrunn. It is most probable that we shall find Mrs. Hartmann at home so early in the day."

Lanz stammered, "How can I thank you, Doctor. . . . It's a real sacrifice. . . ."

Laudin waved the thanks aside. He arose and accompanied Lanz to the door. There he stopped for a moment. "I can see that woman," he said; "I know that woman, trait by trait and I know what she is going to say, word by word.

It is a type that is to be found in all its varieties and that is multiplying at an appalling rate."

"Undoubtedly you know the type, Doctor, but I am afraid that this individual example will furnish you with surprises," the student said shyly.

Laudin nodded. "That is precisely what these individuals have a habit of doing. Good night. Remember—Saturday at ten."

Pia had already gone to her room. When he entered she was sitting before her mirror and combing her hair which, despite its length and abundance, yielded obediently to every gesture of her hand. She turned to him the calm light of her eyes in which there was no shadow of questioning or curiosity in regard to his late caller and said: "It has taken a long time."

"Yes, it has," he sighed, and drooped into an armchair.

"You must be tired, Friedrich. Go to rest now. I have had an apple and a glass of milk put beside your bed."

"Your thoughtfulness puts me to shame, dearest Pia," Laudin said in a tone that was obviously wearier than he had meant it to be; "I had intended bringing you flowers. But when I left the office I found the shops closed. That's the misfortune of people who have to confine their chivalrousness to mere theory."

"Well, instead of that, you bought the little rubber donkey for your son," Pia answered, and looked at him jestingly.

"She forgets nothing, this woman," Laudin lamented in mock despair. "She forgets nothing." Suddenly, he took his handkerchief and pressed it to his face. When he looked at it he found it full of blood that had come from his nose. He ascertained by a glance that Pia had not noticed this. He arose and kissed her very carefully on the forehead and left the room. She heard him cheerfully whistling a tune from an operetta and nodded to him in spirit. But before he could have reached his room the whistling broke off abruptly in the midst of the melody and silence fell.

5

In the upper story of the villa were the children's rooms. In one of them lived little Hubert with his nurse; in the room opposite lived Marlene and Relly.

Marlene sat in her white nightgown at the table and wrote in a copy book which was marked "Diary." Her pretty round little head with its rounded cheeks, round little nose, its forehead like her father's and its mouth that had both charm and expressiveness, was bent over the page. She kept her eyes as close to the paper as a child learning to write. Her two thick ash-blond braids hung down on both sides as far as the legs of the chair.

Relly lay in bed with her arms folded behind her head and winked wearily. "When will you be through with your scribbling?" Her voice broke the long silence resonantly. "I want to go to sleep."

"Who keeps you from sleeping, little roughneck?" Marlene asked in her clear, gentle voice. "Do you have to scold? Why don't you sleep? I'm as quiet as a mouse."

"In the first place, mice are not quiet," Relly replied belligerently. "In the second place, your pen scratches, and in the third place, this whole business of scribbling irritates me. Why do you always have to be writing? I don't understand.

"And because you don't understand it, you try to pick a quarrel," Marlene answered with a smile in which there was the calmness of her sense of superiority. "I've explained to you over and over that I try to account to myself for things, and that's why I write down whatever interests me. If no one else will answer my questions I must seek an answer myself. You, of course, have no ambition to keep your thoughts in order. You let them come and go. But that's not being any more responsible than the baby."

"Oh . . . but that's . . ." Relly was enraged and unable to find a proper characterization. "I really don't know what to call that!"

"You mean I'm trying to be grown up and didactic," Marlene answered mockingly, "and so you want to convince me by the method of the 'Upper Dogs' who fight with indignation and not with logic!"

"Upper Dogs" was an expression which Relly herself had invented and which meant: dignified grown-up ladies and gentlemen who feed young girls on moral precepts and irrational remonstrances.

Relly leaped up. Her honest blue eyes flashed. It enraged her horribly to be put on the same plane with the Upper Dogs whose lack of sincerity and sound reason in controversy often made her so indignant that Marlene, more restrained by nature, had difficulty in soothing her. Because, of course, in the presence of the Upper Dogs it was necessary to behave oneself. One had to pay them the respect that seemed to be their due and thus one fell into a condition which was a painful blending of apparent attention and inner scorn.

Relly was not a girl who could accept an unjust reproach in silence. She defended her view that it was an unseemly thing to attribute an undue importance to your own affairs even in the privacy of your thoughts. To be sure, you had to gather experiences, but you mustn't be always analyzing and criticizing. To observe was one thing. But it was sheer spiritual arrogance to try to make generalizations. Also it was confusing. You should watch life and act from inevitable impulse, not on the basis of a scheme laid down on paper.

She grew violent, even insulting, and in her youthful vigor recoiled from no energy of expression. But she was Marlene's equal only in the tempo of her speech; in all other respects she cut a sorry figure. For Marlene was precise and subtle and could arrange her words like a very rhetorician. Thus Relly lost ground constantly like one who should oppose an agile fencer with an awkward club. And, of course, this circumstance increased her vexation and when she saw that she had lost the argument she threw herself back among the pillows, turned her face to the wall, pulled the coverlet over her ears and lapsed into stubborn silence.

Marlene, too, had grown warm in the course of the dispute; her cheeks and ears glowed. She seemed to regret the wounding observations by which she had challenged her sister. She seemed about to make efforts toward reconciliation; but she got no farther than a peaceful clearing of her throat. Relly paid no attention to her; soon she stirred no more and Marlene gave up any further attempts.

The vivid discussion had not been confined to the matter of its original starting-point. The question whether Marlene had the right to record and analyze and pass a written judgment on her conflicts with the world, her opinions and experiences, had of necessity led to a dispute concerning those conflicts themselves, concerning those small, profound, intense and usually very secret experiences, and had thrown upon them a more or less treacherous light.

First of all Relly had criticized Marlene for her insolence in edifying their father with her opinion concerning Dr. Egyd Fraundorfer. What made her do it? What right had she? Surely she had seen how disagreeable that had been to their father; she was aware that Dr. Fraundorfer was father's best friend. Marlene seemed to be crushed for a moment. Then, with an assumed innocence, she could not help asking her sister whether in this matter she was not substituting moral indignation for jealousy? Unconsciously, of course; she didn't accuse her of actual craftiness. But she had grown red as a cherry when her father had teased her about Nicolas Fraundorfer. . . . Relly flared up and defended herself violently against this perfidious suspicion. "Oh," she cried, and "Goodness gracious!" She, Relly, jealous! She asked Marlene to have the kindness to recall how shamelessly she herself had flirted with Nicolas the other day when he had sat playing the piano. She, jealous? Surely she had something better to think of. Now, if Marlene were to accuse her bosom friend, Laura Arndt, of jealousy—that was comprehensible; there was some reason in that. This annoyed Marlene and she drove Relly mercilessly into a corner, so that Relly took refuge in certain gross indiscretions and crude references to her sister's impulses toward rebellion and independence. And Marlene, frightened at the expression of things which she had barely considered in her secret thoughts, finally commanded her sister to keep within decent bounds.

Now she sat there, alone with her thoughts, gnawed at the penholder with her little teeth and, contracting her brows, began once more to write.

"Relly has divined that a discord exists between mother and myself. That hurts me. I've tried so hard to let no one notice it. But she has the eyes of a lynx. Just as she suspected that time how little enthusiastic I was over the birth of our little brother. But how could I have been? Suddenly an intruder presented himself, a funny little tyrant who greedily bit off a huge piece of our private little world. But what horrified me most was to hear her say that about father. It slipped out, of course, to her own utter dismay. She got quite pale herself. Poor, impetuous Relly. She always lets her temperament run away with her; that can lead to no good. And is it really true that I am beginning to question my father's right to his authority, and that I can no longer give him the unconditional respect which he has a right to demand and which he surely deserves? That is what she asserts. She says she feels it. She says she reads my expression. Is she really right? I must examine myself. Surely, she must be wrong. Only, alas, I cannot deny that for some time past something in father's bearing depresses me—even that characteristic courtesy which is his, that considerateness which he shows not only our mother and ourselves but everybody with whom I see him speak. It seems to me sometimes as though he were sparing people only because he knew something ugly about each one, or as though he were himself fighting a heaviness in his own soul and had not the courage to admit it to himself. Mother is utterly unsuspecting and that is really what I blame her for. Of course one is never sure about her. She listens to every one and lets every one state his case. And yet I have the impression that her interest in father does not have quite the right quality. My notion of human relationships is a different one and I want my life to be differently built. But that may be a vain effort. It may be that one can do nothing by mere willing. How one is surrounded by riddles. My worst quality at present is that I am full of distrust toward people and therefore seem to scent evil everywhere, especially hypocrisy and oppression. I hope God isn't angry with me on that account, and, like Relly, considers it a wicked curiosity."

In this young soul, as can be seen, there reigned an unquenchable longing for truth, a longing that had no stamp of selfishness, no motivation in mere prying, no breath of conscious sophistication. The condition of the world has obliterated the boundary between the generations. We see a generation awakening ten years before the natural period of its maturity, and if on the one hand we see children becoming criminals, so on the other hand the seriousness of our age produces spirits enlightened before their time.

All of Marlene's actions bore witness to an instinctive rejection of moral sloth—the very manner in which she wrote, in which she reflected concerning what she had written, even the physical gesture with which she finally closed her book and locked it in a drawer.

With a glance of smiling indulgence, she slipped into bed beside her sleeping sister.

6

The great reputation of Friedrich Laudin had had its origin in a sensational suit for divorce in 1910 in which he had been the attorney of Prince K., a magnate by rank, as well as a millionaire manufacturer. The litigation had involved extremely difficult questions of law, problems of property, the ascertaining of paternity, and had led to diplomatic complications and finally to an interpellation in parliament. Through all these dangers and difficulties Laudin had managed the affair with incomparable tact, with the result that not only his client but even his opponents had every reason to appreciate his judicial acumen and profound learning, and above all the distinction and restraint of his attitude.

He had since been considered one of the leading lawyers of his country, especially in matters of domestic difficulties, controversies concerning guardianship, suits for alimony, for inheritances and other dispositions of property. In the course of the years the professional activities of his office had become so extended that he could give his personal attention only to the most important and difficult cases. The great majority of cases he left to the gentlemen in his office, all trained men, some of them schooled by himself, and reserved to himself only a supervisory capacity.

The attorneys, the notaries, the copyists and the secretaries who were associated with him loved and respected him without exception. They never heard a harsh word from his lips. He was never irritable, never impatient, never tempted to make a scapegoat of any one in his employ. He had an exact knowledge of the capacity of each and therefore avoided equally moods of undue demanding or of mere slackness or of indulgence through cowardice. In that office confidence never begot weakness, because all relations remained clearly defined. Associates of long years' standing found intimacy definitely halted at a certain point. Laudin's very courtesy preserved a certain distance, if nothing else. His ultimate opinion often remained obscure. But what he expressed sufficed to determine the appointed lines of action.

He had never touched cases that seemed to him unsound or even doubtful. He refused to represent a client unless he felt that he could make that client's cause his own. He was in a position to choose. His reputation and his large income made it possible for him to refuse all questionable cases. If he could not be the guide of conscience where he had consented to be the advocate, he refused his assistance and no material temptations, however great, had ever been able to affect a decision of this kind. But the fates and confusions of men are not always so simple, nor their characters so easy to judge, that any man, even the most experienced and the most schooled in knowledge of the human heart, can, by the mere purity of his own character, avoid situations in which he finds himself at variance with his own convictions. This happened to Laudin quite often, oftener as the years went on, and usually in precisely such cases as prudence had bidden him hesitate about too long. Suddenly he found himself involved; the threads could no longer be torn; he had been deceived and self-deceived and realized it now and had neither the right nor the power to retrace his steps. He attributed this to overwork, to the accumulation of harassing obligations, to the decline of his own powers, of his insight, of his judgment. But these were not the true causes. Perhaps he reflected too little upon the part which the spirit of his time had in these matters and, amid the noise of business and under the pressure of a thousand engagements, was capable of less awareness of certain changes in the world than other men who were less involved in the actual actions and passions of the day.

He was considered a model by the bar, and an ornament to his profession. He was highly esteemed by the authorities, and judges of the highest courts of appeal regarded with initial favor a cause represented by him. Many members of the judiciary had been his friends at school or college. In the years 1911 and 1913 the government had appointed him chairman of a large commission which was to negotiate a loan in England and America. Although in both cases the negotiations had failed in their essential purpose, he had shown so much skill and wisdom that he had earned the appreciation of his employers and had been decorated on various occasions, a circumstance which he preferred to ignore. Seven years later these services of his were remembered, and it was believed that he was the right man to protect the economic interests of the wrecked, crushed state and be the advocate of his country at the bar of foreign powers. It was proposed to establish a position for him as plenipotentiary with almost unlimited discretionary powers and corresponding emoluments. He declined the offer. It was more pressingly renewed. He declined once more. He assigned many reasons for his refusal. He kept the most decisive to himself.

Friedrich Laudin was the son of a Silesian country schoolmaster. He had grown up in the narrowest circumstances and his years of study had been a continuous battle with want. His rise, accompanied by constant privations, had been slow. He owed everything to himself, nothing to chance. He despised low diplomacy, the influence of acquaintances, the favor of those in power, the advantages of mutual secrets. In a country where every official advancement was habitually gained by personal influence, mutual favoritism and paid partiality, he went silently and confidently upon his lonely and independent path.

In 1906, in the interest of the widow of a certain councillor Rossi, an official in the institute of military geography, who had met his death in the Bukowina, he carried on a litigation by which the lady was forced to claim her inheritance from her husband's brothers. A year later he married Pia Rossi, the daughter of the councillor's widow. The latter had since been living in the house of her daughter's husband.

7

Laudin was surrounded by an atmosphere of such silence and isolation that there was really no one in his circle who had his entire confidence. This secretiveness which his calling had made necessary and which his strict conception of the honor of that calling had made complete, had gradually communicated itself to all the circumstances of his life and was now a very part of his nature.

No one, in fact, could have told you anything definite about him. People knew his characteristics, or at least those that met the eye and influenced his environment, but no one knew the groundwork of character from which they sprang. Many people called him impenetrable; others called him mysterious; there were even a few who blamed him for being a juggler of false mysteries. Even exact observers of his life and conversation failed to gain a permanent opinion concerning him; on the contrary, they were forced to revise their views and impressions at every meeting. Most people found that troublesome, of course, and in their association with him could not get rid of a certain psychical discomfort. This became more pronounced, because in the course of the years he exhibited an ever more definite inclination towards pedantry which expressed itself in precise punctuality and love of order.

Yet a magic went out from his personality which those who had entrusted him with their affairs felt most strongly. It could not be said that this magic consisted in goodness, for he was neither soft nor frank. During professional conferences his attitude was far oftener one of vigilant seriousness than that of amiable *bonhomie,* which the majority of his colleagues adopt as their favorite rôle. Nor was it his native courtesy; for this was evidently only the external form into which he cast his human relationships. The atmosphere of confidence that surrounded him did, no doubt, attract and calm others, but it had no relation to the activity of a sovereign and persuasive will. Perhaps it was something stamped upon his glance and features—a knowledge of the souls of men, of the intricacy of their fate; an experience of men and of the way in which men live with each other that had been confirmed by a vision of the endless variations and distinctions of mortality; a knowledge that had irresistibly penetrated his very soul and blood and brain, concerning every form and every degree of human fraud and craft and cruelty and misunderstanding and falsehood and greed and slavery and avidity and passion and crime. Perhaps it was that.

For no one's insight had penetrated as deeply as his own into the machinery of our social life. For more than fifteen years it had been his almost exclusive occupation to search out the untenableness of those social relations which had been entered into in the name of the law and in the name of religion, with a claim—and this claim was usually sincere at the time—upon an eternal endurance. Thus there had opened before him a gigantic vision of the combinations of men in society in general, the mixtures of the different strata of the social world, its nervous and arterial system, so to speak; the interests by which certain groups are chained to each other or by which they are divided in combat. More than that: he had an insight, which in its wide embracing wealth was comparable to no chronicle or memoir, into the private affairs of all callings, classes and professions, the rise of some, the downfall of others, fantastic events and tragic complications, strange mutabilities of fortune, guilty and guiltless wretchedness and a fullness of absurdity, mere silliness, madness and shame.

Before his eyes, as before those of a priest in the confessional, the motives of human action were laid bare; he had to seek out the ultimate origin of decisions and to pass judgment upon their final effects. He had to acquire a knowledge not only of what had happened; instigation and development were not hidden from him. He had to know the process itself, the *curriculum vitæ* of the acting characters, their daily ways of life, the quality of their attitudes, their plans, their habits, their vices, their diseases, their associates, the sources of their money, their reputation for good or ill. He took no account of shame, nor could he spare that feeling.

It was a part of his office and of the execution of the tasks that were required of him that men had to strip in his presence and that he, careless of their sensitiveness, brooded over every wrinkle, over every pore, over every secret woe.

One might think that he would gradually have lost the capacity for astonishment, that no curiosity would ever stir him again, nor any horror nor any revulsion, nor even pity. But this was not the case. In a letter to Egyd Fraundorfer—a letter of recent years, written in Berlin whither one of his great cases had summoned him—he had written: "Surely the soul can become inured to hardships even as the body can. But I have no experience of any such process. If ever I had a psychical callous I have lost it in the course of my activity. This seems to be connected with a characteristic which I find it hard to describe but which I observed in myself even in my childhood. If any one struck me I immediately got a clothesbrush and kept brushing my coat for fifteen minutes at a time; if I happened to witness some brutality in the street I hastened home and in all the rooms in which there was a timepiece I placed the hands of the timepiece upon the hour and minute in which the thing had happened. I did not know then how to motivate this curious impulse and I don't know to this day. Later in life that kind of impulse caused in me those attacks of mere whimsicality which you have often teased me about. For instance, I can't possibly go to bed without first having arranged the objects on my desk in the precise order in which, year in and year out, I am accustomed to seeing them. Sometimes, after an exciting session in court, a fever of exactness seems to come over me. I can't rest until I have counted the pen-points in the drawer and noted down their number; or else I will erase the spots in a book that I happen to take up, or I will be impelled in the middle of the night to get up and shave. I could tell you many strange things like that, but what purpose would it serve? I suspect that we are here dealing with an automatic transference and sublimation of inner

processes into external habitual acts. Thus a crust is gradually grown whereby the kernel of one's nature remains un-
wounded or is, at least, less vulnerable. Don't you agree
with me?"

Had he been a historian of morals or a social philosopher,
he could have written the most thorough of treatises concerning marriage and its development in the twentieth century. He could perhaps have disclosed the motives which
led to marriages and those which led to their dissolution.
With equal dryness and objectivity he could have set down
the innumerable unions which were rooted in frivolity and
credulity as well as those that were the fruit of hasty passion
and lying sensuality; others which arose from ambition, vanity, the desire to get on, the greed for money, the weakness of
mere good nature or a passing common fad, as well as those
which people entered in utter indifference or inconsolable
resignation. He could have sketched the figures of men who
gained themselves a woman by craft as they would secure
themselves a job or a tip on the money market; of others
who go into marriage as one goes into a coffeehouse or to a
card party; of such as had the choice between marriage and
suicide and preferred the former; of men who kept
mistresses with their wives' money, or forced their wives to
become prostitutes and with these earnings played the part
of great gentlemen in a society that had knowledge of all
things and closed its eyes to all things so long as there
was no open scandal; of those who had been deceived for
years and yet would have pledged their souls on the fidelity
of their companions; of the morally slothful who found
it easier to overlook the obvious and retain the comfort of
their lives; of the impotent who became the helots of women
and of men who ruined the bodies of women because they
knew as much concerning them as a butcher knows of the
weaving of silk.

He could have told the stories of women to whom a ball
dress outweighed the welfare of their children, and of others

who lowered themselves to the plane of domestic animals, sometimes out of fear of their husbands and sometimes out of deluded fascination; of those who adored their husbands as a god and in their idolatry would rather have torn out their hearts than become convinced that he was a wretched little mortal with a streak of the rogue. He could have told the stories of women whose strength is sapped in an annual child-bed while the husband and begetter, with a feeling of duty well-fulfilled, passes his nights in taverns, in clubs or with mistresses; of others again who carelessly waste their husbands' hard earned substance and of those who clung to every farthing while the man heedlessly lost hundreds of thousands in senseless speculations. He knew the story of the furies of charity whose houses were as inhospitable as a railway station and of the immature in mind and soul who were driven into marriage and bled to death therein.

He could have told and explained how all these people, couple after couple, plunged into marriage, frivolous and ignorant, half-strangers to each other, often without any adequate sense of responsibility or firmness of mind; the deceived and the deceivers who signed contracts which they had already determined not to keep before the pen was out of their hands or the ink dry upon it; how they begot children to whom the lives of their parents was a disturbing and tormenting dream; how they came to him, the woman or the man, and panted, one or both, to be free of each other again; how they brawled; how short their memory was; how shamefully they spoke of each other; how they betrayed each other; how hatred, contempt, satiety and the desire to hurt had obliterated from them every vestige of human dignity, every memory of the exchange of vows that were supposedly sacred.

All this he could have set down and in the end he could have had the pleasure of the statistician in incontrovertible facts and the laws of their grouping.

But it seemed as though his breast were an abyss into which every single event and its protagonists and originators dropped, even as a stone drops into a deep well. It remained in the depths; it was no more either to be grasped or seen.

It is a fact that the repetition of the similar often has a paralyzing effect upon the soul. It is scarcely to be assumed, however, that this constituted the pressure which so obviously weighed upon Laudin and which had nothing to do with the mere burden of work. Circumstances which he himself did not take into account complicated the problem and these circumstances were stronger, more wearisome, more painful than his constant sessions, examinations or conferences with his clients. It may be that a protocol with its dry list and registration of facts, often spoke to him more eloquently than the most diffuse descriptions, or all the wretchedness and dissatisfaction which men and women brought him personally. Behind all this lay more. The decisive, the enormously disillusioning, the distorting thing was not what they said. Not that, but what lay behind it all. For it is to be remembered that he knew and had to know these obscure backgrounds, these intricate labyrinths of the disconsolate—great heapings up of material, in writing and in print, proof and documentation of treachery and deceit made permanent in all sorts of documents which were first flaunted and then stored away and later grew yellow with age in some depository of records. These documents were like keys with which he could have opened the houses of men, these dwelling places of contention and hatred, these sleeping chambers in which their kisses had turned to poison and their embraces to convulsions of rage. He knew their secret paths and their activities which dreaded the light. Such was his task. In this arsenal of his were stored up all the proofs of dissension, and memory and imagination were filled therewith, as the booth of a huckster is filled with worm-eaten trash, with unclean and bizarre things, trivial and repulsive, from the defiled marriage bed to the unpaid milliner's bill, from the dregs of arsenic in a coffee-cup to a garter lost in a house of assignation, from a forged passport to a forged check. Then there were letters, mountains of letters, mountains of lies, mountains of suffering and mutual insults and hypocritical promises; letters in which people haggled and vowed and swore and accused and flattered and jeered and cursed and begged; letters that were illiterate and letters written in the most exquisite style, business like communications: "I have the honor to inform you" followed by the coldest perfidy, as well as poetical outpourings; threatening letters, spying letters, blackmailing letters, profoundly moving documents of love and of forgiveness and others bursting with irreconcilable hatred and diabolical calumny.

And upon all these the silence of Laudin had set its eternal seal.

8

It was not his habit to groan under his burden. The only complaint which he had been heard to make in the last few months was something like this: "Affairs are accumulating to such an extent that I sometimes get frightened. Where will it lead to?" He always hastened to add: "I don't say that on my own account; I'm thinking of social conditions in general." And when he said this he did his best to look carefree and contented.

However exhausted he was from discussions, advisory sessions, conferences, long hours of dictation, attempts at reconciliation, telephone calls and the sessions in court, there was always that smile on his face which was not only kindly but seemed to desire to deny the measure of his exertions. This was at least true so long as he knew that people were watching him and that he had to be prepared to communicate with them.

But when he was alone in a room and safe from all observation, a dim veil seemed to fall over his face. The tension of his muscles relaxed and the smile died, and between his eyebrows appeared a deep furrow and he threw himself into a chair and stared motionlessly in front of him for many, many minutes.

At the beginning of the previous autumn Pia had once come upon him in this posture. He had not heard her coming; she had remained silently on the threshold and watched him and then disappeared without a word. When she was out of the room she pressed a hand against her cheek and there was consternation in her eyes. But she betrayed by no syllable that she had watched him in his loneliness. If a man falls from a high tower it may come to pass that in a few seconds he can have a vision of many years of life, and be aware of long forgotten details that stand out in a far sharper light than when they were part of a fluid present. Similarly it is possible that while a man is crossing the hall of his house or going up stairs or opening and closing the door of his office, there may race through his mind a thronging flight of faces, forms, words and events.

In the smallest and most accidental of human actions the entire warp and weft of things is probably involved. External action is the symbol of inner being, but that inner realm is like a black river whose shores are enshrouded in darkness. Occasionally a torch flames above that river; occasionally a tremor of fear makes the waters to shiver, and all these things blends together. From this may arise a dream, or a decision may arise; or perhaps decisions are but the consequences of dreams, and the fear of decisions, the fear of a dream which has been forgotten or has not yet ripened into consciousness? The soul often works as long in the building of its dreams as the mind in the construction of its ideas.

When Laudin looked at his bedroom and the things therein to which he stood in a relation of slavery, his thoughts were lonely and discouraged, and when he extinguished the lamp, all these objects melted into a darkness which had yawned for them in this very room at this very hour five to six thousand times. Out of the distance of the years when forgotten freedom had winged his tread, there arose the cry of a living experience. But the way back to those years was peopled by ghosts.

One day his daughters and their friends were playing a game of questions and answers. He played with them for a while. The beautiful Laura Arndt asked him: "Who would you like to be if you weren't yourself?" He answered with a smile much to the girls' astonishment: "I'd be perfectly satisfied if only I weren't myself; I wouldn't have any other wish left." Later Marlene tried to cross-examine him on this subject. He was embarrassed. "It isn't worth your while, dear, to think about it. At your age you'd better stick to what's reasonable. At my time of life one may occasionally indulge in the irrational." Marlene shook her head.

On sunny mornings he would send the car ahead and walk a piece of the way. The tread of his feet was lonely and discouraged. He shrugged his shoulders over a tasteless advertisement or smiled indulgently at small boys playing in the street or lifted his hat courteously to an acquaintance, and all the while was probably lost in brooding over the foolish notion that he was so tired of being himself, and the question of whether one could not strip off one's own character even as one can a worn-out garment. (Why? We repeat Marlene's question. Why should he not want to be himself? Who else could he be? Why is he so wretched in his own identity?) He would hear himself saying: "I might tell the dream to Egyd; it would give him something to interpret."

What dream? It was no dream at all yet; it had not yet been dreamed; it was about to be; it was for the present only a feeling of discouragement and loneliness.

It is difficult to puzzle out the lives of active and practical people in their unchanging outlines. Laudin helped people to see their errors and to file away their shames. And it seemed as though there lay about him so many chains of which he had relieved others, that the walls of a prison had grown up about him out of these chains.

He presented the image of a superior, calm, benevolent, well-disposed and often witty man. But was he all that in reality? Who was he in truth? At breakfast his daughters would appear in grayish-brown frocks. Why did those frocks vex him so? "Again those nun-like garments," he said. It was the grayish-brown color that annoyed him: it evidently reminded him of the fact that Marlene and Relly were equipped for school and were to be trained to useful activities. Did he hate the useful? To be sure these frocks made them like the sparrows that sit in winter on fences along the path and twitter, frightened and frozen. But Marlene's clear, intelligent eyes were fastened upon him. And these eyes were so thirsty after knowledge and at the same time so experienced, that this man of practical life was ashamed of not being equal to their demands. His inadequate answer to them was only a glance which was shattered before the power and the veracity of youth.

The room was fragrant in its cleanliness. Pia sat at the table and buttered the rolls in her sweet deliberate way. She said: "It's freezing to-day, girls; you must put on your heavy coats." The nurse brought in little Hubert; he had just come from his bath and his rosy face gleamed like a freshly buttered bun. The little donkey of rubber stood there, patient and melancholy, for he knew that he could not escape his fate, which was to be piteously maltreated by the hands of this huge human child and to be destroyed at last. Radiantly Laudin arose and took his little son into his arms. A few jests, the same ones daily, a few familiar tendernesses. . . . Then he affectionately said good-bye to them all.

And what is the man really like? Who is he at bottom? We ask it once again. . . .

9

Suddenly, on the stroke of ten, Konrad Lanz appeared in Laudin's office. The office was in an ancient building that had many passages, stairs, gates, inner and outer courts. Most of the rooms were so dark that the electric light had to burn even by day.

The young man sat in the waiting room. There were also a lady and a gentleman in that room who exchanged no word or glance during the whole time, although they were obviously man and wife, and a white-haired, shabby man who read a paper and coughed uninterruptedly.

But he was not kept waiting very long. An old serving man ushered him in. In the hall he met Dr. Laudin in his fur coat and heavy gloves. From within could be heard the metallic rattle of the typewriters.

When they had sat down in the car, Laudin said: "You will forgive me, won't you, if I look over some documents while we're driving? I've got to be in court at noon and I have no other time."

Konrad Lanz bowed shyly. He was obviously oppressed by the favor which the famous lawyer was conferring upon him and found no words.

Laudin opened his brief-case. "You see," he said, "this is the same old mysterious bag." His expression was pleasant. "You can amuse yourself by looking at it once more." He laughed deep in his throat, took out some papers in a blue cover and was soon lost in reading them.

At the end of forty-five minutes the swift car had reached Kottingbrunn. The chauffeur inquired of several people where Hartmannshof was and in five more minutes they were there.

It was a villa-like house near the public road. Across the first story stretched a balcony of wood; a second smaller balcony projected from the second story under the pointed gables. The yellow plaster showed rents and tears, especially on the west side of the house. They passed through a vegetable garden in which the beds were covered with straw. At the left, where there was a little rise in the ground, they saw boards and stripped tree-trunks. In front of the entrance of the house a lad was splitting wood. He had only a hostile glance for the two visitors. Two boys had rushed excitedly out of the house; they passed Laudin and Lanz, and gave their whole attention to the automobile in the road.

Laudin turned to the woodcutter. "Is Mrs. Hartmann at home?"

The fellow shrugged one shoulder indifferently.

A woman appeared in the doorway. "What do you want?" she asked harshly and observed the visitors who were so unlike each other—the one inspiring her with respect by his height and his urbane distinction, the other in his thin, shabby coat, gaunt, shy of glance and more than modest in his bearing. Accustomed to estimating men according to their appearance, she could come to no conclusion here.

When Laudin gave his name she raised her narrow, almost colorless eyebrows; when, indicating his companion, he uttered the name of Lanz, she grew pale. She pointed with her arm in the direction of the interior of the house, murmured something about not being prepared for company and its being cleaning day. In the narrow hall she looked about hesitatingly, as though she were wondering into which room to usher the guests, and at the same time she seemed to be considering what might be the purpose of this visit and for what she had better be prepared. At last she opened the door of a large room full of old, massive, well-preserved furniture, with faultlessly white curtains at the windows and a large green tile stove. She regretted that there was no fire, but there was no other room into which she could take them; if the boys had been at school it would be different; there would be a room free upstairs; but the school had been closed yesterday for a week. Several cases of chickenpox had occurred and a sanitary inspection was taking place. She said all of this in a cold, hasty, absent-minded way with which she tried to conceal her suspense. She moved two chairs away from the table, ran her flat hand over the upholstered seats and with a dry gesture invited her guests to be seated.

She wore a gray sweater buttoned to the throat, a woolen skirt, and over it, a blue apron. She must have been about forty, but since her full face had few wrinkles and since her rather stout figure was kept in constant motion by a series of nervous and superfluous gestures, she seemed considerably younger than her years. Everything about her was remarkably neat and, for a woman who did her own work, her hands were notably well cared for. Only her hair, of an unpleasant brownish red, straggled somewhat loosely about her head and down over her low forehead.

Laudin sat down after he had courteously waited until Mrs. Hartmann, too, had taken a seat. Konrad Lanz remained standing at a little distance from those two and looked at the porcelain cups and plates in a china closet, with assumed interest. "I hope you will pardon us for our intrusion," Laudin began with an extreme and almost exaggerated courtesy, "but what justifies me is that I come here in the interests of my client, Miss Caroline Lanz. Unfortunately Miss Lanz was prevented from accompanying me, and so her brother has been so kind as to come in her stead. The thing that I am forced to trouble you about is of no great importance— the establishment of a very simple fact. Two words and we are done. I am interested in discovering where the will of your late husband is deposited and I should be very much obliged to you for the information. That is all."

Mrs. Hartmann sat straight as a poker on her chair. Not for a second did her eyes leave Laudin's face while she was listening, nor did her expression change. Since her whole attitude betrayed the utmost vigilance, it was obvious that she was not for a moment deceived by the lawyer's conciliatory tone. She answered in a rough voice: "I know nothing about any will. Why have I got to be bothered with that again? Didn't I let the Lanz woman go and look for herself? She used her own eyes. I said to her: Please go ahead and look. She looked and she found nothing. So why do you come and annoy me?"

Laudin nodded in apparent agreement with her. "It is most unpleasant for you," he answered. "I know that. But the will was in existence. There is no doubt at all. Your late husband expressed himself to that effect in a way that could not be misunderstood. In spite of that, we would not trouble you by a renewed search here if for the moment, we had not unluckily lost trace of the duplicate. It is only right to tell you that we have every reason to assume the existence of a duplicate, or rather of a later draft, and of the fact that it is in the hands of a definite individual."

There was nothing in Laudin's face to betray the fact that he promised himself any effect from these apparently careless statements. Nor did he seem to observe that Brigitte Hartmann's right hand closed convulsively over her knee. Her expression did not change. She even brought a thin smile to her lips.

"I am quite indifferent to the whole matter," she said, with a contemptuous movement of her head. "I have nothing to do with it, anyhow. He was free to do what he liked with his money. I don't see what any one can do to me. The cash, as you know, is still in the bank. His estate has not yet been probated, so do as you like. The court appointed a guardian for my children; I have got my lawyer; so what do you think any one can do to me?"

Laudin assumed an astonished air. "What do you mean, Mrs. Hartmann?" he asked, with that suave assumption of social equality which had evidently served his purpose in similar cases before, "what do you mean, precisely, by assuming that anyone could possibly 'do' anything to you? You seem quite to misunderstand the purpose of my call."

"Oh, no," Brigitte Hartmann interrupted him harshly, "I understand very well. I wasn't born yesterday, you know. You're trying to pump me, that's all. But who was there except that Lanz woman, to whom Hartmann would give a copy of his will? Not a soul. Why, he was so crazy, God forgive me the sin if it is one, that he didn't confide in anybody. You don't fool me, Doctor, if you'll excuse me for saying so, but out here in the country we just say right out what we mean. If you've got a duplicate of the will, I'd advise you to get hold of it first. Till you do, I don't see that there is anything to worry about." Her voice had grown loud and shrill and she looked at Laudin like a woman whose consciousness of the justice of her cause was such that she intended to move no hair's breadth from her appointed path.

"The situation is not quite so simple," said Laudin, in his most ingratiating manner. "Your view of the thing is naturally somewhat unprofessional. Even assuming that the duplicate is lost—and we can safely drop that consideration for the moment—you are in no position to know whether we have not a witness who would be willing to reaffirm under oath the statements of your late husband concerning the original will. Assuming, however, that such a witness does not exist, so soon as the matter is brought to court—and it will be, rest assured of that—the judge will make use of his power to examine you under oath. This means that you would have to swear that you had neither seen nor touched the will, nor even known of its existence. And there the matter would end. It would end, that is to say, until we recovered our proof to the effect that, contrary to your sworn oath, the will existed and had been in your house. Without any question of a third party you would then have been guilty of perjury, with consequences that must be clear to you. I must ask your forgiveness for this explanation, but you yourself seemed to stand in need of this bit of legal instruction. So I have given it to you and therewith fulfilled my duty." He got up and bowed.

Brigitte Hartmann still sat up very straight in her chair. But now her left hand, too, clasped her knee. For a little she seemed petrified. Then, rising slowly, and slowly folding her arms across her bosom, she spoke: "Fine things you're telling me, there. Thank you most humbly for the instruction, Doctor." Twice she curtsied jeeringly. "But why should I be treated to legal instruction? Did I run away from home, or he? Did I leave my children in the lurch, or he? He was up and gone one fine day and it was the devil take the hindmost. It's just as I am telling it: one fine day he was up and gone without saying a word and his wife and his children and his house and his farm could go to hell for all he cared. Does a real man act that way? Or one that calls himself a father? Is that written down in the law, too? Maybe you can give me some instruction about it! Did you ever hear of such a thing, except among the heathen? And I don't believe it happens with them that the father of a family, married eleven years, picks up and leaves as if he were leaving a tavern; that he picks up the first woman he sees—you'll pardon me for being honest about it, young man—and disappears with her and is never seen again. And then he goes to strange parts and dies there like a dog and treats his own flesh and blood as though it were dirt under his feet! Is that written in the law that you want to instruct me about?"

She had talked herself into a wild rage. Her lips had suddenly grown white and thin. As she talked more loudly and swiftly one became more and more aware of a gap in her upper teeth. With flaming glances she measured the two men. Konrad Lanz had turned his face to her and regarded her with a somber expression. Laudin's face was attentive and vigilant, with a superficial assumption of surprise. "You do, indeed, deserve a great deal of pity, Mrs. Hartmann, if things are as you state them," he said, and his tone was most sympathetic. "From all that I have been able to learn concerning your late husband, he seems to have been a very conscientious man and not at all inclined to frivolous and impulsive action. One would, I should think, have expected such a man to make adequate provision for his family before seeking refuge with another woman. I am very much astonished. And, above all, one would have thought that he would have come to some understanding with you concerning a possible divorce or separation and would have asked you to set him free. That, surely, was the least he owed you. Didn't he do anything of that sort? I confess it surprises me."

Brigitte Hartmann flushed slightly. It was like the breathing on a pane and disappeared at once. For one moment she lost her composure. She regarded Laudin suspiciously; then a strange, somber smile glided over her features. Several times she opened her lips to speak and closed them again. She began to pace up and down the room, as though she were alone. Without apparent motive she pulled a curtain cord, and the curtain opened. "Divorce," she said suddenly, in a harsh dark voice, "I could tell you a whole lot about that. Liberty. I've heard that word. Haven't you enough liberty, I used to ask him. By night or day you can go wherever you like. Do I try to stop you? If he had wanted to keep a woman? All right! He could have, as far as I'm concerned. Go ahead, if you can't help it. But a divorce? I hadn't the right to that. Is holy wedlock a scrap of paper to go and tear up, if the whim takes you? But he talked and talked and talked. Fine, I said, all right, I said, if it'll make you any happier. But only under such and such conditions. I've got to have my security. The world's got to know that it's not my fault. Fine. All right. That was all done. But I've got a conscience. I'm a woman. I'm a mother. I couldn't. It was too sinful. How am I going to face my children, I asked him. And I asked myself, too. To the end of my days they could have reproached me that I had robbed them of their father. There was a voice in my heart that cried out to me—No, Brigitte." With a strange passion she beat her fist against her breast. "The boys appeared to me at night, in my sleep, and begged me on their bended knees: Don't do it, mother. So I went and visited the grave of my parents and there I heard a voice: It's a sin; don't do it!

Wasn't it my duty to cling to my own husband and fight the evil spirit in him? Why, one would have no religion, if one gave in to such weakness and wickedness. Oh, no!"

She walked up and down, up and down, ever more excitedly, turned utterly in upon herself, or as though she were talking to the man who had long been a shade. It was the stifled recollection of contention, the re-arising of bitter old conflicts, the revengeful tearing open of old wounds. "I can never forgive him, never! Not in death, as I couldn't in life." The words came forth from clenched teeth and there was so much sincerity of hatred and of unquenched bitterness in them that Laudin was visibly impressed, in spite of all he knew, and wondered whether he was not in the presence of a human being whose cause was still doubtful and who could not yet be condemned.

"It's not for me to discuss all that," he said, concluding the interview. "You said, just now, Mrs. Hartmann, that you were employing an attorney. Take counsel with him. Or, if you prefer, you can settle the whole matter with me. I should be very glad. Merely send me a message. I shall wait until you do."

"As you like," said Mrs. Hartmann, standing up straight before him and regarding him with wrinkled forehead and a penetrating look. She seemed to want to speak again, but her tongue would not follow her bidding. She seemed to feel with vexation and disgust the compelling power of Laudin's personality and to fear his going, as though it were a danger from which she must protect herself. But she said no more.

During the drive back to the city Laudin leaned back with closed eyes in the corner of the car. Konrad Lanz, although he was intensely eager to hear his friend's opinion, was careful not to break the silence.

Finally, without opening his lids, Laudin said softly: "There you have her, living and breathing, the tigress of legality."

"And is there any hope for us at all?" the young man asked sadly.

"We shall see. She will come to me. Then we shall know more."

"You do truly believe then, Doctor, that she will come?" Doubtfully, Konrad Lanz shook his head.

"I not only believe it; I know it. And if I am not wholly deceived, we shall have some extraordinary revelations."

10

On Sunday morning, Pia, according to her weekly custom, gathered the bills which she could not and was not supposed to meet out of her household money and took them to her husband. Laudin sat at a desk in the library. Outside it had begun to snow.

"I'm sorry to bother you, Friedrich," said Pia, "but you know—our regular Sunday examination."

"Of course, my dear chief of all departments," Laudin tried to joke. "Duty is duty. Any very bad surprises? Let's see your horrible documents."

A storm had damaged the iron fence in the garden and it had been repaired. A water pipe had broken in the cellar and had been replaced. There was the telephone bill. The kitchen had been plastered. A new washing machine had been bought, and an electric iron for the laundry. Coke had been ordered for the conservatory. The bills mounted up to thirty-five millions and a half.

While Laudin was looking through the bills, Pia stood beside him, leaning her arm against his shoulder.

He expressed no criticism. He had absolute confidence in Pia's management and would, in fact, have considered it unworthy of them both to remark upon purchases which she thought necessary and which commonly proved to be far-sighted means of economy. He looked after her as she was leaving the room, awaiting her cheerful nod as she

[51]

turned back once more at the door. And when she waved her hand he had prepared his features in the right expression. Then he bent over the desk once more, but instead of continuing the letter that he had started, he drew all sorts of bearded and aquiline profiles upon the blotter.

Pia sat at the telephone. First she complained to the dairy of the inferior quality of the milk; next, because it was Sunday, she asked to be connected with the home of the upholsterer and asked him why he had delayed repairing the sofa in the dining room. He had had the material in his shop for two weeks and had promised either to come himself on Friday or to send his assistant. She was annoyed, finally, and hung up the receiver.

She looked thoughtful. All these things, fences, water pipes, washing machines, stoves, coal, milk cans, kitchen tiles, sofa coverings, besieged her. And each thing had its special claim upon her. She could not rest; she could not think. Always something, craving attention or help, appeared before her eyes. The house was stuffed full of these things. They hung or lay or stood in every room. People were generally of the opinion that man needs things. But this opinion seemed utterly foolish and perverse; in reality, the matter stood quite differently. It is the things which shamelessly and impudently and importunately stand in need of man, and demand and misuse his strength and his time, as seems fitting to them.

Books demand to be dusted; doorknobs demand to be polished; carpets demand to be beaten. Cupboards demand to be set in order; beds demand to be supplied with linen; floors demand to be swept, and stockings to be darned, and garden paths to be covered with pebbles, and flowers to be watered. And in all these processes there was neither spirit nor reason. It did not suffice to grant these demands once or to grant them ten times. All things came again and again with their insolent and equally implacable demands. And if you pretended to be deaf or took refuge in some excuse, the result was dirt and disorder and increased trouble and a bad conscience.

Pia was the slave of things. They rose like a barricade even between her and her children. Marlene would call for her snowshoes; Relly could not find her French grammar; the baby's nurse shouted for her luncheon; the chambermaid wailed because she could not find the key to the wine-cellar; the cook complained because her oven would not draw. And though Pia did not personally hunt for the snowshoes or the grammar or the key of the cellar or cook the luncheon or repair the oven, yet she was the court of last appeal to whom all in the house came with their needs. She had to advise and soothe and encourage and consider and pay; and praise some and blame others and never think of herself.

Guests came not to her; but to the house. When she went to the theater or to a party with her husband, the things seemed to follow her, chattering and quarreling, as though she were living in one of Andersen's fairy tales. If some one paid her a compliment, saying that she was pretty or charming, all that she could think of was that she had to send to the apothecary the first thing in the morning, because the milk of magnesia for little Hubert had given out.

When the letter carrier came she knew perfectly well that he had no letters for her, nothing, at all events, that concerned her alone, no secret, no shadow of anything that belonged to her alone. One might well have asked, where is she? Where is this woman?

Is there such a person as Pia? Was she not rather absorbed in the fences and water pipes and sofa covers and milk cans and snowshoes and carpets and doorknobs? Did the afterglow shine for her? Did any singer sing for her? Was she still capable of joy or sorrow or longing or sympathy with the world? Or had she not rather become a repository in which the names of things were written on slips of paper one after another, each with its price, or the damage it had sustained?

But Pia was unconscious of all that. Just as she was unconscious of how little she was still capable of feeling, so she was equally unconscious of her wants. She neither asked nor quarreled with her fate, nor philosophized about it. Her task was to watch and labor, and by evening she was weary. Hitherto, at least, she had not been summoned to any other way of life; she knew of no other; the way appointed for her seemed the only possible one and she tried to meet its demands.

II

As they were about to sit down at table, Fraundorfer had sent a message that he could not come to dinner, since he was going to an early performance, but would drop in for coffee at two o'clock. They were accustomed to his little rudenesses, no one paid any attention, with the exception of Pia's mother who in her morose and sickly manner, could not reconcile herself to the insult, as she called it under her breath. But since she forgot any subject she was talking about at the end of two sentences, she branched out in her monotonous plaintiveness to a discussion of people and matters a thousand miles removed from Fraundorfer. It was rare for her to share the family meals. She suffered from as many complaints as the day has hours and with the egoism of old age regarded herself not only as the center of interest in this house but in life itself, insofar as it came to her through newspapers and conversation. Whenever Laudin turned to her, as he always did with the tenderest considerateness, she gave him a scared look out of her dull black eyes, as though she had to recall to whom she was talking, and then gave him a melancholy nod and a reply that had no connection with what he had asked or stated. Relly and Marlene who, in their attacks of irreverence, called her "mother weeping-willow," looked the while like innocent angels who were thinking sorrowfully of the miseries of earth.

Fraundorfer came earlier than was expected. Pia's mother, as well as Marlene and Relly, had just withdrawn when a scraping and snuffling and blowing was heard and the huge mass of flesh and fat that was his body pushed itself across the threshold.

He was like a stove that seems to occupy a disproportionate quantity of available space. And like a stove he radiated heat uninterruptedly, endlessly; warmth and good-natured noise; at times also smoke and soot, very often indeed; that is to say, very daring cynicisms, equivocal remarks and corrosive comments which horrified well-bred people and were the reason why, at his approach, children, young girls, and all creatures that were immature, were hastily taken to a place of safety. Pia, to be sure, by her mere glance and gestures, had gradually tamed him to the point of being careful in her presence. Whenever he was about to say something particularly disreputable, she looked at him with great amiable eyes, whereupon he would scratch his head and make a gobbling noise in his throat and look about him half embarrassed and half enraged, out of his tiny eyes, and roll his eternal cigar from one corner of his mouth to the other.

He was quite forty-five years old and looked like a schoolboy afflicted with general elephantiasis. His hair was blonde and tightly curled and was tufted at the back of his neck into an artist's mane. He had fat, moist, beardless, negroid lips. A deeply-cleft chin, spongy cheeks, enormous, rectangular ears and enormous, hairy hands. His movements gave the impression that he had to talk persuasively to his body, as you would talk to a stubborn or lazy horse, before he succeeded in changing his position or taking a step. If he once sat securely in a chair, you felt sure that nothing could pry him out until the house burned down.

In directories and other official lists he was put down as a scholar by profession. But no one knew exactly what he lived on. He was half gypsy and half hermit. He had once had a fortune but had lost it during the inflation. He owned two houses in town which now brought him no income; he wrote scholarly articles for papers and magazines which no one ever read because, although they were often witty and amusing, they were never popular. He was extraordinarily frugal, utterly careless of luxury, never asked any one's help, and yet, in spite of the narrowness of his circumstances, seemed suddenly able to raise large sums either to satisfy a whim of his own or to help a friend in difficulties.

He had a tiny white dog who was his inseparable companion. He had brought him along to-day, too. He told a melancholy tale of how he had once checked the dog in the coat-room of a theater and there the poor animal had been so overcome by horror at the numerous human coats and hats that he had been subject to nervous attacks ever since. You had only to look at his little face; disgust and wretchedness were written upon it. And why not? For when you considered what an evil smell men have for dogs, it is not surprising that all those human clothes should have been insufferably disgusting to so delicately organized a creature.

He called the little dog Herr Schmidt. The animal had the mouth and the legs of a guinea-pig. But it is not to be denied that its behavior was infinitely sedate and discreet. Herr Schmidt almost never barked but only growled gently. Fraundorfer asserted that the dog was a stranger from afar, that his original home was Odessa, whence he was brought westward through many astonishing adventures and that he had no fondness for his new home. He always spoke to the dog in tender and respectful terms and vaunted his chastity and the pure, not to say Christian, character of his life and conversation.

Fraundorfer's relation to his son Nicolas was subject to very varying interpretations. Some asserted that he could not endure him and had certainly become estranged from him since the young man's irresistible inclination to music had become unmistakable. All appearances seemed to bear out this view. Fraundorfer almost always spoke of his son in terms of disesteem, shrugged his shoulders at him, called him, with malicious laughter and forehead red with rage, a useless strummer and a sentimentalist and lyrist who had certainly abandoned the ways of his kind. He quarreled with him about money, about his relations with indifferent people, about a book or the meaning of a word. He insulted him. He made ill-natured jokes, especially in the presence of others, about the youth's timidity, about his unshakable faith in himself and his talent, and refused to take seriously anything that Nicolas either did or said.

There were other people, however, and among these was Laudin, who were of the opinion that all this rage and sarcasm and deprecation was comparable to the trickery by means of which a prestidigitator, babbling and gesturing, tries to detract the attention of the audience from what he is doing. Sudden, unnecessary exaggerations, sudden looks and intonations, however carefully they were guarded and retracted and hushed, could not be hidden from an acute observer. And yet it was hard to explain the reason for this emphatic quarrelsomeness and contemptuousness. Were these rooted in an innate dislike of all emotional activity or did they spring from mere queerness?

Nicolas was the child of a union which had lasted not quite three months. When the lady in question had left Fraundorfer she had done so with the remark that, if one had to, one could live with a fool, one could also live with a miser, and at worst even with a misanthropist. But to live with a mad and miserly misanthropist—that was beyond human endurance. Fraundorfer told this anecdote to any one who would listen. Shortly after giving birth to the child she had brought it to him and had been heard of no more. Whenever he spoke of her, which was rare, he said dryly that his relations with women constituted that part of his life of which he was ashamed, but that the one who had fooled him most grossly had belonged to the order of infantile egoists with a morbid tendency to slander. Unluckily, she had bluffed him for twenty-four hours. Hence his son. Had he regained his judgment at the end of twenty-three hours, he might yet have extracted his head from the noose.

One day, during the winter before the war, when rebellion and dissatisfaction fermented dangerously among the people, Laudin was leaving the parlor, where he had had a conference with a deputy, and found himself in the midst of a meeting of more than three thousand striking workers. They were mostly very young men, wild and threatening in proportion to their youth. Boys of sixteen and seventeen were roaring and whistling and throwing stones at the mounted police. In a moment Laudin was in the thickest of the crowd and, trying to make his way, he became the witness of a strange scene. An extraordinarily obese man, caught in the crowd like himself, had become the object of various insults on account of his well-fed corpulence. A few rabid fellows were about to lay hands on him. Laudin hastened to help the man. But the latter, puffing and blowing mightily, had succeeded in escaping his immediate pursuers and with astonishing agility had mounted an ash can which happened to be near him. Standing on it, he addressed the crowd somewhat as follows:

"Fellow citizens, or rather, comrades! Why do you presume to think that fatness is the result of gorging goose-livers and truffles? Who among you has observed me in my favorite inn and has seen me devouring beefsteaks, loins of pork, roast venison and chocolate tarts, instead of eating a lean bit of boiled beef and greens amid my sighs and tears? Let such an one step forth! Let him arise and accuse me! My belly, you will answer? The question is, how I got to have it and what is its natural history? It is not the belly of a heavy eater; it is a starveling's belly, a belly fed on fasts and on grief—a wholly uncapitalistic belly. For all you know, comrades, dill pickles are my favorite dish. Perhaps at a time when the latest improvements in popular suffering had not yet reached this land, I was already a victorious supporter of the slogan: Long live herring and sauerkraut! And, just among ourselves, comrades: Do all the voracious maws in the world sport my roundness of figure? Haven't most of them, if you examine the question closely, a deceptive emaciation, a feathery unobtrusiveness? If you had, like myself, made a study of the stomachs and entrails of those classes that grow fat upon the sweat of the people, you would regard my poor belly with affectionate sympathy; for it is an innocent belly, a conscientious belly."

He had been like some caricature of Mark Antony as he stood on the can with a jovial smile, cigar in mouth and defended his Falstaffian shape with a stentorian voice.

Some of the men grumbled in the belief that he was making fun of them. But the crowd laughed and let him go in peace.

Laudin, who had been amused by this scene, addressed the speaker. They walked off together and met regularly, from that day on, in Fraundorfer's favorite coffee house. Later Fraundorfer came to see Laudin, who occasionally returned his visits, and there arose one of those masculine friendships which are based less upon the communication and exchange of ideas and experiences than upon a half silent but sympathetic harmony of mood and a certain instinctive well-being of each in the moral atmosphere of the other.

12

In spite of Fraundorfer's assurance to the contrary, Pia guessed that Fraundorfer had not yet dined, and ordered the maid to serve him. He devoured considerable quantities of meat, vegetables, salad, compote and pudding, drank a bottle of Chambertin that had been warmed for him, and now and then, under Pia's silently disapproving eyes, gave little bites to his dog. Herr Schmidt crouched, tiny and modest, at the enormous feet of his master.

He told them that he had been in the theater for the sake of a certain actress; rather for the sake of Nickie, who had an extremely high opinion of the actress. Her name was Louise Dercum. She was imported from Berlin. Personally he didn't think much of these importations from Berlin, but he had gone to see her because Nickie had given him no peace. The boy had evidently known her since last summer. For a long time his every other word had been Dercum. Dercum this and Dercum that. The name itself had made him nervous. Dercum! Didn't that sound exactly like a tonic or a substitute for liquor? Well, then for weeks the boy had not mentioned this odious name. But this very morning he had suddenly turned up with a ticket for his father. This was her first big part; she was appearing in a new French play. He hadn't felt particularly drawn toward the whole thing. All right then, father, if it doesn't interest you, you don't have to go. This hypocritical indifference had annoyed Fraundorfer senior and had also made him a little curious. As Laudin was aware, he considered curiosity a virtue, the virtue of the discoverer, and since he had long had his suspicion that there was something going on between Nicolas and the aforesaid Dercum, he had pumped up some energy and strolled into the playhouse.

He couldn't deny that the little female had pleased him. The public, to be sure, in its usual manner, had shot far beyond the mark and had been quite noisy in its indecent enthusiasm. What any one might admit was a pretty little talent for the kind of rôle attempted: female devil with an angel's soul; a sweet kernel in a bitter shell; the whole done with a subtle, modern sophistication. His play within the play was furnished by stupid little Nickie. The boy had been pale; the sweat had gathered on his forehead; he had trembled the whole time, and scarcely had the curtain finally fallen, than he had rushed off as though he had a sudden bellyache.

Fraundorfer rocked his head from side to side and blinked with his wine-moist eyes, first at Laudin and then at Pia. He seemed to be uncertain of himself, to be trying to find out secretly whether his anecdote had won their approval or not. "By the way, the boy promised to come out here this afternoon," he said; "he seems to have promised Marlene he would play some duets with her. . . ."

"No, Marlene was going to sing something to him," Pia said; "an Italian aria. She's practiced all week with the intensest zeal; the child really has a charming voice. You ought to hear her."

Fraundorfer raised a frightened and protesting hand. "Please," he said, "not I. All singing sounds to me like the scraping of chalk on a blackboard, which is certainly the worst of all noises."

The two men retired to the library. Fraundorfer settled himself in an armchair, lit a cigar, folded his hands over his belly and looked comfortably about. Herr Schmidt had followed him and slept at his feet, his little head between his paws.

Laudin walked up and down.

There arose a strange conversation. It sounded like a monologue on the part of Laudin. Fraundorfer's answers were sleepy. Apparently, at least, he seemed to pay very little attention to the words of his friend. He looked slothful, given over to the joys of digestion, puffed blue smoke into the air and bent forward from time to time to address a question to his little dog: "What is your opinion, Herr Schmidt?" Or: "We are not quite clear about that yet, are we, Herr Schmidt?"

Whenever Laudin turned his back, however, he spied forth attentively and with astonishment from under his half-closed lids. For what he heard was comparatively new to him and obviously forced him to uncomfortable reflections.

What did Fraundorfer, who set up to be something of a philosopher, think of the problem of personal identity? Laudin asked and smiled shrewdly from behind his mustache. What did he think of the selfhood of a human being, of the unchangeableness of individual character? What, at bottom, was this thing that was called character, this frequently heterogeneous combination of qualities which, in their totality and common functioning, constitute the ego, the self? How annoying it was, and at the same time how frightening, to be forced, all one's life long, to represent the same individual self, endlessly to react to the same stimuli in the same manner. It had all the appearance of an imprisonment. You, Friedrich Laudin, are sentenced to be during fifty or fifty-five or sixty years, this precise creature and no other; you are sentenced to this city and to no other, to this house, to this activity, and you cannot stir your little finger in any manner that does not correspond to that aggregate of qualities and conditions which is labeled Friedrich Laudin.

Suppose, for example, that a man were to become tired of his I—thoroughly and unmitigatedly tired of the despotism of his own character, of this conglomeration of habits, inclinations, preoccupations, idiosyncrasies of speech and of thought. Couldn't one conceive of such a rebellion against oneself? Wasn't that precisely as though an image in a mirror were to take on life and march forth to act on its own initiative? Imagine this case: A physician was thoroughly disgusted by the ever-changing hypotheses of his science; he was deathly sick of practicing a profession which forced him to conceal the inadequacy of his means and his own complete skepticism beneath a deluding assurance; he was through with the beseeching looks of those who are destined to death and whom he cannot help, with the questions to which there is no answer, yet which he must pretend to satisfy, with the prescriptions and methods and rules and prejudices of a profession into which he has become embedded by tacit and reciprocal agreements, even as a pebble is embedded in a block of ice. Suppose he wants to step out of his own life. Life's framework holds him fast. If he wanted to turn to another calling the discovery awaits him that he hasn't as much skill as a carpenter needs to plane a board. Perhaps he has a family, perhaps he has children. Every free decision is checked and all decisive knowledge throttled. To his last hour he must continue what he began in his earliest hour—implacably, unchangeably, and even though he go mad.

Nothing in Fraundorfer's face betrayed the fact that his friend's words made any impression upon him or that he drew any inference from them. An observer would rather have said that he was bored. If the boredom was assumed it was done very skillfully. He stretched himself lazily and remarked in his careless, colloquial way: "I've always said that the whole damned planet is a failure. This institution called humanity, so far as we can survey it up to date, is a piece of clumsy bungling. One ought really to hand in a complaint. But to whom—that's the question. People will answer naturally: to God. But the only good thing about God is precisely that He doesn't exist. Isn't that your view, too, Herr Schmidt?" He laughed a brief, sleepy laugh.

Laudin took a book down from the shelf, turned the pages absent-mindedly and put it back again. All the wisdom of the sages, he continued, never got one ahead; not so far forward that one could loosen one's professional chains to the point of a decent freedom. The teacher was in the same case as the physician; the priest in the same case as the teacher, the lawyer as the priest. In each one of these social domains men erect an ideal of unselfishness (Ah, Egyd Fraundorfer, do you hear that word? Do you mark how language thinks for us and signalizes our secret griefs?), a wholly hypocritical ideal of unselfishness—yes, wholly so, for every attempt to embody it in action is penalized by society with its cruelest punishments. What a wretched business it was, for instance, to be the representative of justice in a world in which justice did not exist. Wasn't it a devilish hollow and dishonest business to speak and act in the name of laws which were only written and had never been tested by experience? It was quite as though a man were in the service of a jeweler who sported a handsome sign and had magnificent pearls and precious stones in his show window, while in his shop he carried on the business of a loathsome usurer. And yet he had sworn an oath, which had been forced from him in ignorance of the true state of affairs, to share in these nefarious dealings. The bitterness of it all! If all the gathered-up bitterness could be poured out, the very city would disappear as in a flood.

He paced up and down, up and down, his hands behind his back. Fraundorfer smoked and said nothing. Folds of fat stood out on his forehead. He had evidently lost all desire to interpose his diverting sarcasms. If, by a sudden miracle, a wall becomes transparent, one cannot help being curious as to what happens there.

From the music room could be heard the hushed tones of Marlene singing.

What more could Laudin have said? What more could he have dared to say? He paced up and down, up and down. He straightened a picture that hung a little crooked on the wall. With his foot he smoothed out an upturned corner of the carpet. He opened a portfolio on the library table and looked at an etching without really seeing it. Then, hands behind his back, he began to pace again.

Suddenly he stopped close to Fraundorfer and said: "It always hurts me, dear Egyd, when you make fun of your son, as you did just now at table. It always seems to me like a man who would jeer at the fact that an inspired painter had held up to him a purer and more beautiful image of himself. And why do you do it? Because you have artificially constructed a rigid notion of your own character, not of its reality but of that character as you believe it to be, and as you believe it impresses others. And this conception of yourself pleases you better and flatters you more than the reality—God knows why. Don't do that, Egyd. Why should you needlessly diminish that young man's worth in our opinion? Why try to reduce to fragments what is still a whole? Look, these youths of sixteen and eighteen are in reality our creditors and we are deep in their debt beyond words. But you know that without my telling you. Who should know what the clock of time is striking, if not a man like yourself? If I had a son like that I would try to insinuate myself into his friendship as though he were a king and appeal to his imagination as though he were a woman. A son is a guide into the land of the future. We who presume to teach succeed only in giving crutches to those who can fly. Daughters must be protected; at fifteen they're complete human beings over whom we have no power. One fine day an unknown man appears and takes possession of them and the most sensible thing we can do is cheerfully to consent to that outrage. My little Hubert is still in his cradle and what the future holds for him no man can yet tell. But you have a young eagle in your nest and you act as though he were a jackdaw. And all that for the sake of a favorite bit of psychical juggling."

Fraundorfer looked at Laudin with dull irony. But almost immediately he gazed at the floor again. He smacked his lips in satisfaction, but tried all the while to look morose. And all this made a curious impression, as though for a moment he had feared that his friend had suspected his true inwardness, had at once dismissed this fear as groundless and was silently amused at it.

"Fine, grand," he squawked in his throat; "a sermon after dinner, mitigated by the opulence of the aforesaid dinner. Very fine. You're heaping golden words upon my head.

Or should I have said, coals of fire?" He laughed resonantly as Laudin turned away in irritation and apologized. It interested him, oh, interested him extremely, Laudin's passionate partisanship of youth. That a man like Friedrich Laudin whom one had every right to regard as a well-tested observer of the world and of men—when a man like that decisively entered the ranks of the optimists, it certainly was startling. Psychical juggling? No. He, Fraundorfer, could make nothing of this aforesaid younger generation. To him it seemed the very geometrical. point of confusion, of the darkening of counsel, of foolish vanities and vain pretenses. Average young people to-day, and probably in all ages, were as inconceivably stupid in judging life as they were impudent in self-assurance and incapable of self-mastery. Why present them with a halo? In his shop there were no halos at all. Before the beginning of his premature old age he had gotten rid of them all at reduced prices.

Since Laudin was taking so warm and unselfish an interest in Nickie's ways and errors, it might interest him, too, that he had found a photograph of Louise Dercum on his son's desk and had put it in his pocket. He had really done that out of annoyance. The creature gazed out into the world with such a lost, romantic look, as though she couldn't harm a fly. To-night when he got home he'd put the thing back in its place. Otherwise the boy might think that he was being mysteriously pursued. Well, we would like Laudin to exercise his incorruptible spiritual penetration on this face, remembering all the while, of course, that he had the picture of a play-actress before him. Unless he made the appropriate deductions he would make a fool of himself, of course.

Fraundorfer rummaged in his coat pocket and produced first a few bank-notes, then a piece of chocolate to which breadcrumbs were sticking, then a few cigar stumps and finally the photograph, which he handed to Laudin and which bore visible traces of having passed through his pocket.

With a smile Laudin blew the dust, ashes and tobacco from the photograph and gazed at it. His expression grew serious. He dropped his arm, raised it again and looked more closely. "I must confess . . . ," his manner was hesitant and strangely thoughtful, "that this is indeed a face of indescribable, of quite astonishing veracity and innocence."

Fraundorfer grunted. He was obviously making fun of his friend's remark. Laudin returned the picture to him and he stored it away again in its former unclean receptacle.

13

When Marlene had finished the aria she stood leaning against the piano, pale and palpitant, and looked at Nicolas. He let his fingers rest upon the keys and spoke no word. Absently he gazed at the keyboard, as though he had heard no note of her singing and as though it were not he who had accompanied her but some other into whose place he had accidentally slipped.

Marlene could not but believe that he had not liked her singing. Her eyes filled with tears which she strove bravely to conceal. She went over to the sofa on which Relly and Laura were sitting and said with forced indifference, "I knew it wouldn't amount to anything to-day. It's my bad day, anyhow."

Energetically Relly shook her head and declared loudly Marlene had never sung so well as to-day. Laura, who was unmusical, consoled Marlene after the manner of a girl who, well inclined as she may be toward her friend, can yet endure that friend's failure without pain. Laura Arndt was very beautiful and tall and well developed for her age. Yet she was a little ungainly in bearing and gesture and thus fell into a constant state of tormenting embarrassment concerning herself, her body, her speech or silence.

In the meantime Nicolas Fraundorfer had aroused himself

from his state of unnatural numbness. He jumped up, went up to Marlene, took both her hands in his and said cordially: "Do forgive me, Marlene, if I seemed not to be attending. But it was only at the very last and I have so much to bother me and my head sometimes aches badly. Relly is entirely right. You really surpassed yourself to-day. There is something very lovely about your voice, something very genuine. If you are careful of it and especially do not strain the high notes you are sure to go far."

Marlene looked at him incredulously. But she saw that his face did not lie and she at once glowed in her gratitude. To Relly, however, Marlene's singing was true perfection and though she was as happy over the young man's praise as though it had been given to herself, she thought it far too tepid. One could see that from the disappointment in her face.

"I don't want to play any more," said Nicolas, and closed the piano. "I'd much rather that we'd talk. Anyhow, I have to go soon. And rather than talk, even, I would like to read you something. I would like to read some beautiful poetry. You must have some here."

His delicate and passionate features were somewhat blurred by the thick lenses that his eyes required. His skin was pale, almost white; the beardless lips of his rather wide mouth were compressed like most musicians'. His dark hair, smooth across the crown of his head, drooped in a long curl over his right temple and a part of his transparent forehead. He was tall and slender and in his movements and gestures alternately vivacious and inhibited. He bore so little resemblance to his father that strangers, seeing them together, never suspected that there was any kinship between them.

Since he had entered the room to-day his eyes and bearing had been full of restlessness. Marlene had felt it from the beginning and consquently she had been restless herself. But she had the ability to conceal her feelings under an equable cheerfulness. Laura Arndt, who admired Marlene no less than Relly herself, now glanced at Nicolas and now at her friend and seemed fearfully and almost humbly to want to discover whether anything went on between those two, of which she was ignorant. Although she was far inferior to Marlene in both the vigilance and the acuteness of her observation, she could not help perceiving how disturbed Nicolas was, how unsteady was his mood, how, either in sudden fright or as though to drive away a tormenting thought, he would grasp his forehead and not hear what was said to him.

Later, when the two sisters were alone, it pleased Marlene to pour out the vials of her scorn over that trio of female adorers. She considered it in the highest degree ridiculous that they were all three courting the favor of a young man whose heart was probably far above the advances of three bread-and-butter misses. She never spared herself when she considered that she had good reason to be dissatisfied with her behavior. But Relly remarked dryly that she didn't consider herself included in any trio of that sort. As far as the behavior of Marlene and Laura was concerned she was quite ready to share her sister's opinion.

At the present moment, however, she, too, was delighted with Nicolas' proposal. On the table lay a volume of the tales of Stifter. He took it up and turned the pages. Then he closed the book again and recited from memory the poem, "The Castle of the Lost," by Konrad Ferdinand Meyer.

"Beautiful, but sad," said Relly with her incorruptible objectivity.

Nicolas stroked her hair. He still treated her as though she were a child. The two other girls looked at her contemptuously. Again Nicolas opened the volume by Stifter and read as naturally and yet as broodingly as he had recited the poem: "The Tourmaline is dark and what shall here be told is also dark. . . ."

Marlene nodded. She knew every word of the story.

But he had not yet read three pages when he lost patience and put the book aside and sat down at the piano and began to improvise. What he played lacked neither passion nor inspiration, but was a little formless. He sang to his playing, in a hoarse voice, and gradually subdued the passionate expression to an elegiac melancholy which, in its turn, melted into a dull, staccato pianissimo.

He jumped up with a laugh and declared that he must hurry on.

"Too bad," Laura sighed.

"It was all false and stupid what he had done there," he said, "too dreadfully stupid!" Marlene shook her head and gave him her hand which he pressed so hard that she cried out in pain.

As he was approaching the door, Pia entered the room. His appearance made her look at him in surprise. After he had courteously answered her few simple questions, he took leave of her, too. On the threshold he remembered that he had not shaken hands with either Relly or Laura and swiftly returned for just a moment.

14

The next morning, around nine o'clock, just as Laudin was getting ready to drive to town, a message came from one of the tenants in Egyd Fraundorfer's house, which had no telephone, begging Dr. Laudin to come and see Dr. Fraundorfer at once. Laudin had a session in court which he could not put off. Since, furthermore, he suspected nothing ill and rather attributed the telephone call to one of Fraundorfer's sudden whims, he got a servant to answer that he would like to have Fraundorfer call him up again at his office toward noon. He was uninterruptedly occupied until then.

At eleven o'clock Pia called him up at the office. He was taken aback by the very sound of her voice. She begged him not to lose a moment, but to drive out to Fraundorfer's apartment, where she herself was waiting. What, in heaven's name, had happened, Laudin asked. She hesitated. There was a pause. Scarcely audibly, she then told him that Nicolas had committed suicide during the previous night. With a trembling hand Laudin hung up the receiver.

He had let his chauffeur go for two hours. He sent for a taxi. Fifteen minutes later he climbed up the four flights of stairs to Fraundorfer's apartment. The building was one that had gone to wrack and ruin in every respect, a huge barrack in an obscure street. On the landing of the third story stood a small group of people whispering to each other. On the fourth floor stood Pia, near the door of the apartment. From within could be heard the enraged voice of Fraundorfer; he was having a violent quarrel with some one.

"It is a good thing that you have come," said Pia, with pallid lips. "I seem to be helpless and useless here."

Laudin's face assumed a questioning look, since he could not understand the brawling within.

"I don't understand it, either," said Pia, shrugging her shoulders and suppressing a sob. "He is scolding the janitor on account of some weather stripping while the body of his son lies in the next room. I don't understand it."

She pressed Laudin's hand and went down the stairs. He entered the apartment. In the middle of the living room, which was cold and disorderly, stood Egyd Fraundorfer in a spotted coat that had once been brown. His hair stood up wildly, his face was distorted with rage, and he roared, as though beside himself, at the janitor who stood before him, bowed but blinking maliciously, turning his cap about in his hands, letting the storm sweep over him. It appeared that an imperfectly fastened window had been lifted from its hinges by the wind the night before and had crashed into the yard. The janitor and his wife took care of Fraundorfer's house for him.

Laudin knew his friend well enough to recognize at a glance the true character of this outburst. He had scarcely entered the room when Fraundorfer fell silent and looked at him a little strangely, a little surprisedly, with a contortion of the lips that might have been taken for a smile. And now Laudin became aware of the terribly ravaged look on Fraundorfer's face. From that face one might think that the man had been in a fight; there was a long, bloody scratch on his forehead above the left eyebrow.

The janitor slunk out. The little dog, which had been hidden behind the stove, came out and growled softly. "That's right, Herr Schmidt," Fraundorfer murmured breathlessly, and wiped the sweat from his forehead with his sleeve, "don't ever let this brute in human form cross my threshold again, Herr Schmidt." Then he turned at once to Laudin and said, with the strange beginning of a laugh that trailed off into something confused and wild and inarticulate: "Have you been in there? Have you seen him? Go and look at him. All the official representatives of society have been there—the physician, the casket-maker, the coroner's man. We have had many callers, Herr Schmidt, disagreeable callers. But it was nice of Pia to come. Unluckily we couldn't pay her the attention which was her due. Go in there, Laudin, and look at him. . . ." He would have gone on talking that way indefinitely if Laudin had not laid a hand on his shoulder. At that he fell silent and hung his head. Then he turned away and with heavy steps walked into his bedroom.

Nicolas's room adjoined the living room on the other side. Its windows were wide open and offered a view over courtyard, walls and windows, gray under a foggy sky. On the bed lay the body of the young man covered to the chin with a sheet. On his right temple, over which a lock of hair fell down, Laudin saw a tiny, red, round spot. The bullet had pierced the translucent forehead here. On the face was a winning peace, a gentle and amiable restfulness. The white of the cheeks already showed a bluish tinge; about the nose were traces of the swift effects of death. But the fact that the spectacles had been removed gave to the frail, delicate, not yet wholly formed features, a solemn and, as it were, indestructible loveliness.

Laudin stood there erect, without moving, his hat in his hands. From all the courtyards in the neighborhood one could hear the chattering of the maid-servants, the rattle of dishes, the splashing of water on the stones. In a loud voice Laudin said one word: "Why?"

This "why" remained standing before him like a pillar, cleaving the distant fog, and toward that pillar he would have to wander involuntarily and almost unconsciously.

15

When he rejoined Fraundorfer he found the latter lying on a sofa. This room was precisely as disorderly and un-homelike and cold as the others. It was half bedroom and half study. The broad, old-fashioned, green rep sofa evidently served as a bed by night. On the walls could be seen a couple of old family portraits, two crossed fencing foils under a student's fraternity cap, a half ragged oriental rug, a few Chinese masks, a bookcase, and from the top of a wooden chest of drawers grinned the skull of a little dog. A tea service, wine and beer bottles, plates with remnants of food, stood on the desk, the table and even the floor. Scattered everywhere were garments, sheets of manuscript and empty cigar boxes.

Laudin sat down on a chair with a torn seat.

Fraundorfer, his mouth contorted, pointed to a newspaper which he affected to have read. "It says in that paper that an American prophet has foretold that Europe will be swallowed by the ocean in 1945. Rather a hopeful outlook. Couldn't the man petition certain higher authorities to have

the catastrophe come a little earlier so that we might profit
by it, too? Don't you think so?"

"Let be, Egyd," said Laudin seriously. "Why this farce?
We are alone, you know."

Fraundorfer was silent and turned his face to the wall.
The silence lasted long.

"When did it happen?" Laudin asked finally.

Fraundorfer replied that he did not know. He still kept
his face to the wall. At a quarter of nine the janitor's wife
had rushed into his room. She had taken Nicolas's breakfast
to him, as she did daily. The coroner had declared that
death must have occurred between four or five hours previously. He himself had heard nothing. Perhaps he had
slept more soundly than usual. But no one else in the
house had heard anything, either.

Had not Nicolas left a letter behind, Laudin asked now.
No, none. Or had Egyd found notes of any sort. No, not
that, either. Was there any starting point for inquiry to be
gathered from the young man's last conversations or any suspicion from his demeanor? No. Since noon yesterday
when they had gone to the theater together father and son
had not spoken to each other. Did not Fraundorfer, in spite
of that, have his own theory concerning the motive of the
deed? None, except that perhaps his passion for the play-
actress had gone to the boy's head. He was quite capable
of these emotional excesses.

Again there was a long silence.

Then Fraundorfer began to complain that for hours he
had had wretched pains in his chest. Would Laudin bring
him the woolen shawl that hung over his desk chair yonder?
Laudin fetched the shawl and while he spread it over his
friend and tucked it in on both sides, Fraundorfer's hands
suddenly grasped the two hands of Laudin with an agonized
strength and held them as in a vise. Laudin did not stir.
He looked at Fraundorfer. The latter had closed his eyes
and his teeth were chattering.

But half a minute later he assumed his usual expression of morose unconcern. And he communicated a very strange fact to his friend. First, he asked whether Laudin had left the body covered. Or had he lifted the sheet just a little. Laudin said he had not. Fraundorfer explained that on one shoulder, between the upper arm and the collarbone, there was a wound caused by a burn, a wound that had barely begun to heal. It could not be older than four or five days. What, he asked, could be the significance of that? A wound the size of a man's thumb, burned deep into the flesh.

Hesitatingly Laudin suggested that it must have been an accidental injury.

Fraundorfer was almost angry. How the deuce, he wanted to know, could the boy have burned his shoulder? They ought to find out about that wound. Perhaps that Dercum woman could give information. Why should she know? Well, if the boy had had an affair with her, she ought to know. Didn't Laudin think so?

It was hardly to be assumed that there had been an affair between Nicolas and Miss Dercum, Laudin replied. Doubtless the photograph of the actress was now present to his inner eye and he saw again that face full of an indescribable veraciousness and innocence, as he had characterized it the day before. No, he didn't think that was likely. Fraundorfer fell silent; he gnawed at his finger nails. Suddenly he laughed—a long, thunderous, malevolent, convulsive laugh. Laudin started. He did not try to cut short this laughter of a man half-maddened by an insupportable pain. His lips twitched.

Then there was another silence; and again Fraundorfer gnawed his nails while Laudin stared at the wall.

Just before he started to go, promising to return that evening, a woman appeared whom Pia had found and sent hither to manage Fraundorfer's household for the present. The woman's name was Pauline Blum and she seemed agreeable and unobtrusive. Fraundorfer made no objection.

Then other people arrived—friends and acquaintances who had heard of the catastrophe.

16

On the day of the funeral Marlene did not get home until six in the evening and went at once to her room where she found Relly sitting at the table busy over her tasks. Marlene sat down opposite her, supporting her head with her hand. She was pale and her eyes were a little red.

"How is Laura?" Relly inquired.

"She weeps and weeps and weeps," Marlene exclaimed. "For two mortal hours I have tried to console her. She won't listen and goes on weeping. Mrs. Arndt has telephoned for the doctor."

Elaborately Relly blew her nose, shook her head and went on writing.

"The Castle of the Lost," whispered Marlene.

And Relly said: "Marlene, don't." She looked about her and shivered.

They scarcely ate; they scarcely slept. Their conversation had but a single theme. They saw nothing but that beautiful face in the rigidity of death, more beautiful in death, since they did not yet know what death meant. They recalled his last words and how he had stopped at the door and had come back once more to shake hands with Relly and Laura.

Not only did they not know death; they could not believe in it. It seemed to them to partake of a pretense or a game. They dreamed of a secret flight and a secret reappearance after long and incredibly haunting years. They could not quell the pain of that leave-taking; they could not withdraw themselves from the tormenting riddle of that deed.

They listened to all the guesses which were ventured anywhere. They read all the clippings from the newspapers. They asked each other in dread and yet were shy of the thought of any revealing word. The happening was discussed at school and more or less mysteriously the name of the actress was mentioned. There were those who pretended to know that other men had gone to their death or to their destruction for the sake of that woman. There was a young girl from the senior class, more experienced than the others and interested in life, who was in a position to tell the story that a very wealthy and highly esteemed industrialist, a certain Consul Altacher, whom her parents knew very well, had abandoned his wife and three children for the sake of the actress.

The girls discussing this attributed no shadow of guilt to any one involved. This generation bowed with a gentle awe as before an heroic tale. The time had gone in which adolescents derived their judgments concerning the great and ultimate sacrifices of passion from the examples of a stale and sterile literature. This was a new period. Life bore its own norms within itself and spoke straight to the soul, without a blurring intermediary. They had eyes, they had senses, and they used these in spite of outworn precepts.

By a tacit agreement, the sisters dedicated themselves to the memory of the friend whom they had loved. In order to speak of him they had to be sure that they were alone, and even then Relly locked the door. They recalled the characteristics by which he differed from other people; they remembered conversations that they had had with him and also certain quaint and amusing habits which he had had—his way of cracking his knuckles, the little defect of speech like a heaviness of the tongue, which had been more noticeable on some days than on others.

It would happen, during the exchange of these recollections, that they would suddenly laugh heartily. "Do you remember how silly he used to look when he took off his glasses and polished them with his handkerchief?" Relly would ask. And Marlene would merrily add: "And how he tried to put his handkerchief on his nose, instead of his glasses. . . . And they laughed together heartily.

Yet in the night, when the light was extinguished, Relly slipped into her sister's bed and for hours, fearful and silent, they lay in each other's arms.

It could not be denied that Relly showed a heightened sensibility toward the common impressions of daily life. A loud noise would make her wince. She changed color often; she was startled if any one called her. She was afraid of passing through a dark room and had unmotivated attacks of anger or of depression.

Marlene became visibly more reserved and, in her association with her fellows as well as with adults, more watchful and withdrawn. Even before this Pia had had occasion to resist her daughter's premature desire for independence with a gentle decisiveness. It was now a question of struggling with a constant inner rebellion which offered no direct point for attack and to which it seemed impossible to offer any resistance, at least any rational and wholesome resistance. Toward the end of the week Marlene came home once more at a very late hour. And when Pia asked her why she had stayed out so long, she replied that she and Laura had taken a long walk and had not been able to pay any attention to the passing of time. Pia pointed out that she couldn't accept this excuse if for no other reason than because it was neither safe nor proper for the two girls to gad about alone at so late an hour. Perhaps it was this ill-considered expression: gad about; perhaps the sense of Pia regretting having used it; at all events, Marlene's reply was surprising in its arrogant harshness: "I'm not concerned whether anything is approved of or not," she said. "Anyhow, each of us was taking care of the other."

"Marlene!" Relly cried, shocked and indignant.

Marlene shrugged her shoulders and both stubbornness and hardness showed on her lovely mouth. Pia gazed at her. Softly, she asked: "Would you answer your father in the same way if he had asked you for an accounting?"

"Assuming that he would take any interest in how I

[78]

spend my time—I would," Marlene replied. "The question would then arise whether we could come to an understanding with each other."

Pia was amazed. "Then you demand that he come to an understanding with you? Hasn't he the right to exact obedience?"

"No such right exists," Marlene said. She was very pale and her lids were half-closed. "If he chooses to command, I must obey. But such obedience is evil and useless. What does he know about me?"

Pia looked at her and said nothing.

"What does he know about me?" Marlene repeated more urgently and clenched her right hand without raising her eyes.

Pia left the room.

"Marlene, how could you?" Relly whispered in a hurt manner.

Marlene tore off her coat, hat and gloves, threw them on the bed and began to sob unrestrainedly. Relly, who was frightened, bent over her and stroked her head and tried to soothe her with many tender words. "You can't make anything clear to them," Marlene sobbed into her pillows; "it is as though they never had felt any pain, as though they had no soul. They know nothing and understand nothing. . . ."

Pia heard all this. She had stopped outside of the door, not to listen, but in an access of sorrowful reflection. She turned and went back into the room. She requested Relly to leave her alone with Marlene and Relly obeyed with a glance which was meant both to cheer and to thank her mother.

"Get up, Marlene, and come here," said Pia, without any attempt to hide her helplessness.

Marlene arose and approached the table. "Don't tell me I've been in the wrong, mother. I know it," Marlene whispered, with sad archness.

"Well, and—Marlene: Do you think it suffices to admit your fault? Isn't that a cheap way of being relieved of responsibility?"

But it became clear at once that Marlene felt no need of any such relief. She thought it her duty to admit that she had committed an offense against the mere forms of acceptable behavior. Pia didn't think that this reached the root of the matter, although she was more than willing to be indulgent, seeing how things were, and seeing that any sort of solemn inquisition was alien to her own character.

Marlene, on the contrary, was passionately eager to have it out. She was in no mood to assume any guilt or to appear crushed, as perhaps her mother expected her to be. She herself needed to be the accuser and to pour out what she had at heart. But for her, too, language was so difficult and the worn words were so dangerous to handle. She said she didn't feel well and that she often felt the atmosphere of the home to be oppressive. Could she speak more clearly? However considerately she tried to word her complaint, she knew that it must wound her mother. It was useless to try to allay the hurt by an accompanying look or gesture. A strange situation: the unsuspecting mother—the child full of perceptions of truths that had not yet come into being, the woman imprisoned in dead things; the girl who had knowledge of the unworthiness and the weight of these things, who pointed hesitantly to her father as to a mysterious, unrecognizable and strangely isolated figure and, by this act, called forth disquietude and even a first flash of fear in the heart of the mother and wife. Marlene, becoming aware of what she had done, tried with all possible skill to blur and retract what she had said. No, she hadn't meant precisely that . . . nor was it to be understood after this fashion . . . and so on and so on. Sadly she hung her head, despairing of the possibility of human communication.

But there was still another subject, that of education and its feebleness and outmoded quality. This word she emphasized again: outmoded. Oh, she wasn't rebelling against compulsion, as such; she could conceive of compulsion being helpful, but against superfluous compulsion that had its origin in mere habit and the desire for ease. "Is it a crime if one wants to escape what is false and wrong-headed in order to avoid unnecessary suffering?" Her demeanor was that of a tribune of the people. And then she came to what she boldly characterized as downright dishonesty: "Because my parents give me food and clothing and care and a home, must I, in exchange, barter my liberty and my truth? Isn't that a trade that speculates with my weakness and my dependence? Am I less a human being, a creature of will and knowledge, because I am compelled to submit to a biological necessity?"

Happily, this sounding tirade was not without a tinge of self-irony. Without it, Pia would have been hopelessly embarassed. Half in vexation and half ironically she looked into her daughter's glowing face. "I can't compete with you, Marlene," she admitted with a sigh. "I suppose I should be ashamed, but you silence me with your eloquence. Tell me precisely what you're driving at. What's to be done? What's to be changed?"

"Oh, a great deal," Marlene cried, "a great deal ought to be changed and ought to be done." But it just couldn't be discussed; the words had a way of eating each other up. One always heard it said, even by clever people: things are as they are and human nature is what it is and there was nothing to be done about it. But if that were true one would perish of the dreariness of it. "Are you really convinced of that, mother? Are you thoroughly convinced that everything must be as it is? For instance, frankly, mother, do you believe that Nicolas had to die? That there was no way of preventing it? That there was no one in the world who could have kept him from it?"

"But who and how, Marlene?" Pia asked hesitantly.

"I can't tell you, mother." Frightened at herself and

with trembling lips, Marlene sought evasions. "Only everything seems so, so—extremely cruel. Did his father really know him? A human being like Nicolas—he isn't so easy to decipher. Did his father ever take pains to do so? Or did he really know nothing about him? Maybe he never even reflected about him. And that is a terrible thought, mother, so terrible that it's hardly bearable. Father says that Doctor Fraundorfer loved his son. I can't tell. But what do you think? And if he did, was it in reality love? For if it was that, then it is clear that love does not suffice. There must be something more and different that grasps us and controls us—compulsion, too, oh, yes, but a wonderful compulsion, one that grows out of a reality. Do you understand me, mother? Do try to understand!"

Reality! This recurrent word! It seemed to be a magic word on the lips of this girl of fifteen. What did it reveal or what was it meant to prophesy? Pia was silent and perplexed. The passionate grief and rebellion in Marlene's speech overwhelmed her, as much as some element of truth in it—a truth that coincided with some dark presage of her own.

"And what are we to do, my child?" she asked helplessly.

"Dear mother," was all that Marlene answered. The girl's smile was almost compassionate, as though the two had exchanged the natural rôles which the years had assigned them. Marlene put her arm around Pia's neck and kissed her cheek and wept again, but now with a release from all tension.

17

Laudin arose and laid the documents aside. It was a new set which had just been begun. At its head stood the name of Altacher. An hour ago Mrs. Altacher had been in consultation with him. It was a somber record of family life that she had brought to his attention. Fragmentary up to this point, for shame and grief had scarcely let her speak. She had come for his advice. But he had said very little, at once aware of her own profound indecision. Experience had taught him that people who demand counsel fear nothing so much as being shown the right way. Finally she had promised to send him a written account.

She had named the name of Louise Dercum, too. In the rôle of instigator? Or seducer? Of villain in the play? Some such accusation arose from the tentative hints thrown out by Constance Altacher. But Laudin never formed an opinion without sufficient proof.

He was rather exhausted. It was past seven-thirty. He arose and was about to go. At that moment it was announced that Mrs. Brigitte Hartmann begged for an interview. A tormented look appeared upon his face. "Quite impossible," he said. Then, after a moment's reflection: "Let the lady come in."

She was dressed in city clothes. She had on new gray gloves. But her shoes were broad and countrified. Laudin courteously asked her to be seated. She seemed depressed and at the same time annoyed with herself at being so. From the first moment she kept watching the lawyer as though he were a wild beast whom she had determined to tame. Her glance was piercing and restless. She said that she had been on the way to her own lawyer, but had finally determined first to have a conference with Dr. Laudin. She had intentionally let a whole week pass; all sorts of thoughts had gone through her head. She could tell him right off that she looked forward to any legal action with the utmost calmness; she had a clean conscience and she defied anybody to say more than that. In the meantime, however, she had sent the lawyer packing whom she had consulted during Hartmann's lifetime. The man's fees had been, to say the least, excessive. How was she to get hold of so much money? It would be like robbing her own children. Children were expensive these days, especially if you wanted to give them a decent education, which was surely a mother's duty. She was sure that Dr. Laudin was a reasonable man and would be considerate in this respect also, especially seeing that she had come in a spirit of good will, ready to make a decent arrangement with that Lanz woman, provided always, of of course, that the woman's demands, which could certainly be discussed, remained within proper limits.

She talked ahead confusedly, though she had obviously considered previously what she would say. Her words were a tissue of all kinds of slyly concealed intentions, play and counterplay of avarice and prudence, of lies and terror, of respect for the mysterious apparatus of the law and a determination to slip craftily through its meshes, of willingness to compromise and of immediate retraction until the compromise sank to zero, above all, of the naïve trick of seeming to put herself wholly at the disposal of her adversary's attorney in order to get information for nothing or cheaply, and perhaps even to ingratiate herself into his good will and have him involuntarily defend her from the enemy at her back.

Undoubtedly she was impelled, too, by a superstitious notion of the knowledge of this man to whom she ascribed something like omniscience because he saw through her. Probably a consciousness of guilt had awakened in her only at the moment when he first confronted her. In her flickering eyes there was an expression that told of sleepless nights, a morbid desire to confess, if only half-heartedly and untruthfully. Such confessions, she evidently believed, would give her certain advantages as well as a possible appearance of justification. Women of her type have little opportunity to speak of themselves or their lives; when once they do so, all dams are swept away and they lay bare all things, to the point of shamelessness.

Laudin was prepared for this. He had merely to listen. She had guessed that he must first find out how far her willingness to make a settlement with his client went, so as to submit her proposals to the latter; she seemed unable to wait, she was aching to talk about all that was heaped up within her, the wrong she had suffered, the misunderstandings to which she had been subjected, the sacrifices she had made —of the whole martyrdom of her union with Hartmann.

He had not respected her. That had been enough to destroy everything from the start. He had never known what was due a woman. He had been a weakling through and through. Dumb and deaf he had gone through life, had had a look for no man, had trusted no one but himself to accomplish anything. It had never occurred to him that a human being could want to be cheerful or go out in company or have some simple pleasures. He brooded and complained the whole day, year in and year out. It was enough to make anyone go to pieces and lose courage. He had been no good in any respect. Didn't even our holy religion command man and woman to dwell together? Wasn't it written down in the Bible: be fruitful and multiply? But from the very beginning it had been a matter of torment and persuasion with him. Later she had consented to do without. But she had been a young woman when he had married her; didn't nature have any rights? Much he had cared. If he had a warm room, a warm meal, a warm bed, he hadn't looked around. But such a situation implants a poison in the soul. And the poison comes out like boils. No self-respecting woman wants to beg for what is her due. A woman has her own pride. But you can't jest with God, nor with the devil, who sits in each man's breast.

"Do you know what time is, Doctor?" she continued with increasing haste and convulsiveness. "Time is the threshing flail that beats us down. We get no farther in our own souls nor in our relations to each other; each makes life bitter for the other; time tears our souls into shreds. Had he spoken out before the children came! No one forbade him, you know. I would have been the last one to stay where I wasn't wanted. I know what I owe myself. My father was a government inspector. But as it was? Oh, no! One fine day he says: Things can come to no good between us. Thank you, no. Did you pick me up on the roadside? I was an honest virgin when the minister blessed us; I thought I had builded my house on a rock. Now I'm to be thrown out, eh? Well, that was like pouring oil onto fire. Nine o'clock in the morning and my fine husband was gone. Didn't show up again until nine o'clock at night. Then I was worn out and ready to go to bed. For I did all the work and took care of the house and the farm. He had furnished himself a bedroom by himself in the attic, which is in itself an offense against good morals. You heard him dragging himself upstairs. You heard him stamping up and down. I used to jump up and cry out: The children are asleep, you know! There'd be quiet for a while. Then it would start again—tramp, tramp, tramp. Then he would come down to my door and call, Brigitte. What's the matter? I want to talk to you. Very well, we would talk. I'd be half dead for sleep; it didn't matter. He would sit down on a chair and begin to talk. And he would begin from the beginning of things and come up to his present unhappiness and wretchedness. How I had done this thing wrong and mismanaged the other thing; as, for instance, he asked me to remember what happened once when my late brother-in-law was visiting us. Well, I couldn't remember. You can't remember every lousy trifle. He wouldn't stop. He said that I had said so and so, and so and so, and that, if I had said differently, everything would have been different right along. Naturally, my patience gave out and I flew up at him. Then he said: Look at you now; this shows what you are and how it's hell to live with a woman like you. And so it went on, night after night, all the seven days of the week and all the weeks of the year. Sometimes it went on to eleven o'clock and sometimes to midnight and sometimes as late as two in the morning. And like other people I have only two arms and two legs and one head, God help us all, and the upshot of it all each time was: Divorce me! But why should I, I'd like to know? Why don't you get a divorce, I used to ask him. What have I done? Why should I have an evil reputation? A divorced woman—no, thank you! But, by and by, if you torment and vex a human being long enough, you can get them to consent to anything. And a day comes when you almost take your two boys in your arms and get ready to plunge into the river. And another day you get hold of the old fowling-piece to shoot everybody and last of all yourself. But he catches you at it. He's behind you day and night. Rotten pretense, he says. Oh, ho, is it? I got shards of glass one day and cut open my veins before his very eyes and everything swam in blood. Pretense, eh? You can see the scars to this day. Here they are. Then he cried: I'm going to America; I'm through! Is a man a slave for life because he's married? Oh, ho! I told him, marriage was no joke; he ought to have thought it over beforehand. But anyhow, being a good-natured woman, and because I myself had no rest or peace any more, and nothing but confusion in my head, I went to a lawyer. But I just couldn't; I couldn't bring myself to it. What is a woman without her man? A poor creature for all the world to jeer at. God had punished me enough. So there I sat alone with the children, when he finally went away with his woman. And the neighbors gossiped and gossiped. All the evil tongues in the village wagged. You know how everybody looks into his neighbor's windows in a place like that. But I'm coming to the will, Doctor. Don't worry. And I'll tell you the truth, the honest sacred truth. And if one word is a lie, may my eyes wither in my head and my children never see a happy day again. Well, it was the night of October 17th, the very night during which Hartmann died. You see from this coincidence that I can't be mistaken. I woke up around three o'clock. It was the very hour of his death. I found that out later. And my heart seemed to beat up into my very throat and something seemed to be stirring.

I asked: Who's there? Suddenly Hartmann stood beside my bed, Hartmann just as he used to be. And I tried to ask him where he came from and what he wanted. But my throat was like leather and I couldn't utter a sound. And so in my mind I just sent up a little prayer to my patron saint because I saw now that it was not the living Hartmann, but his ghost. He beckoned to me and I got up, and again he beckoned me to follow him. And he went on into the upper room, and I behind him, and when we got upstairs he pointed to the desk and to the locked drawer. He touched the drawer and it flew open. And on the top was lying a piece of paper and he pointed to it and said: Get rid of it, Brigitte; I've sinned against you and the children; what is mine is yours and man and wife are one flesh. And that's the way it was, Doctor, and I don't know to this day what the paper was. How can I tell whether there was a will or not? Next day there was nothing to be found. I've seen nothing and touched nothing."

Suddenly she flung herself upon her knees and grasped Laudin's hand before he could resist and drew it to her lips. She cried out in a high, shrill voice: "Have pity on me, Doctor! I'm a lost creature without any reliance on any one in life! I've done no evil and things have come upon me." But when she saw his rigid expression which betrayed none of the emotions she had hoped to evoke, she grasped his hand again, and added almost whiningly that on her soul and honor she knew nothing of the will and had never seen it, but that if he wanted her to she would search through the whole house again and look into every room and closet and cupboard and wardrobe, only she begged him to think no evil of her. . . .

In this ugly room with its ugly furnishings and its padded doors, with its hundreds of legal documents, and its shelves reaching to the ceiling, which were packed with folios and law books and decisions of many courts—in this room the catharsis of innumerable human fates had taken place; innumerable somber reports had become vocal here, delineations of suffering and crime, confessions dictated by hatred and love, by vengefulness and remorse. But this room had probably never before witnessed a scene in which contrary elements of human nature had blended into so dark a confusion—despair and untruthfulness, slyness and hysteria, exorbitant passion and peasant canniness, theatrical grief and sincere grief, humility and rage, hypocrisy, and yet an aching conscience.

Laudin kept a little bottle of salts of lavender on his table. He took it up and sniffed at it. "Get up, Mrs. Hartmann," he said coldly. All that you say has no bearing on the case except the expression of your willingness, under certain circumstances—and I emphasize this, for we seem to have gotten no farther—to come to an amicable agreement with Caroline Lanz. You might tell me how much money your husband actually left."

Brigitte Hartmann got up. "I think it's in the neighborhood of eighty millions," she answered, thoroughly disappointed by his cool objectivity.

"I think that that is far too low an estimate," said Laudin, replacing the bottle of smelling salts on the table. "I happen to know that a hundred and fifty millions is nearer the truth. But that's a matter that admits of no discussion, since the facts cannot be concealed. I therefore put to you as a purely provisional question, which leaves the rights of my client totally uncompromised: What is your idea of the amount for which you would conceivably be willing to settle with my client?"

Brigitte Hartmann's face grew dark with stubborn craft. In a low voice she declared that she didn't know, that she couldn't say at present, that it would have to be carefully thought over, that she would see. She had thought about ten millions. Oh, well, if that seemed too little to the Doctor, she added quickly, seeing him shrug his shoulders, she might raise the sum a little in consideration of the child. She'd like to know whether she could come back after she had thought it over? Or would the Doctor mind coming out to see her, as he had done the other day? Then one could talk it over in peace. No? Well of course the Doctor had very little time. And of course she was a very humble person. Of course! Then might she write? Very well; she would write within a few days. Then she would go now, thanking the Doctor very humbly and cordially for all his kindness and patience.

And so she went. Laudin bowed and looked after her until the door was closed behind her. He dug his finger-nails into his palms and on his face was an expression of immeasurable disgust.

18

He had sent word to Pia that he could not be home that evening. In a little tavern which he had occasionally frequented during twenty years, he took a frugal meal. Then he drove out to the suburb where Fraundorfer lived.

Since the day of Nicolas's suicide Fraundorfer had not left the apartment. He received no one but Laudin, denying himself to every one else. Thanks to the activities of Mrs. Blum the apartment was in a more orderly condition. Few words passed between Fraundorfer and his new housekeeper. Pauline Blum went silently about her business. Fraundorfer grumbled now and then, but put no obstacles in her way.

He worked, or at least let it be understood that he worked. When Laudin asked him what he was doing, he answered that he was working at an old and favorite project, a history of human stupidity. When Laudin dryly suggested that no possible span of human life would suffice for that undertaking, he agreed with a laugh, but contended that the very overwhelmingness of the material offered an excuse for the temerity of his attempt. Since no single human being could hope to master the sources and the evidence, it would require the coöperation of many, of an entire areopagus of exalted spirits. Flaubert had evidently had a similar plan in mind, but he had scarcely touched upon his task and, having barely begun, had had to lie down in his grave. A great pity, too. Fraundorfer had concentrated all his thoughts during several decades upon this gigantic work and his notebooks were as swollen as torrents in the spring.

When Laudin entered, Fraundorfer was busy brewing grog. He wore a shabby green dressing-gown held at the waist by a girdle of leather. The color of his hair had changed somehow; it hadn't grown gray, but grayish green, like hay. At the sight of his friend he uttered a strange thick laugh of greeting and stretched out two fingers of his huge hand. Then, silent as before, he addressed himself to watching the kettle on the spirit lamp. Laudin took up a book, sat down at the opposite end of the table and began to read. It was a treatise on the philosophy of religion. On the margins of the pages Fraundorfer had scrawled penciled comments: Idiocy . . . the degraded fool . . . the mad chatterer . . . unsupported rot . . . imbecile. . . . Other invectives were less printable.

The grog was done; a full glass stood before each of the two men. Fraundorfer lit a cigar stump, looked out of the window and growled: "Snowing cats and dogs, isn't it?"

"Yes, it is snowing," said Laudin, and laid the book aside.

Continuing in the same tone and sipping at his glass, Fraundorfer declared that that circumstance of the wound on his son's shoulder should really be investigated; he couldn't get it out of his head; it was like foreign matter in his flesh or else like a premonition to complete some unfinished piece of business. He had harbored the intention of looking up the Dercum woman and getting an account from her. But the thought of the streets was repulsive to him. Was it not possible, too, that she would come to him? One might even say that it would have been the proper thing to do, the decent thing, the appropriate gesture. Quite possible, on the other hand, that she had inhibitions in the matter. Not surprising. Even a touch of bad conscience. Not surprising at all. Perhaps it was better that she had not appeared. What would have been the result? A bit of play-acting. He would rather hear nothing. He was making a fairly successful effort to dismiss the matter from his mind.

Laudin said: "I have determined to call on Miss Dercum. I am going to write to her and ask for an interview. I thought myself that you might . . . but perhaps such a meeting would hardly be agreeable. It's no fitting situation for you to be in. I'll drop her a line to-morrow. My only trouble is that I'm so busy. All hell has broken loose during these past few days."

"Yes, do go," Fraundorfer replied, and lit a fresh cigar. "Go and then render me a report concerning what you call her veraciousness and innocence." He laughed a goat-like laugh. He opened a drawer. In it lay the photograph of the actress, the same photograph; it lay amid bills and letters and banknotes. He threw it over to Laudin. "Take it," he said, with ill-restrained rage, "it may serve you as an identification."

Laudin regarded the picture. The expression of the face seemed as gentle and thoughtful as it had on the day when he had seen it first. He talked as though to himself. "It is easy and obvious to assume deceit or self-deception, but the very illusion of certain qualities is a delightful thing. How much there can be in a human countenance! And think of the masks that we have to put up with in daily life. Every evening when I leave my office I feel like washing my body with a powerful acid and laving my eyes and scrubbing my hands."

"You have become Dyskolos," Fraundorfer murmured. "Were you not once Eukolos?"

"It may be so," Laudin admitted; "there are words enough with which to label conditions." He went to the sofa and sat down, supporting his head in his hand. For a long time he gazed into vacancy, and the muscles of his cheeks and forehead were strangely tense. "I must tell you about a dream of mine," he began in a muffled voice, "which really connects rather well with the conversation we had last Sunday. I had dreamed the dream even then. Only I didn't know. . . . I wasn't clear in my own mind as to its character. It may happen, as you know, that one only imagines having dreamed a certain dream, or, at least, that one unconsciously revises or changes it. However, I have dreamed the same dream again; I don't think that I have added anything to the dream as I now remember it. In this dream it seemed to me that I suddenly awoke and became aware of someone standing by my bedside, brandishing a knife. But in the midst of this awareness I seemed to fall asleep again, and in this sleep within my real sleep, there arose a vivid discussion between this man and myself. I tried to prove to him that there would be no advantage in killing me, since there were neither gold nor jewels in the house—an untruth, by the way—and what other motive could there be for the deed? I couldn't harm him nor was I an obstacle to him, in any way. But he only shook his head and sarcastically shrugged his shoulders. The room was so dark that I couldn't distinguish his features, but kept seeing the knife's edge threatening me. From this sleep within sleep I awoke again and again, and each time the question tormented me, first, whether he had driven the knife home, secondly, whether he was still in the room, or, whether he was in fact only a dream of mine. And each time that I sank into that second sleep the violent debate with him began anew. Finally I seemed to lie there with open eyes, and I thought of argument after argument with which to dissuade him—what I had accomplished, how necessary I was to my family and how well esteemed in my profession. But suddenly he came very close to me and bent so near me that I could feel his breath and saw, to my immeasurable terror, that it was I, myself. What did that mean, tell me? What do you think of a dream like that? You are

[93]

fond of rummaging in the hidden corners of the human brain."

A malicious grimace was Fraundorfer's answer. "A genuine lawyer's dream," said he, "a trial, a plea and the whole thing perfectly rubber-stamped. Take a vacation. Your system needs ventilation."

Laudin evidently knew that no serious answers could be expected from Fraundorfer until the alcohol had gone to his head. But he seemed not to care whether his friend answered in accordance with his real thought and feeling, or out of a mere sarcastic whim. Perhaps for this very reason he found it easy to talk to Fraundorfer concerning himself and his difficulties. "A lawyer's dream," he said, "that ought really to be the most wildly confused dream in the world." He leaned backward and stared at the ceiling. "Such a dream would scarcely be describable in words. Ever since I saw a famous painting in an art gallery representing a witch's Sabbath, I have had to smile at the feebleness of the artist's imagination which cannot even succeed in bringing a shiver to a normal human being like myself. Life, which has the reputation of being prosy and flat, has quite other revelations to give us. In both insolence and somberness it outdoes the imagination of madmen. It seems to me that there must be certain fibers in the tissue of my brain which need only to be stirred by memory for me to be automatically transferred into a world in which hope is dead in very truth. A lawyer's dream, indeed!"

He went on talking while Fraundorfer heated more water for his grog. He proceeded to unfold this world without hope and to roll it out, a little for his own benefit, too, as though it were a map. The impulses that led to this explication must have been of long standing, must have fretted their channels through his brain long ago. For everything he said sounded finished and precise. All that the moment added was the translation into the audible. It was a summing up, a bitterly ironical, general view: behold, friends and fellow-citizens, what I am doing and what comes of it. Out with it just this once! You can turn away if you want to, or put your fingers in your ears. It's not essential that you should say yes or no, or have any attitude. . . . In this man's soul there must have been fermentations of the extent and consequences of which he was himself not wholly aware. It was very curious that he arose suddenly, walked over to a little shaving mirror that hung beside the window, looked at his image in it, laughed a little to himself and then resumed his former position on the sofa.

Fraundorfer, brooding over his grog, did not once interrupt him. He went on, and from his words there arose a huge delineation of life in which human figures were interwoven into an inextricable snarl. These creatures had no names. Instead of that they had occupations, offices, missions and distinguishable external fates. They were merchants, judges, physicians, public officials, small shopkeepers, mechanics, writers and women of all kinds, ages and degrees. This mass of figures was lost in the mists of the background. You could but guess at stranger phenomena beyond the reach of the eye.

All these faces were lacerated by definitely directed greed, but their lips were slack with the weariness of words spoken in vain. There were those who would not relax their grip upon each other, and those who were fleeing from each other in hostility or fear. There were those who cried out, yet could not make themselves understood for all their crying, and those who whispered and feared to be overheard. There were some who were panting for justice and others triumphant in their consciousness of having done it violence. And none was satisfied. And all continued to plunge forward or rage on. And the picture takes on the character of a cinema. Generation after generation races by. There is pursuit and clutching and separation. It is a pitiless hunt, a hunt for the purpose of annihilation or booty. This moment's victor is the next moment's sacrifice; tenderness and passion are succeeded by hatred and disgust. And nothing has any meaning. It is often only some change in lighting that alters the meaning of the images. Ultimately no one knows what truly serves him or what his duty is. The man who calls life a battle of Titans, has merely taken it into his head to see dwarfs in supernatural dimensions. The judge's sentence is an accident, and decisions are favoritism or empty formulæ. There is no vital spark within, no daimon, no flame of renewal. It is like a cobbler's shop where for a thousand years, shoes have been cobbled in one identical way. Work is a pretext for idleness and necessity a pretext for making a machine the master.

And the sounds you hear are forever the same. There are five or six hundred words with which they manage to express demand and encroachment, justification and resistance, remorse and confession, reproach and calumny, truth and falsehood and all their daily needs of speech. Unbelievably absurd—this ever recurrent verbiage of rubber-stamped formulæ, as though men's brains consisted of newsprint. Without becoming aware of their poverty, they label their deepest and most painful experiences with an empty embrace. Couple after couple lacerate each other, and always with these same five or six hundred words—the very excreta of the spirit. So it is all like breaking cripples on the wheel or like the dreary moaning of the dumb, and if you watch the evildoers carefully, you find that they do not even know their own sorry business. Punishment, expiation, equity, justice—all ground out of a mill—made of stage-fire—puppets stuffed with paper phrases. He had, recently, brought suit against a man on behalf of his wife. The man, a crude parvenu, puffed up with power and possession, a small-town tyrant, at once weak and sensual, had fallen in love with a cocotte and had simply left his wife and children in want. While he wasted his substance with this woman, his family didn't have enough to eat. Not satisfied with that, he sued his wife for a divorce on absurd and trumped-up grounds. The man's suit was hopeless, of course. The wife, typically enough, refused to make an amicable adjustment. He became brutal and threatening; he beat her and slandered her and came home at all hours of the night, noisy and enraged. Scenes took place which caused the maid servant to run to police headquarters, and the children to kneel down before their father beseeching him to spare their mother. The worst of it was that the family was really in frightful want and there was no power on earth to make the man fulfill his obvious duties. By the help of an astute lawyer he always succeeded in finding a way out. So Laudin arranged for an interview with the man in the presence of the latter's attorney. And it was of this colleague that he wanted to speak now. He had never met him before. He was one of those talented men without conscience, who have brought their calling and its service down to the level of a dicer's game. Their stakes are the varying interpretations of doubtful or equivocal legal enactments which are possible under their astute scrutiny. They are past masters of all the arts of delay and procrastination and they are capable of defending obvious injustice and trickery with more emphasis and passion than their opponents can bring to the support of the purest cause. At all events, Laudin met this man and had a discussion with him and at the end of fifteen minutes had to own himself completely beaten. His feeling of powerlessness turned, in fact, into one of somber admiration. Thus one ought to be made, he thought, and thus view things and thus turn falsehood into truth and cover every shamelessness with a shamelessness once sanctioned. Everything else, he confessed to himself, was mere helpless bungling. Of what good were conscientiousness, decency, strict honesty, humane feelings, moral responsibility—of what avail were these if such an one could triumph? And he would triumph. Compared to him, Laudin was a sorry clown fighting with weapons that could not even scratch the other's skin.

And at this point—was Fraundorfer asleep or had he but temporarily submerged his mind below the level of consciousness?—at this point Laudin seemed more wrought up than he had been for years and years. He asked: Why not become that adversary? Why not identify oneself with that hostile nature since one did not, after all, achieve either the perfection or the transcendence of one's own? Why not throw aside this old and weary and threadbare creature that one was and become and be another? Vanish from one's own self, as it were, and be reborn out of that vanishing. Is this a lawyer's dream, too, he asked Fraundorfer. But Fraundorfer was dumb. Either he did not understand his friend or did not choose to follow his mood.

Laudin seemed abandoned to himself. He got up and paced to and fro. His eyes flickered and his body seemed unsteady. Yet he had fought his way to a certain clearness concerning himself, and he had suddenly and tormentedly conquered that habitual sloth which makes a man stay in a certain groove and embrace voluntary blindness. He spoke as follows: "Who am I, then, and what? A man who loosens bonds, a man whose office and whose bread it is to hammer the iron hoops from rotten barrels. A destroyer by vocation, one who demolishes as a matter of habit and routine, under the protection of public opinion and the law. And so, in truth, I am even now that despicable adversary. No wonder that I am the man brandishing the knife above me in my own bed. It is senseless to continue this self-deception, senseless to try to evade the brutal fact. Either one is citizen, professional slave, draft animal, father and husband, or . . ."

Or what? What? What is this alternative, Friedrich Laudin? You cannot proceed an inch upon that road. Beyond that "or" the ground collapses under your feet. One more step and you no longer know—anything!

During the last words Fraundorfer had looked up and

squinted morosely over at Laudin. "People who are always dealing with irreconcilable contradictions make me quite tired," he growled. "They are usually pirouetting on the dash that separates their antinomies. Look here, by nature you are really a man prone to admit all obligations. These wild contradictions are not in your line. Draft animal, you say? All right, perhaps. Then, draw. If you can salt away your expenses and your fees, don't let the other considerations bother you. I wish I had your means of inspiring clients with respect. And the load that you are dragging in your cart is, after all, a very estimable one."

Laudin stood beside him and laid his hand on Fraundorfer's shoulder. "Stop," said he. And when Fraundorfer looked his morose question, he said: "Don't try to shake me, nor to take me too literally. I am concerned with things that lie beyond love, beyond custom and duty, perhaps even beyond the concept of honor——"

"Ah, ha, all in the service of the well-known firm, Veraciousness and Innocence, *un*limited?" Fraundorfer cynically interposed. "I doubt whether the aforesaid firm is solvent."

But Laudin continued: "Within the endless variety of forms assumed by human life, it must be easy enough for a distinguishing mind like yours to recognize a type of relationship so far above the ordinary as to make any unworthy suspicion of it an impudence and a sin. Question any hundred people in this city upon the subject of the Laudins's marriage and they will answer that they do not know a more successful one. And they will be people of insight and experience, high-minded and just in their perceptions. Should I contradict them? Am I in a position to do so? For do these people err? Never has there been a quarrel between Pia and myself, not even any serious cause for friction. In brief, she is a model wife. Not for an hour, nay, not for a moment, does she forget what she owes her husband in considerateness, care, loving-kindness and devotion. But look. . . . Well, how can you explain that. It is so frightfully delicate and at the same time so frightfully painful. Rather, it has become so, become so—as all things do become. There is no activity in the process. Life flows into character as the water into the basin. I have always adored Pia. She was to me like a being of a higher type. She was to be saved from the meanness and the spottedness of every day. She was, as it were, to be carried across the puddles in the street. Such notions cling. One comes to hold the woman constantly in one's arms and to carry her across the puddles of life. The gesture of adoration becomes petrified. If you join to yourself a fellow pilgrim, and you persuade him from the beginning that he must not, at any price, wet his feet, you cannot complain if he grows used to depending on your muscles. And thus all one's work and conflicts are taken for granted. She does not notice that your breath gives out, nor that your arm grows lame. She takes it for granted that you work, that you support the household, that you satisfy all wishes, that you pay for all display. She takes for granted your conflicts and your vexations. She has her own conflicts and vexations and is not beyond the reach of care. But one day you stand there and ask yourself : How is this to go on? Gone are free impulse and stimulation. Nothing is left but a follower or companion. The common pilgrimage is over. The things that remain are matters of course. Each specializes cheerfully in the appointed tasks. You are out in the world and she is in the house. Ah, if you were a locksmith and came home some day with a crushed finger—then things might come to life. Otherwise, you have the peacefulness of a domestic bliss that is sixteen years old, and life is like a dish of coagulated milk, sour and thick, and you drown in it like a fly, sober and unintoxicated."

Fraundorfer laughed approvingly. "To drown in a state of sobriety—that is hell."

A long silence ensued. On the table lay a heap of paper fragments. A letter had been torn up. Laudin carefully gathered up these fragments and it looked as though he were going to count them and then gather them into a heap. In the meantime Herr Schmidt crept from his basket in the corner, tripped up to Fraundorfer's chair, stretched his four paws and looked up at his master with something between a whine and a lament.

Fraundorfer bent down to him. "My compliments, Herr Schmidt. You evidently think that your opinion ought to be asked occasionally. Quite right, too. You probably have a sounder one than we bipeds. What do you say now? That a certain hour approaches? Quite right. The hour of eleven. At eleven o'clock our young man used to come home. You used always to be heard from then, being of a punctual and vigilant nature. True—true. And how are we to account for it that he hasn't shown up now for the sixth successive day? What rotten mismanagement, Herr Schmidt. For the present, however, you had better calm yourself. We bipeds are about to search out the causes of his non-appearance. And our friend is willing to take an interest in the matter, although in a certain respect it is probably too late. But he says that he has an intimate knowledge of such cases. Be calm, Herr Schmidt, be calm. . . ."

With a few inarticulate sounds he dropped his chin upon his chest. Herr Schmidt stopped whining, went to the door, sniffed about there and then lay down at the formless feet of Fraundorfer.

"Yes, there is a problem to be solved here," said Laudin, deeply moved, and stretched out his hand across the table to his friend. Fraundorfer took it slowly and without looking up.

Then Laudin went. Mrs. Blum carried a light through the hall for him. "He sits and drinks all night," she said. "Occasionally he makes a croaking sound and you can't tell whether it's weeping or laughter; sometimes he talks to the dog. At five o'clock in the morning he begins to write."

Laudin saw that there was still a light in Pia's bedroom. He went in. She lay on her back under the canopy of the broad bed, her hands peacefully crossed over her bosom, and smiled in welcome. But she was pale. The lamp beside her bed was shaded.

"Are you not well, Pia?" he asked in some anxiety.

No, she said, she didn't feel especially well and since to-morrow was Sunday she thought of spending the day in bed. She loved the thought of being able to rest twenty-four hours.

"So you must, darling," said Laudin, "though I confess that I wanted to take you to the theater to-morrow. I never get a chance during the week, you know. I wanted to go to see that young actress. . . ."

"Oh, yes, I know," Pia nodded. "Ah, well, you had better go alone, Friedrich. I really don't feel like it. Marlene and Relly are invited over to the Arndts'; otherwise you could have taken them. You know how they love to go out with you from time to time. But that isn't possible now. Marlene wouldn't disappoint them at the last moment. And as for Relly—of course the play would have to be a suitable one. What are they playing?"

" 'Kätchen von Heilbronn.' I can't say that this play is a great favorite of mine. Its romanticism is rather morbid. And Relly's impressions are so violent, that I should hardly care. . . ."

"That is true. You had better go alone."

Laudin drew up a chair and sat down beside the bed.

"After all that has happened, you understand that this Miss Dercum doesn't interest me merely as an artist. Within the next few days there will have to be a personal interview between her and myself. I thought that I might, in a way, prepare myself for that by seeing her on the stage. It might give me some notion of the woman with whom I am dealing."

"Do you think so?" Pia's tone was gently skeptical and she laid her hand on his. "Do you believe that the performance will tell you anything? The performance of Kätchen? I doubt it. From her Kätchen you will learn nothing. I'm afraid you're too naïve, Friedrich."

Laudin laughed. "Quite possible," he replied. "I wish I could rely upon your sharper or, let us say, more incorruptible vision."

"You haven't been able to persuade Fraundorfer to dine with us, have you?" Pia inquired. "His dining with us on Sunday had become a sort of pleasant habit. I believe you enjoyed it, too. How did you find him to-day?"

"Hardly in a condition to make his presence at the family table advisable," Laudin answered. "It's very sweet of you to think of it, but I don't think it would be wise, at present. The man is shattered. The tragedy has shaken him to the foundations. He fights against it and denies it to his own soul. He clings desperately to his dog and to his work and tries to deaden his feelings with wine and whisky and strong cigars. But nothing helps him. He's going under."

Pia's eyes were thoughtful. An impulse to ask many questions seemed to struggle within her. She had probably given more thought to the suicide of Nicolas Fraundorfer than she had let any one see. She had told Laudin nothing of Marlene's passionate outburst; she never took the liberty of submitting to him or discussing with him those things which, in her opinion, came within the domain of her duty. She had listened with an expression of cool interest to the rumors that had been brought to her, and the excited suspicions of her acquaintances. In this matter, as in all others having to do with the world, she did not abandon a habitual and apparently quite conventional bearing and attitude. To express in words what was in her mind or in her heart, would probably have appeared as unseemly to her as to go out into the streets of the city without gloves.

Yet in the past few days you could observe in her an uncharacteristic air of introspectiveness. Perhaps Nicolas had made a deeper appeal to her than other young men of his age. She was not generally fond of youths and most of them seemed to amuse her quietly. Or else the sudden determination to die, on the part of one so full of life and fire, had puzzled her and she could find no adequate explanation in any of the various motives that people had suggested. Possibly, too, the continuous restlessness and secret rebelliousness of Marlene had given her food for reflection. However these things were, she did not break her silence and at the very mention of Nicolas's name her soul seemed to withdraw itself from the conversation.

Now she still remained silent, although her unsaid words were clearly imaged in her eyes and features.

She looked very attractive as she lay there curbing her emotions and reflections. It seemed as though she, who was so imprisoned, had gained unexpected youth from beyond her prison walls, when that strange event made a breach in them. Perhaps that breach, through which she suddenly surveyed the world about her, would soon close again. Perhaps to-morrow the things that filled her life would mend that breach. It was, at all events, not pleasant to be exposed to the draught that blew in through it. She shivered.

For a second her glances and Laudin's met. He bent down and took her left hand and held it between his two hands. Pia was passive but she looked away from him and said softly: "Ah, Friedrich, we are old people, now."

He touched her hand with his lips and arose at once. "Good night, Pia," he said amiably. Not a shadow of vexation had appeared upon his face. Pia's searching eyes were well aware of this fact.

But as he walked to the door she looked after him with tender pity.

20

Laudin wrote to Fraundorfer:

"Since I shall be very busy during the next few days, I just want to tell you briefly that, in answer to my written request for an interview, I received a note from Louise Dercum asking me to call on her at five o'clock on Monday afternoon. It goes without saying that I will accept the invitation. Moreover, I saw her on the stage yesterday and I cannot deny that she made a most unusual impression on me. If any one had asked me I should have said that it was utterly out of the question for any actress, by acting the Kätchen of Kleist, to give the spectator so intense a feeling of being in the presence of a contemporary and a living passion. I am no critic by profession. On the contrary, my attitude especially toward the theater, is wholly unprofessional. During the overwork of the past years I am more and more rarely able to share the delights of a good performance. This does not seem to me to be a case where the habitual weighing of merits and faults is in place, but rather an opportunity to refresh oneself with the highest type of artistic delight after the weariness of the common day. I doubt very much whether in the contemporary theater there is another example of such charm, of a personality so moving, a voice so soulful, a power so great to move the heart—in brief, so complete a blending of nature and of art. I was infinitely refreshed and stimulated. Anyone who, like myself, is much concerned with the world's filth, must be grateful if, even for one short evening, there arises from that world a thing that is a torch and a delight. To my astonishment I learned that Louise Dercum.

contrary to your opinion, too, is a married woman (nothing seems more incredible when one sees her on the stage). Her husband, an actor named Keller, is said to be in an asylum in Berlin. The ugliest rumors are abroad concerning the situation. But I won't even mention them for fear of sharing the world's guilt in its habitual lust for slander. Take care of yourself, my dear friend. I hope to see you soon."

21

Wednesday morning Laudin received a few lines from Louise Dercum, written in the large, firmly wrought handwriting which had impressed him the first time he had seen it. She asked him to postpone his visit until the beginning of the following week; she would let him know the exact day later. She said that she was too busy to receive him until then and was, moreover, being summoned out of town during the last days of the current week.

On the same day he found simultaneously two letters from Brigitte Hartmann on the desk of his office. Scarcely had he begun to read them, when Konrad Lanz was announced. Before receiving him, however, he had to talk to a young attorney who came to him in behalf of Mrs. Constance Altacher. Like many women of the upper middle classes Mrs. Altacher seemed to have an almost morbid fondness for lawyers, and for thorough discussions with them. In spite of this well-defined partiality she seemed really to trust no lawyer or, at least, lent her ear and poured out her heart only to that member of the profession who, at a given moment, catered to her desires and agreed with her opinions.

When Laudin was alone again, he picked up Mrs. Hartmann's letters and read them with a shake of the head. He even called in his partner, Dr. Heimeran, in order to get the latter's opinion concerning these documents. Heimeran, a tall, lean, care-worn man with a skull as bald and elliptical as an egg, advanced the opinion that the person in question was a dangerous "querulant" with a tendency toward imbecility.

Dr. Heimeran was always inclined to attribute psychical or intellectual anomalies to the majority of human beings. According to him, there were not three adults in a hundred who were normal in this respect, and his view concerning their moral qualities was by no means more favorable.

The letters of Mrs. Hartmann were composed in a curious style: cultivated and even pompous terms of speech alternated with trivialities and dialect; mistakes in spelling were corrected now and then, but they were never eliminated. So, for instance, she had written "resolt." She had drawn a line through that and had then written "result." A line or a paragraph of almost servile obsequiousness and humility was followed by an access of insolence or a veiled threat or a jeering challenge. Self-torment alternated with morbid arrogance. Laudin had often had occasion to observe that women who had in some way been able to ruin the man to whom they had once belonged, and who had disappointed and deserted them—that such women were habitually subject to an indescribable conceit, even though they had ruined themselves in the bargain. The same trait characterized Constance Altacher, although he had not as yet any definite reason to suppose that she was guilty of the collapse of her married life. It was the perception of that conceit in her that had at once aroused his suspicion.

Brigitte Hartmann informed him that after mature reflection upon all the circumstances, she did not feel that she could consent to any settlement of the supposed claim of Caroline Lanz. The woman was evidently a woman of loose morals who had simply persuaded and seduced poor Hartmann. She, Brigitte, didn't feel impelled to set a premium on human depravity. Furthermore, she had pecuniary worries of her own. She was willing to send the Lanz woman some cast-off clothing and some linen. If the woman were a decent woman she wouldn't have taken up with a married man. She would at least have waited till he had his divorce. She didn't see why she should take any interest in the child. Who was going to give her satisfactory proof that it was really Hartmann's child? Wenches of that sort were quite capable of trying to hide one sin by committing another. The Lanz woman had destroyed her home, and she cursed her and the child, too. Surely Dr. Laudin would be able to appreciate the feelings of a mother and of a womanly heart.

Later on Laudin said to Dr. Heimeran: "If God were to protect all the women who try to shelter their crimes and inhumanities behind their motherhood, then the fact that a woman has borne children would suffice to send half of all men to the galleys."

Her second letter was quite different in character; it was incoherent and almost eerie in effect. It had evidently been composed later, for it started by proposing a personal interview with Caroline Lanz. She said she was willing to see the Lanz woman and to be guided in her own attitude by that individual's bearing. Here, of course, you had that mad arrogance in its most striking form. Brigitte Hartmann wanted to play the rôle of judge. She wanted to be both arbiter and executioner. But the condition of this kindness on her part—she made no concession without conditions— was that Dr. Laudin was to be present at that interview. He was to decide; his word was to be decisive; she was willing to submit herself to him; if he considered her guilty she would be willing to expiate (as though there could be any question of her guilt!); she saw in him, so to speak, her ideal of a man (she had spelled it "ideel"); but he, too, had better be careful before he tried to tell her any more rot about a copy of the will; she was at the end of her endurance. She had been hounded long enough and was ready for any desperate act—oh, yes, she was. She didn't care much about life and she wasn't going to be tricked or fooled; she insisted on being treated sincerely, even as she was always

open and aboveboard; one conciliatory word and she was all
kindness; but if she were harshly treated she could hold her
own, and she would see to it that her enemies were put to
flight and shame. She had her own pride, too, although
she was always ready to bow down to Dr. Laudin. She'd
do anything for him, but not for the concubine and bastard
of Hartmann. No, not a thing! It was in this spirit that
she begged to sign herself his very devoted *et cetera*. Then
came a postscript. Her lawyer, whom she had seen after all,
had advised her against making any compromise with the
Lanz woman. Since no will had existed, as far she knew,
she could obviously have destroyed none. She had no hesitation in taking her oath to that effect. If Dr. Laudin
wanted to force her to take an oath, let him go ahead. She
would accept the inevitable calmly. Finally, she wished to
inform him that she had rented the house and the farm and
would be staying during the next few months with her cousin,
in the Josefstadt.

"An exceedingly dangerous woman," Laudin murmured
after he had finished reading the letters. He was far too
wise to despise these documents in which the writer's in-
sanely exaggerated self-esteem was blended with a somber
delight in engaging the attention of others. He knew these
to be the characteristic symptoms of raging instincts, of repressed vengefulness and poisoned eroticism. He knew that
the consequences of such conditions were wholly incalculable.

He rang for the office attendant and told him to usher in
Konrad Lanz.

The appearance of Konrad Lanz had changed considerably. He wore a new coat, a new suit; his hair was cut, and
his face was carefully shaved. Yet his features had a strange
immobility, almost rigidness, and his skin had the yellow
pallor of one who had just arisen from a sick-bed. Laudin,
observing all this, asked Lanz how he felt. With downcast
eyes the young man replied that he was very well, that his
circumstances had undergone a marked improvement re-

cently; he had found new pupils and had been able to charge better prices. He was very grateful to Dr. Laudin for the latter's sympathetic inquiry.

Not once did he raise his eyes. When he sat down at Laudin's invitation, it was the pattern in the carpet that seemed to arouse his uninterrupted interest. Laudin looked at him searchingly before he addressed him.

"You wanted to know how your affair was progressing. I'm sorry that I can't say anything definite, yet. Mrs. Hartmann's behavior is that of someone not wholly responsible. She is now planning to arrange for a personal interview between your sister and herself——"

"I don't think that will lead to anything," Lanz interrupted.

"Neither do I. But I have the impression that a sort of retroactive terror has stolen upon her, and it may be that there is some hope in this circumstance. I am fairly sure that we will be able to get a moderate sum out of the lady in the end. But we must have patience."

"Certainly, Doctor. We are not lacking in patience. What a sorry figure I would cut, anyhow, if I were to be impatient in this matter. It isn't any such motive that brings me here. I have something on my mind. I am attacked by evil premonitions. There is something wrong with my heart. If anything were to happen to me, Caroline would be left quite alone in the world. I wanted to beg you from the bottom of my heart, Dr. Laudin, not to abandon her wholly under such circumstances. It may be only a hypochondriacal notion on my part; it probably is, in fact. And heaven knows I hate to make this further demand upon your kindness. A person is so utterly alone in the world. So few people can be relied on; and if you could give me this assurance I'd be inexpressibly grateful."

Once more Laudin's searching glance rested on the young man. "Don't worry," he replied, "I won't abandon your sister." He waved aside the young man's gratitude: "You mustn't make life more difficult by conjuring up non-existent troubles; you have enough real ones. Courage, my boy. By the way, I seem to remember that when you were a boy you could draw exceedingly well. I suppose you haven't lost that talent. Now I happen to have been told yesterday that at the Anatomical Institute they are looking for an assistant who can make drawings of certain types of preparations which are not suitable for photographic reproduction. Would you like me to recommend you for the vacancy?"

Lanz, who, at the mention of his talent for drawing had grown pale, so that the yellow of his cheeks had turned to gray, and who had drawn his handkerchief across his forehead, said hastily: "During the next few months I have but one aim, Doctor—that of passing my final examinations. I am devoted to the science I have chosen—entirely devoted. I can say that truthfully. I must finish. I must finally be able to show what is really in me. Now, if in addition to my tutoring I were to——"

"I understand you," Laudin interrupted him. "Then there is nothing more now. If I hear anything more about the Hartmann case, I'll let you know at once." He pressed the young man's hand and, with a deep bow, the latter withdrew.

After a while, as he was rising from his chair, Laudin observed an envelope on the floor. It lay under the chair on which Konrad Lanz had been sitting. He picked it up and, since it wasn't sealed, he drew a sheet of letter paper out without considering that the student must have inadvertently dropped the envelope when he was pulling out his handkerchief. To his amazement he read the following words: "Dear Madam, Since I have determined to devote my entire time, from now on, to my studies, I regret that I can no longer tutor your son. I have given up all my tutoring engagements because of an immediate and necessary duty to myself. With many thanks for your kindness, I am, yours very sincerely, Konrad Lanz."

"How extraordinary!" said Laudin to himself. "He talked most emphatically about new pupils . . . about the many hours of tutoring that made it impossible for him to do anything else. . . . What curious lies? What's their motive. . . . ?" Since the letter was stamped and addressed, he sealed it and threw it on the table where a pile of letters was waiting to be posted.

On his way home he had the car stop at a florist's. But the very moment he touched the doorknob of the car, he shook his head and murmured in an almost frightened voice: "No, that won't do at all." He leaned back in the car.

22

"I'd like to talk to you for fifteen minutes this evening," Marlene said to her father. "Have you that much time to spare me? Or are you too tired?"

Laudin put his arm around the girl's shoulder and took her into the library. Relly looked after them with curiosity, turned up her nose and then, in an access of tenderness which was demonstrative without being pointed, snuggled up against her mother.

Marlene, first of all, very courteously asked her father to forgive her for disturbing the peaceful "hominess" of his evening. This she said with a tinge of irony. But she didn't know how else to get hold of him, and it was a very serious matter concerning which she was anxious to hear his opinion.

With equal courtesy and with an equal tinge of irony, so that the resemblance between father and daughter became emphatic at this moment, Laudin assured her that he was entirely at her disposal and begged her to speak her mind. With a grown-up attempt at being informal, Marlene crossed her legs. Her attitude dropped back into the childlike when she took hold of her two braids with her little hands.

She asked whether her father had heard that a suicide had taken place in her school, too? Laudin had not, as a matter of fact, heard of it. Marlene related how one of her schoolmates, named Maria Feldner, had taken an overdose of veronal three days ago. No one knew how she had obtained the poison. She had died at the sanatorium yesterday. The case, like the story of Nicolas Fraundorfer, had naturally caused a great deal of talk. Most of the talk had been idle and pointless. But what had shocked all of the girls was the apparent lack of motivation of the act. Maria had been the child of wealthy parents, had had everything she wanted in the world and no one had ever observed any weariness, or even sadness in her. However, she had had one favorite chum among the girls, a girl named Berg, whose first name was Maria, too, and the tragic young woman had asked so insistently for this chum during the last day of her life, that her friend had been brought to see her. So Maria Berg had been present when the other Maria, sick unto death, had addressed her father and mother, who stood weeping at her bedside, as follows: I couldn't go on living, because I was so afraid of life. You never told me what life is really like. You hid everything from me and made everything about me seem lovely. But I found out from the newspapers how horrible the world is, how cruel men are to each other and many, many other things, which I didn't even understand but which gave me such a heartache that I couldn't sleep any more. And since my terror grew and grew, I determined to die. "That's what Maria Berg told me, quite literally," Marlene said and looked full into her father's face.

"This Maria Feldner," said Laudin, "was evidently a very unhappy being. But she was sick, too. Healthy natures defend themselves against the world like animals that are attacked, and even find a certain pleasure in the combat against evil and pursuit. Such weakness or, if you like, such sensitiveness as afflicted your young friend is a very frequent phenomenon in our age, as frequent as dipsomania or madness, as brutality and bloodthirstiness. This means that the demands upon capable people are higher than ever and that it is the duty of the strong and brave to put forth all their powers. Don't you agree with me?"

"That is true," Marlene replied with uplifted forehead. "Greater demands are made upon the capable. How do they meet those demands? With what? And do the strong put forth their best? And where are the brave? I wish you would point them out to me, father, and name them to me. I know that you yourself are capable and strong and brave. That is why I have come to you. But are you profoundly convinced that you accomplish anything? I mean for human society on the whole. I mean to say: have you the feeling that the world is growing better because you are what you are?"

"A difficult question, my child," said Laudin, oppressed by Marlene's implacable logic and shrinking from it within, as a flame shrinks from the wind. "A man tied to a profession is in a groove which he is not free to leave, bound for a goal in the determination of which he had no voice. You are touching a sore spot in our social order. We seem to will, but that is appearance, not reality. Free obligation and sordid compulsion have become identical. And few of us attain a spiritual height where will and duty merge into that higher compulsion which is the impulse of the master, not the obedience of the slave."

"I understand very well what you have said, father; oh, very well, indeed," Marlene answered with delight. She was truly delighted at hearing from him, beyond all expectations, a living echo of her words. "But you cannot simply let things drift. Not every one can be satisfied in his groove. Not in the long run, certainly. Because if that is so, things are bound to go from bad to worse and the young, who know little of practical life, despair of those who are older and who govern the practical life. Despair and distrust lead nowhere; they are negative qualities; that's why I thought—" she flushed and hesitated.

"Well, what did you think, Marlene?" Laudin was encouraging and kindly and bent closer toward her.

That was hard to formulate. Her lips opened and closed

again. Her braids were crossed over her chest. But gradually, as she added sentence to sentence, the germinating thought seemed to flicker through.

She said she knew that what she was saying was neither definite nor sharp in outline. She was groping and seeking both outline and foundation. It seemed to her that the whole educational system to which she was being subjected was sterile. She had no faith in the school nor in the teachers. She had often said to herself, of course, that with the appearance of a real personality on the faculty faith would appear, too. But that was exactly what was lacking. Possibly that was the reason why she never had any feeling of satisfaction but rather a sensation of emptiness about her. And that made her impatient. She felt as though some one had slammed in her face the very door through which she must inevitably pass. Who was to open it for her? Who had the key? Her father commanded so enormous a section of contemporary life that she had imagined he might help her. Perhaps salvation lay in the direction of the humblest tasks, polishing windows, sewing, doing housework? Maybe she ought to go into a factory and earn her living? All that she was doing now was the color of baby-ribbon or cheap lemonade. She thought she was realistic enough to know that the plan of working in a factory had its fantastic side and that a thousand reasons could be urged against it. But then she was just using it as an example. At all events, it was clear that she wasn't afraid. She was no Maria Feldner. She wanted to be a woman and a mother and learn to know the responsibilities that she must assume. Now could it ever be too early to do that? And most of her young contemporaries felt no differently. They wanted something new, radically new. At any cost they wanted to make the world happier and better—those among them, at least, who could be said to have brains and a heart. Didn't her father know that? Didn't he believe it? He ought to listen to such conversations some time. He ought to be present when they were discussing their parents and brothers and sisters and religion and science and authority and the state. They see through lies and out-moded laws and are aware of the contradictions between what is taught and what is done. Perhaps father might laugh at them. But upon reflection he will be convinced that the matter is no joke. On the contrary, she often had the impression that she and her fellows in age and attitude, were like foreign troops quartered upon this adult world, and that they had their stores of weapons hidden in secret places. It was no fun to walk about your father's and mother's house like a soldier from a strange land. It was no pleasure to know and to perceive that though this father and mother are living beside each other and are fond of each other, they are not really together and at one (at this point tears came into her eyes); she detested secrets; she wanted openness, clearness, light, everything except mystery. For every mystery is like a trapdoor beneath which a murderer lies in wait.

Laudin was overwhelmingly perplexed. His face had grown pale. Suppose that suddenly a charming picture on the wall, the likeness of a human being, which one has looked at with much pleasure day after day—suppose such a picture were suddenly to walk out of its frame and begin to speak, to speak strange words, words that strike boldly into the carefully concealed hiding places of life. Laudin's consternation was like that of a man who has just been addressed by such an image. First of all he had to pull himself together and reflect on an answer. But what could he answer that would not be in the nature of evasion, of embarrassment, of an attempt to gain time? Had he not himself pronounced the saddening axiom of the five or six hundred words with which your average philistine manages all the situations in life? Now it was for him to see whether his range of expression went beyond them. For there was no denying that this was a serious hour, face to face with this daughter who had granted him an insight into the hidden fires of her soul, and who came to him, to use her own image, as the emissary of a hostile army.

He did his best to strip his vocabulary of all faded verbiage and carefully avoided such expressions as immaturity, confusion, insufficient experience, the necessity for guidance and so forth, yet he knew that his drift was the same as though he had used these words. And he was immensely aware of his own entire ineffectiveness at this moment. It was even more difficult to answer her criticism of the conditions of marriage and to attempt to differentiate, in her remarks, between childish supposition and the amazing sharpness of her womanly intuition. Armoring himself with an expression of kindly indulgence, he assured Marlene that in this particular matter she was not competent to judge of essentials; the refractions of life in this mirror were too delicate to be measured by a wild passion for veracity, however honorable. In every river there were rocks and sudden depths, and only the boatman who had been familiar with the waters for years could steer his vessel through. Hardly the youthful excursionist who wanted to catch fish for his lunch. The question of competence derived from experience did enter into the problems of life. He gladly acknowledged the entire sovereignty of the rights which were Marlene's by virtue of her very youth. But first he must in her own interest beg for an adjournment, a brief delay for her stormy appetite for life. On the other hand, his answer in regard to her reference to the relations between himself and her mother must consist in an appeal to her tolerance in recognition of his own. For any defense on his part would be granting the validity of her accusation. And that he was not prepared to do.

His elaborate legalistic style of speech, pervasively ironic in character, disappointed Marlene bitterly, as he could see from her expression. But it showed her, too, that her urgent demand for truth had led her beyond all bounds. She seemed to feel that the rebuke hidden in his words was a deserved one, for she hung her head in shame. But one cannot revoke what one has seriously uttered. The spoken word is irrevocable. Perhaps a humorous dissimulation can heal the wound. She said she would wait and do nothing without her father's advice and approval; she kneeled before him with an almost kittenish gesture and looked up at him smilingly as though symbolically to express a momentary subservience. Thus the interview ended as it had begun, in mutual courtesy and apparent agreement. If looked at closely, it marked a vain effort of these two to find a path to each other.

"Good night, father," said Marlene, and brushed his forehead with a kiss and went out. Upstairs in their room Relly was waiting for her and Relly was one mass of restless curiosity, as though Marlene had done some hurt to their father which she, Relly, as protectress of the house, should have prevented. But since Marlene was silent and not inclined to communicativeness, Relly began to sing with deliberate intent to annoy. She hoped that the singing would lead to a quarrel in the course of which, if only she could vex her sister sufficiently, involuntary confessions would follow.

But this hope proved deceptive, too. So she only murmured: "Mother Weeping-willow is stalking about again this evening."

For several days the girls' grandmother had taken to the queer habit of wandering by night through the upstairs halls, as though she were looking for something. If she was questioned, she gave no answer, peered into all corners, muttered incomprehensibly and finally, shaking her head, returned to her overheated room. This behavior frightened the girls. Marlene opened the door a little and listened, but Mother Weeping-willow had disappeared. The dwarf Uistiti was wailing and his nurse could be heard scolding him.

For a long time after Marlene had left him, Laudin sat without changing his position. It was late when he arose. Very slowly his face brightened. After walking up and down for a long time he went to his desk, arranged his penknife, shears, stationery and ash receiver in their accustomed order. Then he took the ivory case in which he kept stamps, emptied the stamps out, arranged and counted them according to their denominations and marked the result in pencil on a page of his calendar.

23

Constance Altacher came in person to give Laudin the written report which she had promised him. It was clear that she wanted to dramatize the situation. Her tragic bearing obliged the lawyer to adopt a sympathetic attitude. Laudin's experience had made this ceremonial conventional. Most women would rather sacrifice a clear advantage to it.

Constance Altacher was delicately built. She had a feline face; black, piercing eyes set far apart, black, heavy hair, a somewhat turned-up nose—not unattractive. Her voice was deep and gentle and she had the habit of saying insignificant things significantly. That was tiring to the listener. She gazed persistently into the eyes of any one to whom she spoke, as though she wanted to nail him down with her glances. Her entire bearing was pregnant with a constant, unspoken expression of her wretched lot. And that awakened an instinctive contradiction.

The report, written with an evidently practiced pen, was as follows:

My marriage to Edmond Altacher was contracted amid the happiest circumstances. Even then Edmond was rich, and occupied an important industrial position; I came of a good family, had an ample dowry and was not devoid of personal advantages. I had also enjoyed an excellent education, was mistress of several languages and had frequented the philosophical seminar of the university for several terms.

We founded a home that befitted our station, dispensed hospitality and went out a good deal in society. I may say that during the early years, the harmony of our union was broken by no discord. I cannot say that we were always turtle doves; we were never less than good comrades.

So far as I can recall, our first differences arose when the children became old enough to enter school. Our three daughters had been born at intervals of one year; hence their development had been about the same. I wanted the children to be taught at home; I had many reasons for this desire. First of all I feared the danger of infectious diseases for them. I did not desire needlessly to expose to harm these beloved beings whom I had surrounded with such endless care and devotion. Since it was possible to protect them, I considered it my duty to do so. In addition, I did not like to expose the children to the moral influences of an average school. The ordinary disciplinary measures and methods revolted me. My whole trend of mind is aristocratic, and I have always hated the uniformity of mass instruction. Perhaps I overestimated my daughters' abilities. But no one could blame me for wanting to save them from those common molds in which all individuality is obliterated.

Edmond did not share my opinions. He did not believe that our girls had any distinction of character or mind. I could not but forgive him this; for what do fathers know of their daughters? But he ended by denying that our children were in any respect different from those of other people. Yet I could adduce the testimony of many people whose opinions are worth while, that this was precisely the case. As a wife, as a mother, I had a deeper and acuter insight into the children than he could have. His professional cares and preoccupations did not permit him to be with the children sufficiently. His relation to his children was an essentially playful one. A professional man desires his children to vex him as little as possible. If the world depresses him he sees his home as through smoked glasses. Wherever the girls went they aroused admiration—sometimes by virtue of their musical ability, sometimes by their natural intelligence and spontaneous charm of disposition. But Edmond considered people's admiration to be mere flattery, and my own justified pride he called parental delusion. I had definite pedagogical ideals; my friends approved of these and experts came to me for advice; they assured me that my notions were uncommon ones. Edmond was the only one who refused to appreciate me; in his eyes I was an eccentric blue-stocking. Need I say that that annoyed me bitterly?

Gradually it came to a point where he opposed me in all things, found fault with me uninterruptedly and sought to rob me of freedom of action in every respect. I repeat, in every respect, and not only in what concerned the children. He disapproved of my friends, disliked my frocks, distrusted my management of the house, objected to my choice of servants and was annoyed by the books I read. The little essays on the history of art which I wrote in my rare hours of leisure, and which my friends unreservedly praised—these he denounced as the idle attempts of a dilettante. The fundamental trait of my nature is an enthusiasm for the Great and the Beautiful. In this respect I have not changed since my girlhood and it is this quality that has often helped me to endure the difficulties of life. Why was it that Edmond always strove to deprecate this quality in me, even in the presence of strangers?

Why, I asked in my sorrow, why this unfairness? Why does he try to insinuate himself into the peaceful domain of my activities like an acid which, growing ever more concentrated, becomes ever more corrosive? I did not yet doubt his love as I was, alas, forced to do as the years went on. But in the early days I had no reason, at least no deeper reason. I constantly forgave him his whims and his rudeness and I can safely assert that I have known no second instance of a wife so absolutely devoted to her husband as myself. And this obedient devotion in the least as well as in the most important affairs of life, is to this day, after all that has happened, an ineradicable part of my nature. He and my children—I was concerned with nothing else and interested myself in nothing else in the world. His well-being, his comfort, his success, his happiness, were the constant objects of my undivided solicitude.

And how did he reward me? He seemed to distil a poison from the proofs of my love—the poison of ill-humor, of distrust and of self-isolation. Every disappointment which others inflicted upon him, he visited upon me, whether it arose from public affairs or from the inadequacy of his assistants and employees. As time went on he failed me in the most superficial considerateness and seemed no longer to be conscious of our children's surprised or saddened eyes. Was he aware of the thorn that he implanted in their souls? Did he realize how he smudged the surface of life for them, and distorted the natural image of him in their hearts?

He began to avoid the house. He treated our common home as though it were a mere lodging where one passes the night. He took his meals at his club or with friends—with those whom he supposed to be his friends. He had leisure for the most trivial people; none for me, none for us. He was too weak to resist the importunate. But he had no perception of his own children's needs. How was that to be explained in a man of so much intelligence and justice, of so thorough an education of the mind and heart? I have passed innumerable nights of sleepless and agonized brooding over this riddle—in tears, in prayers, in plans. Was I too weak to hold him? What was he striving for? What did he desire? What was the cause of his—I cannot call it otherwise—degeneration? It was as though we had lost him. Many and many a time I asked him, begged him to explain. He was by no means silent; he adduced numerous reasons, but how could those reasons convince me. I saw that they were artificial and constructed merely for his justification. I reproached him with his insincerity. And at that point our discussions usually ended in outbursts of rage in him, of despair in me. One could not go on living after this manner.

I had, of course, known for a long time that he was exposed to certain evil influences. I do not assert that his association with Ernevoldt and May Ernevoldt and later with Louise Dercum were the only causes of my unhappiness. The estrangement between Edmond and myself reached much farther back and had its origin in a period that long preceded the appearance of these people. But since they entered his life, all things grew rapidly worse. I cannot but attribute to them the chief guilt in the swift collapse of our married life, and it is they who must answer for it before God.

It was about eighteen months ago that Edmond first mentioned the name of Ernevoldt. After that he frequently brought the man to our house. But since I could not conceal my dislike for him, and at once suspected that his friendship would have evil consequences, they took to meeting elsewhere, generally at Ernevoldt's house where Edmond made the acquaintance of the former's sister, May. If I remember correctly, Ernevoldt had been introduced to my husband by a business friend. I know little of his character; I only know that he is a confirmed failure. His father is said to have been a Swede who married an impoverished noblewoman, was able to establish himself nowhere and finally died in America. Ernevoldt himself has a wife and child. But he lets them live in want while he wallows in plenty. I have been told that he got rid of them legally. They live somewhere in a small south German town and the woman must earn her bread in the most menial way. Bernt Ernevoldt had been at various times war correspondent, agent, commercial traveler and film director. Recently he has been living in a suburb here, in a rented villa, with his mother, two aunts, a brother and his sister May.

It is this woman who was destined to interfere so fatally in the life of my unhappy husband; this woman first, and afterwards the actress Dercum. For I believe her to be but a blind tool in the hands of Louise and of her brother. For the sake of human decency I shall make that assumption. Nor must I be blamed if what I am about to relate smacks of the sensationalism of cheap fiction. It is a sober fact that the complications of life surpass the imagination of the teller of tales. I will make an effort to delineate the state of affairs as concisely as possible. For it is not easy to make clear the intricate interdependence of events; it is not easy, and if my narrative arouse doubt I know I can bring proof enough to confound the most skeptical.

As things were, I was not surprised that Ernevoldt, with his pleasing appearance and his ingratiating manners, won my husband's regard. To conquer people by his charm is almost the only trade of this semi-adventurer who, at the age of thirty-five, still looks like a youthful athlete. Nor must it be forgotten that he came into Edmond's life at a time when the latter, now in his fiftieth year, had lost his grip on himself and on his relations with the world and was undermined in his faith, or rather in his unfaith, but certainly in the value of his activity and its aims. He was frantically looking for a new foundation, for a new content for his life. I had known that a long time. But I was powerless to bring any remedy. My voice no longer reached his mind.

Among other things and probably under his sister's influence, Ernevoldt occupied himself a good deal with occultism and theosophy. Being a dilettante to the bone, his interest in these things probably had no great seriousness. He told Edmond about a community, a certain group of people, of whom he was but the ignorant pupil, who had transcended the material and the earthly. He told him of his sister May, whom he described as one of these illuminati; he attributed to her visions and magic power. Edmond swallowed the bait. His first meeting with May sealed his fate. From the first moment on, he gave her his boundless confidence. She became his private secretary; soon her influence permeated all he did or thought. At this time Edmond began to sicken. The serious affection of the heart, from which he now suffers and which forced him two weeks ago to take refuge in a sanatorium, had its inception during that period. He had become, as I have said, unsure of himself in every respect; now suddenly he was enmeshed in that misty, pseudo-religious, falsely-mystical activity. He became a member of the sect and became more and more deeply involved; in the pursuit of hypnotizing conversations and the reading of confused and confusing books and periodicals, he neglected everything else. This woman and her followers not only alienated him from his wife and children; their mystical bearing, their impudent deception, also brought it about that Edmond, who had been so sensible and saving, who had been so prudent in spite of his wealth, began to finance Ernevoldt's questionable undertakings, to put large sums at his disposal and, furthermore, supported the entire family. But it is my firm conviction that things would never have gotten to this pass without Louise Dercum. It is she whom I regard as the real demon. It is easy to jeer at these so-called fantastic notions of mine. Edmond has done this on many occasions. Others have done it. Let them! I see what I see, and know what I know.

No one can deny that Miss Dercum has a scandalous past; her name has been dragged sufficiently through the newspapers to prove that. In Berlin the most unpleasant rumors concerning her abound. It is commonly reported that she succeeded in ruining her husband, the actor Arnold Keller, mentally and spiritually. It is credibly affirmed that it was she who caused him to be interned in an asylum for the insane. She simply considered that he had become a nuisance, and in order to get rid of him, there being no other way, she managed by subtle practices to obtain medical testimony in regard to his mental health which led to his internment. People have protested vigorously in order to secure his release, but she opposes it with the plea that Keller has threatened her life. What a crowd! What a world! I had never dreamed that a breath of that world could blow upon our faces.

I've been told that it was Ernevoldt who discovered the Dercum woman when she was seventeen and was playing on a provincial stage somewhere in Bohemia. He was so enraptured by her talent that he caused her to be educated at his expense. At all events, he has always interested himself very actively in her, and there can be no reasonable doubt as to the extreme intimacy of their relationship. But it was not until, some months ago, that she gave up her home in Berlin entirely, and moved here, and Ernevoldt introduced her into the circle of his family. It was there that Edmond met her from time to time. I say from time to time, for I don't know how often. It is clear that we are dealing with a woman who requires no long preparations to throw out her nets and secure her booty. This may sound heartless and unjust. I am sorry. Has not every one been heartless and unjust toward me? The indignation in my breast may well drown all gentler emotions.

Boundless as May's power over my husband was or, rather, is—for these conditions have not changed—so is the power of the actress over May. The latter seems actually to regard Louise Dercum as a creature from another sphere. She executes her commands unresistingly, obeys her slightest nod, and it is not necessary to assume that she is privy to the selfish intentions of her brother and his friend. She is evidently, like all other people who are in any way connected with Miss Dercum, under the sway of a personal magic. In her case that sway is so complete that she has been robbed of all power of self-determination. For this and other reasons I cannot help considering May Ernevoldt to be a creature at once hypersensitive and weak-willed. I have seen her several times, though never for long, and I believe that my judgement is a sound one.

I am convinced that no illicit relations exist or ever have existed between May and my husband. I am persuaded of this not only by the solemn protestations of my husband which I have no reason to doubt, but I am confirmed by my womanly intuition. But precisely this is the mysterious element; Edmond's helplessness in those toils is only the more inexplicable to me and other clear thinking people, on that account. He is her helpless victim, and thus equally the victim of Ernevoldt and Louise Dercum. He does not dream that he is the victim of these people. He seems to be asleep and in a state of well-being while they suck his blood. Until the end of autumn I nursed the hope that he would awaken and grasp his humiliating situation. On his birthday, last October, I adjured him in the most passionate terms; I appealed to his honor; I spoke of the sorrow and shame of our daughters who are now too mature not to be aware of their father's inexplicable defection. He listened to me in somber silence and stayed away from home for a week. Then, several days before he went to the sanatorium, he suddenly brought up the question of divorce. For the first time. I was thunderstruck. Divorce at the end of twenty years of marriage? From the man whom I loved above all things, and who was ill, perhaps incurably so? Nor was I conscious of any guilt, nor did he desire, by his own assertion, to marry any one else. What was going on within him? Was it not justifiable actually to believe in an accursed bewitchment? But who shall describe my indignation and my despair when, three days later, I was credibly informed that he was on the point of executing a plan by means of which he was to turn over to May Ernevoldt one fourth of all he possessed in order that she might, even during the remainder of his life, be secure from all material cares. It was now that I determined to act. The time had passed when I could calmly watch events and let them take their course. What was this May Ernevoldt to him or to me or to my daughters, that she should profit by his work and hold the just possessions of my family? Could one imagine anything more absurd? Also, I had had my fill of suffering and humiliation. This senseless and frivolous waste had to be prevented. I thank God that there is still time to prevent it. It would be a slap in the face for me and my children, and an unparalleled lowering of us all. I summoned a family council. All my kinsmen agreed that, if my husband continued to insist on a divorce, I was to grant it to him on condition that he bound himself legally to abandon all thought of this gift. In case of his refusal it would be necessary—nor will I shrink from this necessity, bitterly as my heart and soul rebel—to have him declared mentally incompetent and petition the court for a guardian of the estate. I will not see the triumph of those who desire to profit by the physical and spiritual weakness of an otherwise noble character. In addition, the three oldest members of my family have declared that they are prepared to seek Edmond out and to attempt to persuade my sorely and unhappily infatuated husband to give up the idea of divorce entirely. They will seek to reach his conscience and to open his eyes concerning the ultimate consequences of his purpose. This step will be taken as soon as the physicians in charge of Edmond give their permission. If that last plea remains fruitless, God help me and my daughters.

With deeply furrowed brow, his piercing glance still on the last page he had read, Laudin sat there motionless. The ringing of the telephone startled him as though it had been the blow of a hammer.

24

Louise Dercum lived in a spacious studio apartment which occupied almost the whole top floor of a new building in the center of town. Yet it was a rather silent street and the house stood among rococo palaces that had either been abandoned or turned into government and administrative offices. The lift carried Laudin upstairs, and even in front of the oaken hall door he heard laughter and the hubbub of many voices.

He was unpleasantly impressed. According to Louise Dercum's last note he had expected her to receive him alone. The occasion that led him to her must have seemed of little importance to her.

Yet he hesitated to turn and leave.

After he had given his card to the maid he entered a high and broad room which would ordinarily have been lit by windows both on the sides and in the ceiling. On this dark December afternoon the windows as well as the walls were hung, like the interior of a church, with brownish-red hangings of brocaded velvet. There were several standing lamps with shades that seemed as large as tents. In spite of them the room lay, probably intentionally, in a dim twilight in which Laudin's eye distinguished first of all only carpets, tables, couches, garish pictures on the walls and the figures of six or eight men and women.

One of these figures detached itself from the purple background and approached him vivaciously. At the same moment the other guests, their faces hidden in clouds of cigarette smoke, turned curiously toward him and for a few seconds the chatting and the laughter ceased. He at once recognized the gong-like, swift, and slightly husky voice. But her features seemed strange to him and her figure smaller. He felt a cool, mobile, muscular hand; he heard rapidly articulated words. He bowed.

Louise Dercum made the introductions. Among these names that meant nothing to him two met his ear that made him look up; Ernevoldt and May Ernevoldt. He saw a tall, extremely robust, rather fat man, whose beardless face might have been called handsome. But when one regarded these energetic features more closely there suddenly came to one an impression of sloth and unintelligence. And he saw a slender little figure with a narrow head and silken hair that fell in sudden curls only to the shoulders and which was so blond that it had almost the effect of spun glass.

Already Louise Dercum had left him. She stood beside the tea-table and gave directions to the maid. Then she immediately turned to a young fellow actress and spoke to her insistently. Two gentlemen, an actor and a journalist, whose names Laudin had already forgotten, joined the ladies and he heard Louise laugh. She bent back her head and one could see the brunette skin of her throat. Her laugh was sonorous and had the infectious quality of laughter that comes from the very heart. The next moment she was standing beside a heavily rouged woman who sat on an armchair near the fireplace, and bent over toward her. The Fortuny silk shawl that covered her shoulders made her look like a great, mobile and fantastic flower. A new guest appeared, at whose entrance she exclaimed with delight. It was a man well along in years, dressed in the latest fashion, whose expression was affected and whom she addressed as Baron. He treated her with familiarity and whispered in her ear, whereupon she tapped the back of his hand. Seeing Ernevoldt, the Baron went up to him with outstretched arms. Laudin heard him asking after the state of health of Consul Altacher; several times he heard him say, "Our poor, dear friend." With a smile Ernevoldt answered. Laudin observed that he had a curious habit of smiling, that is to say, he smiled at stated intervals without any apparent reason, whether any one addressed him or not, whether he was alone or talking to some one. It was a good-natured and dreamy and at the same time shame-faced smile which, upon the whole, impressed one as rather simple-minded.

Laudin stood aside. He was both embarrassed and annoyed. He was neither accustomed to such society nor to such a situation. Tea had been served. He stood there, his cup in his hand, and seemed to reflect. He heard again that low swift voice, that voice which had so charmed him from the stage, and which alone had seemed to remain true to itself, and when a young man asked him a question in a familiar tone—they all seemed to insist on a strange familiarity, almost as though reserve were something indecent—he answered absent-mindedly and looked at his watch.

At that moment he felt a hand upon his arm. Another example of their familiarity, he thought, and turned with a frown. But it was Louise. "Won't you join me for a few minutes?" she asked, and he could see that she had deep brown, gleaming eyes whose glance was violent and impatient. He bowed. She preceded him. Some one cried: "Come here a minute, Lou!" She waved her hand and said: "Later."

They entered a small room. A hanging lamp of red and yellow glass depended from the ceiling. This room, too, was twilit. Louise did not close the door. "I didn't remember that people were coming in for tea." She turned to Laudin and that violent, urgent glance struck him again. "You must forgive me. We can talk here. What is it precisely, Doctor? Can I serve you in any way?"

"I have tried, Miss Dercum, to give you a brief explanation in my letter," Laudin said courteously but dryly. "I am here in behalf of, and by the request of my friend Egyd Fraundorfer. You can realize that he is not in a state to endure an interview which could not fail to evoke and renew emotions of the most tragic kind."

"Yes, I remember your having written that," Louise Dercum said almost in irritation, and raised her head and looked searchingly at Laudin. "What am I to do? What do you want of me?"

Laudin answered: "We are in a somewhat painful position in regard to yourself, Miss Dercum. We are strangely helpless; my friend is in a confusion of torturing suspicions, self-reproaches, somber torment. The only human being to whom his whole heart clung, has been suddenly and fearfully snatched away. Perhaps I need not tell you what high hopes died with Nicolas—not only for his father, but for us all.

Furthermore the case is rendered more grievous by the fact that Fraundorfer, a character of a strangely stubborn kind, was driven to a certain secrecy concerning his love for his son, a case of emotional self-consciousness almost indistinguishable from emotional paralysis. The result is a delirium of despair, a silent misery that drags through the sleepless nights. What was repressed during the years bursts irresistibly forth. We have believed, and still believe, that you can shed some light on the tragedy for us, on its motives, at the very least. Nicolas had won your friendship. It was perfectly evident that he regarded you with a devout adoration. Hence you can hardly take it in ill part if I ask you for some clarification, for some light in our darkness, provided that you are willing and able to help us."

Again that penetrating glance, then a dark wrinkling of the brows. She joined her hands behind her back like a man. And that gave her shoulders and her head a determined air. "Won't you sit down?" she said. He waited for her to be seated. But she remained standing and so he pushed the chair away again. Twice she measured the room with her steps. In those bold and violent eyes there gleamed something like vexation. When she passed the open door again she closed it, and the rumor of those other voices died. She stood with her back against the door and leaned back her head with its thick, brown hair so far that her body grew more taut than ever.

Without any gesture, with that deep music in her voice which compelled the hearer, she began: "In order that there may be no misunderstanding, I shall tell you the whole story. So far as I remember I made the boy's acquaintance at some memorial festivity planned by a colleague of mine. He played the piano and it was his music that brought us together; he came to see me, rarely at first, then more frequently, during the last period every day. Of course I soon saw that the boy was on fire. And then one day the natural confession came. I made it entirely clear to him that I could not be his. I told him that he was still a child, that I was an experienced woman who needed peace and order in her life. My twenty-four years had been so filled that they seemed far more in number. He wouldn't see that. He was not to be reasoned with. He was really a great nuisance, but what was I to do? I could hardly forbid him the house. I wasn't his governess. It's not my business to make philosophers of the young people who come here. And many come. I need to have people around me. I love their society. I dislike loneliness. Furthermore, don't imagine that I wasn't fond of the boy. But he finally became so unmanageable and exacting that I had to say, quite brutally: Listen, Nicolas, either you're content to have us be good friends or I'll simply have to have you thrown out. I've got something better to do than to waste my time in interminable scenes with a kid like you. I don't want to bore you, Doctor, with what happened afterwards. He declared our friendship at an end and yet came back and made scenes, and then begged my pardon and stood around for hours in front of my dressing room in the theater and tried to pump my colleagues about my movements. I'll simply tell you what happened on that last Sunday. That will interest you chiefly."

Laudin nodded. A magic proceeded from that face, a magic from that voice. Everything that she said was admirably clear; each word was firmly placed and seemed to be chosen with a kind of sovereign freedom. In ordinary life it is rare for people to be able to express themselves, to make use of the right word and the right inflection of the voice and the right sense of measure; it is rare for the voice to rise and fall agreeably without becoming hoarse or careless or slothful. Laudin was too experienced in the use of words not to appreciate such qualities. Perhaps he even enjoyed them and found it difficult not to forget the sadness of his mission here. Under his bushy mustache, there almost flickered that smile by which a master salutes his fellow.

Until now Louise Dercum had preserved a complete composure. Now, at the recollection of that fatal evening, she seemed unwilling to conceal her excitement. Again she walked up and down the room, took the beautiful shawl from her shoulders, wrapped herself in it again, glanced at the ceiling, smoothed her hair with her hand and finally continued. "It was after the Sunday matinée that he appeared. I was tired and resting in bed, and could not receive him. He talked and quarreled a long time with my maid; suddenly, he rushed off. That night at eight o'clock he reappeared. I had friends to dinner. I went into the anteroom and said to him: If you'll behave sensibly, come in and join us. Otherwise, you'd better go. A strange look came into her eyes. After all, he had dedicated a song to me and I wanted to be kind to him. He promised to behave himself and came in. All evening he sat there, as though self-absorbed, and uttered no syllable and grew paler and paler. The others left. He stayed. I hated to see that because I foresaw that there would be another scene. No sooner were we alone than he grasped my hands and said: We must get married, Lou. I couldn't help laughing. Why, you little fool, I said, in the first place, you know I am married and in the second place, I wouldn't commit that folly over again. You must get a divorce, he said; I can't live without you and I won't. Good heavens, what was there to answer? The boy was eighteen. There was no room for any serious discussion. So I said: Get out of here, child, and go to bed, and when you've had a good sleep maybe you'll be more sensible. He stood before me with uplifted arms and begged and wept and threatened until I lost patience and left the room. I went to bed, but carefully locked the door of my room; in his madness he was capable of anything. But I couldn't sleep and after an hour I thought he must be gone and went back into the studio to fetch a book. I found him there sitting at a table and writing. I wasn't very friendly, I confess. What the deuce are you writing there at this time of night? I asked him. He got up and said, I'm through.

He gave me the letter and left. I went back into my bedroom and suddenly the whole thing disgusted me so that I rang for my maid and said to her that she was never to admit young Fraundorfer to the house again. Next morning, or, rather, at noon when I woke up my maid came in with the terrible news. An acquaintance of mine, a conductor, had telephoned. Then, I confess, I spent a couple of hours that I shall never forget. And since that day a shadow seems to hover over me and a fatality darkens my path."

She whispered these last words, and the fingers of her loosely hanging hands played nervously with the fringes of the shawl. Her face had grown pale and her eyes had become shadows. She breathed deeply. The telling of the story, which had constantly accelerated in tempo so that the last words, all but that final whispered sentence, had poured forth like a cataract, had obviously exhausted her. She stood there with averted eyes, as though she wanted to speak no more and hear no more.

Considerately, Laudin let several minutes pass. Then he asked hesitatingly: "And that letter? May I go so far in my indiscretion as to beg you to communicate to me the contents of that letter or even to lend it to me for a short time? Consider, my dear lady, that it was his last communication, his last utterance. . . ."

The actress shrugged her shoulders. "The letter has disappeared," she answered. "I put it away that night and haven't found a trace of it since. I didn't even read it. I could imagine its contents; I have since looked for it everywhere; it is as though a ghost had been here and had fetched it."

Laudin regretted the inexplicable disappearance of the letter. Gently he waved aside the theory of the ghost. Remembering his interview with another woman, as far removed from this one, to be sure, as earth is from heaven, he was yet unpleasantly impressed by the absurd coincidence that here, too, a ghost was accused of having stolen an important document.

"I am most cordially grateful to you for what you have been good enough to tell me," he said with an inclination of his head. "Even though the mystery is not entirely clarified, I feel that my mission here is at an end."

"Mystery? What about?" Louise Dercum asked and looked at him with large eyes.

"One mystery is this: Friday morning Nicolas conducted the rehearsal of his choral work with a passion and an absorption which made the deepest possible impression on the interpretative artists under him. Several of them have since confirmed this report. On Saturday, on the other hand, at the next rehearsal, he was absent-minded and disturbed in a measure that no one could fail to observe. Now Nicolas was the reverse of moody. I have rarely known any one with such an equable temper. So I am bound to assume that this catastrophic change of mood took place between Friday and Saturday, that is, certainly before Sunday."

"I am sorry that I can't give you the missing links in your chain of evidence," said Louise Dercum, and her figure seemed suddenly to take on added slenderness and severity. "That chapter in my life is finished. I have burdens enough. I feel no responsibility; I will have none imputed to me. My mournful recollection of him is my own. You cannot expect me to expiate a guilt thrust on me from without. Love knows no compulsion—least of all the compulsion of a revolver held against its forehead. Nor must I let ghosts trouble me, else I should be lost every time I open my eyes. I belong to no one. I belong to myself. I belong to all."

Silently Laudin lowered his head. It had been a vehement outburst of righteous self-assertion and of pride. One could not but bow to that. The lawyer felt a wind from a world of the unconditioned which convinced him that there were no compromises to be made here, nor half sincere reconciliations, nor any half-truths to be talked to death with that conventional vocabulary of five to six hundred words. All that was spoken here had the sharp edge of glass that is cut with diamonds—it was measured, complete, perfect. Nothing was left him except to withdraw respectfully. Louise Dercum gave him her hand in farewell and out of the depths of her repressed feeling, looked at him with a smile that reminded him, almost to terror, of that photograph of hers out of which veraciousness and truth had seemed to speak to him so triumphantly.

She took him to the outer door without passing through the studio. As far as the second flight of stairs below he still heard the voices and the laughter of her guests.

25

Two days afterwards, around four o'clock, just while he was dictating a letter to Brigitte Hartmann who had missed him twice at the office and had seemed very much excited on that account, the attendant brought in a card. It was that of Louise Dercum. He was astonished and interrupted his dictation and sent the typist out.

In the door, held wide open by the attendant, appeared Louise in a mink coat and white gloves, her face rosy with the winter air, and strangely radiant. She came up to him vivaciously and begged him for the privilege of using half an hour of his time. Courteous to the point of magnificence, Laudin brought up a chair. He assured her that he was utterly at her service. He asked her if she wouldn't remove her coat; the room was hot, he admitted, but lawyers must be kept warm; they suffered more from the cold than ordinary people.

She slipped off her coat and let it fall on her chair. She had on a dark gray street dress; the color gave her a distinguished charm. Her lips had their natural color.

In spite of her elegance, which was a shade too new to be entirely genuine, there was an indescribable something about her, not explicable even to the trained perception of Laudin, by which she seemed more like a disguised boy than like a woman. It was not in her costume. It was in her bearing, in the swiftness of her gestures, in the slenderness of her figure and in a certain frank unsecretiveness of countenance.

This bearing of hers was utterly different from that which she had shown Laudin in her own home. It is a very different thing whether some one comes to you and desires something of you, or whether you go to him and desire something of him. And she evidently had a precise conception of this difference which she made no attempt to conceal.

She avoided preliminaries. The reason for her coming was a simple one. His personality had inspired her with confidence. She belonged to that order of persons who needed several days to have the impressions which they receive reach their intelligence. For all her cleverness she was as slow in judgment as a peasant woman. She wanted to know whether he was willing to guide and represent her; the thing she was concerned with was her marriage with the actor Keller. A turbid, saddening, tormenting affair.

Laudin made the observation that, so far as he had heard, the marriage had been consummated in Berlin and that the life based upon it had been led in Berlin, too. Such knowledge as he had, he said, was due of course to the fame of her name. Whatever legal measures were therefore taken would, especially since her husband was still living in Berlin, have to be officially entered in the Berlin courts. Hence the engaging of a lawyer in that city would be unavoidable.

She spoke hastily and shook her hand. "I have a lawyer. I have three lawyers. They're all idiots. I beg your pardon, but these professional gentlemen drive one quite desperate. They drag themselves along step by step, and none has the courage ever to take a leap. One can't live with such people and can't work with them. In a book I skip the pages that bore me. Don't you?"

"My whole profession is, I fear, based on boredom. You are very impetuous, Miss Dercum," Laudin said indulgently.

"I know I am," she admitted. "But I don't want you to put me off with forms of speech, Doctor Laudin. If I can't have your assistance, at least give me your advice. Don't tell me that I was deceived by the intuition that pointed you out to me not only as a man but as a human being. Don't imagine for a moment that I am trying to flatter you. All my friends call me the rough-neck. But it is equally true that I am enthusiastic whenever I find true superiority of heart and spirit. But I must really find it, you understand." She laughed. She bent back her head and he saw that slender brown throat as he had seen it two days ago. It was pleasant to hear her laugh. It was like an enchanting surprise.

Without words he thanked her for being apparently the object of one of her enthusiastic appreciations. A gesture of his hand invited her to tell her story. He offered her a cigarette. She talked while she smoked. She had crossed her legs and bent forward her trunk. Her whole attitude bespoke her confidence; her glance was confident and open.

She had married Arnold Keller to protect herself against the implacable pursuit of a man who, soon after, met his death in a falling airplane. In those days she had been as inexperienced as a child. She had been warned against Keller, but she had not heeded the warnings. He had amused her enormously; he had been so extraordinarily funny that she had imagined living with him to be an uninterrupted pleasure. Furthermore, she hadn't .had the slightest notion of responsibility in those days; she had thought of marriage as merely pooling one's salary with some one else's, and having some one to complain to if the director or the stage manager happened to be impudent. She thought the word frivolous couldn't be used at all to describe her state of mind at the time; it couldn't, in fact, be understood without taking her youth into consideration, the story of her earliest years, which she intended to tell him some day: the story of lightness floating up from the terrible heaviness of life—an iridescent soap-bubble out of thick ordure. Ah, yes. But the lovely bubble is aware of its own fragility; it glitters and waits for its inevitable end. . . .

She threw her cigarette away. She smiled and drew herself up elastically.

Arnold Keller turned out to be jealous to the point of mania. He proved to be a delusional psychopathic in every respect. Even his ability as a comedian was derived from his inferiority complex. The process was something like this: he was so frightened at the thought of meeting himself that he tried by constant grimaces to distort himself beyond any likeness of himself. In connection with this Louise had made the most astonishing observations: comedians are the most pitiful creatures in the world. Their whole being is flight from themselves. She seemed not to realize that this description could really be applied to all members of her profession.

She wondered if Laudin could fathom the depth of her martyrdom. To recover from such a fate as hers and to be able to forget it, life must simply be regarded as a lottery. Well, she was grateful that she had a talent for forgetfulness. She was born anew every morning, born out of the old day which died at that new birth.

She lit a new cigarette. Laudin was fascinated by her gestures and held in suspense by following her speech from sentence to sentence. Language suddenly seemed like a bunch of wild flowers.

If jealousy is a disease, it destroys anyone who is its object—generally the woman. An individual so afflicted has no eyes or ears for anything except his hallucinations, and spies and listens and seeks and creeps and rages. Tenderness and rage are one. He will tear you out of your sleep because he suspects that you are dreaming of a rival. He shatters the windowpane because the postman has delivered a letter; then he falls on his knees and howls when you show him that the letter was your dressmaker's bill. If you look at people in a restaurant he suddenly acts like a mad dog. Madness, cruelty, oaths, beseechings for forgiveness—such are the rule and conduct of the day. Finally, he is horrified at himself and takes refuge in cocaine. Then the lowest hell is reached. The second vice joins the first and both attain incredible proportions. If this had gone on nothing would have been left of her but a whimpering heap of bones. She succeeded in having him confined in a sanatorium. This, at the end of three years of torment. That doesn't mean that she is rid of him, heaven help her. By an apparent cure he might regain his liberty at any moment and her old burden would be upon her back. Hence she could hardly draw a breath of relief even while he was under lock and key. She had scarcely escaped him when her first great successes came to her. It was as though he had chained her with diabolical chains. Of course, gossip reported that she had caused him to be locked up. It was easy for envy to buy up a few yellow journalists who were willing to describe her as a fury because she thought a madman ought to be put where he belonged. But as long as he was where he belonged, she couldn't get a divorce from him because the law was so funny as not to permit it. Yet if he were out in the world a divorce would be a mere illusion, because he wouldn't leave her alone and no one could force him to do so. A nice situation! She wanted to know if Dr. Laudin had any advice to offer.

He was silent. He was accustomed carefully to arrange in his head the facts that were communicated to him, and to weigh the arguments.

"Maybe one could buy the man off with a large sum of money," he said, joining the tips of his fingers.

"He's not interested in money. He's quite Spartan-like."

"I'll have to think it over and get in touch with a colleague in Berlin."

"Yes, do that," Louise Dercum said quickly, and got up. "At this moment I don't care about taking any steps. The witches' cauldron is still seething too violently for me to want to dip my hand in. I think the time for legal action hasn't come yet. All I wanted you to tell me was whether, theoretically, at least, justice could be obtained in such a case as mine. Or am I condemned to be the prey of this mad creature to my death? Is that the fate to which your laws condemn me?"

She looked at him challengingly, full of scorn and contempt. He lowered his eyes as though he were aware of his inadequacy. "Justice!" He shrugged his shoulders. "You mustn't seek justice from me. The best I can do for you is to lead you through dark alleys with a flickering lamp so that you do not drop into unsuspected caverns and trapdoors."

"And that is all?"

"All!"

"And that satisfies you?"

"It's a case of having to resign myself."

"Frightful!"

"I could tell you a good deal about that, Miss Dercum."

He helped her on with her coat. She seemed to be thoughtful. At the door she turned around once more and asked, as if the thought had struck her suddenly: "Aren't you Mrs. Altacher's attorney, too?"

He said that he was.

"I should like to have talked to you a little about that affair. But I don't know if that's proper, or if you would consider it so. I'm afraid, anyhow, that I've bothered you long enough. . . ."

"If you please, Miss Dercum," said Laudin with some reserve and offered her a chair anew.

But she remained standing. She looked at him searchingly and a mysterious smile curved about her expressive lips.

"In that case, too, I should have liked to appeal to justice, had not the folly of such an appeal already been pointed out to me. Or if I were facing a friend, now, Doctor Laudin; if you, so famous and so clever, were my friend and not the inviolate ruler of an office with all sorts of considerations and anterior obligations, I would say to you: Take the picture that has been presented to you and lay it aside for an hour and impartially examine another picture, the reverse of this, which you ought to see. After all, that would be interesting, wouldn't it?"

"I don't quite understand. . . ."

"Well, I can make myself clear. Constance has composed a written accusation. This is no secret that I am giving away. Not only did she talk about it everywhere, but she passed the manuscript around among her acquaintances. It happens that, really without knowing the circumstances, really out of the depths of an inner urge, her husband, too, has composed a little memorial—a little account of their marriage and of related experiences. This document is in the keeping of my friend Ernevoldt. I wish you could read it or hear it read. It would be worth your while. Ernevoldt keeps it very quiet, of course. But if I asked him, especially for your sake, he won't hesitate to let us have it. What do you say to that proposal?"

"Since it is your wish and since the reading of the manuscript will evidently bind me or obligate me in no way, I shall be glad to read it."

"That's nice of you, although you formulate it very carefully. Don't be afraid. We won't violate your professional holy of holies. But what I like is confrontation. The drama consists of speech and counterspeech. And I am curious to know what you will say, both as a man and as a jurist. I am a woman and full of curiosity, and once in a while I like to smash the shell and get at the nut. Could you call on me after the performance to-morrow night, at ten-thirty?"

Laudin promised to do so.

When he was alone again he looked almost like some one whose hat has been blown away by the wind.

26

When Laudin entered, Egyd Fraundorfer was sitting at the piano. With high, hunched back he was sitting on a little piano stool, his head nearly on the keyboard, and playing with one finger a melody which he was deciphering with difficulty from a page of manuscript music. His little dog was crouching beside him and following the activity of his gigantic master with attentive astonishment.

Mrs. Blum had discovered that the manuscript had belonged to Nicolas, and was a sketch of a composition that he had made shortly before his death. She had betrayed to Laudin that Fraundorfer passed hours and hours trying to decipher it and to express its melodic motifs on the piano.

"You wouldn't believe how God damned hard it is to play the piano if you don't know how to play," growled Fraundorfer. Then he got up with a groan and went with Laudin into the next room. "I thought all you had to do was to sit down and be a Busoni. But that's the way it is with everything. Vanity can be sustained only by complete ignorance. Retire to your chamber, Herr Schmidt. Sit down, Laudin."

He drew the curtains, put whisky and soda on the table, pushed the electric lamp from the middle to the edge, lit a cigar, and, puffing, faced Laudin. He indicated the room with a wave of his arm. "What do you say to the cleanliness that now reigns in our house? Do you notice the tyranny of the broom wielded by Mrs. Blum? She is a fury whose mission it is to exterminate dirt. Not a bad woman, in other respects."

Laudin smiled. "I see. But why is your face covered

with stubble? Don't you shave any more? Or do you feel better in this condition?"

Fraundorfer rubbed his chin. "Does my young harvest bother you? You associate too much with smooth articles. You cannot serve two masters. You can't learn how to play the piano and shave, too. Especially if music gets on your nerves and if you possess only one razor into which the tooth of time has bitten. I'm giving the razor a rest. It seems to me that we use all the common objects about us far too much. We never give them a chance to rest. If they do rest and consult their souls, they start to function again. That holds true not only of razors but of boots, shirt buttons, cigar cutters and pens. You try it, Laudin. All the things that in our folly we consider unconscious, will rise up and bless you. In my history of human stupidity I have devoted an entire section to this discovery. The chapter is called: Concerning the Justified Resistance of the Objective."

He went on discussing this theme and talked, too, about the revengefulness and actual revenge of things which manifested itself, for instance, in the form of rust or of stains on books or tears in fabrics or the sudden refusal of locks to close or open. All these phenomena were the expressions of the spirit of the thing in question, the expression of its dissatisfaction at misuse or overuse, in short, the rebellion of the slave. Finally, Laudin, well knowing that Fraundorfer was only waiting for it, abruptly changed the subject, and gave an account of his interview with Louise Dercum.

He was able to reproduce what she had told him quite literally. He made no comment.

From time to time Fraundorfer shook his head. When Laudin had finished, he protruded his nether lip and said in a snuffling fashion, "A nice little fairy tale. But only a fairy tale."

"What motive would there be for inventing stories?" Laudin asked with a frown. "Am I the sort of man for whose benefit one invents them?"

"Pah," said Fraundorfer. "You're not the first, nor the last, either. In that region you've lost the ground from under your feet. The brilliant plumage dazzles you. The improbable is not the visible. It lies within, in the mechanism itself. One hears the wheels crunch and the screws rattle."

"I undertake to deny that Louise Dercum kept the truth from me," said Laudin, and laid the palm of his hand upon the table. "I think I may do so justifiably. I am not even ready to admit that she veiled the truth. I am quite sure of my impressions. If you appeal to that experience which may guide one aright in ninety cases out of a hundred, I, on the other hand, appeal to an intuition which has never deceived me in even one case out of a hundred. The world which we are touching is a strange one. True. Stranger, perhaps, to me than to you. It is an unsound world in many respects; it has the phosphorescence of decay; its moral equilibrium is not our own. Granted. But this woman is like an arrow which cleaves that world and never touches it. I am not without respect for prejudices. Prejudices arise often enough from the witness of bloody wounds that have actually been inflicted upon the body of society. In these low levels upon which we live, repute and character are not easily to be divided. But one must respect the free judgment, too. Appearances bear undeniable evidence. I am free to confess that I cannot altogether grasp this extraordinary woman, and have as yet no path to the heart of her mystery. Nevertheless, this is no reason for a negative judgment; nor is the fact that she belongs to a stratum which, generally speaking, arouses distrust. One should rather exert oneself doubly and not forget that one is dealing with a creature of genius."

Fraundorfer regarded his friend attentively. "H-m," he said, after a long pause. Then, after another pause, he said: "And how about this?" He took out the page of music which he had been trying to play and which he had rolled up and stuck into his coat pocket. He unrolled it and handed it to Laudin and pointed to a place in the midst of the notes where the following words were clearly to be read: "Ah, Lou, how can I ever thank you for having given yourself to me?" And a few lines below was written: "And your marvelous body which I have held in my arms. . . ."

"Well?" asked Fraundorfer, with a grim smile at Laudin's silence.

Beginning on his forehead and creeping down his face, a yellowish pallor glided over the features of Laudin. "I hope that you don't take that as a reliable proof." He uttered the words with difficulty. "At the first moment it takes one's breath away. But it is a phantasmagoria of love, the dream of a passionate soul that assumes its wishes to have found their fulfillment. Young artists are accustomed to identify yearning and reality. That is it. That must be it."

"You insist that their relations were platonic, at any price?"

Laudin arose. His tall slenderness seemed to take on an added nobility in contrast to the crouching mass of fat that was his friend. He spoke: "Give me one reason why that woman should have lied to me? She is free. She is independent. She has nothing and no one to appeal to. What is there to hide? What reason is there for silence? What is there in such a confession that could dishonor her or put her to shame? Such inhibitions are disappearing even among the conventional middle classes. Why, then, should she mystify us in regard to a matter that is of no particular importance in her eyes? Merely for the lie's sake? That's nonsense."

With half-open eyes, his cigar clenched between his bared teeth, Fraundorfer called: "Herr Schmidt, come here a minute!"

Morosely the little dog left its basket and trotted to Fraundorfer's chair. "Pay attention, Herr Schmidt," his master said, and with a snort bent over toward the animal. "Pay attention, now. Our friend here is wholly ignorant of the true character of lying. He neither knows its power nor its significance! He is aware neither of its shameless self-sufficiency, nor of its eel-like slipperiness. All he knows is the common or garden variety of lies, which can be aimed at and hit at a distance of three paces. He does not know the lie which is implicated with the rooted evil at the core of space and time, the lie of the world demon, the lie for its own sake! Now, what do you say, Herr Schmidt? There are still children left in the world! Full-grown, famous, hardened lawyers are still in the conceptual kindergarten, and babble: 'Now I lay me down to sleep. . . .'"

"Egyd!" Laudin was startled and horrified. "Are you drunk?"

"All right, all right," Fraundorfer said soothingly and threw his dead cigar on the floor. "I was only trying to relieve myself. It was only a variation on the D string. An apocalyptic ride. By the way, did you ask this genius of yours about the burn?"

"It was hardly possible, under the circumstances," Laudin answered almost reprovingly, "to put so intimate a question. You seem to see the situation in a wholly false light. Moreover, the way to her is by no means closed. On the contrary. She has asked my advice in a matter that concerns her closely. I am sure to see her several times more and if there are any further researches in our affair that I can honorably make, I shall be glad to do so."

Fraundorfer nodded. His head sank down upon his breast. He seemed to be asleep. Herr Schmidt trotted back to his little shelter. A profound vexation took hold of Laudin. He remained but a short time. When he took his leave, the hand that Fraundorfer gave him was limp and nerveless.

27

Ernevoldt and May Ernevoldt were already in the studio when Laudin arrived. Louise Dercum sent May to fetch a book; this was evidently done by a previous and mutual agreement. Ernevoldt gave Louise a manuscript. Laudin moved his chair out of the light of the lamp and heard the actress's marvelous voice read as follows:

Rarely, I suppose, has a man entered upon marriage with expectations as high as mine were. I regarded Constance not only as the builder of my home and the nurse of all my comforts; my wishes and my faith seemed to be based upon an even loftier security. Although only in my thirtieth year, I was somewhat satiated with the world. Concerned with great undertakings and extensive affairs I had seen too much of selfishness, of evil, of mean ambition, and had been their victim on more than one occasion. Marriage presented itself to me in the nature of a fortress in which I could be protected against the harshness and the tumult of the world. In this essential respect I was soon to recognize my error, although at first I had no ground for any more serious complaint. The first years of a marriage, though they may symbolize its tendency, contain nothing of a decisive character. Two personalities must first have a chance to develop through each other even though this process involves friction; both must show consideration and have a right to demand it; the common life is still new and common interests are added each to the other. The man feels himself to be the master and no one questions this fact. The soul and mind of the woman are employed in the development of her personality and it is only later that one gains a view of the path which she will take when her development is complete. It is at this point that men commonly make their great mistake of imperfect guidance or lack of intervention at the critical hour. And one day they are amazed to see beside them a human being utterly different from her whom they had imagined to be developing while they were slothful and unseeing.

What I mean to say is this that, in the middle strata of society, unless indeed, qualities and passions show sharp and immediate contrasts, the true success of a marriage can be judged, even by the two people most concerned, only after the lapse of a considerable period. In Constance I early discovered an inclination, which rose to the point of being hectic, to surround herself with swarms of so-called society people. She loved to be the center and the object of admiration of this crowd. She loved to shine, not by her elegance and taste, but by her mind and culture. She was well read and valued this quality above all things. And if I say people of so-called society I should add that they were always people of a certain standard of education, scholars, lawyers, physicians, writers and artists with whom she busily filled our house. These associations, one would think, were not open to any criticism, and her ambition was no vulgar or superficial one. But a point is reached when intellectual interests no longer express a true inward reality and are only composed of restlessness and of a superficial zeal that gives one an excuse to neglect one's duties. It establishes relations where none would naturally exist. A revolt against the supposed banality of daily life which arises from vanity and self-deception leads to a breaking of all proper rules and a denial of all sane necessities. My objections were not those of the thoughtless egotist when I came home in need of self-recollection, of peace, of friendly counsel, and found my house, evening after evening, full of guests. Yet it was difficult to dam that flood. If a man but seeks to protect his essential rights, he is at once stigmatized as a tyrant and a dog in the manger. If, on the other hand, he lets things go, the merely vexatious soon becomes a heavy burden. In the first admonition lies the seed of discord and the earliest contradiction marks the beginning of complete division. When looks and expressions play one false, happiness is gone beyond recall. It is strange how all of the shortcomings of a human being arise from that human being's changeless relation to some ruling passion in the depth. It was no different in this case. The deliberate and artificially heightened tensions of mental interest led to an undervaluation, and later to a complete failure in evaluating the daily round of life. The household creaked like unoiled machinery. The servants knew there was no guiding hand, and had no respect for a mistress who alternated between outraged arrogance and moody condescension, between stubbornness and weakness. But the welfare of a house depends upon the people who serve that house. The common tasks involved are subject to the psychical atmosphere that prevails. Let no woman imagine that she rules her little kingdom if she does nothing more than issue commands to her servants and pay them when the wages are due. Constance was always a prey to the comfortable delusion that if anyone were in her service she had bought that human being body and soul. Hence every little failure or neglect at once aroused her measureless rage. It soon became apparent that, like an evil magician, she had the quality of eliciting unpleasant characteristics even from the most kindly and good-natured. She suffered all the more in this situation, since she was utterly in the dark concerning its real value. I saw through it, of course. But if I tried, however considerately, to point it out to her, her rage was at once turned against me. Whenever there was conflict or rebellion, the chambermaid or the cook or the butler or the nurse or the gardener or several at the same time left the house amid disgusting scenes, uttering threats and imprecations. When others took their places and seeming, at first, to be better, failed; Constance, for some mysterious reason—whenever this alternation took place, went so far as to accuse me of a silent and hostile conspiracy with these various groups of servants. This unfortunate tendency to scent plots and conspiracies everywhere is a trait which characterizes many people who are inexperienced and constitutionally unsure of themselves. Bitter experience has taught me that it can develop to the point of persecution mania if the individual in question is incapable of objectifying himself, and if he is so lacking in insight or vision that he is accustomed to make his unobserved individuality the measure of all things. Advice does not help; the kindliest leadership does not help. On the contrary, anyone stricken with this blindness will necessarily regard as hostile even those whom he loves or thinks he loves, whenever they try to stop his downward path, or to open his eyes to the sad results of his actions. But I was never fit to be, in that sense, teacher and guide. I have an impatient heart, though a patient disposition, if one will grant me this distinction and try to understand it. In the course of time, to be sure, my impatience turned largely into resignation. I came to see that people cannot really be reached and that they cling as fiercely to their qualities as though they must perish without the least and ugliest of these. But there were years during which I often lost control of myself. I sometimes became unjust myself, especially when my sense of justice was wounded. This confession is not as paradoxical as it sounds. The passion for justice assumes so precarious an equilibrium of the soul, that the slightest disturbance of this equilibrium ravages and disorders the inner man, and he feels as though his universe were caving in. We seem to be overvaluing our powers and our rights in the very act of passionately embracing an ideal, so that even the good within us contains an evil.

There is only one sufficient motive for the recording of these memories. I would revive the past in order to lay bare the errors which led to the destruction of my marriage and the darkening of my best years. If one would undertake such a task in genuine honesty, he must dig deep into the intricate roots of existence and, if one test oneself thoroughly, he will discover that the decisive mistake was made at the very point where instinct once raised its warning but unheeded voice. There is no life in which, be it but for a moment, God is not present and speaking; if we understand neither his presence nor his admonition there is no further grace in our purposes and we have lost the right to bewail our fate. Every choice must be accomplished with the consciousness of a sacred responsibility. And the meaning of this responsibility is an answer to that infinite, all-penetrating being at the moment when it puts a question to our souls. It is unnecessary to be more definite; watchmen stand guard lest the slightest indication penetrate. . . .

Since I come to the question of the children, I must confess that it has only now been given me to recognize how difficult it is to disentangle and to illuminate. In all questions of upbringing and education, Constance's opinions and my own were diametrically opposed. This fact was clear even during the infancy of the children. The lack of agreement increased with the years and broke out in open contention. To describe this process step by step would be to get lost among unimportant and trivial details. Anything in these matters which is subject to a great law or, rather, to a great fatality, would degenerate into hair splitting accusations and destroy the substance of the action accused. This searching for cause and guilt whenever a child was not quite well; this immediate desperate appeal to a physician; this dissatisfaction with any physician who could not at once diagnose and cure the trouble, and the summoning, behind his back, of a second physician or even of a third; this utter faith in the power of official science and corresponding unfaith in either nature or fortune; this sickly tenderness to which all mankind and all the world were a single evil element, and which depended for all development and success upon its delusion of its own perfection; this refusal to acknowledge any institution for these growing creatures which their mother had not first thoroughly approved; and no teacher, no school, no influence from without could satisfy her exorbitant demands; finally, this conviction that beyond the circle of her immediate influence there was nothing but danger, disease, moral ruin, utter inadequacy, unmitigable misfortune. And how curious and sad to see this same mother, who believed that she could guide the lives of her children like omniscience itself, open to the whispered suggestions of the lowest of human creatures and pliant in the hands of all who flattered her absurdest notions or confirmed her in her extraordinary idea of her own importance and of the confusion and turbidness of all the world beside. If no one contradicted her she was capable of a child-like and charming appearance of sincerity. In utter repose, in fact, she exhibited harmless and kindly qualities. But at the slightest motion the evil thoughts arose. And since, in the course of the years, constant mobility and busyness grew more and more to be her element, she gradually lost these redeeming traits and everyone was horrified but herself, as she plunged from error to error, from disappointment to disappointment. Strength failed her; authority failed her. If a child's will rebelled, contentiousness was followed by defeat. She obeyed fancied higher laws and lost all touch with those that guide reality. She stumbled when she thought she was soaring. When the inevitable fall came, she poured out reproach and blame upon the husband, protector, guardian, who had not been present at the right moment to stop her or bear her up. Then she would unravel the past to seek proof for accusations that could not be proved, because guilt did not lurk where she sought it. She would tear the tissue of life to shreds, often in the few painful hours of a single night, in order to support these accusations, which no defense can weaken. Yet what she wanted was a defense that was an admission of the legitimacy of her reproaches. There is more corrosive misery in the world that has been brought about by conciliating, explicatory talk than there is harsh misfortune born of breaking another's heart by an eternal separation. But hearts are not so easily broken. That is a legend.

Strange, how people can get drunk on a lie which justifies their walk and conversation, their commissions and omissions in their own eyes, and which seems to give them a halo of nobility and self-sacrifice. They can get drunk to the point of utterly abandoning reason, almost of abandoning consciousness. Irrevocably this lie becomes cancerous. Poisoned excrescence is heaped on poisoned excrescence. The soul ceases to exercise its divine functions! There are women, obviously, for whom the burden of motherhood is too heavy. As isolated creatures they might come to no grief. Their feeble energies might suffice for that. They might not even be wholly useless as members of a society whose demands are modest. But once they bring forth children, they seem to themselves important beyond their fondest hopes. It seems to them a true miracle that while they are themselves still struggling after reality, and are uncertain of themselves and their relation to the world—that they have brought forth life. At once kindly care becomes a raging passion, natural duty a solemn service; vigilance becomes terror, and in their hysteria, their child becomes an angel. The umbilical cord is severed in only a physical sense; it is the fate of this new being to be inseparable from its mother; of the mother to be inseparable from it, in every respect, at every moment, or, at least, to feign this condition in the eyes of the world. All this is nothing but essential weakness puffing itself up into a Hercules, assuming rights, in the sick fancy of the woman who is so afflicted, which can be admitted only if one conceives of life as a hothouse, of marriage as a prison, of the family as a fenced-in poultry yard. . . . Matriarchate involving the complete subjection of man. . . . Ah, this hen-woman, who covers her chicks with her wings to protect them from some vulture of the air or some pole-cat of the fields—how often have we met her in all ranks of society! How often have we heard her shrill clucking when she has sat upon her fancied throne in order self-righteously to substitute her power for that of Providence. Her devotion is boundless—up to that fence; her philosophical vision, her feeling for art; her social consciousness, her idealism—all are magnificent as far as that fence extends! At the fence stands her outpost and demands password and identification. She is the foundress of the clan, and the spirit of the clan is the only power she admits. Do not try to count as an active personality; do not appeal to your works! You will be asked to name your clan and its password and totem. It matters not of what blood you are, only what clan's blood you acknowledge. First be father, husband, son, son-in-law, uncle, brother-in-law, cousin, nephew. . . . After that they will permit you to be man, workman, human being. . . .

And that is the triumph of the hen.

Ah, these good women; how well they mean! They assure you of that often enough. And why should we not believe them? At bottom they know very well what they owe their children. Even if they have paid for their birth with many pangs, they have an unending compensation through them, in that they have obtained innocent and unbreakable hostages by whose virtue they have, forever imprisoned and wholly at their mercy, the man and husband and father. They seem not to know it; they know it very well. They seem not to misuse the circumstance; they do so without ceasing. Knock at that iron gate and ask to have it opened. Unless you have arms of iron they will fall in weariness out of their sockets. Above all, like those knights in the Arabian tale who were turned into stone by reason of the mercifulness of their ears—do not look back. But we are beloved of them. Aye, that's the rub. Yes, they love us. Alas, this conception of love has been brought into human speech and into our human world like a piece of stage scenery that hides a country side in bloom. At best it is the boastful title of a gigantic and mysterious book which few have taken the trouble to decipher. Or would you make your happiness dependent upon the pleasures of the senses and measure it according to that delight? Then you will be like that wanderer in a frozen world who tries to protect himself from a polar death by the flame of a match.

I would have died that death—without that match even—if I had not met May Ernevoldt. It would not be seemly to go into the details of the process of my salvation; nor is it fitting in this place. All that I need do is to thank her, and I do so every day and every hour. She has opened to me unknown countries of the soul. A turning point had come to me—the end of all paths; I could only plunge into bottomless inanity. She was the soaring bird who showed me, surrounded by that fence on all sides, the only way out—the way upward. She helped me to discover the fact that the ethical and religious person retains no memory of the evil that has been done him—no general and no individual memory. He is magnanimous, that is to say, he is free of the tribe and its spirit. He is bound to his kind by profounder, nobler and more silent laws. If I undertake to protect this being who has enlightened me from mere material need—I am not even fulfilling a duty. It seems as inevitable to me as that I should protect myself. The stubborn spirit of the clan and sib will, of course, be beside itself. Yet what I give is the fruit of my work alone and therefore intimately mine. May that hand wither which is outstretched to prevent me!

When, for the first time, with all the considerateness that was possible and appropriate, I spoke to Constance of the advisability of a dissolution of our marriage, she had a maniacal fit of despair. I shall never forget this hour nor the sight of her. And this is what must occur, I said to myself; after the most irrevocable and unhealing breach, this utter hopelessness of bridging the fatal cavern, this long, slow death of all marital affection! What unbelievable blindness must be and must always have been present here. As though a man set free could not grant much more than one who is chained; as though it were better to trample upon another's quivering corpse rather than open the iron gate through which he can return at times, a friendly guest.

The fatality is inherent in the institution. Its forms no longer correspond to anything that lives. And I do not believe that these forms can be revivified or propped up any more. But what is to come to pass when these forms are utterly destroyed and even the wretched illusion of them is gone, and what will be the nature of that new force which will rebuild our being—that I do not know. Nor will I live to know it.

28

Louise gave the manuscript back to Ernevoldt. He smiled in his good-natured, shamefaced way and put it back in his pocket. The maid came and announced to her mistress that some one had called up twice. Louise ordered tea to be served. Ernevoldt chatted about a new play, whose première he had seen, and said he had gotten in touch with the author in connection with the film rights. He looked at Laudin as though the latter had a particular interest in this matter. Laudin did not seem to have heard him at all. When Louise began to speak he looked at her almost greedily. But an expression of disappointment came over his weary features when she turned to Ernevoldt and made a contemptuous remark about the playwright in question. She used certain technical expressions which left any one unaccustomed to them uncertain of her meaning. While Ernevoldt was making an evident effort to draw the depressed and silent lawyer into the conversation, Louise seemed to be careless of doing that. Her words, at least, seemed simple and spontaneous.

May Ernevoldt entered the room. She put the book which she had been reading on the table, went over to Louise's chair with soundless tread and leaned tenderly against her friend. With a smile Louise looked up at her and caressed her cheek. Searchingly Laudin observed that pale girl with the silvery silken hair and the figure like a swaying reed. May frowned and involuntarily nestled closer against Louise.

Louise said that May looked tired and that she ought to be sent home. Courteously Laudin offered the use of his car. "And you, yourself?" Louise asked, and turned her face to him with a glance that seemed markedly strange and cool. He answered that he could easily get a taxicab. Ernevoldt, with great familiarity, asked Laudin what type of car he considered the best. Ernevoldt had recently been offered a Daimler car, cheap; cars could be freely bought now at a small percentage of their value. Laudin's answers were polite but absent-minded.

He finished his tea and carefully, almost timidly, placed the cup back on the table. Then he got up, since May Ernevoldt had in the meantime gotten ready to go out. Laudin was strangely inhibited, as though the mere act of articulation were difficult, and he said to Louise: "I am under infinite obligation to you."

Louise looked at him expectantly and smiled with a touch of hidden scorn. May and Bernt Ernevoldt also gazed at him expectantly. Curiously enough this seemed to embarrass him. Hesitantly, stopping at the end of every sentence, gazing on the carpet, he said that in that manuscript thoughts had been expressed which were, in many respects, identical with his own. It was not even necessary to take into consideration the exquisite reading of the manuscript. All praise of it was vain, and admiration almost like impudence. No beautiful rendering of it would have been required to impress him. It was hard for him to express precisely what had stimulated and excited him so strongly. He was profoundly conscious of the fact that the manuscript dealt with a force that absolutely demanded a decision from society, and with all possible urgency. Like cowards, we had all hitherto slunk away from that decision. As for himself, he hoped some day to gain a final clearness and to give an accounting of his own thoughts.

Doubtless they all realized that these weighty and far-reaching words on the lips of a man like Friedrich Laudin bound him to an intellectual responsibility and would even, in a certain sense, determine the lines of his action. Hence the deep silence that followed them. Louise Dercum was the first to break the silence. She gave her hand to Laudin and turning her head at the same time in May's direction, she said: "You see, May, I was sure that we would find a friend in Doctor Laudin. Well, Doctor, we shall be waiting for you as the heathen waited for an apostle."

The pressure of her hand was comradely and her glance vivacious and intrepid. Perhaps these words were thoughtlessly uttered. Laudin had no such suspicion. He bowed without speaking. Ernevoldt smiled his good-natured, shame-faced smile. May looked thoughtful.

29

Doctor Heimeran was in the habit of playing bridge at his club on certain evenings each week. His partners were Doctor Kappusch, another associate in Laudin's office, Professor Weitbrecht, a noted dermatologist, and a wealthy merchant. It was on a Saturday, after the closing of shops and factories. They had not been playing very long. But Heimeran made such uncommon and annoying mistakes that he subjected himself to the reproaches of his partner.

Suddenly he threw down the cards in vexation, passed his hand over his bald crown and said: "I can't help thinking of other things to-day and I'm amazed, Kappusch, that you can sit here in cold blood as though nothing had happened. I can't get this business about Laudin out of my mind. I've reflected about it and talked about it and it becomes more and more incomprehensible."

The emotion behind this complaint made it quite clear to what an extent the watchmen of the ordinary had already been shocked. This is what they repeated: A man like this, who has been all his life a model of normality, faultlessly correct in all his dealings, refuses a case to which he has formerly committed himself and turns away a client to whom he has given his word. And this client is a highly esteemed lady of very good society.

"You gentlemen all know whom I'm talking about. Mrs. Altacher has quite naturally not hesitated to spread the news, and I can't say that the astonishment of the public is very pleasant. The office will be sensibly hurt; we shall lose a great part of our good repute through this idle, curious, malevolent gossip. Did Laudin have to do that? Was it necessary?"

Questioningly and challengingly, Doctor Heimeran looked around. They were all of the opinion that a thing so unseemly, so contrary to all use and custom, should never have come to pass. Heimeran had warned Doctor Laudin most insistently. Unluckily, it had been too late. He had begged Laudin to tell him his motives. The answer had been that Laudin could no longer reconcile Mrs. Altacher's cause with his conscience; he had had occasion to change his opinion, had been forced to do so, in fact, and had told the lady so.

"But, gentlemen, he should have taken thought first. A lawyer has no right to change his opinions within twenty-four hours. He is like a lighthouse on a stormy coast; people have to know where to find him."

It transpired from Heimeran's narrative that Laudin's change of mind was connected with an entire series of sensational happenings. Consul Altacher had died two days later, as though he had only waited for Laudin's decision to flee from whatever miseries life still held for him. And scarcely had his grave been filled than his widow instituted a suit for the restitution of a considerable fortune, against the consul's friend, Ernevoldt, and the latter's sister. She demanded sixty thousand gold crowns which, according to her, these two had succeeded in wheedling out of her late husband. As if there were not enough of scandal, what does Laudin do? He undertakes to defend these people. More than that: he brings suit against the widow for almost ten times the amount stated, namely half a million gold crowns, which, he asserts, the dead man had promised the Erne-voldts.

"Promised, I say, gentlemen! There isn't even a formal will. Laudin argues that undue influences were at work and appeals to a letter which Altacher wrote Miss Ernevoldt. I ask you whether that isn't juridically untenable and humanly disreputable. The whole case is disreputable. How can a man like Laudin lend his assistance under such circumstances? What is happening? Rather, what has happened?"

But that isn't all, by any means. Heimeran's troubled thoughts had another, entirely different subject. Of a private and personal nature. Doctor Kappusch would bear him out—he did—that Heimeran had, at the very first symptoms, called his colleague's attention to certain facts calculated to arouse the astonishment of any one versed in human nature.

"You take a man who for twenty years has been accustomed to hanging his coat on a certain hook. One day he stops. He carelessly throws the coat on a chair, across a table, over the side of a cupboard. Haven't we the right to infer from that, specific changes in the state of his soul? Here we've got a physician among us. I ask him to judge. For twenty years this man has addressed his old office attendant as 'Mr. Ruediger.' One day he simply calls him Ruediger in the harshest tone. For the same twenty years this same man has missed no office hour, never been late in court, never delayed a conference, never left a letter unanswered. Suddenly this exemplary order and accuracy come to an end. And what an end! The letters are mountains; at the last moment another representative of the office has to run to the courtroom; clients who have been promised interviews for weeks have to be turned away or put off; he won't see some of them at all. He'll read documents for thirty minutes and then throw them aside. We are scarcely told that he is at last in his office—and he's off again. And you've seen him. Almost unrecognizable. I tell my colleagues that it is as though a hen with inky feet had walked over a fairly written page. You can't blame me for being badly worried. He and I have been colleagues for years. We won our spurs together and what stains the escutcheon of the one, does not leave the other's clean."

Doctor Heimeran took up the deck of cards and began to shuffle with nervous gestures.

The wealthy merchant, a morose and ill-humored old man, said: "It's come to my ears, though I won't say that I credit it—but it has undoubtedly been the subject of common talk—that behind Laudin's curious behavior in the Altacher affair there is the hand of the actress Dercum."

Doctor Heimeran was angry. He declared this to be stupid gossip. In all his long practice Laudin had never even been touched by the wiles of any woman. There was no example of it and there was no justification for assuming such a thing.

Doctor Kappusch remarked quietly that, according to his knowledge, Doctor Laudin's acquaintance with Miss Dercum was due entirely to his friendship for Egyd Fraundorfer and was connected with the suicide of the latter's son. That the Dercum woman had been mixed up with this was an open secret. Laudin's intervention in this matter, far from being open to criticism was, on the contrary, but another proof of his unselfishness and of his loyalty to his friends.

At the mention of the name of Fraundorfer, Professor Weitbrecht had looked up. "That's that young musician," he said with a very serious look. "He came to see me. Two days before his death he was in my office. A charming chap. Infinitely to be pitied."

Sadly he nodded to himself, as though he were talking about an experience too common and too frequent to give one pause, but one which in this special case had, nevertheless, clung to his memory. No one paid particular attention to his words except Doctor Heimeran, who united with his legal acuteness the qualities and the ambitions of a detective. He pulled out a notebook and on an empty page he scrawled the two names: Fraundorfer—Weitbrecht. Then he dealt.

30

That very day Pia had been forced to keep the dinner waiting for Laudin. He had promised to come. But at one-thirty his office had telephoned that he couldn't; he would certainly be home for supper. At a quarter of eight that evening the telephone rang again. It was he himself who spoke this time. His voice, as it had had for some weeks, had a different sound—a harsher, drier sound. He begged Pia on no account to wait for him; by the time he could get off it would be too late.

Pia answered sweetly, although with a tinge of regret in her tone. She was unwilling to express more than a kindly regret for fear of annoying her overworked husband.

This thing had been going on for four days. They had seen equally little of him on the preceding days. Relly occasionally remarked that she'd almost forgotten how her father looked. She explained a plan she had to Marlene. Very early in the morning, holding the dwarf Uistiti on her arm, she intended to appear at his bedside—a living reminder of his family. He would probably not be able to resist such an admonition. But Marlene was busy with more important things and took very little interest in Relly's jokes. Pia feigned not to have heard either the plaint or the plan. She did not even show that accustomed smile, forgiving even while it reproved, which Relly loved to see upon her mother's lips.

When, toward midnight, she heard Laudin come in, she kept her light going for quite a while, in spite of her unusual tiredness. Perhaps she was a little exhausted by the gnawing of her many duties, of the demands upon her, by the insistent quarrelsome, impudent babbling of the things that fill the world. Perhaps she thought that he might still visit her and sit for fifteen minutes at her bedside. She had every reason to hope that, for it had happened on many, many days in the course of many years. But it did not come to pass to-day, as it had not done yesterday and the day before and the day before. A few minutes after half past twelve, she put out the light and tried to sleep. But when sleep came at last it was no real sleep. For there is a kind of sleep that is like a room with open doors and the drafts blow in and there is no feeling of comfort.

31

A few days later a series of queer annoyances began to overtake Pia. An individual, who refused to give her name, telephoned in the morning, in the afternoon, in the evening, even during the night. It was a sharp, resonant voice—a woman's voice. She demanded to speak to Mrs. Laudin on a very urgent matter which, according to her, intimately concerned Dr. Laudin. Pia knew, of course, that such intrusions, closely looked upon, were apt to be mere impudences; that they proceeded from people whom Laudin had refused, for some reason, to represent and whose importunities at the office had been rebuffed. Out of sheer good nature, she had gone personally to the telephone the first time this stranger called up. Each time she asked for the name of the speaker, there regularly followed a pause which was then succeeded by a curious kind of chatter, half confused, half insolent, a mixture of threats and complaints and dark hints. Finally, Pia sent the chambermaid to answer the telephone calls of this woman. If the girl refused to deliver the various messages that were given her, the voice became stridently insulting. Occasionally the connection was suddenly cut off in the middle of a sentence; at other times there were only inarticulate noises. In the late hours of the evening there was no escape for Pia, except at the risk of missing important messages or even a communication from Laudin himself. And so that voice came to her ear more and more frequently in the late hours of the evening— twice almost every evening. The first words were usually uttered in a disguised tone; then the unsympathetic sharpness of the tone revealed itself and as soon as Pia recognized it she hung up the receiver. She was seized by an abhorrence for the entire mechanism and the malevolent featurelessness which it brought her. She was tormented by a wire and a bell; there was no effectual resistance to be made; she was helpless under that treacherous violation; she was forced to yield to the wire and the bell, senseless and annoying though its messages were. Gradually things reached a point where she was frightened at the very sound of the signal and even listened nervously in the stillness of the night for that shrill sound.

One evening it seemed to her that she had suffered enough. With indignant impatience she called into the black funnel: "You will either give me your name and state your business or I will appeal to the police." The word "police" seemed to have the desired effect at once. Something sweetish stole into the voice. Very well, then, said the unknown individual, she would tell her name. She had thought it useless until now; she had hoped that, by trying so many times, she would succeed in getting the doctor himself. She had to talk to him, privately and at length. Would Mrs. Laudin be so very kind as to tell him who had called up. No further explanations would be necessary. She need merely say that it was

Mrs. Hartmann. He would know all about it, then. She would be glad to come out to his house; there was no trouble she would not take; she only begged for an appointment. The letter which the doctor had caused to be sent to her had excited her frightfully; for a whole day she had had to stay in bed without stirring a limb; such letters were worse than poison for her; she would mail the letter to Mrs. Laudin so that the lady could see for herself how unjustly she, Brigitte Hartmann, was being treated. It was an outrage that cried to high heaven—and to think that it came from a man like Doctor Laudin, on whose honorableness she would have staked her life. Mrs. Laudin might answer her when she had read the letter, or telephone her at 56-2-13; a great deal might depend on Mrs. Laudin's keeping in touch with her; she would be very willing, too, to call on Mrs. Laudin and talk to her alone; certain conditions would have to be observed, of course; she ventured to say that it was not to Doctor Laudin's advantage to refuse so stubbornly to receive her and listen to her; no, on the contrary, and Mrs. Laudin would live to see it. Things had come to her ears which might be of decisive importance to Mrs. Laudin herself. She herself felt much easier now that she had been able to pour out her overcharged heart to Mrs. Laudin. She had a great admiration for Mrs. Laudin. She had seen her last Sunday in town. Her cousin had pointed the lady out to her. And so she took the liberty of saying good night.

All this bubbled into Pia's ear like water from a spring; she endured it dumbly. It did not bother her. It did not penetrate to her mind. These were Laudin's affairs; that domain was foreign to her; people with whom Laudin had dealings—vague silhouettes. The names of these people were stamped with no more significance to her than the random names on a directory page. Their fortunes meant no more to her than the rattling of plates in the kitchen. Yet something ugly seemed to have been squirted at her; involuntarily Pia looked at her hands, as though they had been soiled.

On the following afternoon she received the letter which Laudin's office had sent to Mrs. Brigitte Hartmann. "If by the fifteenth of January you have not made a satisfactory arrangement in the matter of our client, Miss Caroline Lanz, we shall be forced to institute a criminal action against you. We shall proceed at once to submit a memorandum to the court of chancery and cause you to be summoned and put on oath by the aforesaid court. In the meantime we shall, in the name of our client, institute an investigation at the bank in which the moneys of your late husband were deposited and discover whether, since his departure and subsequent death, any funds have been withdrawn by you. At all events we shall immediately have the account declared under the surveillance of the court. Awaiting an early answer, we are, etc."

Brigitte Hartmann's commentary to Pia was as follows: "You now see, dear Mrs. Laudin, how I am being treated. I am determined that no one shall use such a tone to me. I am not the first comer, if you please! No, I am a mother, just as you are, Mrs. Laudin, and both as a mother and as a wife I have nothing with which to reproach myself, unless, indeed, that I always took my duties too seriously. I know of some who disgrace the holiest feelings of man. And they are people, too, of whom you would expect it least. But facts are facts, dear Mrs. Laudin. Ten times I went to the office; the doctor had no time for me, simply no time. I have no words for this insult, especially in view of my boundless esteem for him. But then I hear that a great many of his clients complain of being neglected. Well, they don't know what I know and what I will take very good care, dear Mrs. Laudin, not to breathe. But maybe later on I won't be so considerate. I've never been one to hide my light under a bushel, and I see what I see, and I don't see but that we humble folk had better look around in the world and watch out and see whether the high and mighty people are as wonderfully moral as they like to make us believe. I wasn't born in a workhouse—not I. I come of a good family and had a good education, facts which nobody seems to consider. Hoping that you will not make things worse by neglecting the voice of public opinion, I am, yours very faithfully, Brigitte Hartmann."

Of all this Pia, of course, understood nothing. But as on the day before, she had the sensation of having been physically soiled. Next morning at breakfast she asked Laudin: "Who is Brigitte Hartmann?" and handed him the letter and related to him briefly the strange annoyances to which she had been subjected for over a week.

Laudin read the letter, held it in his hand longer than seemed necessary and, with an angry tenseness which also surprised Pia, said at last: "We must discover some way of rendering this idiot harmless. It is quite possible that she may go so far in her impudence as to molest you in person. Avoid her if possible, avoid the very sight of her, avoid her as you would a pestilence. But I shall not neglect to put a quietus on her at once."

Pia looked at him with a smile and a gentle shake of the head. "I would certainly not have told you anything or shown you the letter either, if I had dreamed that it would excite you or give you a single uncomfortable moment," she said. "I know nothing about the woman. But she's probably some poor unfortunate devil and you ought to be used to that kind. She seems to have gotten herself into a wrong situation, and so she twitches and whines after you. That should not trouble you. Or does it? Is there some element here that disturbs you? Would you like to tell me what it is?"

Breakfast had been a little late that morning; the children had started off to school; husband and wife sat alone at table. And while Pia was asking him this and looking into his large, serious face, that carefree expression of her own features which she had cultivated so meticulously throughout the mornings of the many years, changed, too. Suddenly there lay upon that beautiful forehead a dim reflection of all that had furrowed his forehead and whitened his hair. But she was quite unconscious of both the phenomenon and its cause. It seemed to arise like an act of inner obedience. It is through such acts that the faces of married people come finally to bear a resemblance to each other. For several seconds their glances met, and after an unduly protracted silence Laudin began to speak.

It was an entirely erroneous assumption that the person in question was deserving of any compassion. Sympathy was distinctly out of place here. The woman was flourishing and well able to take care of herself, and was the representative of an entire class. All that she did, desired, demanded, her very life and breath, was the final result of regulations and conventions having no substantial nature of their own: of all those iron rules which had gathered rust in the course of the centuries, of all the agreements, bulls, enactments, prescriptions and charters which, from the very invention of the state on, had been decreed and petrified in order to change right into compulsion, security into terror and good custom into the spirit of the eternal penitenitary. It might be asserted without fear of contradiction, that through the slow and industrious digging and corroding of this representative and her followers, all noble spontaneity had been destroyed and was being destroyed more and more. To her and to her like, the whole of humanity, men, women and children, were but a single debtor. She conceived of herself as having a perpetual lien on law, morality, love, fidelity, good faith, on God himself. And in so far as she conceived of herself as having been disappointed in her claims upon happiness and satisfaction—in precisely that measure she believed all human society to be in her debt. She carried about a bond concealed in her bosom, ready to show it at every opportunity. Ceaselessly outraged in her fancied and inalienable rights, she was the Shylock of society—Shylock demanding his pound of flesh.

It was doubtful whether Pia understood all this. Such philosophical criticisms of society, having only a symbolical content, went beyond the reach of her vision. Yet her eye rested with intense attention on her husband's face and what had struck her was evidently less the substance of his words, than the bitter, weary, secretly excited tone in which he spoke. And it seemed to her, too, as though the words were not spoken so much to her as to an imaginary audience. This impression was deepened by his appearance and gestures. He sat there with lowered eyes, his chin resting upon his hand—a strangely distant and unfamiliar figure.

Nor had he finished. . . . It is a matter of daily observation with what bitter stubbornness this female Shylock insists upon the privileges denominated in that imaginary bond. He advised Pia, for instance, to take the trouble to study the characteristic document that had been sent her. This one, or others coming from similar sources. She would find substance and intention extraordinarily identical. She would find the same flags fluttering and the same trumpets blowing and the same aiming at the same targets and the same mad implacability. The appeal would always be to duty, honor, conscience, motherhood, sacrifice, faith, religion, heart and home. Never to pride, to dignity of mind, to nobility of heart. She is insensible to reasons—this Shylock in petticoats! she does not hear them; she does not hear other human voices nor see other human faces; she flourishes her bond and wants that pound of flesh denominated in it. She is deaf to all else. She keeps the police busy and wastes the time of the courts. If she herself comes in conflict with the police power and the courts, she pours forth in a resistless flood her attempts to make an evil case appear good, wildly summons all men to be the witnesses of her complete innocence and succeeds finally in crowning her crimes with the halo of the martyr. Laudin said that it amused him grimly, that it delighted him with a profound sense of irony to imagine this creature's performances over the telephone. It is so amusing—this vision of Mrs. Shylock at the telephone: she uses all modern improvements and inventions in order to make them subservient to her ruling passion of taking people's breath away and making them the tributaries of her misfortune. Mrs. Shylock wants to see all the world about her in turmoil; she carries in her bosom a pained, contorted image of herself and she desires all men to share that vision with her and to mourn over her. And Mrs. Shylock is especially fond of such impersonal projections of the self as the telephone; she adores the telegraph, air mail, radio, for these make possible an incomparably heightened business on her part, compared to the dragging methods amid which she grew up. They make possible a swiftness of manifesto, of projecting news, of setting people at odds, which surpasses anything that she had ever thought of in her modest dreams. Modest! For though she may have risen in the world and may finally be found in the highest ranks of society, she remains a plebeian by the very constitution of her soul. For what is it to be a plebeian except to emphasize the letter and the bond, the convention and the rubber stamp—with an eye fixed upon some pound of living flesh.

Pia had lowered her head, as some one overtaken by a rain of stones. Her cheeks had grown pale and her eyes large and round. It was as though she were thinking: what kind of a man is this who is saying these words? Do I know him? Do I still know him? Or have I lost all knowledge of him? As though she desired to clear their path of what she had heard and to introduce a healing commonplace, she said softly: "The tailor has sent word that you're to come for a fitting, Friedrich. I'm so glad you're having some clothes made. I think it must be two years since you had anything new. It was a shame. Even when I was scolding Egyd Fraundorfer the other day for his dreadful shabbiness he told me that at his age no man would go to the tailor unless he were absolutely forced to do so. Whenever he did go it was an attempt at either flight or fraud. Characteristic, sophisticated Fraundorfer nonsense."

Laudin looked up. "Yes, it is nonsense," he said. "And yet, and yet, there may be just a grain of truth in it. But let's not investigate that, Pia."

He got up and kissed her forehead. Yielding to an impulse which was not clear to her but which made her feel as though she must somehow protect him on this day, she asked whether he wanted her to go into town with him. He shook his head.

32

For months, Laudin had been representing a large stock company in a suit against the state. It was a complicated and long drawn out affair and very large sums were involved. Every step had to be taken with extreme caution, for the slightest mistake could have had the most fatal consequences.

When the matter came to court for the fourth time, Laudin was half an hour late. This was observed not without astonishment. The opposing attorney had cleverly used this delay by persuading the judge to omit the reading of a protocol which would have been of the utmost importance in determining the decision of the court. It would be difficult to make up for this omission. The incident gave rise to a debate between Laudin and the judge. Laudin emphasized the imperfect instructions with which his representative had come to court. In the course of this debate, quite contrary to his custom, he became unnecessarily violent. The opposing attorney remonstrated; Laudin replied with an impatience, and a contemptuous scorn which were very unfavorably commented upon, especially in view of the fact that his almost ceremonious courtesy had for years been proverbial.

The judge, who was an experienced and jovial person, succeeded in calming him and the court continued its business. However, it seemed to the audience, composed almost entirely of experts, as though Laudin, in his management of the case, lacked all his usual clearness of judgment. He overemphasized the trivial and at the same time overlooked decisive arguments. Once or twice he had even to apologize for crass failures of memory. It was as though he found it impossible to master his material and, conscious of the feebleness of his leadership, wanted to obtain his results by violent measures although he knew that only the most flexible and carefully calculated diplomacy could bring him to his goal.

The representatives of his client, frightened by the possibility of an unfavorable outcome, begged for adjournment. The judge, who had occasionally cast a thoughtful and questioning glance upon Laudin, consented to this maneuver.

33

Three new clients appeared in the office on that same day all wanting divorces. In all three cases, the differences were utterly beyond hope. These marriages were rotten to the marrow, and an examination of the facts left no doubt but that in all three cases the men were the guilty parties. In one case the morbid avarice of a notoriously wealthy man had driven his wife to despair. The second case concerned a man with completely shattered nerves. He was a banker, and his raging ambition for power and position and influence had driven him to work year in and year out, for sixteen to eighteen hours a day. His health was completely destroyed and during his ever more recurrent fits of profound depression the only thing that gave him any satisfaction was to beat his wife. All the while this man's wife, whose spirit was wholly broken, emphasized the kindliness of his original nature.

In the third case both husband and wife appeared. The man was an engineer and upon first impression seemed calm and sensible. But when the conversation turned to the question of the confusion of his married life, he gave vent to a shameless cynicism both as regards the details and the theory of marriage, which was the more monstrous in its effect because his description was constantly and almost appreciatively confirmed by his wife. He not only admitted quite frankly that he had deceived and betrayed his wife, that he had seduced his young sister-in-law, carried on affairs with two of the latter's friends, gotten a servant girl with child, and spent his nights in bars and dance-halls. He was proud of his goings on. He had a whole bag of magniloquent justifications. He talked about the very proper desire of self-expression, of the necessity of sensual delight in the life of a hard-worked man, of the folly and harmfulness of the monogamic ideal in general.

They were both people who no longer took the trouble to curtain the windows of their souls. They had lost the ability to be surprised at each other, and had utterly lost the ability to make each other suffer. They had stripped off suffering and secured themselves against it. In so far, their fate was typical of the age, and unimportant. They lived together like Bushmen; but, like well taught and progressive pupils of their time, they did not neglect the analysis of their relation and the careful stripping of each other to the buff. And they said something like this: We didn't harmonize with each other. Harmony—that most ill-used word. As though their feeling and their thinking had ever known even the breath of the knowledge of such a thing. As a geologist can estimate the effects of an earthquake, so could Laudin gage the conditions of minds amid this social collapse of which neither the beginning nor the end nor the true nature was as yet recognizable. His path became ever more a pathway among ruins.

"Have you any children?" he asked.

Yes, they had children; two of them. One had come along, the wife declared with cheerful zeal; it was in the anteroom; she would fetch it in to show the doctor. The child was a girl of four, and lovely beyond description.

The profound emotion which Laudin experienced at the sight of the child's beauty, sickened him deep in his soul. When, a little while later, Bernt Ernevoldt and May, who had been announced, came in to him, he said suddenly, in the midst of conversation, as though this had been in his mind the whole time: "I'm almost coming to believe that children are of different blood, of different chemical constitution from adults. They are as different from us as we from the fauna of the deepest seas. And suddenly they become ordinary human beings. And we know what that means. Up to their fifth or seventh year they are elf-like creatures; incomprehensibly high, pure, tender, good beings; miraculous in their possibilities. Suddenly they become mere men. Common men; hopelessly average, empty, stupid, inarticulate; utterly God-forsaken. How does that come to pass? And why? At what point does the break come? By what dark magic is the crystal transformed into ordinary window glass? At what moment? On what day does it begin? And for what reason? One could think oneself to destruction over this problem."

May, who was, as usual, in deep mourning and had very little to say, raised her veil, and her moonstone gray eyes gleamed mysteriously. "In the souls of children die their father's and their mother's unkept promises to life." Her voice was soft.

Laudin looked at her searchingly as though he were waiting for an explanation. But she relapsed into silence.

34

Ernevoldt and his sister had come in order to sign a power of attorney. Furthermore, May had had a meeting on the previous evening with Constance Altacher, at the latter's emphatic request. She was to give a report of the interview. But it soon appeared that she was not capable of doing so. She had given such a report immediately afterwards to Louise Dercum; she could not bring herself to do so a second time. Louise had declared herself quite ready to inform Laudin. According to Bernt Ernevoldt's indications the scene had been a painful one. There had been tears and reminiscences and imprecations and adjurations and an offer of reconciliation and a demand for renunciation—all in one and the same breath—with the result that May had come home quite ill.

Laudin would have liked to get at the concrete facts. The character of Constance Altacher had begun gradually to inspire an interest in him which was rather dark and in its whole extent not quite comprehensible to himself. In another way and in regard to another social stratum he found himself cultivating an equal interest in Brigitte Hartmann. It seemed to him as though the endless procession of women who, in the course of years and decades had passed like shades before his eyes, had gradually reached a symbolic embodiment in these two figures. He had the perception that these two embodiments were the symbols of a crisis in human society. They first clearly emphasized the now indestructible fact of his consciousness—these crowning and symbolic figures—that in his implication with such fates and fortunes an unfathomable evil had been done to himself.

Through Ernevoldt as well as through actual witnesses, especially a notary whom he knew, he had been informed of what had taken place in the sanatorium one or two days before the death of Consul Altacher. In the presence of two brothers-in-law and an older brother of her husband, Constance had appeared beside his bed and embraced him with sobs and almost smothered him with caresses, and had acted in general like a dangerous hysteromaniac. On her knees and with lifted hands, she had besought him to give up his decision to try to get a divorce, to which she would consent under no circumstances. His kinsmen had agreed to talk calmly to Altacher. They were disagreeably surprised when Constance suddenly burst into the room. The more so as she had given her solemn promise not to endanger this intervention in her behalf by her unexpected personal appearance. But somebody must have told her that Altacher had summoned the notary. And she dreaded nothing so much as the dictation of a will. She fancied that she was the only person who could prevent that. For that reason she had come. But she had not come alone. In the corridors waited her three daughters whom she had forced to accompany her. They had gone daily to see their father, but without their mother, for they knew how unfavorable her presence was to his state of health. It was much against his will that Altacher had finally consented to receive the delegation of his kinsmen. The physicians, moreover, had duly called his attention to the possible consequences of unusual excitement. Their objection, however, was more apparent than real since they had really given him up and thought that the opportunity of putting his affairs in order might even have a favorable influence. This was the reason why Constance found it possible to be admitted. She thought it was her duty to disobey his insistent demand that she should not visit him for some time. A man dare not close his door to his wife, she said to his daughters when they ventured gently to remonstrate. Whenever she determined on something definite, her will was utterly unbending, and since she nursed the delusion of a plenary inspiration from on high, inhibitions of any kind did not exist for her. The sick man attempted in vain by gestures and whispered words to calm her wildness, her loud pain, her stormy appeals; equally in vain were the persuasions of his kinsmen who felt that, under these circumstances, their mission could come to no good. The calculatedly impassioned outbursts of Constance increased in ferocity up to the moment of the notary's entrance into the room. Dramatically she summoned her children and cried out in a very convulsion of despair: It now depends on you whether your father plunges you into eternal shame and makes over to his mistress that fortune which belongs to you alone and to no one else in the world! The girls burst into tears; they were thoroughly ashamed; they would have liked nothing better than to flee. But the iron will of their mother robbed them of all thought and of any power of determination. The power of Constance, to which Edmond Altacher, too, had always succumbed, lay in her ability to summon and exploit the grandiosity of such scenes. A human being capable of being inflamed at will by the highest degree of passionate excitement can pull down heaven and earth, and pry open the jaws of hell. Altacher, according to his own sad confession, had never been able to guide this possessed creature. Hence she had lost all discrimination between above and below, between light and darkness. Once more he resigned himself; at his silent gesture the notary withdrew; with no hope but to insure the peace of his last hours, he gave his word to Constance to desist from making the legacy which, according to her conviction, would forever have tarnished the honor of the family. It was clear that, in his state of health, any discussion of a divorce would have been futile, anyhow. In return for this, Constance, who seemed utterly melted and crushed in her emotion and in her gratitude, vowed that, so far as she could prevent it, his friend should never know a care in life. She also contritely apologized before those present, including her own children, for the insulting and emphatically unsuitable epithet which she had used to characterize May. In the second night following this day, Edmond Altacher died. Constance, a faithful wife and nurse, sat at his bedside. May had not been admitted to see him again.

Laudin said that this whole story gave him a feeling of dizziness. Good and evil, unhappiness and calculatingness, love and business instinct, piety and greed, were here so inextricably intertwined, that each seemed now to intensify, and now to destroy the other, so that the faculty of judgment could find no handle and the moral consciousness no starting point from which to operate. In his entire practice he had not come upon a similar case. The knowledge of all these events inflicted a deep wound upon his sense of what was fair and right. He said that reflecting upon them there overcame him a ravenous hunger after cleanliness and human dignity. Awakening in the middle of the night, he told May, he was filled with a burning and impotent rage. No one about him was able to estimate in how far his actions arose from calm determination and objective responsibility. The immediate motives lay on the surface. But what happened in the depths, what employed his whole nature, what slowly spun its undeterminable web in his bosom—this remained hidden from him. He was not accustomed to analyzing himself. He was one of those modest natures who take but little interest in their own inner life, and who let the unknown forces of their own souls operate freely out of a certain self-respect. This much is certain, that he felt the death of Altacher as though it had been that of a dear friend. It was chiefly under the immediate impression of this event that he took the fatal step of undertaking the legal representation of the Ernevoldts. When, thereupon, Constance Altacher hired to represent her one of the most skillful, astute, and in a certain sense notorious lawyers, namely Doctor David Kerkowetz, it became to Laudin a matter of honor and conscience to throw over this doubtful case the mantle of his authority.

He seemed to forget that, by so doing, he endangered that authority, and perhaps even the honor of his name.

35

In order to fulfill, at least formally, the promise that she had made her dying husband, it is most probable that in the course of her interview with May Ernevoldt, Constance had made the girl a definite proposition concerning a pecuniary settlement. But, as we have already said, May was not to be persuaded to give a report of this interview—whether out of a feeling of contemptuousness or because she felt that a humiliation had been inflicted upon her, it was impossible to say. When Laudin insisted that, in order to interfere with propriety, he should be informed of all details, she begged him again and again to go to Louise, who had her authority for making the necessary communications.

"I have a great deal more to tell you," she said to Laudin with that confidential gesture which she had but for very few people, "and I have long made up my mind to do so. Edmond's marriage and his experiences within marriage—I can't get rid of the impression of all that. It has become to me the symbol of all the guilt and suffering of man: the Passion of Man. If only I had the power to tell you! So much is implicated in that—all that there is of pain and of somberness. What he succeeded in writing down can give you only the faintest notion. The knowledge I gained from him, although we never talked about it directly, has completely changed my opinions about marriage. Only now, that he is gone, it comes to pass now and then"—at this point her voice sank to an almost indistinguishable whisper and her eyes seemed to disappear—"that I summon him in order to question him and to take counsel with him. For to me he is not dead."

Laudin had heard from Louise Dercum that May had become wholly involved in the idea of and the belief in a living spiritual relationship with her dead friend. To hear it confirmed from her own lips, however, surprised him and even gave him, for a moment, a noticeable and unpleasant feeling of shame. He had always to combat this feeling whenever he saw that people really tried to transcend the natural order of things, really existed in a super-world of dreams. In a word, whenever he came face to face with these phenomena, he felt that they could not be dismissed with a mere shake of the head.

It had been reported to him that, since the death of her husband, Constance Altacher was instituting something like a cult in commemoration of him. She was gathering all reminiscences, having all his letters copied, repeating his opinions and sayings as though they were oracular, and displaying photographs of him in all the rooms of the house, precisely as though his person had always been the object of her veneration and she had never dreamed of not making his character and his opinions the guiding stars of her life and conversation. In his reëmbodiment, in this attempt to re-summon him who was gone, there seemed, in Laudin's opinion, to reside still another insolent attack upon the law of both morals and nature. This attack was not, like that other on May, one that estranged man from his world, but one that distorted and defamed a life that had been. But even while he asked himself this question, Laudin could not help wondering whether it was for him to call that a lie which most people would consider praiseworthy piety. Nor was it to be denied that this pious tissue held a special truth of its own. Yet he was determined to despise it, together with its probable content of truth, since this sort of piety meant nothing to him but an impudent suppression of old sins. The whole thing illustrated once more that unbelievable female conceit— disguise, mask, scarcely to be identified, and yet as odious in this form as in any other.

This feminine conceit and rancor, found in so many forms, had become like a nightmare to him. It seemed to symbolize to him all the essential evil of our social structure. He suffered at the thought of it; he shuddered. To fight it and destroy it, seemed to him to have become his mission.

He spoke very kindly to May in order to deceive her in regard to the considerations which left their almost convulsive marks upon his features. He wanted to understand. But like a plant that opens its blossoms only in the dusk and whose manifestations of life are confined to the vague groping of its membranes; even like such a plant she was not touched by his reactions and seemed not to dream with what acute vigilance he had received her declaration of the "appearance" of her dead friend and how anxious he was to discover what was the attitude of Louise Dercum toward this encroachment upon the irrational. The saddest kind of obscurantism—such was his judgment in his character of one who had always trodden the path of enlightenment. And in his resistance there was a good deal of the unimaginative hostility of the academically trained intellectual liberal. From his standpoint, then, the friendship between Louise and May seemed mysterious. He told himself, to be sure, that he was committing the common male error of believing that a friendship between women was based upon like-mindedness and intellectual harmony. Yet in this instance, the differences of the two characters were so striking that, even without intellectual harmony, a cordial relationship seemed hardly credible. On the one hand there was a shy, timid, isolated, bloodless, sensitive plant; on the other hand, a woman all mobility, fire, presence, vividness, energy. No speculation concerning the attraction of opposites seemed sufficient to explain this case.

This confrontation of the two, concerning which he speculated with characteristic thoroughness, bore witness to the light in which, at this period, Louise Dercum still appeared to him. In his own thoughts about her he doubtless granted her rights which he would have denied to any other human being, certainly to any other woman. Perhaps it was her independence that impressed him above all things. According to his well-tested experience really independent characters are the rarest things in the world. Wherever he met such a person, he would forgive a certain arrogance and proud hardness which, even as in Louise's case, was a constant characteristic of the type. Louise's specifically feminine genius, the miracle of her ability to intensify and transform herself—these qualities did not make the path to her easier. Laudin seemed to himself to be compelled to an attitude of venerating reserve, of constant wordless reverence. To subordinate himself to the mission of her genius, to let no criticism nor idle comparison nor blame nor offended feeling on his own part arise to tarnish it—such seemed to him to be his duty. A few days after his last conversation with Fraundorfer, he wrote to his friend for the purpose of refuting in one defiantly concentrated argument the ugly suspicions of the actress which Fraundorfer had expressed:

"At last a woman in the fullest sense of that word; a free and soaring heart and therefore a veracious one, somehow and in the deeper sense guiltless, if it is proper to see guiltlessness in the power of a human being of rising instinctively from its own seed and root. In her, at least, there is nothing of that element of the distorted, the crippled, the greed-bent, the stickily secretive of those slave women who are condemned to legal cohabitation and are proud of their damnation."

Yet were not these the words of a bourgeois who seeks a way out from his own region of life and either does not observe or is unwilling to observe the character of his own pretexts?

36

A conference with Louise had really become necessary. Not only on May's account, but for many other reasons. But she was hard to get hold of, and a confirmed enemy of definite appointments. Her situation was as follows: She was not only having a quarrel with her present manager, but was being sued for breach of contract by her former manager in Berlin. In addition, she had now made up her mind to accept Laudin's legal assistance in the matter of getting a divorce. But since the interview when, after some hesitation, he had promised her his assistance, he had not succeeded in getting out of her the minimum of necessary material and data. From day to day, she either forgot or made impatient excuses, such as important appointments or her artistic plans and tasks, or annoyances in the theater, or controversies with newspapers and editors and authors. It seemed to her that her career was not rapid enough; her ambition was not satisfied; what she achieved did not fulfill her expectations; the unfed flame smoldered; everywhere she saw obstacles, conspiracies, envy, faithlessness, distrust. "It is unendurable," she cried out, and ran through the room like an imprisoned creature, her hands behind her, her shoulders thrown back, "wading in slime and grasping the wind; all the fools and sluggards are in a conspiracy against any one who both wills and accomplishes. I have no time; I have absolutely no time; I can't sit around in your musty corners and make grimaces for your entertainment; I will smash all your windowpanes. I will, by God, I will!"

And in the very moment after one of these bitter outbursts she was capable of shaking with laughter, her hands clasped and her body bent far forward.

One of her plans was to buy a theater of her own. But for the present she had no money. "Get me the money, dearest Doctor!" she cried to Laudin, and looked at him in irritation, as though she were amazed that he hadn't already started on his way to get it. "All these important people whose chestnuts you pull out of the fire, are known to snore on their money bags. Can't you at least make that money come alive? The creatures themselves can go on sleeping. What I need is living money."

"We haven't gotten our Crœsuses to the point of fetching and carrying like well-trained dogs," Laudin replied. Her magnificent demands embarrassed him. Other people were present, the featureless loiterers and half acquaintances who drifted into the actress's house and without whom she was rarely to be seen. It annoyed him when Louise made her appeals to him in their presence.

Another plan, which was already fairly definite and seemed nearer to realization, was the founding of an international film company with Louise Dercum as its chief star. Bernt Ernevoldt was to head the undertaking; according to Louise he was the most suitable man. He had both the experience and the knack. She was sure of this. (She had the occasional habit of making an assertion with all possible emphasis and at the same time of letting you subtly see that she didn't believe a word she was saying.) The intention of the company was to attract foreign capitalists. The interest of several, who were willing to put considerable funds at the disposal of the company, had already been gained. So, at least, Ernevoldt asserted. And he really believed what he said.

Thus, in addition to the Altacher affair, to the suit brought against her by the Berlin manager and to the question of her own divorce, there was now added this business transaction to keep up the vivid relationship between Laudin and Louise Dercum, and to make necessary a continual stream of messages and communications between them. Almost daily Ernevoldt appeared in the office with a brief-case full of documents, so that Doctor Heimeran once remarked acridly to a colleague that, if things continued after this fashion, they would have to establish a separate office for the affairs of Miss Dercum. Unless, indeed, the entire practice of the firm was gradually to be confined to the quarrels of the aforesaid Miss Dercum. Everything seemed to be headed in that direction.

It was a fact that Ernevoldt, awkward and heavy as he was, put Laudin's patience and indulgence to the severest tests. It saddened him that this woman with her breathless swiftness had this habitual sluggard as path-breaker. It took a great deal of time to make Ernevoldt understand the terms of a contract, and more to get out of him any objections that he might have against the provisions of the contract. At last he raised his objections. Then he had telephone conversations with Louise. Next he broached the plan of a tour and Laudin had to prove to him that it was a bad plan. He seemed to yield to argument. Fifteen minutes later he would begin to talk about it as if it had never been mentioned before. All the while he looked comfortable and benevolent, smiled good-naturedly and shamefacedly, and seemed delighted with the consciousness of his own good looks and well-being. He never lost his faith and never doubted the success of even his most fantastic plans. At the end of every failure he discovered, without any effort of thought, a new and more radiant vista down which he trotted with the composure of a Newfoundland dog.

Laudin could not help communicating to Louise his doubt of Ernevoldt's reliability. Louise laughed. "Don't you worry about him," she said. "He's the kind that wins because he doesn't know how to play, and out of sheer absent-mindedness forgets his old umbrella and takes home a brand new one instead. I love these brave and sanguine fellows. Luck is what a man should have."

This short conversation, which was an introduction to a much more significant one, took place one night after the performance. Laudin had been to the theater. Whenever Louise played a new part she sent him a ticket. But he would often drop in to see her in the same part a second or a third time, if but for an hour, in order to let some special act or scene renew its marked impression upon him. His visits to the theater were secret visits; they grew more secret as they increased in frequency; one might have said that he concealed them from himself. They furnished him with emotions which he had not hitherto known. These emotions seemed to him welcome and unexpected liberations from the pressure of life; as he became more accustomed to these emotions, so their effect grew to be like that of a powerful narcotic, the danger of which lies in the undue relaxation of soul and body between doses. He was not deceived in this matter, since self-control had become a habit with him. Certain swift, telegraphic records in cipher which, for some time, he had been accustomed to make in the late hours of the night were like superficial monologues, in which he strove to give an accounting to himself, to issue warnings to himself, to ask himself in amazement whither he was steering, and at the same time to confirm himself with a growing and most strange stubbornness in the bonds of his own activity. In these notes he never mentioned the possibility of a personal and private relationship to Louise Dercum. He would probably have been both frightened and indignant if some superior spirit, who had an insight into the meaning and kernel of all things, had whispered to him that this very omission was the surest sign of the fact that he was sailing under a false flag in treacherous waters. It must not be forgotten that the majority of men who have been hardened and sobered by the practical life have an almost superstitious notion concerning the radiance of such a world as that in which the Louise Dercums move, and never dream that disillusion and sobriety have stolen even deeper into those hearts than into their own. Apparently distrustful, but full of yearning in their souls, curious to the point of lustfulness, they see in that supposedly higher world a marriage of freedom and beauty, of fairy magic and noble passion, of liberation and of bliss. In some such fashion Laudin gave the actress his idolatrous admiration. At this period, when he was still keeping the real truth from himself, she became to him the conqueror of our disconsolate working day, the genius who had the power of making tormented humanity forget its wretchedness evening after evening. He had come to a conclusion something like this: that he had denied himself these noble relaxations from the ordinary slavery of life on principle; that he had been too cowardly, too confused, too downtrodden, to enjoy them; his education had petrified him, and the uninterrupted expenditure of strength without equivalent inspiration had disillusioned him. Thus the overburdening of his motor system had revenged itself by crippling his capacity for impressions and for inspiration. Thus a hunger had come upon him in which, to be sure, there might slumber harmful germs. It may be dangerous to long so for that unknown other shore. But was he not infinitely weary of and disgusted by this shore which his feet trod? Had he not himself defended the venture of flight and transformation in words of blood and pain? Unless he wanted to lower himself in his own eyes as a mere spouter of empty phrases, did he have the right, of all people, to be abashed by the consequences that a journey into the uncharted dark might bring? No loss was to be feared, least of all that of personality.

Here the question arises whether one who is determined, under given circumstances, to risk his very personality, should not be quite ready to sacrifice a part of his fortune as a small advance payment?

On this very evening Laudin was to be put to the test.

37

She had been playing the title rôle of a Russian play called "Natascha." A young girl is faint with longing after a true and great love. She experiences several disappointments and, unable to endure the last and severest of these, she shoots herself while the rhythms of a waltz resound through the house, in which a ball is taking place. This was the rather poverty-stricken content of the elegiac play. But Louise Dercum, in the part of the young girl, had created a figure of tragic melancholy and of penetratingly sweet and morbid charm. Into every gesture she had poured that sad and moving story, into every break or raising of her voice, that innocent woe that trembled above her fate. The end had been like a gliding on moonbeams down the river of death and common, banal words had been transfigured into music.

Louise had invited Laudin to come to see her after the play. She had told him over the telephone that she really wanted to discuss business with him thoroughly. He heard this with pleasure.

The profound emotion, which he had experienced in the theater, had by no means disappeared when, toward eleven o'clock, he entered her studio. The place swarmed with people. With a tormented smile he remained standing near the door. It seemed as though his innocent expectation was to be disappointed again. To-day, at least, he had hoped to find Louise, if not alone, then in a small circle. If any one had paid any attention to him, he could have read on his features how annoying all this was to him: the brightness of the room, the laughter and chatter, the glasses and plates hurriedly passed around by servants, the mixture of familiarity, wit, zeal and self-importance that marked the bearing of all these people. For he was probably the only one of the guests who came from a higher sphere, the only one upon whom the art of the actress had had the effect which was necessarily the aim of her exorbitant ambition.

Perhaps Louise knew this. Assuredly she felt it. When she gave him her hand and he bowed slowly and silently to her, there was a proud glitter in her eyes. She held and pressed his hand in a way that made him very happy because it seemed to express an understanding of his inner state. It could at least be interpreted as a wordless mark of distinction. Nor, in spite of the irony of her flattered smile, did she fail to interpret his glance—that astonished and questioning glance which seemed to say: Is it possible that you who stand before me, concrete as common clay, are not Natascha? That one can return from such regions and associate with people, with ordinary, colorless, unmeaning people?

After a few words about Ernevoldt he did not see her

for a while. He only heard her laughter now and then, or the sound of her deep, husky voice. Several people addressed him. He answered courteously but without grasping what they had said. Then some one uttered the name of Nicolas Fraundorfer. He listened and approached the group in which the name had been spoken. The group consisted of actors and actresses who were slouching about on sofas and armchairs and were carrying on a lively conversation. They were talking about Louise, who was sitting scarcely three paces away listening to a theatrical agent who was trying to persuade her of something, while the overdressed baron with his affected expression was trying to whisper to her from the other side. The people whom Laudin had joined were talking about the humble beginnings of Louise's career, of her unparalleled rise and of the incomparable good luck with which she now hastened from success to success. With all the usual ceremonies they shied away the evil spirits, knocking on wood and spitting. A very fat fellow, who in spite of his jovial and satisfied smile, didn't seem to want to admit all this and seemed to intimate that after all, among colleagues, no one was in much doubt as to how things like that came to pass, raised his fat forefinger and said that only six months ago Louise had been able to please neither the public nor the critics; people had shaken their heads at her; then suddenly the devil seemed to have gotten into her and, be it remarked, precisely since she had had the affair with the little conductor Fraundorfer. He had evidently become her mascot, all the more so since he sent that bullet through his head. A handsome young woman, who had a feather boa about her neck, agreed excitedly and declared that she knew many similar cases. Even the late so and so— she named a forgotten actor—had told her that the death of a lover brought success. She, by the way, had been present when Lou and Nicolas Fraundorfer had met for the first time. There had been something elemental about it, something like a thunder clap on both sides. "Well, Lou didn't waste any time on nonsense," said the fat man, and took his glass and raised it in the direction of Louise. "She didn't have to be asked twice but devoured him whole. Isn't that so, Lou?" he called over to her. "In that respect you always did have a magnificent appetite. Your health, Lou!" Obviously, no syllable of this conversation had been lost on Louise. Laudin, who stood motionless behind the chair of the lady with the feather boa, looked over to her in dumb expectation, prepared for an outburst, for a flaming eye, for an indignant contradiction. None of these things appeared. She emptied her glass, beckoned carelessly with her hand, and, turning her head a little, said as though she were bored and absent-minded and indifferent: "Don't bother me with your silliness, good people." That was her only answer, and her absent-minded smiling look even brushed Laudin, whose pallor and immobility must surely have aroused her attention.

Dumbfounded, he crossed over to the opposite side of the room. He leaned against one of the pillars which supported the roof of the studio and, since he felt his forehead becoming moist, he drew out a handkerchief. He gave a start when, at an uncertain distance from himself, he became aware of a tall, distinguished-looking man in a dinner coat, who seemed familiar to him.

It was his own image in a crooked mirror opposite.

He heard a gentle voice asking him whether he was not feeling well. It was the voice of May, who had been watching him from a corner in which she had been sitting the whole time, lonely and unobserved. He looked at her sharply but did not answer, and when he stretched out his hand after a glass of water on the tray which the footman was passing around, his hand trembled. "Did you hear," he asked, shyly, "what those men and women are saying about our friend? They're dragging her into the very mud and she doesn't even defend herself."

"What were they talking about?" May asked with a reserved air.

"They were talking about a young man, the son of my friend. . . ."

May's face grew even more reserved. She arose and came close to him. "You must forget everything that you hear about Louise," she said, and her moonstone eyes suddenly had an air of sorrowful unsteadiness. "It does not count, whether for good or ill. Louise burns, and fire is not good and not evil. You can neither grasp it nor mold it. At times it will warm you and at other times destroy you. Cruel or beneficent, loveless or inspiring, true or deceptive—it does not matter. It is, and it lives. Thus it is with Louise. It suffices that she exists. If you take her differently you end in despair. I know that, I know that well." She hid her face in her hands and one could see a shiver running down her body.

Laudin raised astonished eyebrows. He had many proofs of May's almost slavish dependence on Louise Dercum. But he had tried to explain the relationship on natural grounds and as based upon natural processes and feelings. Now, as his face showed, he saw it in a different light. He saw it as something uncanny, as something belonging to that order of phenomena which had always seemed to him unsound, obscure and unseemly, and through which any human being seemed to him excluded from the company of the right-minded and the morally responsible. He was rooted in another century. The people of the 1880's are allied by their attitude toward the world, as though they were members of a single family. Any effort on their part to liberate themselves only serves to abrogate the law within them but does not extend the forms of their mentality.

"It is probably as you say; there is at least that possibility," he stammered in his effort to be courteous and even agreeable; "undoubtedly we must admit the existence of exceptions." A short time ago he would probably have rudely refused to entertain such an explanation as May's, such an interpretation of a character which, though contradictory and obscure, nevertheless had its definite place, as well as its passionate ambitions, within the given social order. He would have answered somewhat as follows: I grant you that she is gifted, of the elect, a creature of genius; this only increases her obligations; all the more is it our duty to stay within definite outlines and not slide into a conceptional chaos. Let us give her all due appreciation and the applause which she deserves and on which she is nourished. But let us be very careful to grant her no special rights and not to transform the artist into a saint. If we did, she might well be tempted to treat our superstition as a farce.

Only a few weeks ago this, or something like this, would have been his reply. But to-day his judgment had been incurably darkened; he had been torn out of his path by Natascha and by all that came to him from Natascha's origin, mind and character. So that the present Louise Dercum was but a shadow in his eyes, and Natascha or Kätchen or Hannele or Ophelia were the real originals— the burdened, sensitive, soulful, innocent and ill-starred creatures—the blending of all of whom produced, so to speak, the imminent Louise Dercum.

"You can do me a great service," he began, but stopped again as he became aware once more of May's reserved expression. With her curious intuitive power she had evidently guessed what he was driving at. He bit his lips. Three words more and he would have gone too far. He would have seemed a spy in her eyes, and a coward in his own. All this was incomprehensible; it was as though all paths became the passages of a labyrinth.

Louise interrupted them. Familiarly she put her arm into Laudin's and walked up and down with him. Guests still kept coming, but the room was large enough not to seem crowded. From the corner where the actors sat you could hear salvos of laughter. A few young men were leaning across a round table in the middle; an outer circle gathered about these while one of them, amid shrieks of laughter, read aloud a

comic poem. By one of the tall windows a group was playing poker. Once more Laudin took out his handkerchief to
dry his forehead. Walking by Louise's side he had the
sensation that he must step over the bodies of men. He
said in a modest and gallant but difficult tone that it was very
kind of her to take pity on him. He had been on the point
of fleeing.

She answered that she wouldn't have it, that he must stay.
They could promenade about here quite calmly and privately.
First of all she intended to tell him what had taken place
during the interview between May and Constance Altacher.
Her features seemed to relax; something like an impatience
for words, something like an appetite for words, appeared
upon her mobile lips as she began to speak.

Aside from that performance accompanied by tears and
cries of shame which belonged to the inevitable repertory
of Mrs. Altacher, the concrete result of the interview had
been as follows. She was willing to give May an annual
pension—the amount to be determined later—for the space
of ten years. The condition was that May was to obligate
herself in writing, first, that she would never make any
further claims upon the Altacher family; second, that she
was to hand over to Constance the memorandum which the
dead man had written concerning his marriage as well as all
the letters which he had written to May; thirdly, that in the
document in question she was to declare under oath that no
illicit relations had ever existed between Altacher and herself. These were the conditions, Louise continued, in a contemptuous tone. And these monstrous demands had not even
been made with businesslike objectivity, but to the repulsively
sweetish accompaniment of all sorts of jabbering about their
common fate and their common grief. Constance had even
had the impudent bad taste to desire May's friendship and
mutual confidence since, as she said, a sorrow such as she
had suffered broke down every prejudice, and a life of misunderstanding and vain sacrifice such as she had led was

apt to render the heart of a woman—or at least her heart—milder and more capable of love. She added that her emotional life had never been chilled in any way and that it would be a joy to her to stand guard over a being who had been as close as May to her unforgettable husband. And so on and so on. Louise felt sure that Dr. Laudin would be glad to do without a literal repetition. It would be clear to him that the woman was always emphasizing herself—her grief, her fate, her magnanimity, the generosity of her spirit, she, her, her, she, nothing else. Yes, Laudin said with lowered head, that same conceit, that unbelievable conceit. Very well, Louise continued. Two days later a letter had come from her in which, after a thoroughgoing conference with her lawyer, she had stated the sum of the pension. That was her tasteful name for it. (They are so tactful, aren't they, these ladies of good society, so considerate and delicate?) And what did Laudin think was the sum that this lady had mentioned out of her magnanimity and her newly discovered friendship for May? What did he think? She was ashamed to tell him. It was too laughable. It was the equivalent of what the state would give a superannuated brakeman, a regular charitable contribution.

Louise stood close to Laudin. She grasped both of his arms and looked at him with glowing sarcasm as though she meant to say: There you have your fellow-citizens, your class, your world. Now, advocate that you are, advocate them and their ways. Her look and gesture were entrancing. They were, at least, enormously successful.

He had no reply.

"Yes," she murmured with contemptuously bent lips, "they want to pay, they all want to pay. They want to pay for their errors and those of their husbands and sons; for the injuries that they inflict on their coachmen and hairdressers and on the mistresses of their husbands. They are willing to pay. But not much. It mustn't come high. A tip is enough, or a so-called contribution. They will grow en-

thusiastic and swear that one has made a new being of them
and they will send one flowers—Oh, yes, they will—and
even poems. But they are just the same. When it comes
to paying they begin to chaffer and the temple becomes a
mart of money-changers."

Laudin was silent, as though he were really a condemned
criminal, and had not noticed how cleverly she had implicated
May's affairs with her own. Then he said consolingly, and
yet could not keep his bitterness from showing through, that
he had found a statement in Altacher's correspondence on
the basis of which he could inaugurate a legal action against
Constance.

"What an insane noise!" Louise was vexed. "My colleagues have reached the brandy stage. Let us flee. I have
something else to tell you, dear friend. Let us go."

As on the occasion of his first visit she took him to the
little room behind the studio, asked him to sit down and
herself sat down opposite him.

She said that she would disdain any diplomatic preparations. She would come right out with what she had to say.
She wanted to talk to him about the film company. She
could see in this plan the possibility of an unparalleled
development of her talent. This, she thought, was the road
not only to international celebrity but also to wealth. She
didn't care to enter the services of an existing company,
because she had definite and individual plans, the execution
of which would probably collide with the purely mercantile
interests of most of the existing companies. What those
plans were she would confide to him on some later occasion.
She had plenty of ideas; her brain was seething with the
unheard-of. The theater is dying; the theater no longer
affects great masses of men; the future belongs to the film.
She had an offer from a German capitalist. She knew the
man, but she didn't think much of him. He was a recent
parvenu and she had reason to fear both his vanity and
his lust for power. She would rather have the money from

a friend. So she had thought of Laudin. All she needed was thirty thousand gold marks. The security she had to offer was her talent, her name, her luck. She knew that Laudin was rich. She knew, too, that where her success and her cause were concerned, he would have no trivial fears or hesitations. He should tell her how he felt about her proposal. There was no time for lengthy consideration. She must wire to Berlin in the morning. He must answer now: yes or no.

No more cold-blooded holdup could be imagined. Yes or no. Your money or your life. Was Laudin really as rich as Louise took the genius' privilege of assuming? Could he just shake thirty thousand gold marks out of his sleeve? Wasn't he rather the careful father of a family, who had earned his fortune bit by bit and managed it prudently? He wasn't poor, of course. He wasn't without means. Certain sums were invested, others were liquid. He had been an excellent manager. Political experience as well as a certain pessimistic foresight had been of advantage to him in this respect, too. His practice, especially in the last few years, had been a very profitable one. It was common talk that his office collected bills running into the hundreds of millions. Oh, yes, he was secure enough in his position in the upper ranks, in the stronger phalanx of society. But the spirit even of the upper middle class moves, in matters of money, within a relative and traditional circle, and exists by virtue of remaining within limits which have all the power of unrecorded laws. From that point of view, how foolish and frivolous to alienate so considerable a sum from his interest-bearing capital and devote it to a purpose which was questionable and dangerous if for no other reason than that he had no expert knowledge of such matters and could not judge of any results. An adventurer's trick.

True. On the other hand—a demand was made upon him to prove the real content of a human and personal attitude of his, which had, as such, its moral obligation.

Here was Natascha or Kätchen or Ophelia or Hannele and she said: Are you willing to stand by your attitude? Drop the mask! What are you—a mere enthusiast, a guest at the banquet, a spiritual voluptuary, especially if the emotions are cheap, or are you a confessor and defender of your faith? Is this jest or earnest? Are you priest or money-changer?

Louise, who observed the advocate's noticeable inner struggle with malicious irony, lit a cigarette and said coolly: "Of course, thirty thousand won't do it all. It's about one-fourth of what will be ultimately needed. But we can begin on that. We'll rent our properties and write our own scenarios. I, your humble servant, am the chief drawing card. Mr. Max Ortelli, who is sitting out there and who has just sworn eternal fidelity to my plans, will institute an advertising campaign of international proportions. He's thoroughly experienced, head of a big advertising concern, and is willing to take in payment a bundle of the company's shares. You, Doctor, will arrange all these legal and financial formalities. Once the thing is started, once it is known that our backer—the backer of the Phoenix Company —the man who is causing the Phoenix to rise from its ashes, is none other than yourself, capital will be forthcoming from other sources, in any amount. Well, how is it? Have you decided?"

Laudin bowed. "You are extremely expeditious," he said with quiet dignity. "The amount you ask is, of course, at your disposal."

"Good, very good." Louise nodded. "That's what I expected. You are the man I took you for—a real person, a true friend. You don't try to escape; you don't twist and turn; your teeth don't chatter when it comes to really backing your tastes. Splendid! Thank you!" She gave him both her hands and let him hold them firmly in his own. "We'll arrange all details to-morrow," she added.

"May I, too, ask a favor of you?" Laudin's tone was

hesitating; he fixed a serious, penetrating look upon her and drew her a little nearer to him. "May I, if I am really the friend that you have accepted, may I ask you, as a matter of honor and conscience, what was the meaning of the gossip of your various colleagues concerning you and poor Nicolas Fraundorfer? Don't be vexed, my child. Compared to me you are a child—marvelous and adorable, but a child. So I ask you not to be angry with an incorrigible pedant and to take the burden of a doubt from his soul. What really happened? What element of truth was there in that talk? Was all of it mere gossip?"

Louise was extremely astonished. What talk did he mean? What gossip? Oh, what was said in there a while ago? Nonsense! Did that bother him? Oh, such nonsense! She took her hands away and passed one carelessly over his hair, very lightly, yet with an ironic tenderness which caused him to look up, half-awed, half-intimidated, like an animal in a cage. She knew of nothing. Upon her soul and honor—nothing at all. It had all been swept away. Nothing much stuck to her—in either head or heart. But she'd try to remember what it was all about. But for heaven's sake, why should he cross-examine her about that wretched old business! How strange! Suddenly she grew angry. Was he a district attorney? She stamped her foot. An expression of wild suffering came into her face. Was it a crime that she had kissed the boy? Should she have noted down the number of times and the days? Or should she have recited sentimental verses to him? She laughed. She clapped her hands and bent back her brown throat and laughed and kneeled down before Laudin and crouched at his feet and put her chin on his knee and gazed at him with radiant laughter. And he, utterly overcome, dumbfounded, fought for breath and sought to discover the meaning of this play. If it was a play. For it was all impenetrable.

Some one knocked at the door. Some one pulled open the door. Louise threw herself on the carpet and still laughed and laughed. And a drunken voice squeaked that lovemaking was not permitted here. Lou was to come along; she was needed; she was needed in a poker game. Laudin arose and asked courteously that they let him pass. But in the studio he was met by the sounds of a wild revelry amid which he could still distinguish the flicker of Louise's laughter. The anteroom, too, was thronged, and even when he succeeded in getting his hat and his fur coat, he was forced slowly to break a path toward the door. Laughter to the right and to the left—a chain of unmotivated rumbling, high, staccato, trilling laughter. Even on the stairs, even in the lower hall he heard that roaring, giggling, bleating.

38

Since he wanted to go a part of the way on foot, he asked his chauffeur to drive on ahead to a certain street and there wait for him. A cold wind bit into his face. It was a starry, clear night of February. He had not yet reached the nearest corner when he heard steps behind him. At first he paid no attention. But by and by, as these footsteps continued to remain audible at the same distance behind him in the otherwise deserted street, he became annoyed. Listening, he pushed his head forward. Tap, tap, tap, said those footsteps. Was it not as though that laughter had come out into the winter night and had been frozen here until it became dumb, until it became a mere tap, tap, and still persisted in following him?

He went more slowly; those footsteps became slower. He stood still and looked around. He saw a woman, well dressed, apparently quite mature. He stopped under a lantern; the yellow ray fell into the woman's face. Two eyes flared up at him. He recognized Brigitte Hartmann.

He let her approach him. She came up slowly, watchfully, fearfully. "What is the meaning of this?" he asked, and measured her with his eyes. "What is the point of this pursuit by night, my good woman? You are taking to very strange ways. I don't understand. What do you want of me?" She stood before him and looked on the ground and murmured: "I just wanted to know how long you were staying with that play-actress wench." She pointed backward with her thumb and shrugged her shoulders.

Laudin regarded her as though he considered her demented. Hence his answer was tentative and measured: "I've already told you that I don't understand. It is probable that you are drunk. You do not realize to whom you are talking. A few days ago it was necessary for me to forbid you to annoy my wife. I advise you to read the letter I wrote to you more attentively. You will see from it that I am by no means defenseless against such attacks as yours. That is what you must remember." He turned and walked on.

But a very strange thing happened. Brigitte took no notice either of his reproof or of the fact that, contrary to his habits of courtesy, he simply left her standing there in the street. At the end of a few seconds she was beside him once more. And her footsteps went tap, tap. Her heels were probably so high that they made walking difficult. Laudin increased his pace. Rage got the better of him and in addition he had a sensation of the gruesome. The steps became swifter, too, and he heard the woman panting. And soon he heard what she was saying. He couldn't help hearing it. It was an uninterrupted torrent, an incoherent and insensate flood of words.

Yes, she had stood and waited; it wasn't too much trouble at all; for two hours she had walked up and down in front of the house, in the bitter cold. It wasn't the first time either. Twice before she had sent her hired man from Hartmannshof, but he hadn't been steady on the job. It gave her no rest to think of his being with the actress woman. Docton Laudin and a creature like that—those things didn't go together. The whole world knew what sort of a woman that was. You had only to ask the dressmakers and the milliners, whose bills she never paid. Yes, any one can have her—a venal woman, immoral and depraved. A whisky drinker. All the people around the theater knew how she swallowed brandy by the tumbler and could play best when she was half drunk. Oh, yes, she, Brigitte, knew a thing or two! She had once lived in the house of an actress and had seen the disgusting goings on. A man so highly honored and esteemed on all sides as Doctor Laudin had no business to have any dealings with such trash. Didn't he have a wife, and such a very dear wife? What was she to think of it? And why was he running so quickly? Why was he running away from her? Was she just dumb? Wasn't she worth listening to? Her breath was giving out. And didn't he know how devoted she was to him? She had really determined to live a new life. Since she had known Doctor Laudin she had become a different being. He had just to look at you and you got to have better feelings. But he mustn't, for God's sake, have his office write such letters to her any more. She just couldn't stand it. She was willing to give Caroline Lanz twenty-five millions. Only he must have her account released! The shame of it robbed her of sleep. Even her sainted Hartmann wouldn't approve of that. She had been out there to call on Caroline Lanz and she didn't see why those people howled so. They were living very decently. There was no real poverty in that neighborhood. Shabby, yes. They couldn't indulge in luxuries, but there was no want, nor anything like that. She had taken some linen to the Lanz woman and some knitted dresses for the child. But that student brother had shown her the door. A grand gentlemen, eh? Who in hell is he? So she had taken the things back with her again. The people in the house had told her that there was something not quite right about those Lanzes. Something was going on. Well, as for her, it was none of her business. But Doctor Laudin could see how much good will she was showing. And he mustn't, please, take her talk in ill part, nor what she had said about the Dercum woman, neither. She just happened to be a sincere person and she valued morality above all things. It's only because she admired the doctor so and would go through fire and water at a kind word from him that she was watching, and was heartbroken over his pitiless procedure toward her. But she was sure it was not his fault; he was much too noble; it was the fault of his clerks. There was a conspiracy against her; she'd known that for a long time; he had been prejudiced to the point of hounding her; and if these tortures didn't soon come to an end (torturing a poor defenseless widow, if you please, who has to take care of two minor children) and if the doctor didn't pay any more attention to her than to a dog, and didn't even take the trouble of answering her—why, then, if you please, she would have to take certain measures, too, and her decent forbearance could no longer be counted on. Because right was right and where fidelity had been vowed it must be kept, or else the end of the world was coming. . . .

And the ghostly steps said tap, tap.

There was his auto. Swiftly Laudin entered and slammed the door. A somber look, wholly unlike himself, pierced the woman. She stood in the middle of the street as the car began to move. Her mouth was half open and one could see that gap in her teeth.

After a few minutes the car had melted into the darkness. Brigitte Hartmann was still standing there. She did not move. She was a part of the night which lay heavy and black over the city. She gazed in the direction in which the car had disappeared.

The pain that a created thing suffers is something absolute. It is alone with that thing and with God.

39

As Dr. Heimeran was one day turning the pages of his notebook he came, among many other things, upon a note that consisted of two words: Weitbrecht-Fraundorfer. It took him some time until, visualizing the scene at the bridge table in the club, he was able to recall the exact conversation that had taken place. Shortly after this he had occasion to have a conference with Laudin in regard to various matters. He found his chief and colleague sparing of words and very indefinite in giving him necessary information. Hence his tone, which he had meant to make friendly and sympathetic, sounded rather cool and searching when he inquired of Laudin whether the actual circumstances surrounding the suicide of young Fraundorfer had ever been actually cleared up.

Laudin measured him with a sudden, swift look. "How do you happen to ask that?" His manner was not only curt but filled with a sense of disturbance that was but ill-concealed.

Heimeran shrugged his shoulders and looked out of the window. He said he had just happened to think about it; there had been so much vague talk; he knew that Laudin had had particular reasons for sympathizing with the tragedy. Perhaps Laudin no longer remembered that under the first impression of the sad event he had confided to him, Heimeran, how disconsolate both he and the boy's father were. So it was no wonder, Dr. Heimeran said, that occasionally he should happen to think about it. But that was all.

He smiled a rather crooked smile and took his leave. Laudin had answered nothing, but had frowned and gone back to the reading of his letters.

Perhaps there was something both malicious and stubborn in the way that Dr. Heimeran had dropped the subject without making the communication which he had quite determined to impart. He was much too vain of his own talents for bringing hidden things to the light of day and for cleverly combining apparently unrelated perceptions, to be urgent, or to make a point of his discovery. He was fond, on the contrary, of clothing himself in his better knowledge and of chuckling while the laity, whom he thoroughly despised, were making their gawky and stupid mistakes.

He was wounded in his vanity by Laudin's harsh refusal of confidence, although he knew perfectly well the reason for Laudin's unhappy mood on this particular forenoon. It was a communication from Dr. Kerkowetz in the case of Altacher. Suddenly, curiosity began to gnaw at him. He recalled Laudin's relationship to the actress and the latter's to the dead young man. Into this mental web he wove the figure of the unhappy father. There was a possibility here of sending a ray of light into darkness, of testing a mystery, of making a discovery, and Heimeran made up his mind to see this Egyd Fraundorfer.

The very next day he called on Fraundorfer and found him at home. He stood beside the huge man and looked most respectfully up into the latter's small, sleepy, half-treacherous eyes. "I had the pleasure of meeting you one evening last winter at the house of my honored colleague, Laudin."

Somewhat morosely Fraundorfer admitted the fact and asked his guest to sit down. Distrustfully Herr Schmidt slunk around the chair of Heimeran and his master winked at him, as much as to say: Well, we'll see what he has to say.

He started the conversation with somber and rather obscure irony. "How is that highly honored colleague of yours? I don't see much of him, nowadays. He hasn't been here for nearly a month. He seems to be drowning in his legal battles. Well, you have only to observe the world to see that it must keep the lawyers busy. That beast of a janitor of mine nearly beat his wife to death yesterday. What did you say? You'll have to talk a little louder. For several days past I've been hard of hearing on the left side. What did you say your name was?"

Once more and emphatically Heimeran gave his name. Fraundorfer acknowledged the effort with a nod. Next he expressed a desire to know the purpose of this visit. He wasn't used to visits, any more. It surprised him to have anyone cross his threshold. He had forgotten how to behave on such occasions. He was afraid that his behavior could be interpreted as rude, whereas it was only that of a shy cave-bear of mastodon proportions. He laughed. "Go into your basket, Herr Schmidt!"

Although Heimeran was never alone and did not know what loneliness meant, he nevertheless had a sense of the isolation that came to him from these words and this place. He dryly stated what had brought him here. He told of the conversation among friends at the bridge table. He thought he might just as well keep to himself the length of time that had elapsed in order not to rob his experimental communication of its possible weight. He told how, among other subjects, that of young Fraundorfer had arisen, and how Professor Weitbrecht, one of the group, had casually remarked that the young man had been to consult him shortly before his death. Fraundorfer would undoubtedly be familiar with the name of Weitbrecht, the well-known syphilologist. Heimeran had felt it his duty to communicate this fact to the father, even though it might almost be taken for granted that he was already aware of it. Nowadays, thank God, young men no longer regard their misfortune as shameful. Or was it news to Fraundorfer? It seemed to be.

The big man's gesture was like a short circuit. A sudden clenching of the fist motivated the other's question, which was asked with some satisfaction. For Heimeran saw at once that his errand had been justified. No other reward came to him, not even a word of thanks. From this moment on Fraundorfer lapsed into an almost fearful silence, and an ashy gray crept over his ravaged, spongy face. But the dark ignorance of the laity had once more been exposed and Dr. Heimeran's ray of light had found its object. Further effects could undoubtedly be observed by watching Laudin. But since he was here at the house of the man who was well known to be Laudin's friend, it seemed quite natural to discuss the disquieting transformation in the character of the lawyer—a transformation that bore more and more the stamp of a mysterious ensnarement. It is curious that for some time past all of Heimeran's observations concerning Laudin had the appearance of malice, of actual hatefulness toward his once so thoroughly admired and, in fact, exalted friend and chief. How was that to be explained? Because the inviolable had not remained inviolate? Because that bright image had been darkened? The mediocre practitioners of daily life have commonly no other god except some moral and intellectual superior in their own profession. And if he ceases to square with those high notions of him by means of which they cleanse and exalt their own souls, there awakens a revengeful bitterness.

Fraundorfer had been alone once more for a long time, but he had not yet stirred. Nor did he stir when Mrs. Blum brought him his dinner. Hours later the food had to be warmed over and even then he was able to force down only a few bites. During the whole day an iron heaviness was upon him. At nightfall he opened a bottle of powerful spirits; by morning the bottle was empty. He slept for sixteen hours. Then he tried to work. But the janitor's wife came to beseech him to use his influence with the police for the release of her husband. To be sure, the man had treated her with the utmost brutality, as the very condition of her body proved. But she simply could not get the work done alone. For a while Fraundorfer submitted to her noisy lamentations. Then he roared out and told her to go to hell and pursued her with his rage to the top of the stairs. It seemed to relieve him to have found a pretext for anger and noise.

One would think that he would have hastened at once to Professor Weitbrecht in order to ascertain the truth or falsehood of Heimeran's revelation. Perhaps he had considered the matter; perhaps he felt a driving force within and determined upon that errand from day to day and from hour to hour. And yet he did not go. He evidently could not bring himself to go. He was afraid to know. It would happen that, to the enraptured and expectant delight of Herr Schmidt, he would put on his boots and a clean collar and fetch his overcoat from the closet. But he never got farther than these preparations. They seemed to exhaust his strength. At the last moment he would look as though some one had thrown a noose about his neck and was slowly throttling him. A thick, quivering roll of fat made its appearance above the bushy eyebrows. Again and again the huge hands were clenched.

One night Herr Schmidt was lying on the table with all four paws stretched out. It was a particular mark of his master's favor when he was permitted to do this or was, at least, not prevented. And for this elevation of his tiny person in space, Herr Schmidt showed his appreciative understanding by not taking his moist, adoring look for one moment from his master's face. Fraundorfer, with a beam-like cigar in the corner of his mouth, one eye shut, the other sleepily open, holding a glass of hot, freshly brewed punch, delivered himself of the following speech:

"We ought to go tomorrow to that great medicine man, Herr Schmidt. We should do so, by all means. Or day after to-morrow. We ought by no means to put it off longer. But I see already that we're going to shirk the job again. The mechanism of our mind seems to have a serious effect; one might almost call it a disease—the very convulsion of retardation. Anything but accomplished facts! That was always our motto, wasn't it, Herr Schmidt? The irrevocable was always our pet enemy. I see that you quite share my opinion. Bravo, Herr Schmidt. Your intelligence is making progress. For the irrevocable is as sterile as death. Beyond it there is no consolation, not the shabbiest rag of consolation, not the shadow of a possibility of self-deception. That's the fact with which we have to reckon, Herr Schmidt, and by which we must be guided. When the barriers are closed—then look out! It is quite as though some one were to say to you: Will you kindly come along to the knacker; there you will find a swift, pleasing and painless end. Life at old Fraundorfer's is not a bed of roses for you. Would you, in spite of that, rashly plunge into that irrevocable situation? And even if this comparison of your conceivable path to the knacker seems a little exaggerated to you, or even brutal, I must still beg you to consider: What then? Ah, this "then" means that something must, after all, be done. Or else there will be further irresolution and further defects in the clock-work of being. Ah, Herr Schmidt, what problems arise to goad us! First of all, we should initiate our friend, once called Dyskolos, into these new circumstances. But on this whole subject we had better keep our thoughts well caged. Let us be glad that they are behind bars. Let us not deceive ourselves, Herr Schmidt. Equivocal things arise here. Let us look elsewhither. Let us assume an innocent expression. And if by chance the bell should ring and he should enter by that door, let us be as friendly as ever. I desire it, Herr Schmidt, and I expect it of your upbringing. Let us look frankly and openly into his eyes and give him no clues to the disorders of our mechanism. Let us practice the beautiful virtue of dissimulation. Do you understand?"

Eagerly Herr Schmidt wagged his tiny tail. Fraundorfer took a long and greedy draft from his glass. He smacked his lips. "I fear, however, that he will not soon appear upon this scene," he continued with a somber and a bitter expression and with a voice that seemed to die away as in the mumbling of approaching sleep. "We'll have time enough to catch all the fleas on our skin. It isn't even out of the question that we may have time to finish a new chapter in our history of human stupidity. All that, in spite of the fact that between ourselves, Herr Schmidt, we don't consider the scribbling of books worth a continental. All that one does is to write over again what some one else has written better long ago. Very well. We'll not discuss that. No reason to feel hurt or wretched because the Eukoloi and Dyskoloi furnish us with material for several chapters. This particular one who, for certain reasons, is not uncongenial to us, has filled his manger with poison pills. He's like a merchant gone insane who insists on making all his debits mount up to something on the credit side and lets his goods go for nothing to bankrupt firms. You remember what that skinned herring of a lawyer man told us the other day. . . . By the way, it isn't very appetizing the way you're lying all over the table, Herr Schmidt! I endure it because I'm too lazy to punish you. Let it go. Let everything slide, Herr Schmidt; let everything be as it has been. . . ."

His chin sank upon his breast. He kicked the table and the empty glass toppled over. Herr Schmidt went to sleep, too.

40

It was not without difficulty that Laudin managed to raise the five hundred and five millions cash which were to be the foundation of the capital of the film company. Further difficulties arose in the course of the execution of other necessary formalities, beginning with the notarial service to the transference of the moneys and the opening of the account. Three times Louise Dercum changed her mind in regard to the choice of a bank. Her vacillation had the most childish motives. Against Laudin's advice she finally decided upon a banking house of medium size, simply because the personality of the managing director appealed to her. At all events this man had known how to throw dust in her eyes and had lured her on by promising an unusually high rate of interest. All this in spite of the fact that the interest meant very little to her, as she freely admitted, since the money was to be spent and not to be invested. The careless largeness of her gestures in everything connected with money was astonishing. Sometimes, if she was in a vexed mood, she would order four new frocks at once, without thinking of ever paying for them. In her bedroom one simply trod over unpaid bills. In this respect Brigitte Hartmann had by no means exaggerated. In spite of the carelessness with which she managed her affairs, there were quite a number of people who considered her greedy and didn't believe in her openly expressed contempt for money. All sorts of opinions floated to Laudin; he heard whispers, too, that she played for high stakes. A great many people seemed to take pleasure in communicating to him their opinions and estimates of the actress. God knows why. What he heard was rarely favorable.

In the nature of things the bank account should have been in the name of the corporation. Louise resisted this violently. She asserted that in the first place such an arrangement would interfere with her freedom of action. Unless her power of disposition were unlimited, the whole business had neither sense nor purpose. In addition, she pointed out that until the company was incorporated and had agreed upon its provisions and had received its charter and had elected its officers, precious and irrevocable time would go by, during which she would be waiting with fettered hands. Laudin had instructed her concerning the measures dictated by the law. With great hesitation he yielded to her arguments. There were conferences, however, during which he had to veto proposals of obvious silliness. Louise herself was far too deep in debt to make it advisable to put the account in her name. Nor was Ernevoldt to be thought of. Laudin knew that the man's financial situation was a desperate one, quite aside from his unpracticalness.

Finally, and after Laudin had refused to have anything to do with the advertising expert Ortelli whom, and in spite of Louise's impatient protestations, he characterized quite openly as an irresponsible windbag—finally, the plan was adopted to open the account in the name of May Ernevoldt.

Curiously enough, May refused utterly. She gave no definite reasons for her refusal; she only said, and begged every one to believe her, that to her money was the acme of everything revolting and that if they got her mixed up with money matters she would quite simply run away. Nevertheless, her behavior seemed, in addition, to be dictated by a definite fear which she sought to conceal but which, at the very moment when Louise first tenderly and then angrily tried to induce her to change her mind, burst forth with double violence, despite her devotion and affection for her friend. Since all emotional processes affected her with the utmost violence it came to the point that, when her consent had finally been wrung from her, she had to be treated like an invalid and put to bed in a darkened room.

Two days later seventeen thousand marks were transferred in the name of Bernt Ernevoldt to a German banking house. Ernevoldt left at once and wrote Laudin that he had gone to hire actors and to buy apparatus. This didn't prevent him from first paying his most insistent creditors, the accumulated rental of the villa and buying a grand piano and a gramaphone. Louise, too, decided suddenly to pay some of her most pressing debts because she was being threatened with the seizure of her salary. The amounts she drew amounted to between fifty and sixty millions. Although Laudin asked for no accounting, she voluntarily denied that the money had been withdrawn from the account. With the great eyes of a fairy princess and in a tone of child-like gratitude she related how she had won the money at the gaming table. It didn't occur to Laudin to investigate. He had, as he told himself, given this money up as lost. But a few days later the bank made a mistake and sent the notification of the withdrawal of funds to him, instead of to the holder of the account. The sum was precisely that which Louise had needed for the payment of her debts. He forwarded the slip to May.

Anonymous letters of abusive and slanderous content had

always formed a regular part of his affairs. In the same mail which had brought the treacherous notification from the bank there had also arrived the following lines: "If you imagine that that Dercum woman's lackey has gone to Germany to carry out the plans for which you've thrown your good money among that crowd, you're a poor, pitiable ass. We people in the theater know better. Suppose you make inquiries as to what a certain infamous shyster lawyer K. M. and the even more infamous quack R. Z. still get for keeping the unhappy Arnold Keller in a madhouse."

The sheet flew into the waste paper basket.

41

The "point" which, to use his own words, he had discovered in the correspondence between Altacher and May and which was going to be the starting point of his suit against Constance—this same point served him at once as the foundation of his controversy with the lawyer Kerkowetz. It arose from an accident that had taken place two years previously. At the death of his mother, Edmond Altacher had inherited, among other things, a beautiful old miniature set with jewels. He loved this little work of art very much and he determined to give it to his friend May to whom he had shown it and who had been equally enchanted. Several stones were missing in the diamond setting of the frame and in order to have these replaced he took the little picture to his jeweler. Constance had discovered this fact. A few days later she went to the jeweler and asked for the repaired miniature as though her husband had sent her for it. The jeweler knew her, of course, and hastened to give it to her. As soon as it was in her possession she no longer concealed from her husband the motive and intention of her trickery and refused to give up the picture. She said it was the property of the family and as such a symbol of ancestral piety and that he had no right to withdraw it from the family. Since he didn't want the conflict to become acute, he was forced to yield. In a letter which during a journey soon thereafter he had written to May, he told her the story of this incident. The only explanation he could give her for Constance's knowledge of the fact was that, in view of his carelessness, she had probably succeeded in getting hold of and reading an earlier letter of his to May in which he had mentioned the miniature. At that time he and May corresponded a good deal.

This action on the part of Constance Altacher, Laudin interpreted as the illegal seizure of a documentarily recorded gift. Without overemphasizing this incident, which would have been a mistake in tactics, he nevertheless used it as the psychological basis in the preliminary conferences with Kerkowetz. The suit for the payment of the legacy was quite as hopeless as the counter-suit for the repayment of the various sums which Altacher had actually given the Ernevoldts. In fact, the whole affair had from the very beginning the character of a sort of juridical sword-dance, in spite of which Laudin betrayed a stubbornness which was hardly conducive to the success of his measures. And although he became more stiffnecked in his attitude from day to day, it cannot be said that he felt one moment's peace or satisfaction. His attitude was not that of a man who, in the course of a very intricate piece of litigation, represents the by no means wholly defensible, but genuine interests of one set of clients. He acted as though he were on the warpath against the hereditary foe of society and as though the fate and right of many people depended on the outcome of this conflict. It was obviously once more the particular moral phenomenon that spurred him on and that engaged his grim zeal. His image of the world grew more and more distorted. This was evident from his glance, his gait, his somberness and from the altered rhythm of his daily life.

The affidavits of Dr. David Kerkowetz, which were written in reply to his own, were of an incomparable sharpness. The man was courteous as a matter of form. But his veiled sarcasms and biting equivocations and jeeringly humble maxims disturbed Laudin indescribably. He grew white as chalk after the reading of the very first of these fluent, perfidious documents that offered no point of attack on their smooth surface. He felt profoundly that he was unequal to this adversary, that he could not hold his own in this duel, at least not concerning this cause which was more like a catastrophe of his mind than like a professional duty and task. This cause had sickered into his soul; it had been branded upon his forehead somehow, by some hand; he knew not how nor by whom. It was like a dream that dragged itself on into the day. And Kerkowetz, knight of the enemy, opponent and adversary, was made invisible to him by a turbid miasma and thus gained advantage after advantage over him.

The third reply of Kerkowetz was accompanied by the letter of Laudin that had occasioned it. The final sentence of this affidavit which Laudin had dictated was thickly underlined in red and adorned on the margin by two large red question-marks. The sentence in question was hard, dry, unprofessional: "There is no possibility of our reaching an understanding. Between us lies a world which my foot will refuse to tread until you have succeeded in driving me out of my own."

Laudin was petrified. He couldn't have said that! He couldn't have dictated that! How could it have occurred to him to utter such a challenge, such an insult, such an empty boast? His voice was hoarse as he called in his secretary. He pointed with his finger to the passage. The girl did not understand. Then the constriction in his throat was loosened and he roared. For the first time in the history of his professional activity he was heard to roar: "Who put this down? Who is the author of this sentence? Who is guilty of this folly and this madness?" Kappusch, Heimeran, the assistants and the secretaries rushed in. Kappusch tried to quiet him. The girl was frightened. He foamed, "Bring me your stenographic notes!" The secretary disappeared. He walked up and down with great strides, tormented as by something uncanny. After a few minutes the girl came back and silently handed him the book with her notes.

The sentence was there. He had dictated it. He hadn't been conscious of it. He had spoken the words without knowing it. Confused, he looked about him. He frowned and with a strangely sad self-irony he turned to Heimeran: "It almost seems to me as if an inquiry into identity were necessary here."

They held a brief counsel. He tried to explain the matter somehow to his colleagues, who feigned to find his explanation plausible. There was nothing to do except to offer a formal apology. A letter was sent by messenger to Kerkowetz. In that letter regret was expressed that a mistake due to the absent-mindedness of a clerk in mixing up two different dictations had given rise to this unfortunate incident.

An hour later, in the hall of the court building, Laudin suddenly found himself face to face with Kerkowetz. Both were in their robes of office, which gave their meeting a touch of almost unreal solemnity. Silently they looked at each other. Then Laudin bowed; Kerkowetz, a fatty imitation of Napoleon in aspect, responded reservedly. He seemed to have an expression of triumph in his eyes. But he was the kind that is born with that expression.

42

Ernevoldt wired from Berlin: "Arnold Keller discharged from institution prior to my arrival. Present whereabouts unknown. Inform Louise."

Coming from this source, Laudin thought the alarm excessive and impudent in tone. Since a certain pedantic prudence was in his blood he could not help reckoning up at times, how much of his strength he gave without any reward to the affairs of Miss Dercum. The fact that he did all these things voluntarily did not rob him of the feeling of being exploited. But such thoughts stirred within him only in moments of weariness or when he asked himself what was to be the upshot of it all. There were other moments, too, when there came to him the surprised, regretful, many-tongued rumor of the world. Yet if Louise called him he followed, and when she commanded he obeyed; when she smiled ease stole into his heart; when she lamented he found the air too heavy for his lungs. Whenever the golden brown shimmer of her glowing eyes was upon him, he was at peace with the world.

He read all the daily papers in the hope of coming upon her name. The criticisms that appeared about her he cut out carefully and collected them like a college boy, who in his secret rapture follows from afar the phases of the life of some adored star of the stage. He had acquired the habit of very subtly turning conversation with the most indifferent persons in the direction of the theater. And since the name of Louise Dercum was upon all lips, it did not take long before it was pronounced. From that moment on, he fell silent and became all ear.

At this point we can see lips curl in irony, and the wise in their own conceit shrug their shoulders. But they are mistaken. This is not the place to boast of experiences that are as common as blackberries. From a hundred hints and indications it must now be clear that a spirit such as Laudin's, an inquiring spirit, and one that measures the world by its own innate measure, has the right to nullify and to deny the judgment of those who, fortified by some experience, interpret his inner state by means of rubber stamp expressions and conventional estimates. He is beyond both their smiles and their pity. For they forget that Laudins do not stroll up every street, and that a woman like Louise Dercum is, after all, more than a tidbit for sensual millionaires.

In his private notes Laudin himself made merry over the

possibility of his being in love, of his nursing the late passion of an aging man. And although this fact in itself is no sufficient proof of the entire absence of such feeling, since in these matters self-deception knows hardly any bounds, yet the scrupulousness of his mind and his strict and habitual veracity leave room, at least, for the existence of more mysterious emotional backgrounds.

There could, at least, be no question here of empty enthusiasm or of an unbridled imagination. There may have been a moment of this danger at the very beginning. There was a moment in which the sight of her burning pathway dimmed the glance of this merely academically educated man into the belief that here was a priestess of art. The experiences of any three days in real contact with Louise sufficed, however, to destroy that image. And three days are quite enough to raise a kneeling adorer from the dust and turn him into an ordinary admirer of the kind that always follow in the wake of the cart of Thespis.

Let us not forget that the occasion of his seeking out Louise Dercum had been the death of an admirable youth. He had entered the circle of this woman in order to put an end to the dark broodings of a stricken father, to soothe that father's raging grief which quarreled with man and God, and also in order to quiet a tormenting restlessness within himself. In brief, he had acted under the dictate of a higher law. She had willingly given him the information that he had asked. No elaborate investigations had been necessary. The story was apparently a simple one. Closely looked upon, it was perhaps too simple. Did he believe it? Was there no suspicion in him? Did he take it all to be genuine? It is hard to say. But we would be doing this weighty jurist a wrong if we did not assume that from the first, and increasingly, doubt had stirred more and more strongly behind his courtesy and kindliness and had ever since stood strictly on guard. It must, to be sure, not be forgotten that at that very first meeting he had been under the influence of what seemed to him an artistic achievement of overwhelming brilliance, and that this impression did not only not decrease but was heightened from day to day, from meeting to meeting in both extent and endurance. And this enduring and overwhelming impression was made upon a nature modest to its very core, so that it acknowledged another's superiority with delight, almost with a kind of humility, and was thereby persuaded to considerateness, to awe, to a constant show of respect.

Then came the whispers of gossip; they came from all sides. He could, at need, have armored himself against these. For twenty years he had been living in a constant whirlwind of slander. What men said concerning each other and what consequently it was his business to listen to—this had long turned his existence into a muddy puddle and had seeped, in the form of concentrated poison, even into the well-waxed rifts of his private life, if indeed he could still be said to have a life of his own. But gradually there came to him a vision of his own, unveiling itself pitilessly and gradually. He came to see and to hear. And he became aware of a knowledge of things upon the faces of idlers and parasites and flatterers which those people took as matters of course. But these things not only escaped him, but were kept from him by a sort of tacit conspiracy, as one keeps from boys the scabrous adventures of men of the world. Why was that so, he was forced to ask himself. Obviously he did not know that the essentially pure wear an armor that seems to close automatically in the presence of the impure, who are capable of an immediate understanding among themselves, since they commonly inhabit the same dunghill. Much worse and even stranger was Louise's betrayal of herself—this frivolous, laughing, cynical betrayal which was a mixture of forgetfulness, curiosity, high spirits and a mood of challenge. Nor is it possible to say why she dared to sacrifice and to toss aside his reverence and his admiration and to deceive his confidence. Why? To gratify a mere whim? As though she didn't have the slightest regard for what was really magical and divine within her. As though this were something to be trodden under foot unless it expressed itself in plaudits, in newspaper paragraphs, in the figure of her salary.

Nor was it all this alone that darkened his mind, and caused his strange brooding and his strange inconsequential management of the totality of his life. Insight into untruth and a knowledge of untruth are not so bad, good people; it is not wholly destructive, oh, my few friends, and you, Pia, and you, my daughters, and you, oh, small son—nay, it is not destructive even if we became so implicated with unveracity that it seems to become, as it were, a part of ourselves. What is evil? It is the discouraged submission into which untruth weaves us with a subtle lightness of touch, thread by tiny thread; amiably playing with us and —God protect us from that—sustained by an apparently magical element.

It was a lie when she said: I've been in a coffee-house. She had been at a fashion show. It was a lie when she said: I've been at a fashion show. She had been out driving with some rich fool whom she was luring on. It was a lie when she said that she had seen one man beating another in the street. It had been a mere exchange of rude words. She said she had been ill during the night and had had to call in a doctor. It was a lie. Or that she had read an interesting novel and had had such and such thoughts. It was a lie. She hadn't the patience to finish a letter. She never read a book. She had been asked to play in America. Not a word of truth in it. Her emerald and platinum ring, she said, she had inherited from her grandmother. An out-and-out invention. Her grandmother had been a charwoman in Olmütz. She told the story of her early youth: Seven brothers and sisters, all delicate, three of whom died in three successive years; her father was a highly gifted engineer and bridge builder who had been brought to ruin by the persecution of an implacable enemy and who ended by seeking refuge in drink; her mother had been a dancer of European celebrity whom a disappointed lover had shot in the hip on the stage, so that she was condemned to the life of a cripple. All this was the emptiest invention. For several days later her father had become the owner of a circus and her mother a former Baroness Schlichtenfels. Or something like that. She told no incident of her past which had any relation, however distant, to reality. If at any time it was actually necessary to check up on some humble fact—let us say, or the occasion of a court formality or the procuring of a passport—she pretended that her birth certificate was lost and said that she had been born in some famous city and not in the wretched village where her cradle had actually stood. In the end, of course, she had to eat her own words. But she did that with the charm of a fairy-like being whose lips had never known the touch of untruth, and with a smile which forgave those others who had believed her for five minutes.

She pursued this method in higher regions, where there was no possibility of check or discovery. God dwelt in her heart; with profoundly moving devotion she spoke of the holy sacraments, of confession and communion. One could see her pray in some church; she threw herself on the stones and, in the manner of the Italian women, hid her head between her outstretched arms. At some corner she gave alms to a beggar; twenty paces away she turned back and gave him more; she had been absent-minded and given too little. This, with an inimitable upward gaze. If compassion could become incarnate, here was its incarnation. The suffering of the world penetrated her marrow and robbed her of sleep. And yet it was only yesterday that she had been as impassive as a stone when poor little Miss Markmann was sobbing at the door of her dressing room, because the celebrated and all-powerful actress refused to play opposite her without any reason, without any explanation, out of the mere dark hatred of woman for woman. She is for the just division of the goods of this earth; the communistic ideal inspires her to the point of prophetic eloquence and there is no violence, no bloodshed that she is not willing to excuse or even to commend for the sake of this exalted dream. Which doesn't prevent her—since she is never satisfied with gold and silk and brocades and laces—from the senseless wasting of unheard of sums, from drowning every vexation as well as the stirring of every true feeling in champagne, and from planning to make a sensational film of Charlotte Corday's heroic act of arbitrament.

But she probably knows little or nothing about Charlotte Corday. Some scribbler, no doubt, told her the tale.

She was the most impassioned of friends; the most melting assurances, the fieriest vows moved the heart of anyone, man or woman, who pleased her or attached himself to her. And it could easily happen that twenty-four hours later she would pass such an individual in the street without a greeting, for the simple reason that she really didn't remember him. Two or three women had played a real part in her life, and five or six men. For these she did entertain a kind of fidelity, an almost animal gratitude, which was commonly based upon the fact that the individual in question had totally suppressed his own will, had been at her service like a mere implement, had lightened her boredom, soothed her rages and endured any kind of maltreatment at her hands. She treated the majority of her lovers like the useless trash of which she would occasionally empty her drawers in order to provide space for a new supply. This one or that one had been good for something some time—had flattered her vanity or amused a dull hour or satisfied a whim or a thirsty moment of impatience in the flesh. She admitted no claim. A wild night of love. Next morning her companion was a strange gentleman.

Laudin knew all this. He had recognized it and felt it and suspected it and had added up his observations and, without any illusion, recorded their sum. She had sworn eternal friendship to him, too, friendship unto death. In the excess of her gratitude and almost submissive devotion she had gone so far as to assert that her heart was pledged to him forever and that only since she had known him, had she arrived at a proper concept of the possibilities of manhood. And considering the magnificence of her eloquence, considering that voice whose very sound could stir the soul, it goes without saying that he did not remain unmoved. But he knew that she needed him. He knew that in certain respects he had become indispensable to her. He knew furthermore that she bathed herself in the deliciousness of her own speech as in fragrant waters and enjoyed the sound of her voice as though it were the playing of a violin. He knew that her promises were worthless, that she forgot agreements entered upon, literally the next minute; he knew that she lied if she merely said: Let's be alone together to-morrow for fifteen minutes, or: I wrote my brother about you yesterday (she probably didn't have a brother), and that it hadn't the least significance when she nestled against his shoulder tenderly, half daughter, half exquisite seducer and looked up at him with a happy smile. She was capable of denying him the next day without the quiver of an eyelash.

Whatever happened to her or about her was immediately obliterated from her mind. She could retain no image, nor did the image of any action projected by herself retain its features, color, or continuity for an hour. Bribed by a sound, seduced by a vague association, she exchanged both experiences and people as one shuffles cards. Coquettishly, she would plunge into unnecessary expenses for an injured fireman and would be insolent toward people to whom she was indebted. And why? There was no reason. No one could find a reason. She was capable of maligning an honorable man as though he were the most unscrupulous of rogues.

But she did that almost unintentionally. It just slipped out.
The moment seemed to call for it. She liked the resultant
scene. She liked the surprise in the faces of her hearers,
and while she mixed her poison with a melancholy upward
glance she looked like an innocent and astonished child who
makes a hole in her doll and watches the sawdust spill. She
was the mistress of many things, of amazement, harmless
and frightened amazement, of the small, sweet, equivocal
stirrings of mood, of the undecided, the doubting, the questioning, the helpless, the gestures and the looks that were not
yet those of a woman and no longer those of a virgin. She
played upon her personality as a master plays upon an in-
strument and produced one unique effect after another:
grief, fear, delight, scorn. Who, having seen that, could
resist it? She was intelligent when it was expected of her
and ignorant with the sweet ignorance of Marguerite, when
that suited her game. She could be teachable or stubborn,
modest or shameless. She sensed the echo that was expected
of her and gave it forth. She would slip into speech and
speech would extend at her will like a diaphragm of rubber
and she had all that she needed. Through sheer ability,
she could transform herself into images of which there was
no trace within herself. On one day she would be a dear,
small, helpless, heavy-laden creature that must be tenderly
guarded in order that it might be reconciled to this harsh
world. She seemed so humble that one had to give her a
little self-confidence as one gives medicine to a sick and
tired child. And to-morrow—nonsense! An hour later—
with a new public or even with the same—she became the
angel with the fiery sword, a tragic muse, a Jacobin and a
rebel, probably precisely the figure which the momentarily
most credulous and useful of those present expected to see
in her. And for such perceptions her instinct was unerring. . . .

Such was the knowledge of her that Laudin had gained.
He had gained it step by step, like a man who cuts his path

through a bamboo jungle. Not without lacerating his hands. And yet, and yet. . . .

For at this point began the dark backgrounds.

43

When he entered his office one afternoon, he found a visiting card on the table. The name on it was that of Arnold Keller. His hand holding the card trembled. He pressed the electric button. "Connect me at once with 16-6-28," he commanded the secretary, who had entered. It was Louise's number. "The lady is not at home," he was told. "Call up the theater," he commanded. He was informed that the lady was not at the theater. "Then telephone the Ernevoldts and ask for Miss Ernevoldt." Miss Ernevold was out.

He took up the card once more. "She must be told to-day," he murmured. He went to the door. "Ruediger!" The old attendant emerged from the dim anteroom. "Yes, sir?" Laudin held up the card. "When did this gentleman call?" About an hour ago, was the answer. He looked at the clock. It was twenty minutes past four. "Order the car!" he cried. It turned out that Miss Dercum, to whom he had loaned the car for the forenoon, had not yet sent it back. He himself had had luncheon in the city. He ordered a taxi. Just as he was about to go he was called up from home. The maid asked whether Mrs. Laudin could have the car for a couple of hours. She wanted to take her mother on an important errand. He answered that he was very sorry, but that he had for the moment loaned the car to a client.

Then he drove to Louise's apartment.

44

The studio room was thronged with people. They were trying to rehearse a scene for the films. All the furniture had been pushed up to the walls, so that the room seemed doubly large. A pock-marked man was directing. He roared till his voice cracked. Six or eight female supers, barefoot, dressed only in a shift and a short skirt, crowded together near a window and chattered like a herd of geese. Another actress, also half-naked, with disheveled hair and cigarette in mouth, was trying to imitate a pose at the direction of the pock-marked man. The operator of the machine cursed and swore at its defects. Some one stood high on a ladder, fastening a shade to the window.

No one paid the least attention to Laudin. People came and went. He turned courteously to an elderly gentleman who was unrolling a shrilly painted back-drop. He asked after Louise. He was told that she was expected in at almost any moment. He asked where she was. A shrug of the shoulders. He looked helplessly about. The odor of powder and sweat annoyed him. The naked limbs and torsos of the women were unreal and chalky. The yells of the pock-marked man hurt his ears. The man was in a rage over the inadequacy of the machine and the props. If you're going to make a film, he declared, everything had to be A-No. 1. You could have the best scenario and a hell of a good actress. If you didn't have the other things, the whole thing collapsed on you. He gurgled like a dying man.

Laudin went out into the hall. A carpenter was hammering at a scaffolding. A door opened and Louise's maid appeared. When she caught sight of Laudin she turned to him with a bitter appeal. She couldn't stand this menage any longer; she hadn't hired herself out to a booth at a fair; she was going to pack her things and go; this was no kind of a house for her; rowdyism every night till four o'clock; people spent the night all over the place, as though it were a shelter for tramps; well, there were other things she wouldn't mention. Anyhow, she was through.

The carpenter interrupted his hammering and looked up and giggled. Laudin buttoned his coat. "Be so good as to

tell your mistress that I was here on a most urgent matter."
He took out his purse and slipped a bill into the hand of the
rebellious maid. It was a cowardly action; perhaps it was
only one of sheer disgust. He didn't want to buy anything.
He wanted to assure his own aloofness which, he feared,
would be invaded.

Hesitatingly the girl took the money. Perhaps moved,
perhaps astonished, she repeated softly: "Oh, yes, Doctor, if
I wanted to talk . . ."

He waved her aside and left the hall. He felt as though
he must see May. He drove to the Ernevoldts. It was half-
past five when he rang the bell at the gate of the villa. The
gardener's boy opened the gate, didn't understand his question, but let him go into the house. He waited. No one
came. He passed from room to room and saw no one. He
had been here once before with Bernt Ernevoldt. He
thought he could take the liberty of looking about him.
Perhaps, too, his restlessness made him less formal than
usual. Ernevoldt's wire had left him cold; the fact of
Arnold Keller's personal appearance on the scene filled him
with consternation.

While he was waiting here, without proper reason, his
restlessness grew. There was added to it something oppressive from the homelessness that hung over these low and
narrow rooms. A sense of neglect, as though things were
full of mildew. Furnishings, carpets, pictures, bore the
stamps of luxury and ruin at once. A doorknob was broken
here; there was a rent in the wall-paper yonder; the gilding
had crumbled away from a frame and cold ashes lay in the
fireplace and the dust of weeks on a table. And all this ruin
had a spiritual quality and you knew that it had endured
not only for weeks but for years. Dwelling rooms do not
so much tell you what people do, as what they are.

Determined to leave, he rose at last, but passed once
more through the adjoining rooms and entered one at the
threshold of which he had previously turned back. Through

a glass door he became aware of two old women playing cards at a table. A third old woman, who had a green shade over her eyes, sat in an armchair and slept. These were the aunts and the mother of May and Bernt. There was nothing peaceful about this picture. The three emaciated old women, with their white caps on their heads, two of them throwing cards on the table in that strange hush, looked almost ghostly. When he turned away and returned to the first room, which was a sort of writing room that one would find in a *pension,* May entered at the opposite door.

Dusk had fallen. He could scarcely distinguish her features. Only her silvery hair gleamed. A brown, close-fitting street dress made her figure smaller and more penurious-looking. She still had a glove on her left hand; she was about to take it off and stopped halfway at the sight of Laudin. "What has happened? What brings you here?" Her voice was soft.

He went up to her and bowed and said in his dark, harmonious voice that he must beg her pardon for this visit. He had been at Louise's house and had missed her and had waited here in order to discuss an event with her that was of great importance to Louise. He told her about Arnold Keller's visit to his office.

For a while May was silent. He could not see the expression of her face. Finally she said in an oppressed tone: "She must be told. She must be told right away. I don't know what might happen. I don't know how she'll take it. I don't know the man myself and I don't know much about him. I think there must be something evil in him, and probably dangerous. What do you think?"

He answered that his insight was as imperfect as her own. All he had to go on were the reports of Louise. Still, precautions were undoubtedly necessary. One could never tell what a man like that would do. His unexpected turning up was strange enough.

"Louise is playing to-night," said May, "and we ought not

to tell her before the play. But she is off after the second act at nine o'clock."

"I'll be at the theater at nine," Laudin answered. "I'll take Louise home and perhaps you'll wait for us there. Some one ought to be there to prevent the man from laying siege to the apartment. When will your brother be back?"

May whispered that she didn't know. It was curious that she didn't think of switching on the light. But neither did he. It was as though neither desired to watch the other's face; as though they feared the light.

"It isn't my fault that he went on this trip," May went on. "I begged to have nothing to do with the money. Whenever Bernt has money he becomes utterly irresponsible. It was always so. If he had a single gold coin he played the cavalier and the Mæcenas. When it was gone he collapsed. He can resist no temptation; his reason leaves him completely. I didn't want to have anything to do with it. And now I am responsible. I feel clearly that you think me responsible; you might as well say it."

"Nothing is farther from my thoughts, dear May," Laudin murmured. "You can be quite calm on that score."

She shook her head. Her forehead was lowered; her nerveless arms hung down. With a melancholy, scarcely audible voice, she continued: "You are not conscious of it, I know. But you demand an accounting from me and you demand truth of me. I feel it. You have only to look at me and I feel it. It torments me. I've asked myself sometimes if I am the conscience which has become detached from Louise. Perhaps I am. Louise has no conscience. I am that conscience. I am condemned to walk beside her and to suffer." She wrung her hands; Laudin, moved and amazed, was silent.

"But I am equally condemned not to speak," the young girl continued, her attitude unchanged, "that is to say, until to-day, until to-day. For to-day you demand speech of me so imperiously that I would rather run out of this very room. And that other time, too . . . when you asked me about Nicolas. . . . How could you do that? The truth, ah, dear God. . . . When the dead come to one they demand the payment of all the debts one owes. I see him eternally stretching out his arms after her in vain. And I hear her laughter, her terrible laughter as though he had been a clown. And every night I see him; he appears before me with that woman in his flesh——"

"What are you saying there, May?" Laudin cried hoarsely and grasped her wrist so violently that she had to bend forward.

In the pallid light that came in through the window he saw that her eyes were closed. With the index finger of her free hand she pointed into vacancy and said in an almost singsong tone, with the strange frightening harmlessness of a mad little child: "Yes. Of course. That's what she told me. She told it jubilantly. That she had doubted him. That she had no more faith in his love. No, no; it wasn't that at all. It was only a game. She wanted to play with him. She did believe him, but she had determined to put him to a test. She had wanted to find out how far a human being could go under the influence of a great passion. It is all a game with her. And she doesn't acknowledge the existence of any limitations. He lay at her feet and begged and begged, because things change so from day to day. And she pretended that she didn't want to have anything more to do with him. She had a poker in her hand and was absent-mindedly tormenting the desperate boy with her jeers and sarcasms. And it was all a game, all of it. And then she drew the red-hot iron out of the fire and held it up to him and said: 'If you are real and not only afflicted with calf-love, then press this iron to your breasts.' And, incredible as it may seem, he obeyed her and pressed the red-hot iron into his flesh. There was a hissing; then there was smoke. So Lou told me the story. And she added that the night that

had followed had been the most beautiful night of her life!"
Laudin had stepped back several paces. He groped about
him and took hold of the back of a chair and sank into it.
Cold sweat started out all over his body. "You are talking
in madness, May," he stammered. "You are losing yourself
in phantasms. Let us not waste our time with images of
demons and invented devils. Let us use our reason. I
will forget all this. It shall be as though I never heard it."

"And do you believe that that was all?" May cried out,
sobbing, and pressed both hands against her forehead.

With an extreme effort at self-control Laudin restrained
himself. "It's enough, my dear May," he said, with apparent friendliness, and got up. "I think it's best, now, for
me to leave you alone. Your nerves are in an overexcited
condition. Perhaps you'll be so kind as to turn on the light.
I can't find the switch. I've put down my coat and hat
somewhere, here. I must go. I still have work to do."

May went up to the wall. The bulbs burst into light.
Pale as death she seemed to take refuge in a corner. "Do,
please, stay," she besought him. "Stay ten minutes more.
I'm so frightened at being alone."

Laudin hesitated and considered, and stayed. His mighty
head bent forward, his jaw twitching nervously, he stood
beside a table and mechanically drummed with his fingers
on the cover of a book.

May had folded her hands and pushed them between her
knees. "No, my story is not one of devils or evil spirits,"
she whispered. "You read about such things in books. I
know it. But this reality is utterly different. You can't
explain it. But it is so terribly, so absurdly different." She
raised her eyes and her voice a little, without losing the shy-
ness and depression which had come over her since the
lights were on. "There is only one thing I should like to
know, one thing, and that is, what it is that draws you,
Dr. Laudin, to Louise, and lures you on. A man like

yourself. It is very mysterious to me. If I knew that, it would be like a gleam of enlightenment."

Swiftly Laudin looked up. First there was anger in his eyes. Then his glance betrayed that indecision which is felt when an account must be rendered to some one of whom one is not wholly sure. But at this hour his condition was perhaps such that the character of his hearer was of less significance to him than the obvious opportunity for the act of self-examination. There was a need in him, a dark, immeasurable need. And speech, even though it were comprehensible only to himself, might ease that need.

His hands behind his back, he started to pace uninterruptedly to and fro.

45

He did not deny that the question had irritated him. But then it was his office upon earth to be an answerer of questions. And it was at bottom not May who had asked the question; it was only her voice. It was the world that had put the question and perhaps One above. In his own person he seemed to himself like a man with his back to the wall, whose path was barricaded until he should answer the question. In order to be both clear and exact he would have to go far back into his own past. But he was afraid that that would tire him and he was very tired in many ways. It was questionable, too, whether his attempt would not fail wholly. Cruel as it may seem, it was nevertheless true that, in the last analysis, men of his kind continue to exist only through a defect of memory by means of which they are forced to be entirely concentrated within the present, by day or night, in action or in rest. And this excess of awareness of the present reduces the past to ruins. Worse still—it robs the past of its sanctity. He possessed only his present —nothing beyond; he could project nothing but his present— nothing. Above, below, in front, behind, to the right of him, to the left of him—the terrible emptiness of space.

He could not indicate the precise point in time at which there was born in his soul the yearning to be another than himself. The tangible experience was this: Utter satiety of his own character. Of that steely and unchangeable entity which is called character, that state of being so and so, once and for all, unchangeably, without continuousness or development. This experience was no doubt connected with his professional occupation, with this activity of a digger of spiritual graves to which his calling forced him. Thus it had been his fate constantly to be holding in his hands the rigid spiritual substance of men. And this circumstance had hurled him back into the night of his inner being. His crushed inner man had set up a resistance against this petrification of character, character in the widest sense, and had desired to be transformed. In a dream his own ego had confronted him in the guise of a murderer and with that murderer he had wrestled for his own life and chaffered with him for the earthly part of him, for this lonely, lost, eternally present part. And then again, when he was awake, that wrestling match had gone on in front of the mirror of all deeds, and now the prize had been his future self, his rearisen self or, if one preferred, a self that was passed and lost. For in the end each man is his own prodigal son and returns to his father's house when his wings have been broken.

Thus it had been. Laudin, prisoned in his rigidity, unredeemed from himself, met at the crossroads of life, Louise Dercum, the eternally changeful, the daily changeable. Here was a miracle of fate. Nothing of settled character was here; everything was fluid and discontinuous and this seemed to Laudin, by contrast, tending toward salvation. Since there was no cause here, one could not speak of effect, and since there was no groundwork one could not speak of continuity. There was only a body. Yet this body even, was wholly beyond law. A soul? Can one call that a soul which flows forth from a thousand souls, like water into a basin, in order suddenly, like the mixture in an alchemist's retort, to form a new and ghostly substance? Is there untruth where there has never been truth, where truth is not grasped and can never therefore exist? All forces and blood-streams, all ancestral instincts and obscure natural impulses blend in her fleeting moments of divine self-love and divine self-intoxication to make a form . . . and yet this form is only imago and symbol, eternal liquidness and flow, eternally propagating and changing. Seek to grasp her—she is no longer there. She has neither face nor eye and exists only within the magic circle of Laudin's money and disappears into nothingness, into indefinite qualities and desires when she seeks to descend into life itself. Embrace her; you press a shadow to your breast. Take her to be human and it is as though you would try to mold water in your hollow hands. Confront her with yes or no or with twice two is four—words become ghosts and figures empty laughter.

Thus it was that Laudin had met his fate. And that fate was as though it had been thought out, a thousand years ago, by some intensely speculative mind above the spheres, and as though the Fates had desired to intertwine threads from the uttermost ends of their spindles in order to see how extraordinary a web could be spun, whether for God's sake or for the devil's. It was for him to endure; it was for him to bow down. All he could do was to look upward from time to time and to cry out: What is it, Lord? Whither am I being led? What is it that Thou desirest of Thy servant? And that glance was vain and that cry was vain because he knew only too well that he and his like had long ago sold the Lord upon whom they called for thirty pieces of silver.

He stood there a few minutes longer, carefully buttoned his long frock coat, saw the girl's moonstone eyes fixed insistently upon him, took his hat and coat and left the room without farewell.

46

It was two o'clock in the morning when he got home. He went first into the library, switched on the light and opened a package of books that had been delivered. He looked at the titles of the books one by one, put aside some that he meant to read and stuck the others on a shelf. Then, slowly and thoughtfully, he gathered up and threw away the wrapping paper and the cord, got a brush and brushed the table and then proceeded on the way to his bedroom. On the threshold of the room a thought seemed to strike him and he went back. He sat down on a wooden bench beside the stove and pulled off his boots which were covered with mud, since he had taken his walk not in the city to-day, but in the suburb near his house where the roads had been badly soaked. Absent-mindedly he took up a book from the library table and at once started in sudden fright. A bit of mud had clung to his hand and had stained the fresh jacket of the book.

For a long time he stared wretchedly at the ugly brown stain.

He went into his bedroom in his stockinged feet, drew on his slippers and washed his hand. In the mirror above his wash basin he saw his own image and said aloud, though in a careless tone: "How pale you are, man! Why are you so pale?"

He couldn't make up his mind to undress. First he wandered hither and yon; then he suddenly left the room and went over to Pia's bedroom. He remained standing outside the door and listened. He had the knob in his hand and did not turn it. He could not know that the woman in there lay with open eyes and that her over-acute hearing had perceived the approach of his hollow tread. He could not know that she was waiting with clenched teeth, her fingers convulsively grasping the coverlet, trembling as grass before it is mown—that she was waiting for the door to open, waiting as she had never waited in her life before. He could not possibly know that. He was forced to believe that she was asleep. Perhaps he would have felt her waiting, her waiting of the long days and of the long weeks, her waiting that had become more and more painful and had, as it were, now sprung forth from that cage in which dead things had kept her and was breaking forth in pain and in terror—he might have felt it, if . . . Yes, if he had not by chance stained the white jacket of that book.

So he went back as he had come.

And out there, on the upper landing, in her white night dress, straight as a candle, listening as out of a dream, her young soul laden with a heavy but bodiless presage, stood Relly. Why did she stand there? Why was she waiting there in the middle of the night? What had robbed her of sleep? Or had she lain sleepless, she, too, and waited to hear her father's key turn in the lock and her father's footsteps in the hall below? Why did she stand there in the cold with fear in her large eyes?

Well, that is Relly's secret.

PART III

47

Pia's virginal forehead had lost its clarity. It was like a mirror upon which some one has breathed. Hitherto it had been ageless. Now it showed the grooves of the years.

Pia was not only accustomed to silence, but she had disciplined herself to be silent. She did not possess the gift of communication. Readiness of speech had not been granted her. In general, she used no words except the names of facts and of the small necessities of life. In the course of time and with the unchangeable return of the same daily duties, these words had become mere implements of use and had long ceased to make any demands upon thought or emotion.

And so it came to pass or so, at least, it seemed to her, that all thinking and feeling sank before her very eyes into a deep shaft. Above were stored, like a constantly growing pillar of sand, the household, the general management, the kitchen, the needs of each member of the family, the purchases, the keeping of accounts, the periodic cleanings, the questions of education, the assigning of each one's duties and the consideration as to what was necessary for the food, sleep, comfort and health of all those who dwelt under this roof.

She had no friends. There was no place for friendship in her life. She had never suffered from this want; it had been no active renunciation on her part. Firstly, on account of the natural reserve or, rather, the uncommunicativeness of her character, but also because nothing in the world was of importance to her except her husband and her children. She belonged to them body and soul, and that was as much a matter of course as the fact that her arms and legs should belong to her. Pia, Friedrich, Marlene, Relly and Hubert— these formed an indivisible unity. On this fact of nature she reflected as little as she reflected about herself.

As she admitted quite calmly, her heart sustained no deep relation to her mother. There had never been any open affection between the two. Her mother's interests had always been concentrated upon herself. In the course of the years her lifeless egotism had not only become petrified but she herself had grown ever more morose and quarrel-some. All the members of the house treated her like a property that must be well taken care of, or else like an unavoidable annoyance which was to be shunned whenever possible.

So the outer world impinged on Pia only in the form of social forces and social duties. She was forced to receive visits quite frequently; to return them often cost her a violent effort. But Laudin would have taken it ill if she had not done so. He himself rarely went into society. But in past years Pia and he had accepted the invitation of some family of friends about once a month. That had now ceased, too.

At a still earlier period they, too, had given parties during the autumn and winter, usually on the second Sunday of each month. These evenings had even had a certain reputation on account of the careful choosing of congenial guests and the stimulating character of the talk. It had been something of a distinction to be invited to these evenings. Without any conference between husband and wife, but doubtless because Laudin did not wish to keep up the habit, these evenings had been discontinued.

He no longer expressed any desire to visit a concert, an opera, a play or an exposition with her. He had even grad-ually given up their common walks, which at one time he had urged on her on every Sunday morning, and during which, however the weight of work burdened him, he had once been good-humored and constantly chivalrous. The hours passed with him in the neighboring hills and woods belonged to the dearest memories of her life. She used to walk at his side, listening to him with a smile when he spoke, smiling silently when he was silent. And precisely this stillness of hers seemed to please him and this quietude of hers to cheer him. And when they came home they had come to all necessary inner understanding, although the substance of their speech had been mere matters of the common day.

All this was over. But it was grounded in the very depth of Pia's makeup that the fact did not reach her consciousness for a long time, during all the long months of the winter. But sometimes, as one day gave place to another, and as she stopped to look back and around, it became clear to her. She understood it and digested it and wondered at it and began to brood.

She couldn't help noticing that when she met acquaintances nowadays they greeted her in an eager sort of way. She met many acquaintances from time to time during her frequent drives to town and during her errands in the business streets. And so she observed in others a certain confidentialness of demeanor and in still others an excessive considerateness or else a strange curiosity and even pity. This gradually made her so nervous that at the very sight of some one from afar, she turned into a side street. One day, for instance, a woman whom she could not avoid had inquired after her husband with an excess of amiable emphasis. She wasn't satisfied with Pia's matter-of-fact account but asked a second time. Another one, to whom she had to return a long-delayed visit, assumed the air of a sybil and indulged in dark and tactless references to that fate which overtook even the purest and most devoted of mortal wives. Their husbands simply stepped over them, not, be it remarked, in order to rise to higher regions, but to sink to an undoubtedly unheard-of depth. Pia had looked at her, rather stupidly perhaps, and had begun to discuss the weather. No wonder that in her

own social sphere she was regarded as uncultured and somewhat simple-minded. It was for this reason that women
forgave her her delightful ways and the youthful freshness
of her face. It affected her far more unpleasantly, though
she was careful not to betray herself, when an old gentleman,
a former minister of state, who had a private passion for
the theater, informed her with friendly volubility that he
had seen Laudin three times at three different performances
of the same play. "I don't blame him in the least," he added
enthusiastically, "for the play is a real experience, Mrs.
Laudin, quite incomparable, in fact."

Laudin had never mentioned this so-called experience to
Pia. No doubt it had been an experience to him, too. For
what else could have moved him to repeat it three times?

Added to the intangible gossip which fluttered about her
like nocturnal birds, there were the incessant telephonic
suggestions of Brigitte Hartmann. Whatever attitude she
assumed to them and in spite of the corrosive sharpness with
which Laudin had characterized the woman, these communications left a residuum of the turbid and the uncanny in Pia's
soul. For a while she heard nothing more from the woman.
Then, one afternoon in March, she was told on coming home
that a lady with two children was waiting for her. When
she entered the reception room the caller arose, made a tentative curtsy, grabbed with each hand one of the boys who had
been standing by the window and flattening their noses
against the panes and said: "Allow me, Mrs. Laudin, to
introduce myself. I am Brigitte Hartmann, and these are
my two orphans, I mean half-orphans. I hope I don't disturb
you."

Pia was speechless. She couldn't even get out a question
concerning the motive of these impudent intruders. She
stood stock still and the half-orphans, who were in their
Sunday best, but not properly washed, stared at her open-
mouthed.

"Run along into the garden, boys," said Brigitte Hartmann in a sweetishly tender tone to her offspring. "I've got to talk to Mrs. Laudin; I just wanted her to see you. You've already seen the lovely garden. Maybe Mrs. Laudin's little daughters will play with you for a while. She wouldn't object, I'm sure."

The two boys obeyed hesitatingly. One stumbled over the carpet because he couldn't take his eyes away from Pia.

"You don't mind if I sit down, Mrs. Laudin, do you?" Brigitte Hartmann cooed ingratiatingly and, curiously enough, began to draw on her gloves which she had put on the arm of the chair.

At last Pia pumped up some energy. "I don't know of anything, Mrs. Hartmann, that we could discuss with each other. I think it extraordinary that you should venture. . . . I shall certainly inform my husband right away. . . ."

Brigitte Hartmann raised her arms adjuringly. "Your husband, Mrs. Laudin, the doctor. . . . Oh, no, you'd better not do that. No, no." She seemed half-frightened at the prospect, and half-malicious. "We've got absolutely no use for him. I am so glad that we're alone. It's about time that we had a mutual explanation. I certainly have got something to explain to you. And even if you're not so mighty well pleased by my visit, which is something that, God help me, even a blind man can see, all I can say is that I can't help it. I'm a person that just can't lie, if I may say so, and if there are lies about, I've got to open my mouth even if it is to speak evil, come what may. That's me."

And thereupon followed, starting so swiftly and swelling so torrentially that no resisting and no warning sound of Pia, motionless on that spot, could restrain it, a perfect lava stream of words. And such words! To Pia's eyes the room was darkened, and the sky without, and the innermost chambers of her heart. She could not flee. Something stronger than her disgust, than her bodily horror, seemed to have nailed her feet to the floor and while her cheeks became paler each second, and her eyes grew round and hollow,

Brigitte Hartmann arose again from her chair and thrust her face close up to Pia's and stood there gesticulating and laying bare the gap in her teeth.

Oh, the doctor could have prevented it easily enough. One kind word and she would have been as silent as the grave. No one in the world stood higher in her estimation than Dr. Laudin. But instead of sticking to her, as she had warned him to do a dozen times, he had driven her to despair. Now he could take the consequences. Even the worm will turn if you tread on it. The whole world, to be sure, had conspired against her. She had started out in life with great hopes. She had had fine ambitions and every reason to expect to realize them. If any one thought that she didn't have her Schiller and her Goethe in the bookcase at home, or even that poor Lenau, who had had such a sad fate, she could disillusion them all right. She'd never been one given to boasting; modesty was her second nature; she'd rather bite off her own nose than make a show of her education. No, not even for Mrs. Laudin. Although she wished Mrs. Laudin to know how she had been treated. A married life to turn a heart of stone. And how she had loved that man. How she had catered to every wish he had. People had just been astonished. And then how that sly slut named Lanz had addled his brains and he had demanded a divorce! All right, she had said to him; you go your way; I want nothing more to do with you and I don't need your money either; you can go on with your woman. For she had never doubted that he was going to his end. What else can you expect when a man of his years begins to dissipate? And that was the way things had happened. Suddenly, however, if you please—Mrs. Laudin must excuse her for using hard words, but when you torment a human being's soul out of him you can't expect him to coo like a dove—suddenly that whore and her bastard had turned up and had asked for a will. It's a wonder she hadn't had a stroke. A will? May God strike her dead if ever she'd seen a will. And then the doctor had come along and had scared her to death and had asked her, holy Mother of God, to hand over her personal inheritance. That had given her no rest, nor the evil opinion he had formed of her, and so she had gone to his office and fallen on her knees before him and had begged and besought him to believe her. He had been deeply moved and had believed her and had asked her forgiveness. But that slut of a Lanz woman had conspired with the Dercum woman and the Dercum woman had raised hell with Dr. Laudin. Naturally, since Dercum had been promised a part of the swag. That had changed everything. The doctor, who had the character of an angel, had become a perfect devil and she had been pinched and thwacked, so to speak, until she was tired of life. And did Mrs. Laudin know who that Dercum creature was? Did she know that she was known to all the city as something that she, Brigitte, was too decent to mention? And did she know that Dr. Laudin passed half his nights with that creature? Half his nights in that gaming hell and grog shop with play actors and whores? Oh, she could prove what she was saying. She had waited for him in the street and had asked him to explain and had appealed to his conscience and had reminded him of his wife and his sweet children. It had done no good. He had abused her like an old shoe. And usually he could be as smooth as butter. He could throw thousands of millions into the maw of that drunken witch—he could, could he? The very huckster women were gabbling about it in the streets. To fill the purse of such an actress wench who devours men as though they were chocolate pastries. So it was Mrs. Hartmann, if you please . . . your humble servant, says I . . . doesn't mean anything . . . please, if you please. . . .

With a hoarse shriek she fell thumping on the floor. Foam came from her mouth. Her limbs twitched. Her trunk writhed in epileptic contortions. Her flowery hat had slipped over one ear, so that she looked both horrible and funny. And Pia asked herself whether, in spite of its horribleness, this attack were not the result of a dissimulation, although of a kind which was rooted in an incurable perversion of the mind. Slowly she approached the outstretched figure and kneeled and bent over and whispered hollow, disgusted, and yet compassionate words. But when she wanted to go out in order to get help Brigitte Hartmann half arose and groaned: "Do help me up, Mrs. Laudin. It's my heart, that's what it is. Oh, my poor orphans. It's better now. Please to forgive me. Thank you, Mrs. Laudin. Well, anyhow, I've visited you and seen you. Don't, for the saint's sake, take it in ill part. Don't tell the doctor the story, don't. . . ."

With the gloved right hand she brushed off her skirt, looked sadly about her, stared at Pia's hands and then into Pia's face and murmured: "You're a lovely lady, Mrs. Laudin; you're real lovely." Then she half-curtsied again and went out. Outside Pia heard her call her boys and then slam the garden gate. She herself sat down quietly in a corner.

Had she really needed the revelations of this deluded creature whose behavior bore so clear a pathological stamp? Had she needed them in order to see and to know? Although the medium had been so turbid that, passing through it, truth turned into falsehood and proof into hallucination, yet Pia's heart was like a sensitive photographic plate which registers and brings to the light what not the sharpest eye has been able to perceive. Thus it had been superfluous to annoy her with anonymous letters, whether they proceeded from this same source or from an allied source, like the one which Laudin had so contemptuously destroyed. It had been quite superfluous for the curious to cross-question her, as it had been to awaken her by hints or humiliate her by pity. She had had her forebodings; she had fought against them in vain. Now she knew.

But what would happen if, some fine day, she would find it no longer possible to be content with mere knowledge? She was not clear about that in her mind. She could not foretell that in any way. She did not belong to that order of people who can follow a program. She would have to wait until a decision ripened in her soul. Until then it would be her lot quietly to rule her house, to help her daughters at their tasks so far as she could, to be plagued by all the many things about her, to watch Laudin grow more and more silent and disturbed and restless. Sometimes, quite in secret, hidden even from the watchful eyes of Relly, she would take little Hubert and sorrowfully, with eyes closed, would press him to her bosom. Hubert was now slowly blossoming into humanity. A little while ago he was only an indistinct creature. Now he was becoming a son. Marvelous word—son.

48

"Kindly sit down, Mr. Keller," said Laudin, after the actor had closed the padded office door behind him.

Keller sat down without speaking, with an abrupt gesture of thanks. His figure was thin and badly put together; his head was as narrow as the head of a fish and his whole face seemed, somehow, to protrude forward in a fashion both homely and absurd. Even the eyes, with their constantly winking lids, seemed to spring out. Only the forehead receded, as though frightened, in the direction of the skull with its thin reddish hair. Laudin observed at once the shy and suspicious look with which the man glanced about him, and which was doubtless the result of his confinement in an institution for the insane. He seemed to be expecting the appearance, at any moment, of an attendant or an inspecting physician. Aside from this rather touching watchfulness, his demeanor was quiet and had something of that easy hail-fellow-well-met quality which is common among actors. There was no trace of any real disturbance of his mental equilibrium. The nervous fear in his features was simply the fear that one might consider him unbalanced. Laudin, who was an expert in the psychical treatment of all possible types, adjusted his demeanor, accordingly, to the end of inspiring the man with a degree of confidence.

After a number of trivial remarks in which the matter in hand was not yet touched upon, Arnold Keller began to speak with a rattling Berlinese accent, in a bass voice that had strange funny breaks in it: "Well, now look here, Doctor; I'm in what you would call a hell of a fix. Here I've come and here I am now and Lou—she's nowhere to be seen. Not that I want to force myself in where I'm not wanted, no sir, though, after all, I am her husband, you know. Of course, you might say that the way she got rid of me wasn't exactly fair. They talked me into it, you know. Sanatorium, etc. Abstention from drugs, etc. Well, I won't deny that my nerves were smashed. But it was no sanatorium exactly, take my word for it, Doctor. It was hell, hell if ever there was one. You let them lock you up in a place like that and I'll bet you my boots against a diamond pin that two hours later you'll begin to suspect that you are crazy. And then you get to a point where you might well say: *et secum petulans amentia cercat.* Say, do you mind if I light up?"

Laudin hastened to offer his cigar case. The Latin quotation had caused him to look up in surprise. It sounded a little pompous on those lips; at all events one was hardly prepared for it. "I flatter myself, you know, that as far as the old Romans are concerned—well, I know more than a little," the actor continued with a clownish grimace. "But since I don't want to waste your time unnecessarily and since brevity is notoriously the soul of wit, I shall be brief. All right. You are Lou's attorney. I don't envy you your job. Who should know it better than I? Anyhow, will you be our intermediary?"

"In what respect? Let me know exactly what you have in mind."

"With pleasure. Or, rather, with no pleasure at all. But whether with or without, that's what I've come to explain.

Let me explain it quite quietly to you. *Male cuncta ministrat impetus,* as Quintus Curtius used to say."

He blew his nose, made that unspeakably silly grimace again, something between a dog showing its teeth and a carp coming up for air, and started off again: "I haven't had the face to see Lou, yet. You may well ask the reason. Simple! Her treatment of me was so rotten that it would hardly please her to have me within reach. Yesterday and the day before I started two or three times. I got to the foot of her stairs. No farther. I just didn't have the sand to display before her a biped who had been so unjustly treated. That, sir, is a paradox out of Hamlet. Heroic rôles are, as you have already inferred, not in my line. If instead of the torch of Melpomene I had swung a sword in some antique world the Horatian saying *vixere fortes ante Agamemnona* would not have been applicable to me. However, Doctor, I'm no chatterbox. Proof thereof—I plunge in *medias res.* I should be grateful if you'd have the goodness, then, to tell Lou or to communicate to her or to assure her—you'll know how—that I don't bear her any grudge at all, provided that she on her side is willing not to be revenged on me for the disgusting trick, the lousy trick, the crime—again put it as you like—but by God, it was a crime, which she committed against me. And I would like you to request her, yes, express the request, or, beg her, or—spill your dictionary of synonyms—anyhow, that she doesn't in the future harangue me or annoy me or whatever you choose to call it, any more about a divorce. Because, in short, I can't live without her. That's brief, eh, Doctor? Can't live without her. I'm an artist. Granted. I've got my art. Or my art has me. But think of the saying: *Nulla ars in se versatur.* Can't live without her. That's the briefest form of expression. If you will permit me to use so frivolous an expression in these halls sanctified by the presence of justice, I'd have to put an end to myself without her. But I tell you this in confidence, Doctor, man to man. I'm not trying any psychical blackmail. It's a cold, unavoidable, God damned fact."

Very curiously impressed, Laudin looked into the actor's face with a sudden upward lifting of his own. He saw no real seriousness there. He saw neither jest nor sarcasm; he saw for the third time that clown's grimace which swallowed and concealed all other feelings upon this countenance. But by virtue of his knowledge of the human heart it was clear to him that he was not dealing with the boastful threats or verbal jugglery of a scamp. Through all kinds of undergrowth, through all kinds of intricate shames and self-inhibitions, there came to him something faithful, inevitable, final.

He did not answer; he rested his elbow on the desk and supported his head with his hand, while Arnold Keller continued in his comic basso and with his apparent comfortable ease: "Let me tell you an anecdote, my dear sir. Not uninteresting, either. I picked Lou up in the mire. I dragged her from the gutter. There's a certain Ernevoldt. He may be a man of genius; he may be a man of character. For years and years he has been claimed to be one or the other, being successful in neither capacity. Well, he's been boasting that he discovered Lou. I haven't any intention of denying that. Only—I'm going to express myself carefully—only, he used his find to get out of it what he could. When he thought, after a while, that there was nothing left to get, he was suddenly nowhere to be seen. He didn't appear again until a few upward steps had been taken. Lou, who has, as you know, no moral sense and likes to decorate her boudoir with Adonis heads, promptly fell into his arms again and was happy to have such a handsome fellow to fetch and carry for her. However, to get back to the aforesaid gutter. I won't make the impudent demand upon your imagination to ask you to figure out the particular kind of dung in which Lou was sticking up to her eyes when I gave her a helping hand. I shuddered, myself. She didn't have a stocking on her leg nor a whole shift to her back nor bread to eat. She ran around with a crowd of thieves and rogues, and was drained dry by a lousy cabaret-keeper and white slaver out there in Acker Street. Have you got an idea what that means? I guess you have. Right next door to hell. Whether she wasn't literally lousy and had the itch—by God, I can't tell you. Well, I went down into that muddy hole and fetched the girl out. Was she pale? Well, that was no word for it. First she had to be scrubbed and taken, saving your presence, to a delousing station. Afterwards I put clothes on her. Altogether, it was a sort of a return to humanity. And then first I saw the possibilities of the creature. And then I began to teach her a little. Well, of course, I needn't tell you what I found. The whole world acknowledges her talent to-day. But it was polishing a very rough diamond then, and no mistake. It cost blood and sweat. But it was written in the book of fate that it was to cost even more—more blood, at least. Originally I didn't think that the whole thing would turn out so seriously, that I would, so to speak, get stuck. You see, we actors really feel for each other, for all our public chatter about jealousy and envy. I grant it all. No one wants a heel in his teeth, and the footlights are the devil's flames. But if somebody is down and out there are twenty hands stretched out in helpfulness. There are more noble sacrifices among us than among the ladies and gentlemen out in the audience. Unluckily the comradeship between Lou and me turned into something else. That we got married pretty soon—well, that was like adding salt to butter. I wanted it so. I thought I'd be surer of her. But if I were to tell you the story of that marriage, I'd have to strain your imagination and your credulity even more than I did a while ago. People said it was a farce. Well, it was a pretty sad kind of a farce. Others said it was a tragedy. Especially those who knew me well. They had the better scent. Did you ever happen to watch a cat with a mouse, after the mouse's back was broken? She gives her funny little slaps, right and left, cunning, graceful little fillips, doesn't she?

And each of these cunning little slaps brings the poor mouse a little nearer to its end. All right. There you have the symbol of the funny tragedy or the sad farce. Very effective, I must admit. You'll hardly ask me for details. What good are they? One detail means nothing at all. All of them together are the wheel upon which we are broken. I was like that well-known man who gets lost by night, with his horse, in a swamp. You could hardly call it a marriage. Her bedroom had too many doors. The little men came trooping up as though they had bought tickets at the door. You couldn't call it a love affair either, since we were legally married. So let's call it a marriage plus passion. The most dangerous thing in the world. With all the passion on one side—a hopeless passion, the kind that robs a man of dignity and honor, makes him lower than a dog, turns him into a beggar and a spiritual cripple. Why should I deny it? It happens to be true. And if you ask me: How can a man stand that—day in and day out, the sword of Damocles over his head, and some one else's boots kicking him from behind, and knowing perfectly well that he is being deceived and betrayed and cuckolded and made a fool of—if you ask me that, I'll have to answer you in the words of another quotation. Catullus, I forget the number of the poem: *Si furtiva dedit nigra munuscula nocte.* You'll understand me. Question of the flesh. You get a little bite now and then. Not enough to satisfy you, enough to keep you quiet. You know how the animal trainers throw the beasts a bite. Or else, sometimes, because the stench becomes too scandalous. Then out of fear. But even a sheep of a man—well, a day comes when he gets wild and rages. And for that reason and because I was a bit superfluous anyhow, my salary being no longer needed, this business of the asylum was started. Sly, wasn't it? And damned low, too. Once I was inside of the place, violence did me no good, prayers and tears did no good. I'd be there to-day, if a radical paper hadn't taken up my case with great enthusiasm. And so I'm here. Not to protect my rights as people are fond of saying. For God's sake, what are rights or, if you come to that, right? All I'm after is a sort of peace pact, and you needn't be afraid that I will insist on any fourteen points which, like the famous fourteen points, would go up in smoke, too. I make one point only. All I want is to ask Lou to put up with me. Not necessarily have me around all the time. Just, somehow, . . . put up with me. She doesn't have to live with me. Just let her leave things as they are. Let her, shall we call it, concede me ten days a year, or a week. You make her understand that, Doctor. A week, a year. Not all the seven nights. I'm not as impudent as that. Only to come to her and be with her and see and hear her. Don't despise me as a lost soul, my dear sir, now that you've had the patience to listen to me. Consider—it's like a poison that's in the blood. Look at me. I'm a wreck. One week a year, Doctor. Make Lou see that, any way you can. Tell her it's a question of life and death. What does a week a year matter to her? Do you mind if I light another? Thank you."

Laudin stared at the table. After a while he began to cough. There was a lump in his throat that seemed to interfere with his breathing. He got up and went over to the table and poured out water from a carafe and drank two glassfuls greedily as though his gums had been burnt. His irises were slightly enlarged, his lids slightly swollen, and his jaw quivered. He looked around him as though the walls annoyed him and said at last: "I suppose you know that she is going on tour for a week, to-night?"

"I'll wait till the end of the week. It's a small matter. Sort of a reprieve."

Laudin nodded. "To-day is the 23rd of March," said he, looking at his notebook. "Will you be here on the 2nd of April at five o'clock in the afternoon?"

Keller got up. "So I can hope that you will . . ."

"I will make an effort," said Laudin in a somber tone. "I cannot tell with what measure of success. The risk is great. The very discussion of the question is a daring thing."

"Certainly, I understand. But I have great confidence in you, Doctor. My address, if you should happen to need it, is Hotel of the Three Ravens." He took his derby hat and the yellow gloves which he had put on the brim of the hat and bowed very low and went out.

49

Let us linger a little longer in this *camera obscura* of life and we shall see a woman enter in, oppressed in bearing, about forty years old, well, but unobtrusively dressed. And she, too, tells Laudin her story and this story, added to what he has just heard from the actor, makes the thought upon his forehead almost a vocal thing: it is too much; it can no longer be borne.

The woman's name was Annette Gmelius. For eighteen years she had been married to a merchant who was three years her junior. There had been no issue. She had been undeviatingly faithful to her husband, although he had turned from her to other women, even in the early years of their marriage. But his ways had always been secret ways. She had to sense it each time, then to guess at the signs; then, when the matter could be no longer hidden, there had been an explanation and he had been crushed and contrite, and had begged for her forgiveness, and at the end of some weeks or months the same process had started all over again. Gradually, as one can readily imagine, she had grown very weary, and had given up hope and had resigned herself to losing him. She could not say that he had utterly neglected her. A wife is still good enough for one single thing. The man doesn't mind taking his pleasure; but he never thinks of hers. He pays no attention to the fact that the wife just endures it and feels humiliated and that her kindness turns into indifference and the indifference at last becomes disgust. But why should he take any care? One woman is like any other woman. The only point is that it is always another woman. At moments the wife is easy and comfortable. And so gradually she had become vexed through and through, and sorely depressed. Nothing gave her any pleasure any more and she had forgotten the use of laughter. Well, and then one day he had brought up the subject of divorce. She had at once told him right out that she would never consent. She hadn't looked for any reasons, but had simply given him to understand—no, never, under no circumstances. But why? Why this refusal which looked so unreasonable and which, as she herself sees, can lead to nothing but endless contention and bitterness? Because, she said, men get things too cheaply in this world. He can start life over again; she can't. He has taken no harm. For so and so many years, he has had an obedient housekeeper and bedfellow. Now, at thirty-six or -seven, he is as good as he was at twenty. She, on the other hand, is weary and worn out. She has nothing more to expect from life, has no freshness of inner impulse and is just about good enough to hide herself somewhere and lie down to die. That is why a woman wants a little moral satisfaction and clings to her poor feeling of power and stubbornness. He made several attempts to change her mind. Then he gave it up and seemed to resign himself, too. One day he brought home with him a young employee of his house of business, a handsome, merry chap. The three conversed together very agreeably. She didn't dislike the young man and felt that she had made a pleasant impression on him, too. Soon she had proof of this. He sent her flowers and wrote her tender little notes and while Gmelius was out of town he came to her with theater tickets. They went together to the theater and to supper afterwards and they did this again the next day and the next. It seemed to her as though her youth had reawakened. She was full of a sweet pain; she had not believed that she was still capable of such feelings. She had felt as though all the ice about her was melting and when the young man had grown ever more stormy in his passionate pleas, she had thought: Ah, once more in life I shall drink the cup of life, too; it was but a little thing compared to what her husband had done to her. And she gave herself to her friend. And then it appeared that the whole thing had been a shameful plot. The young man, black to the very heart, had given a previously agreed-on signal. Her husband was at the door. Everything had been arranged. Nor was that all. The fellow had been in her husband's pay. He had been bought in order to be caught with the woman in *flagrante delicto* so that a divorce might be precipitated. Yes, the husband had bought the fellow for this purpose. Now she was the guilty party and would get neither a settlement nor alimony.

"That's the way I've been treated," the woman closed her account, "and now I want to know whether I must just suffer what has been done to me and if there is nothing that I can do about it."

"Unparalleled," Laudin murmured. "Unexampled."

"Yes, so it is," said the woman bitterly. "But as you see, one can do things that have no example."

He dismissed her with the assurance that he would take up her case. But when she had gone he no longer merely thought, but spoke the words: "It is too much, too much; it is scarcely to be endured any longer."

50

Since May had sent him word that she was confined to her bed, he went to see her on the following day. His mind felt numb and his body felt like the body of one who has had a bad fall.

Just as he arrived, six or seven people, men and women, were leaving the room. Among them was an old man, an elderly lady and two very young men. He could not help remarking a certain peace and cheer and clarity in their faces. There was something innocent in their bearing and they spoke to one another in soft and gentle tones as though they feared the wounding quality of loud words. A middle-aged man with a long, brown beard and spectacles had a face of child-like purity, an unburdened face. Involuntarily Laudin stopped and looked at the man in amazement.

These were friends of May; these were the illuminati.

He sat beside May's bed and asked: "How does one gain admission to your community?"

"One must share the faith," she answered.

"What faith?"

"Faith in the eternal, indestructible Being."

"In God, you mean?"

"The concept of God is too deeply implicated at present with the existing religions. But we have nothing to do with any of these, for we have neither dogmas, nor articles of belief, nor a church. We recognize that Being only by a communion with the innermost soul of us."

"Very well. How does one gain that faith?"

"Through renunciation and chastity and patience."

"And do all these men and women live in a state of chastity?"

"Yes, all."

He looked at her. Her usually pale face flamed. She spoke hesitatingly: "When an elemental force thrusts us into the state of imperfection, the power of our yearning grows proportionately. The hostile principle can affect the soul like thunder."

"There is a good deal of pious hypocrisy in all that," Laudin answered. "There are things we make clear to ourselves only because we want to be armed against the voice of conscience or against the voice of the blood."

With a wandering glance, May said: "I often think of you as though you were an omniscient healer. And at such times I would wish to be wholly in your hands."

Sadly Laudin shook his head. For a while there was silence.

"For a long time past I've wanted to tell you about Edmond," May said. "This impulse has been all the stronger, since I have not been able to clarify my mind wholly, nor to know whether I am quite innocent of the collapse of his married life. Of course, the idea of guilt ought really to be excluded. The marriage was rotten to the core. He knew that; she did not. In the beginning I tried to support their common life. I had a sense of awe and could not dream of coming between two people united in wedlock. It had something inviolable, to me. And Edmond, too, when I made his acquaintance, regarded marriage as a sacrament. Not on religious or ecclesiastical grounds, but in consequence of his view of the totality of things. Then, too, he clung to the children. I have rarely seen a man who took his paternal duties so seriously. But beyond this feeling of duty there was the tenderest affection. He told me how, when the children were very young, he used to go and look at them in their beds once or twice during the night. He could not sleep unless he did this. He had a great reverence for childhood; in reality he was always in fear for his children. Now, a very curious thing seems to have happened. Constance became infected with this fear. But because she is a thoroughly rationalistic creature, this fear in her became transformed into delusion and superstition. Instead of bowing down before the unfathomable, she wanted to prevent its decrees, and had a panacea for every mortal ill, until finally she became a prey to the most dangerous quackeries."

"But that is only one of the many symptoms of ruin in which this marriage was so rich," Laudin interpolated. "As I think about this marriage more and more, and hear your account, I am forced to the conclusion that it was almost in the nature of a paradigm. All the phenomena which are necessary for study and arrangement seemed to have existed there in germ and to have become a so called 'culture' in the cases of two typical human representatives."

"You are quite right," May answered. "There was, above all, one thing that Edmond used to talk about. He used to say: the whole problem of marriage is a question of tempo. A great part of his misery arose from a difference in tempo. This started with the commonplaces of every day, with the keeping of engagements and the punctual appearance of dinner on the table. It extended to things—well, to those things between two people of which they alone have knowledge. It is implicated, don't you think, in the very question of keeping step with each other in the street. I have made the observation that if two people walk at the same tempo, the better and the swifter walker gets tired first. The other, if he can't insist on his own tempo, takes refuge in his weakness or in being insulted, and lags behind and rests. But the weariness of him who is really the better walker, is a weariness of the spirit. And one day he discovers that he not only walked faster but that he fled in order not to be lamed by the deadly tempo of that other whom he must leave behind. That sounds quite trivial and is, in fact, very important. Edmond had reflected about it so closely that he could discuss it for hours. Now it was the fate of Constance that in all such matters she cast doubt upon his good will, as though he could have acted differently but had simply made up his mind to victimize her. She persuaded herself more and more stubbornly that she was being sacrificed to him. The real truth was that she oppressed him daily more and more by an arrogant passion for mastery which is, I hope, unparalleled. I must explain that to you, because it is highly remarkable. I've thought a good deal about Constance. I wanted to understand her, because I wanted to help Edmond. Nothing caused him acuter suffering than the fact that his imagination was constantly absorbed by her, and that he could never wholly liberate himself from her. This was more true of her shadow than of herself. She knew her power over him and made every possible use of it. You will say that he was weak-willed. It isn't so. I could tell you of incidents that might make you call him cowardly. That wasn't true, either. Every marriage is determined, it seems to me, by the rigidity of the direction pursued by one of the two people. The stronger of the two is he who can develop some quality, a good or an evil one, to such a point that by virtue of this quality he forces upon the other a relation of guilt. I don't know if I make myself clear. Now Constance is a woman of extraordinary passionateness. Passionateness to the point of savagery and of madness. From the first day on, not consciously, of course—she didn't make herself—she tried to fill Edmond with the fantastic conviction that she existed only through him and that they were bound to each other by a decree of fate. A strange kind of love, a kind of possession in both senses. To be sure, she always knew what she was doing. You should have heard her when she said: My husband. My! It all lay in that word. As though she had devoured him. But such had not been Edmond's feeling when he entered upon marriage. It was not at all this way that he had wanted to plan his life. He found himself suddenly trapped and surprised into this situation and it took many years before he was clearly conscious of the fact. What he needed by his side was a free human being, and one to whom the things of the mind were realities and not merely a handsome pretense. Thus he was gradually throttled by her declaration of unconditional dependence. It was a most curious as well as a most dangerous distortion of the concept of possession, whereby he came to feel that he was a piece of property, and was so, in fact. You comprehend how much inevitable defeat there arose from this situation, how much restlessness, how much flight and inner conflict, especially seeing that in Constance, impulse and calculation, ecstasy and dry cerebration were so inextricably intertwined. The things that I have witnessed! Sometimes he would come, utterly distressed, as though his skin had been torn from him. The vain words that he had been forced to utter clung to him like thorns. I know that he used to stand at her bedside for many hours in order to console her, to strengthen her, to soothe her, to teach her. Until the dawn he would labor to repair the physical connections between her and him, between her and mankind, between him and his friends—to repair all that in her despair and bitterness she had destroyed. But since the occasions were always of the most pitiful triviality, incredible and indescribable—a misplaced letter, a stain on a rug, a misunderstood word—neither of them knew how deep their discussions really were. Nor did they want to see it. Not he, in his dreadful enslavement, his fear of losing his daughters, his natural disinclination to make decisions that would revolutionize his life, above all, in his compassion for her and her unhappy nature. And she would not see, on account of the very delusion of her frightful suffering. For she, too, must have suffered. Terribly. She didn't make herself; she came into being like the rest of us and was forced to act and love according to what seemed to her the inner law of her being. And Edmond knew and recognized this truth and that recognition was another chain about him."

Laudin sat there as though he had heard nothing. An expression of absent-mindedness was on his face. After a silence so long as to become almost painful, he gave himself a jolt and said: "I always remember one remark of your dead friend, that the institution of marriage can no longer bear us up and no longer possesses the principle of life within itself. Anarchy would be better or chaos or universal nothingness. Away with it! We must begin anew, whatever this new thing be. Only let us do away with this lie, this evil caricature, this world-shame. This unblessed mixture of compulsion and revolt, of public morality and of vice, which in a more modest age was secret but which is now perfectly public. It makes people evil; it makes them stiff-necked and vulgar; it does so more and more each day."

He had spoken quite calmly in a strangely dreamy tone, with folded hands. May drew herself up as though frightened and asked him, with the veiled moonstone of her eyes wide open: "But are people to live together like animals?"

"I confess," Laudin replied, "that it costs me a definite effort to imagine that they do anything else, at present. Nor can I grant you the analogy at all without degrading the animals beneath their proper level. For even those animals that are lowest in the scale do not live otherwise than according to the wise laws of nature."

"But what you have just expressed is not a view that can be discussed; it is really an outburst of despair."

"It may be, dear May, it may be."

"A man like yourself can hardly be satisfied with such a statement. Have you any vision of what might be?"

Laudin leaned far forward. "What I have in mind," he replied, still in the same dreamy tone, "what I seem to see is like a great liberation of slaves. There must be something like a year of jubilee for the execution of all laws concerning these matters; there must be the complete nullification of such laws. Then, at the end of a decade or two, one should let laws develop anew. I say develop; they mustn't be manufactured laws. That is to say, a council of the best and profoundest and most far-visioned spirits of all nations must tentatively formulate them anew, in strict accord with the actual facts of contemporary experience and under the guidance of genuine moral insight. Have you ever heard of the so-called Siberian system of marriage? In that country it is customary for a man and a woman to unite themselves by an act of free choice and free decision without the blessings of the church or the approval of the authorities. In the deprecating word forced upon us by the guardians of our morality, it is a kind of concubinage. Surprisingly enough, experience has proved that such unions are not only far more lasting than those that have the guardianship of state and church, but that the two partners whose remaining together depends on nothing but their will, have shown, in the majority of cases, even among people of the humblest kind, a remarkable degree of mutual considerateness and kindliness. But I have still another vision. . . ."

He waited for a moment and passed his hand over his forehead and continued: "I have a vision of something like the transformation or rebuilding of an entire social ideal. It is a thought with which I have wrestled much and which has always returned to me in many forms. The central point of all our thinking and action is the I, is the self. We are drowning in self-assertion and self-consciousness. We are concerned over the extinction of the I or its separation into component parts or its deliquescence and reformation. If an individual is dissatisfied with the form of its existence, it will seek a new one, a more joyous one, one that is more conformable to its needs. I can no longer resist the conviction that the individual personality, in consequence of the modern overemphasis of it and especially since Christianity has ceased to function effectively, has lost its significance. We must prepare a new loam from which new creatures are to grow. I find that the individual is no longer important to society, in so far as we are dealing with society's spiritual and moral state. The pair is important. I am thoroughly persuaded that for each man and each woman there exists but a single possible complementary personality. It surpasses all imagination what human society would gain in peace, in delight, in elasticity, in purity and cleanliness, through the constant multiplication of such truly constituted pairs. And it is for this reason that I want all barriers to choice to fall. Neither men nor women must be hindered in their choices. No moral odium, no burden of paternity, neither motherhood nor premiums on virtue, must prevent them from testing and experiencing all the forms and even the fancies of love that they either desire or imagine. If they possess any true instinct, that instinct will be sharpened; if any social willingness stirs in them, they will be led to some goal. And be that goal what it may, it must *not* be what is now called marriage. Nor should we be concerned over a possible dissolution of morals and a so-called lapse into savagery. Nothing more evil is conceivable than that which now weighs on our hearts and darkens our spirits. No price is too high to pay for the mere attempt at transformation. In every human being, even in the most apparently lawless, there is a natural inclination toward some sort of equilibrium. It is this inclination which will, in the end, conquer all temporary and dangerous forms of eccentricity. It is a mere hysterical convulsion that ties our present world to laws and customs, which were once significant and necessary, but which to-day have left behind them only the empty forms. The abolition of capital punishment decreases the number of murders. Crimes create criminals; penalties create criminals. There is something wonderful in the spirit of man—an inextinguishable longing to trust the good that is in it, even if of that good there is but the tiniest seed." He got up with a sigh. "What is the use? What is the use? These are soap bubbles and empty dreams."

"Perhaps not, perhaps not wholly," May said out of the depth of her thoughts. "Perhaps this thought is slumbering in many souls. Perhaps it need be only expressed and proclaimed. . . ."

"Experience has taught me that whatever is expressed and proclaimed loses its significance two days later. It becomes a theory, and when the theory has been sufficiently babbled about people regard it as a commonplace, and practice remains untouched."

"The twofold human being . . ." May murmured. "It has the sound of something lofty, but will it bear the test of reality? The birth of every child alters the obligations which two people sustain to each other. Does not the child withdraw the mother from the father? I have seen the happiest unions, and when once the children came, everything became gray and difficult. Women can do little to sustain the level of happiness; it is not in their hands. It is in the hands of the men, at least up to a certain point, but they are not careful enough. Either a poor little child is born each year, which makes the battle of life more cruel, and is driven like another wedge to separate the twin souls of the spouses, or else they must resort to the method of killing the germinating life. Now that is what most people do. It has become so common that no one remarks on it any more. But how does the sky curve over such a union? So much mysterious guilt coagulates that it is no wonder that the two people involved become sharply hostile to each other without knowing the reason why. One sees women who have grown homely from sheer sadness. And the reason is this that I am speaking of. But the women themselves have no notion of the true reason. They are tormented and do not know of what they have been guilty, and what they have permitted to be done to them. But what are they to do? Are they to bear a child every fourteen months? And what is society to do with all these children, considering that even now there are far too many people in the world. And such is the reality with which we have to deal."

"Let us not make reality the measure of our possibilities. If we did, we would have to despair of the entire process," Laudin said wearily.

May looked at him attentively and then she said slowly: "And if this vision that you have, this dream, this phantasm . . . if there is a possibility of realization in it. . . . I mean to say if this notion of a twofold being, of the single possibility of complementation . . . if this, for instance, were to be applied, applied to what you hinted to me the other day . . . you must remember. . . ."

Laudin interrupted her with a hasty and commanding wave

of the hand. His face grew pale. "Not that," he said harshly. "No concrete examples, no applications of theory. At least, not in this case. I beg of you; I beg of you. . . ." With lowered eyes he gave her his hand in farewell. He felt suddenly sorry for the abashed girl and forced himself to smile agreeably and mention, quite by the way, the talk that he had had with Keller in his office. He added that he would tell her more about the matter soon.

"I'm afraid that some misfortune will happen," May said.

"Yes. The end will be tragic for one of the two," he replied, and walked out with a heavy tread.

51

When he was out in the street, with his foot on the running board of his car, he seemed to have the impulse to turn back once more. Had he forgotten something? It almost seemed so. Perhaps he had wanted to ask May one other question: What did you mean the other day when you said: "And do you think that that is all?"

On that evening he had interrupted her. Not only that. He had fled with the panic haste of a man who finds himself on a railroad track in the darkness and sees fifty yards ahead of him the approaching headlights of the locomotive of an express trian. He had not wanted to hear or to know or to understand. But that was not his way. And so it had happened that the panic had worked on in his brain, and that he would start up out of his sleep with wretched eyes and look about him and hesitatingly ask himself: What more? What more, if that was not all? That he received no answer when he asked this, was his only consolation, the only thing that still left him the possibility of any sleep.

But this, too, was not Laudin's way. Yet one might well ask what there was left of his admirable and much-admired ways of old? He had once been warm-hearted and scrupulous about obligations, and true to his promises. Would he, in those days, have found it possible to avoid his friend for weeks and to leave him without news—that lonely man out there in his suburb, in the fourth story of that huge barracks, wailing after a shadow and yet pretending to the icy mien of the stoic? It was as though he feared that friend's face as much as he feared the answer to that question: What more, what more could there be?

He had tried several times to write to Fraundorfer. The written word can be more equivocal than the word spoken eye to eye, with its betrayal through expression, glance and tone. The written word can be more broad and general and can be weighed and studied before it is put down. Hence, he had written something like this: Egyd Fraundorfer should be so kind as to consider not only his professional preoccupations but also a certain intellectual numbness that had come over him recently; he begged him to believe that his impulses had not changed, etc., and that at the very earliest possible opportunity he would, etc. As an explanation that seemed to sound quite stale and flat. Therefore, he tried to write in a different form, saying that he was ready to admit the mistakenness of his original assumptions; the interplay of unsuspected circumstances had given a new aspect to the whole sad affair. But his judgment could not yet be final and he, therefore, asked his friend to have patience. But neither one of these letters had been sent. They lay in his brief-case and gradually there came over the author of the letters an inhibition about opening the brief-case. Now what do you do with a brief-case, the very sight of which is reproachful and annoying. You lock it in a drawer and let it gather dust.

But you cannot do the same thing with the image of a living man. It was perhaps in order to evade that image and to satisfy its silent demand by some visible act, that on more days than one Laudin set out in the direction of his friend's house. And once he got as far as the door of the house.

But he turned back. He walked down the street with a look of horror. No doubt he was horrified—horrified at that stairway, at the thought of climbing up the old, cold, desolate stairs, at the walls with the broken plaster, at the window in the fourth floor which was open, and from which one could hear all the more clearly the chattering of the maid servants, the clashing of dishes and the running of the water from the faucets all around. No wonder he was horrified at the memory of the scene, that day, when he had stood beside the dead youth and asked in a loud voice: "Why?"

Yes, and then he would have had to ring the bell. Then, black and thin, Mrs. Blum would have appeared and begun her discreetly indiscreet whispering. An odor of burnt fat would have come from the kitchen; leaden, used-up air would have seeped out from the living rooms, and all the objects in those rooms would have leaped forward, reproachful and demanding, toward him, the caller and the loiterer. No, the horror was too great.

If only things were different at home. Not that horror met him there. Home was still something of a refuge, and a place of well-prepared peace. But it held something akin to horror, something that flickered over it like a deep, dusky, equivocal light. It was the same light that could occasionally be seen in the eyes of Louise Dercum, when the golden brown tones that gave them life and fire were lost, and there arose out of the depth something yellow and wornout, like the light one sees when one dreams that one is under water and the sunshine becomes refracted until it is a fibrous web.

There was Marlene with her radiant busyness. But turned away from him. She seemed to have said to herself: We had better dismiss father from our thoughts for a while. There was something almost hostile, something almost defiantly superior in her cheerful way of talking to indifferent persons. In spite of the courtesy she showed him, she seemed to be saying: I don't need you. Her courtesy had no eyes for him.

And there was Relly, vigilant and earnest, reliable and quick. She would notice at onee if there were no salt on the table; she would flit out and return with the salt-cellar in the twinkling of an eye. But why did she look at him so searchingly? Is putting the salt-cellar on the table a proper occasion for such searching glances? He asked her what she wanted. Nothing, nothing at all. And the sound of her voice was full of sincere surprise. But behind that there was an embarrassment, a repression, an unchanged, never-to-be-silenced question.

How the child was growing up. It seemed to him that he could see her daily increasing in stature. Marlene told the anecdote how, in the bathtub, she would put her feet close together so that the toes stood in a row and would say profoundly: "Ten must undoubtedly be more than twice five." But already in her torso and her limbs you could see the woman growing out of the child; upon her forehead the premonitory restlessness of sex began to tremble.

That is what is dangerous about these beings, this becoming of theirs, and growing and formation into selves and personalities. Soon that mighty paw of fate will be stretched out which will hurl them into the ranks of the finished, the completed, the lost. Such oppressive thoughts did not trouble him when he held little Hubert in his arms. At such moments the gate of the world could be slammed. Here was the entrance to a fairy kingdom, where laughter and tears dwell as close together as the fingers of a hand and where endearments are like the magic potions that bring forgetfulness. It was so pleasant to touch the child's naked body. The whole body was like a strangely warm jewel, a precious stone come to life, and he could hardly bear to believe that this was a form of the same strong, permanent, self-determining life that dwelt in him and in other men and women. Faced with the child, both father and mother play a rôle of singular powerlessness. They desire to mold a substance and to form a spirit that obeys alien and as yet unfathomed laws. And when the day comes on which substance and spirit begin to yield to their molding hand, then perhaps the most mysterious part, arising from the innocence of the primeval world, has been stripped off.

Laudin expressed these thoughts to Pia. She listened and seemed not to understand. Perhaps she was thinking of the torn cord of a curtain. The little daughter of the gardener had thrown her ball awkwardly and broken a window that gave on the terrace. Perhaps Pia was thinking of that. Into Laudin's words there crept a tired tone. Pia got up and busied herself about the room. But her gestures still seemed to be about him, and in her clear light tone she said something that was meant to encourage him to go on, but which had no connection with the thoughts he had expressed. She was evidently absent-minded. "Did you put rouge on your cheeks, Pia?" Laudin asked with a smile at once shy and surprised, as he came nearer to her. "Do you notice it for the first time?" she answered, also smiling, but withdrawing herself strangely. "I've been doing it for some time; I don't want to look so faded in the morning." Everything about her withdrew itself from him—her hands and her eyes. But she herself seemed not to know it. She avoided touching him. She no longer leaned against his shoulder when, on a Sunday forenoon, they went over the weekly bills together. And her face, when she turned away from him, was different from the face that she showed him. But he paid no attention. Even standing with her back toward him, you could see in that back something of discomfort, of resistance, of an impulse toward flight. But he paid no attention. He did not feel with what force she had to hold on to herself, nor what it cost her to greet him so amiably. And, of course, he did not see that her face seemed to be submerged in shadows when she closed behind her the door of any room where he was.

To him she was an accustomed phenomenon. All in life that is custom, that is the regular recurrence of the same, was embodied for him in her. It had come to be utterly a matter of course for her to be there, for her to come and go. He knew how she would sit down and how she would get up and how she would turn her head to one side when she said certain things and what words she would use by preference. He knew her way of thinking and of drawing inferences, her simple, never deeply searching, but quite correct judgments about people; and at the beginning of every conversation with her, he knew how it would end. He knew her words, her smile, her attentively watchful look. He knew all these things in her not only at any given time; he thought he knew them for all time to come. The possibility of a transformation in her did not lie within the range of his imagination.

Now, as always, he was courteous and chivalrous in his treatment of her. But into the old and practiced forms there had stolen something that was at the same time tense and mechanical. One no longer knew precisely what his manner concealed. At moments it seemed like varnish that showed cracks. He was in the habit of showing a certain respect in action even toward his desk, his cigar case, and his paper cutter, and there were moments in which he seemed to lose all sense of the difference between people and things. Presiding at the table with his agreeable dignity, he would suddenly sink deeply into a silence which all could feel like a leaden weight. His forehead would become clouded, his lips under the thick mustache compressed, his eyes fixed and his whole bearing exhausted. Marlene and Relly did not dare to talk about a trip over Easter, which they had been planning for a long time and to which they were looking forward with beating hearts. Their father had recently expressed himself in very strong terms about the increasing expenses of the household. Once, speaking of this matter, his expression had given them a moment of intense dread. He had presented the picture of a man who looks desperately about him to

[271]

see whether there is no escape from the whip that is lashing his shoulders. Perhaps this was only an obscure reminiscence of that saying concerning the draft animal in his old conversation with Fraundorfer.

Throughout all this he had a feeling as though Pia were pursuing him. Not pursuing him in reality, but in the guise of a ghost. He didn't try to account to himself for this feeling, and denied himself any test of the fact. He let the exacerbating perception suffice. Yet he almost nursed the delusion, as though Pia had multiplied herself. That she was walking behind him now here, now there, now in one disguise and now in another. Her great, gray, silent eyes seemed to be uninterruptedly upon him and they seemed to be penetrating to the very bottom of his soul. He defended himself, closed himself in, fled, hid. But there was no escape. She was forever there—in the office, in the theater, in the car, in the courtroom, during conferences, during his waking hours, in sleep or dreams. Uninterruptedly, that great, silent passionately serious glance sought out his soul. That was why he lowered his lids so shyly whenever the real Pia stood or sat opposite him. That is why his features were convulsed in a pain from which, he believed, he would one day have to liberate himself in a great cry, a helpless and embittered and tormented cry: "Let me be, woman!"

On a stormy night four days after his last conversation with May, he came home late. Until midnight he had worked all alone in his office. Then he had gone to a little suburban café and had sat brooding there for an hour and a half. When he opened the door of his bedroom, he saw a figure rise up in the darkness and disappear in silent haste through the door that led to the library. Obviously she had been sitting at the table so lost in her thoughts that she had not heard his step in the hall. He switched on the lights. But of that form, which could have been the form of no one but Pia, no more was to be seen or heard.

He remained standing by the door for a little while. Then

hesitatingly, with lowered head he passed on through the dark library and through two other dark rooms to Pia's bedroom. He knocked softly. There was no answer. He touched the knob. The door was locked from within.

52

Very pale, he came back into the library and turned on the lights. He sat down at his desk and supported his head in his hand precisely as he had done in that little suburban café. After a while he looked up. In the street immediately under his windows, he heard footsteps pacing regularly up and down. First he thought that it was the policeman on his beat. But since the footsteps never went beyond the house, hardly beyond the light of his windows, he arose and pulled the curtain aside and looked out. At that very moment the nocturnal wanderer stopped and looked up. He could be easily recognized by the light of the lantern at the gate of the little front garden. It was Egyd Fraundorfer. On his head was the well-known slouch hat with the enormous brim; a cigar smoldered in the corner of his mouth; below, next to the gigantic feet, like a tiny white shadow, hovered Herr Schmidt.

In nervous haste Laudin opened the window. "Is it you, Egyd?"

"The same. Who would it be?" croaked the nocturnal wanderer's voice, made rough and hoarse by drinking and smoking.

"So late. . . . What has happened? And why do you walk up and down in the street?"

"It's hard to get into a house at two o'clock in the morning without being considered a suspicious fool, and cursed as such by all the inhabitants of the house. I was taking a little walk in order that Herr Schmidt might get a breath of air. And somehow or other I drifted into your neighborhood. It's quite a distance, I know, but after all one has one's

[273]

thoughts on the way. And when I saw the light in your room I thought it would not be amiss to recall myself to your memory."

"Won't you come in?"

"If it doesn't annoy you . . . it's worth discussing. The rest of this night isn't good for much, anyhow. Come on, Herr Schmidt. Make up your mind."

Softly Laudin went down and opened the door and the gate. He led Fraundorfer in, asking him by a gesture to preserve an equal silence. He did not relieve him of his coat and stick and hat until they had reached the library. The storm had violently closed the window, and now tore it open again. Laudin latched it securely. Then he said to Fraundorfer that all he could offer him was cognac, if he would be satisfied with that.

" 'Only' is a grand expression," Fraundorfer chortled, deep in a corner of the sofa. He had assigned Herr Schmidt a place near his thigh.

Laudin brought out the cognac bottle and filled a glass. "What do you do with yourself nowadays? How are you getting on?" he asked with enforced naturalness.

"What I do with myself?" Fraundorfer said and scratched his head. "Honestly, I don't know. How am I to know? Yesterday a gentleman came to see me, a publisher. He had heard that I am writing a book. Wanted it. Offered very decent terms. But he talked and talked until my stomach became uncomfortable, and at last I said to him: You've been here for a considerable while, my dear sir; you might just as well go home now. He got red with anger and jumped up and roared: The devil, Doctor; people are quite right; you're not in your right mind. There you are. There you have the world's opinion of me. In the last analysis, perhaps my own also." He leaned back, stared at the ceiling and twiddled his thumbs.

Since Laudin did not answer, he said after a long period of twiddling: "Excellent. Let us be silent. Until a really significant thought occurs to either of us, we shall be silent. Only proper solution of the problem." His voice sounded hard and almost contemptuous. After another little while he threw his cigar butt on the carpet and began softly to hum to himself and to beat time against the table leg with the tip of his boot.

Laudin picked up the butt and threw it into the stove. Still bending over and gazing into the black hollow of the stove, as though the words he must speak were written there, he said: "I think I may assume, Egyd, that neither chance nor accident has brought you here. I am sure I am not deceived in my suspicion of your intention. I won't investigate that. The hour is strangely chosen. You could hardly count on finding me awake, still less on finding me prepared for conversation. I am tired. I am thoroughly and always tired. If I haven't gone to bed it's for the simple reason that I'm tired. Also that I'm afraid of sleep, for my sleep is one that is a caricature of real sleep. But since you are here now, Egyd, I regard it as a sort of providential arrangement. And that you may be informed once and for all, I'm going to try to tell you the innermost truth about my situation."

"Speak, son of Themis," said Fraundorfer dryly, and acted as though he were suppressing a yawn.

Laudin got up. He went to the door that led to the corridor, opened it softly and listened for a moment; then he went to the door of the adjoining room and did the same thing. Thereupon he returned to the stove and sat down on the carved wooden bench and said: "Since I came to see you the last time things have occurred that blocked my path to you. My way to you would, in any event, have been a difficult one and, since I could not bring you the information you were justified in expecting of me, a way of humiliation, too. It would have been humiliating because, not suddenly, but very gradually, I have gained an insight which taught me that I had been utterly wrong. Yet on the other hand I had neither the courage nor the force to communicate to you the knowledge born of this insight. In the meantime I have been caught in a most lamentable web. I have . . . well, I abstain from all attempts to make the thing seem better—I've lost my self-respect. Ah, if it were only that! I'm afraid it's more. I'm afraid I've lost my self. You smile strangely. I know you think that that is precisely what I wanted and strove after. No, dear friend, to lose my self? No. Unluckily to lose one's self or to throw it away does not mean, alas, to exchange it for another and a higher self; it means an impoverishment that surpasses all imagination and all belief. And it means more than that. It is as though with your right hand you were to grasp your left, and with your left hand your right and to try to tear your own arms out of their sockets. And this is but one phenomenon. I could not save myself from that woman. Without doubt you estimated the situation correctly from the first moment on. I was deluded and sought to be so. I shall omit the painful causes. For I am not now concerned with an analysis of my existence, with an account of how I have been crushed between the two mill-wheels of justice and society. That would lead me too far. There came a point when I became the victim of this woman, when I had to become her victim. With horror I now recognize that it is a passion of the most fatal sort. I am degraded. I am stained through and through. I have become involved in affairs, the very mention of which would once have made me blush. I defend actions and carry on litigation of such a sort, that in hours of self-recollection I am tempted to flee across the ocean and bury myself in some lonely island. It has come to such a pass that I am forced to let the most notorious members of my profession be shameless toward me in a manner that makes my heart turn to ice and poisons every bite of food. I associate with people, whom only luck or superior insolence has kept out of the penitentiary, and press their hands respectfully. I have become the errand boy of loose women and the supporter of more than questionable projects. I have become an object of scorn to my employees and of pity to my former friends. I fear the look of my daughters, tremble at every gesture of my wife, and am a stranger in my own house. I know it and I cannot change it. As things are now, I could become a criminal for the sake of a smile from Lou. When she comes from the stage, clothed in the flame of her genius; when the pain or joy of her voice has stricken me to the heart and the veracity of her impersonation has melted me wholly—at such moments I forget what she is or is not, what she really plans and executes, and the whole world seems to me like a house of silver. It is a kind of fascination. That is the word that one uses when one can find no other. But I have never yet touched a finger of her hand save in reverence. The notion of asking for her favors, of a physical relationship. . . . I don't know that I've ever entertained it. That thought has something dreadful to me, like the end of all things, a kind of death yet unrecorded, the collapse of all the elements of life. Laugh at me if you like. I, too, could laugh if I were not afraid that my laughter would turn into something more questionable. For one thing I am bound to add. I am clear-eyed. No gay veils hide my vision any more. Veracity and innocence—ah, yes, let us laugh, by all means, if the impulse is in our throat. In spite of that! But is it right to say: in spite of that? Let me rather say: therefore. Have you never, when some one has lied to you and deceived you steadily and uninterruptedly—have you never had the feeling that you must go to him and open his bosom and at last drag out the truth? Have you never felt the impulse, the fearful impulse, to follow that degraded creature in order to subvert and convert him until he ceases to follow evil and becomes transformed? The name of that is fascination, too, and it is perhaps the most incurable of all fascinations, because nature itself denies us the means of its cure."

He stopped and arose and breathed deeply. Then he sat down again and pressed his hands to his eyes.

"Hmm," said Fraundorfer, and then no more for a long time.

Then he dragged his heavy body up, put on his coat and slouch hat and grasped his cane.

"Are you going?" Laudin asked in a toneless voice.

"It's past three o'clock," said Fraundorfer.

"I don't blame you for feeling that you've heard enough," the same toneless voice replied.

Fraundorfer leaned with both hands on his stick and arched his fat back. "We might some day attack the matter from an entirely different angle," he croaked. "I mean in regard to your cure. Remember, however, that we would have to raise the question as to how much this sad sort of fascination can endure an enlargement of the knowledge of your original mistake. You did call it fascination, didn't you?"

"What are you driving at?"

"Several weeks ago one of your colleagues came to see me. Man named Heimeran, or something like that. A very vain fellow. Have you nothing in your shop but tailor's dummies? Anyhow, he called my attention to Weitbrecht. On account of Nicolas."

"Weitbrecht——?"

"Of course, you know Weitbrecht? Naturally. Yes, that one. Nicolas had been to see him. Two days . . . before. Don't you understand yet?"

"Nothing. Or do you mean to say that . . .?"

"What else should I mean——"

". . . . to say that. . . .?"

The voices crossed like swords.

"Hold fast to one thing, oh incorruptible son of Themis, namely this: at the beginning of August, Nicolas confessed to me—a remarkable enough confession for his years and station—that he had hitherto never touched a woman. One night he came home later than was his custom. I don't remember what devil got hold of me that night or what had crazed my brain. At all events, I trotted over and delivered myself of a little paternal sermon. Discoursed on hygiene and of the dangers to which, under given circumstances, a young man might be subjected. I was quite informal, quite comradely. He was lying in bed and reading, leaning on his elbow. I can see him clearly there. He looked at me and watched me a bit ironically and blushed and said these words: For the present you haven't any reason to worry about me, father; I am still as I was on the day of my confirmation. I stood there open-mouthed, the picture of a fool, and trotted off again. Do I have to speak more plainly to make you comprehend——?"

Laudin's face looked like the face of a corpse. Only very slowly, sound by sound, he seemed to grasp what he had heard. Then he drew himself up. He smiled a strangely arrogant smile and said icily: "For the sake of our old friendship you will permit me to disregard this monstrous thing. I cannot consent to receive it even as information. I seem to perceive that I still owe a remnant of respect and faith to the humanity within me. I have gone far enough by revealing to you what I have revealed. I cannot follow you into the morass of unproved slanders. It is the instinct of self-preservation. I assume, of course, that you are the credulous victim of evil tongues."

Fraundorfer, still leaning on his cane and arched forward, his massive body swaying a little, looked at him with a dark and malicious curiosity. "Very well," he said. "Assume what you like. Assume it for the present. Till the moment of retraction. We'll agree on that. Herr Schmidt knows that I am not opposed to the notion of proper retraction. I wish merely to add one thing. I have not, up to date, called on Professor Weitbrecht. Why? Well, there is such a thing as the irrevocable. And up to now I've stood in some awe of that. Now, however, I'll have to drag myself to the man's office. Perhaps not right away. Maybe not to-morrow. To do to-morrow what you have determined on to-day, is a species of pedantry. But maybe in three or in four days. Possibly to-morrow, after all. Who knows? But when once I have been there, my friend, and when the die has fallen and we find that here we are dealing with no slanderous gossip but with an irrevocable fact, then . . . well, maybe in that case I, too, will create another irrevocable fact. Good night. I'm sorry for you. Come on, Herr Schmidt!"

He turned. Silently Laudin accompanied him to the door.

53

Next morning Pia did not appear at the breakfast table. The maid said that she had had breakfast with the two young ladies and was accompanying them a part of their way to school.

It was radiant spring weather and Laudin was not surprised. But just as he rose to go, Pia entered the room. "Can you spare me five minutes, Friedrich?" she asked him cheerfully.

"Certainly, my dear," he answered, and sat down again.

She sat down opposite him and folded her arms on the table.

Then she leaned slightly forward and said in the same cheerful tone: "I'd like to propose to you, my dear, that you move into town for a while. Under the circumstances, I believe that that's the right thing for you to do. For your own sake and for ours; I mean for mine and the children's. There are no difficulties at all. We'll tell people that the press of business compels you to be nearer to the office. The daily drives, especially so late at night, are too much for you. I've already solved the problem of where you're going to live. I talked over the telephone this morning with Mrs. von Damrosch. She's a sensible and very worthy old lady, and her late husband was very fond of you. She always remembers that. She has room and to spare in her large apartment and will be delighted to have you stay with her. What do you think, Friedrich? You could move over this very day. I'll pack all your things, of course, and this evening you could simply go to your new dwelling. Wouldn't that be best?"

She looked at him with an encouraging smile. Nothing in her face revealed any emotion except heart-felt care for his comfort, the desire to serve him and to make her words seem quite unemphatic, and the natural result of a practical exigency. Nevertheless, Laudin, who could not answer at once, and felt indeed as though the room were turning with him, perceived something new in her face, something that aroused both amazement and consternation in him, namely, an absolute, unbreakable determination. He took up his napkin, rolled it up, put it back into the silver napkin ring and tried in vain to find words.

"This arrangement is only for the present, of course," Pia continued. "Later, we'll have to see what seems best and agree on that. But just now it seems the simplest and most sensible thing to do. Don't you think so?"

Laudin swallowed a couple of times, picked up a few crumbs of bread that had fallen from the napkin to his knee and replied: "I think you're right, Pia. Since you regard this step as a necessity and as an easement for me, I have no doubt that it's the proper thing to do. I have no objection to make. I shall do exactly as you think fit."

This was the reply that Pia had evidently expected. She nodded. "There's one thing more," she said, and blushed slightly, a thing which annoyed her and made her turn aside as though vexed with herself. "I wanted to tell you, Friedrich, that you are not to consider me in any of your actions. You are free. You are wholly free. As far as I am concerned, I make no claim upon you, not the very slightest. Act as seems best to you and you can be sure that you will have my approval in all your actions, the gravest and the least. We needn't discuss this matter at all. Do not take thought of me. Do what you must; I have confidence in your judgment. You are free."

Before Laudin could answer, even if it had been possible for him to find an answer, she had arisen and had left the room with a friendly nod.

He sat there for a while lost in reflection. Then he drove to town.

That afternoon he paid a call on Mrs. von Damrosch. The slightly deaf old lady of seventy had the pleasant, formal ways, and the demeanor of a vanished age. Laudin remembered her husband, who had been a presiding judge of the court of appeals.

The large trunk with his effects was already in the rooms assigned to him. "So that is Pia," he murmured, with an expression of utter amazement.

When he returned to his office he found Louise Dercum waiting for him.

54

She hadn't gone into the waiting room. When Reudiger had informed her that he was momentarily expecting Laudin, she had simply gone into the private office without observing the consternation of the old attendant. She was walking impatiently up and down.

"You here, Lou?" Laudin cried in his surprise. He went toward her with outstretched hands.

Yes. She had returned three days earlier than planned. She had simply let the rest of the tour go. There had been nothing but annoyance and vexation. Furthermore, she hadn't been in the right mood. Her playing had been rotten. She had gotten into a jam. First she meant to wire him; then she thought she might better come herself. The impresario and the agents were raving, of course. Let them. It was so funny to see those asses go on. It brought out their asininity. The trouble? A question of money—

as usual, of money. She had to have four hundred millions by seven o'clock that evening.

Her pose was ironic as she leaned against the side of a bookcase. The fingers of her right hand played nervously with a bracelet on her left wrist. As always, when she talked about money, a change came over her eyes. The golden brown shimmer turned greenish. The swiftly changing expression of her features, from passionate irritation to watchful calm, restrained tamelessness to utter pliability, was transferred to the expressiveness of her whole body—a rustling of her gown, a sudden turning of her shoulder, a lightning-like face-about, a swift, strong tapping of her toes. All of her was concentrated in uninterrupted movement that seemed to run down her limbs. And she enjoyed restraining this movement at moments.

"Why do you need so considerable a sum at such short notice?" Laudin asked slowly.

Why! That's just the way these miserable things turn out. Adventure and danger. Two weeks ago she had bought an emerald chain of a jeweler named Esslinger. She hadn't paid for it. Just before her trip she had needed money to satisfy some other bloodhound. So she had pawned the chain. She didn't know how the devil such a thing could have happened, but Esslinger had gotten wind of her action and had telegraphed that, if he didn't get the money or the jewels by a certain hour, he would have her arrested for fraud and for getting goods under false pretenses. Imagine! Imagine Louise Dercum arrested! "Now you see, dear friend, why I have to have the money."

Laudin was pale. He had sat down and stared at the floor.

She approached him. Suddenly she sobbed. She pressed her cheek against his hair and her whole body quivered. "Am I not your own Lou, and can't I turn to you when the whole world grows dark about me?" she cried with the grief of a beaten child and clung to his shoulder with both hands.

Am I not your own Lou! Who could have withstood that! And her tears and the grieved quivering of her slender, boyish body; her melting in shame and indignation and remorse; the marvelous beseeching of her eloquent hands! What was there here that was not real, that was artifice or untruth, hypocrisy or studied gesture? Am I not your Lou? And that voice—the very soul of music. As though, in the midst of a frightening dream, a many-colored fountain rose.

Laudin took her hand and pressed it passionately to his lips. He looked up at her as to a being immeasurably far above him. He said, almost with fear: "It is impossible to get the cash to-day, Lou. The banks close at four. It is too late."

"Oh, but you can go to Esslinger and give him your note," said Lou. "Laudin's note is all that is needed."

He was frightened. "That's even more impossible, Lou. I can't personally be mixed up in such a case. . . . I risk too much. You must understand that."

Lou compressed her lips. "I understand," she said frostily, and drew herself up. "Professional standing. High reputation. I understand. I'll see where I can get some help. She shrugged her shoulders and picked up her coat.

"One moment," said Laudin, and arose. "I have not refused to help you. Some way out will be found, though I do not deny that the matter embarrasses me extremely. But first of all there is something else that must be settled between us."

Lou looked at him with cold suspense.

He continued: "Once before, on a similar occasion, I have tried to get a return from you. I hate that. It looks a little like the vulgar swapping of favors and values. What I am after to-day is not, as it was then, a mere piece of information, since I must use this legal term—a piece of information, furthermore, in regard to which you eluded me very skillfully. I am concerned over a living human being to-day, over the life of an unhappy man which has become dependent upon your decision. This consideration forces me to disregard the painfulness of my demand. . . ."

"Well? What? What is it?" Lou asked in extreme impatience, wrinkling her brows.

"Arnold Keller was here to see me, Lou."

"Ah," she said and threw back her head. Her face grew hard.

"If, in return for some not quite unimportant services which I was privileged to render you, dear Lou, and for others that I still hope to render you, I might hope to——"

"Not another word!" she interrupted him. "I know all about it. I know what that unappetizing creature wants. The fool has been bombarding me with letters for a week. If you annoy me with that, Doctor, we'll simply have to part company."

Calmly and firmly Laudin replied. "I repeat that it is a question of a human life. What he told me impressed me as wholly sincere. It moved me, Lou, as few things have ever . . ."

Lou's face was distorted with disgust. "Your feeling of solidarity with that lousy bum hardly redounds to your honor," she said contemptuously. "No more about him or others like him. I wouldn't have him touch the tip of my nails. Spare your breath."

"I have promised him and given my assurance that I would plead his cause," said Laudin in that voice and with that bearing which twenty years of purity and loyalty in the service of causes and of people had given him. "I will not permit you to crush him."

"And why not? What else is one to do with a reptile like that?"

"However annoying his very existence may seem to you, however worthy of your hate, he is a human being. It is a human life, and you have not the right to destroy the life of any human being."

She broke out into laughter. "Oh, really?" she asked, and

looked curiously at Laudin with challenging and sparkling eyes. "But suppose I take that right, in spite of what you say?"

"The man asks nothing but a little toleration," Laudin continued, insistently. "How did he put it . . . what does she care about one week out of a whole year? He would be satisfied to crouch on your threshold like a dog. He has this fixed idea, a sad and unnatural one, senseless and utterly without human dignity. How true that is! But who among us has not at one time or another identified the very weal of his soul with an idea like that? Have pity, Lou. Pity for yourself, as well. Don't assume the burden of this responsibility. The man means what he says. Make peace with him; you are in his debt. If I am to believe that I mean anything to you, that you feel the slightest friendship toward me, do not let me have spoken in vain." He smiled a kindly smile, a kindly and beseeching smile which, by its very character, gave proof of his unfathomable enchantment. That smile faded from his lips. For Lou, stretching forth her neck and head with the gesture of a panther, could not wait to answer him.

"Do you imagine that his life means anything to me?" she asked in evil triumph. "Or that any man's life means anything to me? Not that much!" She snapped her fingers. "Not that much!"

And now a flood of words came from her lips which seemed to tear those words in the overeagerness of mad speed. There broke forth the stored-up, concentrated savagery of the years. It was a mixture of the coarse and vulgar with the absurd and spontaneous; in the midst of brilliant acting, there resounded the loud cry of the heart of the common folk.

Laudin wrestled with this unchained element. The feeling of his own powerlessness did not prevent him from trying to dam and to restrain it. Nor did his feeling of admiration, as at the irruption of a volcano, keep him from a stirring of

shame at the witnessing of this excess. He wrestled with
her by expression and gesture and look and broken words
of adjuration. He fought for a life—for the life of a human
being who was a stranger to him but whose advocate he
had consented to be, and all the while he looked as though
he were a stranger to himself, as though he were standing
upon some hallucinatory stage and playing a pantomimic figure
in a drama, of which only this scene was given him to know.

It was difficult, if not indeed impossible, to fathom why
Louise Dercum lost all form and self-control at this precise
moment and over this precise matter which was really one
of complete indifference to her. Perhaps it was a mere
whim. Perhaps the impulse came from some experience
that had nothing to do with the matter in hand. Or it was
the mere necessity of hearing and seeing herself, or the
temptation to mystify others, or the delight which she
sometimes seemed to take in tarnishing the surface of her
being and making it opaque. The occasion might have been
something either extremely complicated or extremely primitive. Doubtless, the risk was great. For, in a sense, she
overstepped the limitations set by nature to her talent. Her
strength lay in the moving, melting, dreamily idyllic, in the
soulful and, on the other hand, in what was defiant, agile,
sparkling, boyish in its swift energy. That was her range.
It did not include the outbursts of mad passion. But in the
end, creatures like her are unaccountable and inscrutable.
They will risk foregoing an obvious advantage in order to
test that enrapturing power by which they feel themselves
borne up.

It was pity that Laudin demanded? Her experiences
had drained her of that. She had no place left for pity.
She had given her youth and bloom. She had paid with
both. Men! Ha, she knew them. She had run the gauntlet,
and was stripped of all illusions. She had never known
her father (this was a new version of her past!); she had

never had any brothers (this was new, too) ; she was willing to except half a dozen friends although, heaven knows, they weren't always the rare birds that they pretended to be. But the others! She knew the faces and the lures and the baits and the fairy tales and the masks; she knew the hucksters and the princes, the stock brokers and the generals, ministers of state and drummers in wine, officials and parsons, writers and diplomats, dancers and scholars. She knew the respectable, the coarse, the subtle, the pious, the idealists, the hypocrites, the swindlers, the perverse, the misers, the spendthrifts, the dandies, the fathers of families and the green boys, the lambs and the wolves. Why shouldn't she know them all? They swarm about her like roaches. Some pretend to high character. They haven't any. Others pretend to the fires of genius. They're the funniest. Even if the humor is unconscious. Some swear that they will die of love. Take them at their word and they pretend to be deaf. A few really die. They cause the most trouble. And they're not worth it. For of what value is a life that was thrown away like an old boot, simply because a woman would not submit to their will? And you can buy them all with counterfeit coin, with a shameless little pretense of delight—a pretense so coarse that you would be astonished, if you weren't secretly horrified. Looking back upon her life, she knew that she stood here with empty hands. They had stolen the soul out of her body and had disappeared. A woman like herself could never become a mother; the earth beneath her is rotten to the core. She has no faculty for respect left; men have alienated her from mankind. She sometimes seems to herself like a wild animal whose retreat the beaters have cut off. To break that fatal chain she must show off the tricks she has learned. She recalled a night in Posen. It was during the war. The officers at the front were starved in every respect. A crowd of half-drunken fools stormed her dwelling and forced her out of bed. She had scarcely time to slip on a few rags.

Amid shouts and cries they dragged her to the so-called Grand Hotel. She had to sit with them and show off her tricks before them till the early morning. And they fairly raved, because she didn't want to yield herself to them and tossed down at their feet the heaps of money which they offered her. There had been gypsy music, and a few wretched Polish Jewesses had danced the dance of their despair for these coarse louts. Did Laudin want to know more? She could tell him; he could have all the anecdotes he wanted. Did he expect her to be frightened if one of this eternal crowd of hunters, who has accidentally succeeded in driving through her the stake of marriage—if a creature like that comes along, tearful and fantastic, and demands so-called rights and thinks he's a fine fellow for not asking to share her bed as well as her board? Is she expected to shed tears over that? She would not give up a single night for ten such lives as his! A week? Seven days can seem like seven centuries. One can die of disgust in seven days. To her time was neither long nor short; only full or empty. There is time in which she burgeons and time in which she wilts. She throws her heart into the seconds, and that is her eternity. That's the way she is; that's the way she is made; no one knows it nor has discovered it, and that one thing in her which no one has yet possessed she would not sell at any price, however high. That's all she had to say. Except good-bye.

During her last words she had slipped into her coat with the agility of a lizard. Before Laudin could stop her she was gone.

It was an incomparable exit. On the stairs she drew herself up and breathed deeply and smiled over the deliciousness of herself, and as though she were wondering: what will he do now?

Then she went immediately to the jeweler Esslinger, whom she persuaded without any particular trouble to grant her two more days in consideration of her assurances in regard to Doctor Laudin.

55

Ten minutes after she had left, Laudin also left his office. He drove to the bank. It was closed for business. He sent in his name to the secretary of the board of directors and asked whether there was any possibility of his still drawing out four hundred millions. His request was regretfully refused. He knew that he didn't have that much ready cash and asked to be shown a list of his securities. When he looked up the rates of that day, it was clear to him that he could sell none of his papers without considerable loss. He hesitated to give any order to sell and said that he would phone to-morrow when the stock exchange opened. Since he couldn't have the cash to-day, it didn't matter at what hour to-morrow it could be made liquid. But his expression showed that he really felt that he must have it to-day and was determined to get it, too. He drove to an acquaintance of his who had a private bank on the Ring. The office was still open, but the man himself was gone. When Laudin, however, assured the clerk that he must seê the banker on a matter that admitted of no delay, telephone calls were sent out in all directions. Laudin waited, constantly rubbing his fingers with the palm of his hand as though they were benumbed, and gnawing at his lips. Finally, the banker came and took Laudin in his private office. He, too, sincerely regretted his inability to oblige. Great sums had been paid out to-day; there wasn't nearly that much money left in the treasury; by morning Laudin could have any amount he desired.

Again he threw himself into his car and drove back to his office. His face was like wax and his eyes had a feverish gleam. He had evidently lost all inner freedom and all power of reflecting. The strange circumstance that, considering his means, he couldn't in an urgent situation get hold of a sum of money which he needed at a certain hour —this circumstance was tinged by danger and seemed like a foolish and evil dream. "I'll have to go to the jeweler, after all," he murmured to himself as he entered his private office. But this seemed a desperate step to him. His whole appearance showed how he fought against it. Suddenly, he struck his hand against his forehead. He unlocked his safe. At eleven o'clock that morning a client, a wealthy manufacturer whom he represented in a dispute concerning taxes, had entrusted the office with six hundred millions. Laudin had intended to ask Dr. Kappusch to take charge of the money and to turn it over to the appropriate authorities. He had forgotten to do so. It still lay there. His hands trembled as he took out the packages of banknotes. His hands trembled, because he felt himself guilty of a fraudulent action. Perhaps at this moment he was not conscious of the fact that he could replace the money almost at once and that he was only exchanging things wholly identical. But his very gesture seemed criminal to him. This money, which had been entrusted to him, precisely because it had been entrusted to him, seemed to him alien money. It did not matter that he could replace it in the morning. The night that must pass before the deed could be undone was a night without honor, a night of crime. Under the pressure from without and the shredded disarray of his imagination, his soul produced only melodramatic visions and only an insufficient light came from his mind.

He locked the safe. He dropped the keys twice. He had taken off neither his hat nor his coat and left the room as soon as he had gathered the money and slipped it into his brief-case. Scarcely had he crossed the threshold, when there came to meet him the form of a woman with arms upraised, whom Reudiger was trying to hold back by the sleeve. He was startled, and quivered backward as though he were still in that shredded world of the imagination with its insufficient light. The woman was as pallid as death and her eyes were almost extinguished with grief. "Doctor," she stammered, "for the sake of God and of his Son!" And Laudin said: "Who are you and what do you want? I have absolutely no time . . ." And the woman, with those beseeching uplifted arms: "Doctor, something unspeakable has happened; my brother . . ." And still more harshly, Laudin: "But you hear that I haven't a moment to spare." Thereupon, that swaying figure: "I am Caroline Lanz." With both hands Laudin waved her aside. "To-morrow!" he cried to her and left her behind.

But his eyes could not help remembering that pallid, grief-stricken face.

He ordered his chauffeur to drive to Louise.

It was seven o'clock when he rang the bell. The maid—it was no longer the maid to whom he had given money the other day—said that her mistress could not receive any one. She had to be at the theater in fifteen minutes and she was now dressing. Laudin said that he would wait till she had finished dressing. With a good deal of self-confidence the maid objected that her mistress never received any one just before the theater. Laudin insisted that he would wait in spite of that, and went into the studio.

The maid shrugged her shoulders and closed the door. He walked up and down with great strides. Occasionally he glanced about him, like the criminal and cheat, already pursued by justice, that he felt himself to be, from the depth of his distempered imagination. After a while he heard a whispering and a rustling of dresses. Next he heard the outer door slam. He waited a few seconds longer and since all was silent, he went out. A faint fragrance of perfume was perceptible in the anteroom—Lou's perfume. The silent maid appeared. With a shrug of the shoulders, as one who should say: I have done my duty, she announced that her mistress had just left the house.

Slowly, and clinging to the banister as though he were dizzy, he descended the stairs. He stood undecided by the door of the house, his brief-case under his arm, and looked wretchedly about him. Again a vision of that grief-stricken face came to him. He shook his head a little and looked in another direction, away from that vision. Perhaps he had the feeling that the brief-case under his left arm was beginning to burn, for he shifted it hastily to the other side. He saw the astonished look of his chauffeur. He pulled himself together and ordered the man to drive to the theater.

When he left the car he glanced for a moment at the bill of the play posted next to the stage entrance. In just a second he had forgotten the name of the play. What he did know was that, in this particular play, Lou was busy up to the last moment.

He walked up and down in the stony corridor that led to the dressing rooms. Scene shifters in blue smocks met him and passed him. From below he heard roars of command. Two firemen were conversing sleepily. Several young girls, quarreling or laughing aloud, came down the stairs.

The period within which Lou, according to her statement, had to have the money, had elapsed. Undoubtedly Laudin was aware of this fact. No practical good could be done by handing her the four hundred millions that evening. He might just as well wait until the next day. Then he could easily raise the money and send Lou a check. It was wholly unnecessary for him to march up and down here in this dim corridor of the theater, with a brief-case full of money. But the situation was evidently that he could not endure the thought of Lou's believing that he had left her in the lurch. Since, in a moment of unforgettable self-revelation, when she had permitted him to look into her innermost being—as he still potently believed—she had renounced his help, it seemed to him his nearest and most urgent duty to convince her of his devotion and desire to help, and to sweep aside all hindrances, in her service. The money in the brief-case was the visible proof of this intention on his part. Visible and tangible. That he was so sure of this fact and relied so thoroughly upon it, pointed to an instinctive understanding of the actress's nature on his part which would have frightened him, had it been wholly clear in his mind. To see and actually to feel a desired object—that is the irresistible lure which conquers the pride not of harlots alone.

Through an iron door that was ajar he heard applause that lasted for minutes. It sounded like a landslide of stones in a quarry. The act was evidently at an end. He stood still and considered. He said to himself: I will wait till the end of the next act. He went out on the street and sat down on a bench next to the stage door. Half an hour passed. He got up again and walked several times around the entire theater. A newsboy offered him the evening paper. He bought a copy and thrust it into his pocket. Then he returned to the corridor. But this time he went as far as the dressing rooms. He knew which was Lou's, and paced up and down in front of the door. The wardrobe woman, who knew him, an elderly woman in a little white cap, came out of the door that gave on the stage and looked at him with a question in her eyes. He said that he had a very important message for Miss Dercum, not an unpleasant one, he added with an almost servile smile, when he saw the woman's double mien. All the serving people here were, of course, instructed concerning all the special considerations which the star's peculiarities required. The woman offered him a chair and he thanked her and sat down. He moved his lips about as though his spittle was bitter. The completest stranger could have seen that he was tormented to the point of physical pain by the sense of his humiliation.

He took out the evening paper. The first thing he saw was a heavy headline: "Student arrested for counterfeiting." He read the name of Konrad Lanz. He let the paper drop and pressed his left hand to his eyes. Once more he saw that pallid, grief-stricken face. For a while he was too numb to read.   Then he went through the article which told of the affair with considerable detail.

The authorities had been informed that for some months past counterfeit banknotes of the half-million denomination had been issued at regular intervals, from a definite part of town.   A thorough investigation had been instituted; all suspicions had converged upon a single point, and to-day it had been possible to arrest the counterfeiter in the person of the student and candidate for the doctorate in chemistry.   Konrad Lanz.   For years the young man had been living in a poverty-stricken garret; he had always lived a reserved and simple life and was very well thought of by his neighbors on account of his modesty and industry. Originally he had occupied the two-room flat alone.   Since autumn, however, he had been joined by his sister and the latter's illegitimate child.   He had supported them both on his earnings which had once been small but honest, and had only recently increased through criminal methods.   Inquiries made at the university and the laboratory, among professors and fellow students, had resulted in a most favorable account. His life had been quite blameless; his gifts for science were highly praised; he had already published several papers in technical journals, which had attracted the attention of the learned world.   In scientific circles, there had even been a rumor that he had been on the point of an epoch-making discovery of the highest practical value for industry and the economic life of the country.   These facts seemed to render the error, which had now delivered him into the hands of justice, the more incomprehensible.

The report stated furthermore that the counterfeited notes had been made by means of the most primitive technical and lithographical instruments, in spite of which they were of such extraordinary precision and exactness that in a number of cases it was difficult to tell them from genuine banknotes. The most curious circumstance of all was, that although Konrad Lanz, in view of the relative perfection of his notes, could have made enormous profits and robbed the state of huge sums, he had limited himself absolutely to the spending of three of these per month, which was exactly as much as he needed, using the strictest economy, for the support of himself and his dependents, and for the pursuit of his studies toward the doctorate. From all this it was evident that he did not feel the temptation toward wealth and ease; he simply wanted to keep himself above water. His first confession substantiated all these facts. After a youth of the bitterest want, he desired to obtain a position worthy of his gifts and to forget this criminal episode in his experience. That he had, in fact, withstood any impulse to utilize his criminal skill to any dangerous extent, could already be proved with some certainty from the circumstance that his sister, who was utterly devoted to him, who trembled for him, had spent the nights which he needed for the manufacture of the counterfeit notes at his side, and had kept an account of everything they spent, to the fraction of a crown. Hence she had been permitted to remain at liberty.

With brow so contracted that three deep furrows branched across his forehead, Laudin stared into emptiness. Then, almost mechanically, he read the whole account through once more, word for word. But there was at this moment something mechanical in his movements and in his bearing. It became more and more emphasized, as though he were thinking and acting out of a diminished or vanishing state of consciousness, and were able to react only to certain external impressions or to decisions already in the past. The brief-case lay upon his knees; it seemed gradually to grow heavier. He regarded it with absent-minded awe, with a kind of fear; it might have been a block of granite that had been rolled over him; he looked at it as though the leather were transparent and the packages of banknotes something to strike terror to the heart. Is it possible that he was thinking of the want of the student Lanz, of those long years of pain in head and heart, and the vain struggle of worthy and ambitious plans and thoughts? And was he comparing all that with that heap of money on his knees, which he had brought with magical swiftness for the satisfaction of a woman's fleeting lusts? Did he think those things out? Or did they only hectically flicker about in his disordered imagination?

Once more the applause, long and roaring, came to his ears. Figures rushed in from the stage. "Curtain!" some one cried. Painted faces and many-colored garments appeared and disappeared and reappeared. Laughter and chatter and commands and upbraiding. Bass and tenor voices and falsetto. Suddenly, Lou stood in front of him. In her eyes was an expression of strangely equivocal curiosity. Was she nodding at him? He looked up sharply. He got up. He bowed. He said something in a hoarse tone, with an excessively courteous expression. "Curtain!" some one roared again. Lou disappeared. He was still standing there with that courteous expression. It was clear, now, that only a mechanical principle still guided his actions. Lou came back, rushed to her dressing room, called some name, put her head out again and nodded to Laudin. She did not smile; she was almost contemptuous; in her eyes there was a certain fluid scorn, something dubious and lustful, but quite without banal sensual significance. The brown, mobile, bold, boyish face was scarcely recognizable under the mask of rouge and powder, and the outlandish wig. "Ah, you bring me what you promised me, Doctor," she said in a rather metallic voice and with a superficial, unusual politeness, while she beckoned to her dressing woman, who evidently stood behind her, to be silent. "But I can't do a thing with it here, most excellent friend. What do you expect me to do with it here?" She laughed excitedly and the intoxication of the stage seemed to quiver through her whole being; an unveracious, almost insane flame. "You want to come in here with me? (Laudin hadn't indicated any such desire.) No, that can't be done at all. But you really are an angel, Doctor, an angel in human form. Ah, there's Ortelli!" She pointed to the elegant advertising manager with his obsequious smile, who now entered the small, crowded room. "Max, you'll have the goodness to take the brief-case and wait here till we're ready to go home. Do you hear me? And, you, dear Doctor, you must come to see me to-night. I shall expect you. By the way, why are you so pale? I don't approve of that at all. One moment, please; just one."

Swiftly she ran back into her dressing room, came back as swiftly with a pot of rouge in her hand, dipped her fingers into it and, before Laudin could resist, painted two red spots upon his cheeks, laughing heartily. "Now be sure to come, Doctor," she said ingratiatingly. "Any time after ten-thirty." She slammed the door of her dressing room.

Laudin stood by that door. Mechanically he had handed over the brief-case to the obsequiously smiling Ortelli.

A seething emotion of such immeasurable shame flooded him, he felt himself so stained, so utterly drenched in moral mire, that he would have made any conceivable sacrifice of comfort, of possessions, of life itself, if he could have summoned a miracle to make him invisible at this moment.

At the same time he knew with a dark fatalism that he would obey the woman's summons. He knew it as surely as though her wish or her command had been burnt into his brain. With unsteady step he emerged from that stony tunnel of a corridor. In the street once more, he looked up at the dull redness of the sky—this veiled sky of smokestacks and of the unclean passions of the city. Astonished, hesitating, incredulous, he asked himself: "I?"

56

It was not until twelve-thirty that he rang the bell at Louise's door.

He had driven to his office, sent the chauffeur home, and

gone into his private room and lain in the dark, on the leather sofa, for three long hours, like a felled tree. He had neither felt nor thought nor seen. It seemed to him that he lay at the bottom of the sea in a dark green, soundless dusk. Fishes swam about him; fishes of every conceivable kind and form; pair by pair they swam by him; their aspect was morose and stupid and threatening; the whole of space up to the very surface of the waters was filled with these pairs of fishes; far below, their scaly bodies showed glowing colors, purple, blue, red and yellow; nearer the surface the colors grew pale, and those that were highest and farthest away were of transparent white. But in the direction where this huge and intertwined procession swam there was a huge open maw, the gullet of a sea monster. Thither they swam unsuspectingly, and the insatiable maw devoured them, while above, far from all danger, the glassy white fish disported themselves.

When he got up and consulted his watch he was as frightened as a soldier who has missed his roll call. But in spite of that, and although it had begun to rain, he went through the streets on foot.

Even in the anteroom he heard the deafening noise of a large party. He stood there pale and undecided. He was impelled to count the coats and hats which hung on the hooks, and to count them over and over again. Then May came into the anteroom. She nodded in surprise at Laudin and started looking for her coat. She had the air of a fugitive. "I'm going home," she said; "it's quite too . . . too repulsive. . . . I can't stand any more . . . and you come so late. . . ."

Laudin looked at her as though he were searching in his memory for something that had to do with her. Immensely relieved, he said at last: "Ah, yes, dear May, to-morrow we have the first session in the case of Altacher. We will hardly be able to dispense with your presence." This bureaucratic

[299]

form of words was projected by the mechanical principle that still obtained within him.

May looked up slowly. Her glance glided over his face. "It's a long way until to-morrow," she said, and her moonstone eyes seemed to know not only everything that was passing within him, but everything that was ahead of him. "Good night."

In the studio the clouds of smoke were so thick that at first he could not distinguish the faces and remained unnoticed himself. About the round table were sitting twelve persons, men and women, drinking, smoking, talking, crying, and laughing at the same time. In a corner by the stove an absurdly liveried page, pricked out in a theatrical costume, was fast asleep. He had probably served food and drink, and now his services had been dispensed with. Dozens of bottles of wine and champagne and spirits were standing on the table, and a huge array of glasses of all shapes and sizes. The company was evidently planning to play poker. Ortelli was shuffling the cards. The women, mostly colleagues of Lou, including a well-known film actress, had opened or half-dropped their garments. Their eyes, in their excessively reddened faces, had that peculiarly blind expression which comes into the eyes of women when they are in the grasp of their evil instincts. Laudin recognized several actors; next to the eternally smiling Ortelli, he recognized the unavoidable baron, whose name he could never remember, and the film director whom he had met here the other day. But when his dully searching look proceeded farther around that circle, he suddenly started as though some one had given him a blow on the head. He could not believe his eyes. For there sat Arnold Keller.

He sat next to Lou. He sat bent over forward, as though lost in thought, with a brooding expression, yet wholly unexcited, as though it were the most natural thing in the world for him to be sitting there beside the woman he adored. And Lou, too, looked as if everything were as it should be and in perfect order and not as though, a few hours ago, she had acted as if the very sight of this man would drive her mad with hatred and disgust. Laudin could not take his eyes from these two. Had there been an explanation and reconciliation? But when? And if an explanation and a reconciliation were possible, why had there been that unheard of conflagration of passion only a few hours ago?

He didn't know that Keller had simply walked upstairs. That was all. He had just made another one of his attempts, without either expectation or hope. And then, when Lou had returned from the theater, and had seen him standing in the anteroom she had, contrary to all expectation and hope, welcomed him amiably and invited him to spend the evening with herself and her guests. The cause? There was no special cause. Perhaps she was tired of contention. Perhaps she wanted to have peace for a while. Perhaps she had utterly forgotten the whole dreadful quarrel or wanted to forget it to-night. Perhaps she didn't remember either her disgust or her hatred. Perhaps she had expended all the force of her hatred and abhorrence in that burning moment of passion, until there was nothing left of either. Perhaps, on the other hand, her success that evening and the enthusiasm of the public had softened her mood, and she enjoyed playing the part of magnanimity, which usually she had reserved for Laudin's benefit. All these things were possible. Some were more probable than others. The thing, at all events, was neither remarkable nor noteworthy and no member of that company, at least, seemed to find it so. The man had been imprisoned in a madhouse; the woman had gotten rid of him in this way; he came back; for the moment they were again one heart with but a single thought. That was not considered either remarkable or amazing here.

Only Laudin stood there, two paces away from the table, and dared not trust his eyes. At last Ortelli saw him and leaned over to Lou and called her attention to him. At the same time Ortelli arose and bowed. He did not dare to include Laudin in his sloppy comradeliness. Arnold Keller looked up and he, too, arose at once. But his bow was deep and solemn. Ortelli and he were the only ones who were still half-way sober. The other guests didn't take any notice of Laudin at all. Lou beckoned to him with her outstretched arm, invited him in this way to sit down somewhere and held up her champagne glass in the direction of Ortelli. She laughed uninterruptedly; she had a wreath of leaves in her hair; her gestures and her whole demeanor had something open and unchained; as though in token of this, she had torn the shoulder strap of her evening frock and her left breast was almost bare. Her voice was hoarse and deep, and now and then had a gurgling resonance; her brown throat was now turned to this side and now to that; her eyes had the raving glitter of a Mænid. In the midst of an anecdote which was frankly filthy, although charmingly told, she felt Laudin's rigidly searching glance upon her. She hastily finished her story, and while her hearers broke out in thunderous laughter —(it was the story of a man, obviously known to all present, who had come home very tipsy and had wanted to go to bed with his wife. Pulling back the coverlet, he had seen two women and had begun to lament at seeing double)—while all except Keller, who remained very serious, gave themselves up to orgiastic merriment, she jumped up and stamped her feet and cried out: "This is stupid; this is utterly stupid." With a gesture she commanded Laudin to come to her. He obeyed. She said it was stupid of him to stand there like the Commander in the Mozart opera; she would not permit it; he had no right to throw a shadow over her party; he must drink. She had Ortelli fill a glass with champagne, added cognac to it and handed it to Laudin. "Drink it all!" she commanded and laid her naked arm about his shoulder.

He obeyed.

Again she filled his glass and in the same manner; and again she commanded him to drain the glass. And this time she nestled closer to him, so that he could feel the pressure of her breasts, and she put both of her arms around his neck. In order to drink at all, he had to bend his head far backward. His face had become perfectly colorless and quite wilted. But he smiled. It was the smile of a man whose soul was being sucked from him. Was it the intoxication of her breasts? Was it the wild odor of her hair and body which made him obey? He obeyed and looked about at those grinning, cynical, curious or indifferent faces. As he turned his head a little, he suddenly said in a scared and thin voice: "I beg of you; just one moment, please. . . ." And he looked in the direction of the door, which had opened.

Some one had entered. It was Fraundorfer.

57

Fraundorfer, and behind him Herr Schmidt.

He stood there in his coat, his slouch hat on his head, the thick cane in his hand, precisely as he had left Laudin's house twenty-four hours ago. His face had its expression of watchful sleepiness; he looked diagonally at the floor; his long, disordered, hay-colored hair protruded from under his hat; he had not shaved for days, and his chin especially was covered with grayish stubble. His enormous frame filled the doorway; beside him, Herr Schmidt looked like a white insect.

You could not tell from his expression why, having once entered, he lingered in the door. The reason could hardly have been that he wanted to draw to himself the attention of all present, or that he wanted time to observe the company. It was certainly not his custom to try to achieve a calculated effect, and to take pleasure in its intensification. On the contrary, everything about him betrayed extreme hesitation, and grim discomfort. He loved neither tense moments nor dramatic situations. He had a profound contempt for all the apparently theatrical episodes in life. He had a horror

of calling people to account; the notion of being himself
called to account was contrary both to his intellectual pride
and to the lonely habits of his life. Even as it was something extraordinary that had persuaded him to cross this
threshold, so it must also have been at the inspiration of
some higher knowledge that, having come, he delayed. A
last glimmer of light had evidently to be extinguished.

With a gentle whine Herr Schmidt rubbed his head against
his master's leg. Fraundorfer nodded to the little dog and
began to move in the direction of the table. The baron and
the film actress drew suddenly apart. The laughter, the
drunken babbling and crying had ceased. Fearful and
astonished glances sought that colossus. The fact that he
still kept on his slouch hat made an uncanny effect. He
grasped his cane around the middle, and with the head of
the cane beat thrice upon the table so that the bottles clat-
tered and the cards and glasses danced. Then he stretched
out the index finger of his left hand in Laudin's direction and
said in his hoarse, bass voice: "I didn't put it off, after all.
Herr Schmidt and I went to see the great medicine man to-
day. And it is for that reason that Herr Schmidt and I are
here."

None of the people around the table seemed to find anything comical in either these words or the man himself. They
gazed at him as though his face were a magnet and their eyes
were iron filings. With every second the silence deepened.
All felt that something unheard of had come upon them.
Behind her chair, her empty champagne glass still in her
right hand, her brows contracted, her left hand involuntarily
hiding her naked breast, stood Lou, and gazed now at her
guests, now at Laudin, now at that unknown man who
towered but two paces away from her, like a giant.

Laudin did not stir. His eyes, like Fraundorfer's, sought
the floor. And Fraundorfer, now, without looking at his
friend, gasped his cane with one hand, pointed with the
other toward Laudin, and spoke once more: "You must tell

her who I am. Tell the woman who I am!" Oppressive silence. "You will not tell her? She doesn't seem to know. She doesn't seem to know that I am Fraundorfer."

Lou receded a step. Her face twitched. Fear, rage and indignation rose into her eyes. She tried to speak. Then a noise like sharp thunder was heard to crash. With all the might of his powerful arm Fraundorfer had brought the head of his cane down on the table. Two glasses were in splinters. He raised his lids and his steely glance sought out the pallid woman. "You destroyed him with your poisoned embraces, foul slut!" he cried out to her.

She receded farther; her eyes were torn wide open; she held the glass like a weapon in front of her.

"Confess!" he roared in a voice that vibrated through every one's marrow. "Confess, vile wretch! Confess, or I'll throttle you as though you were a wildcat! Confess that you poured the pestilence into his blood, degraded creature! Confess that you robbed me of him! Confess, you harlot!"

The costumed page had been jolted out of his sleep; he stood by the wall with open mouth and upraised hands. The people around the table looked like a group in wax.

A strange transformation came over Lou. Perhaps it was because horror and fear had gotten hold of her entirely, or perhaps it was because the mere bodily appearance of that huge judge and recorder drove her forth from all her accustomed means of defense; perhaps it was because the enormity of his threat, the unthinkableness of an attack upon her body, almost robbed her of her reason (dark pictures from her earliest past undoubtedly rose before her)—whatever the cause, she began to tremble like an aspen leaf; she let the glass fall on the carpet and bowed her head into her hands and began to cry with the whining crying of a school-girl.

"Ah ha, ah ha," Fraundorfer jeered, "the monster issues a draft against our hearts. He who has made it out and signed it is now supposed to cash it, too. Ladies and gentlemen, who wants to cash it? Ha, you know well enough why you won't open your pockets. Forged check. Forged signature. Documentary forgery. You have eyes, Dyskolos; you have ears. Do you need further proof?"

And turning once more to Lou he asked with a terrible implacability in his tone: "Why did you let it come that far, infernal beast? Tell us!"

Weeping more loudly, Lou drew her head in between her shoulders.

"Why did you stamp upon that blossom?" Fraundorfer continued in a voice that broke and became shrill. "Why did you massacre a father's only son? Why did you steal from him all he had, in the insolence of your sin? Why, woman, why, demon in human form, why did you rob the world of such a being? Is this pig-sty of a world filled with his kind? Why had you no compassion upon him, woman? Why give the pestilence to one whom it was bound to drive out of life? Why, I ask?" His last question was thunderous; he shook his fist in the air; thick rolls of fat hung like tumors over his colorless eyes and, strangest of all, out from the crinkled lids flowed tears.

And suddenly those two faced each other weeping—each at an opposite pole of the world.

Lou raised her white face and stammered almost imperceptibly: "He knew it." It was clear that she lied, that she did not expect to be believed, and that she was only groping for a way out at any cost.

Then slowly Arnold Keller arose. He had the air of a man who is going to make an after-dinner speech or appear before the curtain to inform the audience of a change in program. He laid down his cigar in an ash receiver, briefly cleared his throat and said: "I beg your pardon, sir. I'm going to take the liberty, however, of calling your attention to the fact that this is no criminal court which can examine or condemn a culprit. Nor is it very dignified to be so heated and so insulting. I should recommend a measure of reflection. Remember the saying of Seneca, *magnus, animus remissius loquitur.* I venture to ask you whether this pitiable woman was born with the disease in question? Or whether she produced it in her own body out of voluntary wickedness; or is she not also an innocent victim in her turn? 'Fate lets our guilt upon us come,' it is written; and an even more venerable passage says: 'Deliver us from evil.' Therefore, my dear sir, not so fast and, with all due sympathy for your grief: respect the genius in this woman and recognize the fact that her soul is taboo."

Fraundorfer's answer was a thick gurgle of laughter. He turned aside and croaked, still laughing in staccato fashion: "Herr Schmidt, do you understand that. . . . Help, Herr Schmidt. . . . I must appeal to you, Herr Schmidt; it chokes me . . . it cuts off the air. . . ."

While he was roaring down at the dog, giving the impression that he was suffering from bodily pain, Lou had slipped down to her knees and taken the hand of Arnold Keller and pressed it against her bosom. The white, upturned face was that of a contrite Magdalen. The baron who, like several others present, gradually felt the awe that had held him recede and melt away, murmured with delight at this picture. The film director, completely drunk, got up and clapped his hands as he was accustomed to do when a pose satisfied him completely, and said with a clucking sound: "Bravo! First rate! Shoot! Oh, I say, shoot!"

This cry, in its boundlessly naïve vulgarity, had the quality of a sudden revelation. It laid bare a diabolically intricate web of craftiness, self-deception, histrionic exhibitionism, submission to mere sound and momentariness, and a forgetfulness of all reality—an utter and many-sided unconsciousness. Fraundorfer, considering this for several seconds in somber surprise, suddenly grabbed the brim of his hat, pulled it down almost over his eyes and, turning toward Laudin, said with a strange friendliness: "Dyskolos, I am now going to address a sermon to the stones in the street."

Laudin joined him where he stood: "Yes, Egyd, it is time to go," he said. "Permit me to accompany you."·

Who was this man that uttered these words? He had a voice no one had heard and an aspect no one had seen. Permit me to accompany you. He seemed to be in doubt whether the permission would be granted. His face had aged, and it was moist and ashen. His hands made unmotivated gestures. He stumbled over the threshold. In the anteroom he had difficulty first in finding his coat, then in putting it on. Fraundorfer had to help him. It took him several minutes to button his coat.

A candle had been given them to light their way down. Fraundorfer held it and preceded his friend. His huge shadow covered the landings. At the bottom of the stairs Laudin said: "The knowledge that one has walked down a certain stair for the last time is one of the many communications with death that life has to offer."

"How do you know that it is the last time?" asked Fraundorfer in a hard voice.

"How do you know that you have finished a book when you have turned its last page; how do you know that you will never again drink out of a glass when it is broken? The stair; truly, the stair is but a symbol. But a glass, a book or a stair cannot melt into utter nothingness as a human being who is hopelessly alienated from mankind, from God and from the earth and whose nothingness—oh, is there no stronger word; why are all words so obliterated?—whose nothingness we comprehend so little that we do not become aware of it until we look at the clock of our hearts and see that it no longer indicates the time." He pressed his forehead against the banister but immediately thereafter, ashamed of his weakness, drew himself up stiffly.

"That is fantastical, brother. Come," said Fraundorfer, unmoved.

They were in the street. "Well, now we can try to preach to the stones," cried Fraundorfer caustically, and struck the

stone so violently with his cane that Herr Schmidt jumped
backward with a whine and looked reproachfully at his
master. "Look at his contempt," said Fraundorfer, and
pointed to the dog; "look how full of contempt the beast is.
Wretched crowd, he says to us, melancholy starvelings of
illusion, melancholy vagabonds crowding a melancholy
fair."

"That is fantastic, too, Egyd," said Laudin. His body
was bowed again.

And then he said: "I am no longer living at home. I
am living with Mrs. von Damrosch. Pia has arranged it.
Pia and I will probably part."

Fraundorfer murmured something incomprehensible.
Silently they went the short distance which they had to go.
But it was evidently hard for Laudin to walk at all. "I'm
cold," he said. Then he proposed shyly that Fraundorfer
stay with him. To sharp ears the proposal was an insistent
plea. Fraundorfer growled again, but the growl was a growl
of consent. In the same oppressed and overmodest tone,
Laudin then told him that in the morning he would have
to confer with a remanded prisoner. It was a student whom,
quite involuntarily, he had helped to push along the downward path. Some one of whose fate he was not wholly
guiltless. He would have to talk to that man. Then he
had another errand. Then, at eleven, there was an important
session in court for him to attend. He must get to Konrad
Lanz as early as eight o'clock; before that he would have
to see the judge or get him on the telephone for permission
to see the prisoner. Hence the time during which he asked
for Fraundorfer's society would, after all, be only a few
hours.

All these remarks seemed to make Fraundorfer thoughtful. He put his arm through Laudin's and helped him to
drag himself onward. The streets were utterly empty.

At last they came to Laudin's new dwelling. Not without difficulty, they used the several unaccustomed keys.

Broodingly, Laudin looked about him at the room which was hung in blue. At the foot of the bed stood the trunk which Pia had sent. And, considering all the incomprehensible things that had come to pass since that afternoon when Laudin had first stood in this room; he murmured as he had done then, as though the sight of the trunk mechanically produced in him an identical psychical reaction: "So this is Pia. . . ."

He let his coat fall and himself dropped into an armchair. Fraundorfer also took off his coat, threw his slouch hat on the floor, spread his huge body over a chair and bent massively forward, leaning his chin upon his cane.

Herr Schmidt, silent as ever, the moist devotion of his glance upon his master, lay down between the two men.

Hours passed; the dawn came; then the daybreak. The sun began to shine. Neither of the two men slept and neither spoke.

58

At half-past eight o'clock Laudin entered the room in which Konrad Lanz was being held. He had already conferred with the judge. Since a lawyer for the defense had hitherto neither been appointed by the court nor demanded by the accused, Laudin hardly needed the influence of his name to get to Konrad Lanz. The judge had been courteous and helpful and had permitted Laudin to read the stenographic reports of the preliminary examination.

The cell was dark and rather small. The coverlet on the iron bedstead was not quite clean. The barred window was open. It gave on the courtyard around which stood a huge mass of buildings. Aside from the distant rumor of the city starting upon its daily life, all was still.

Lanz sat beside a rickety little table. An open book lay before him. His face was so emaciated that the rectangular cheek bones protruded and the cheeks had become mere hollows. Even the beardless lips seemed to have sunken in.

The face was an ascetic face, severe and silent, no longer that face of a suppliant which dwelt in the memory of Laudin. This circumstance alone gave the conversation a turn which could not have been foretold, but which profoundly confirmed Laudin in the impulse which had brought him here.

He said that he had full information. He was not only willing but determined to act as Lanz's counsel. It was true that criminal cases were rare in his practice. Nevertheless, he would make this cause his own to the utmost extent of his powers, even though he could not appear personally at all stages. To-day, at least, he couldn't say whether he would be able to do so. Various things had taken place in his life which might necessitate a complete change in his arrangements, the precise character of which he could not yet foretell. If, then, it should be impossible for him to be always personally on the scene, he would nevertheless be consultant, and work through a thoroughly authorized representative. He assured Lanz that he considered this his duty. His interest in the matter was not merely professional. His motives were of another kind. It was unnecessary to explain them. He begged Lanz to realize that he had not appeared in order to confer a favor, from the vantage point of his position, upon one who was pursued by and defenseless against society. He had come—he said this hesitatingly—at the urge of an inner necessity and out of a feeling of community in guilt.

Lanz seemed surprised. Not excessively, only superficially. Perhaps it was because at this moment no human communication entered deeply into his consciousness. Laudin was much more surprised when the young man, after staring intently at the floor for a while, declined his offer. Laudin, naturally, asked for his reason. Lanz answered that the notion of any defense gave him a feeling of discomfort. If his wishes and conclusions were followed there would be no defense at all. The thought of implicating a friend whom he so honored in this matter, which he considered quite hopeless from the start, only gave him an additional and unnecessary pain. He was reconciled to his fate. He was wholly at one with himself. His fate was sealed and his life ruined. It mattered little to him what kind or length of punishment was to be meted out to him.

Laudin objected that this mood of spiritual self-annihilation would not last, and ought not to be taken as a norm for the future. The mind has its ebb and flow like the tide.

Lanz shook his head. He was sure that there would be no change in him. He had always been quite clear as to the possible consequences. From the first moment on, in fact. The game had been a dangerous one. The stake had been his head. The head being lost, what sense would there be in trying to save the arms and legs?

With a veiled look Laudin replied that with an emotional logic of this kind there was a danger of undermining the entire structure of justice. Not only the existing and, as he freely confessed, very faulty human structure, but also the very idea of a possible higher justice.

Lanz assured him that he believed neither in a higher justice nor in any possibility of development.

Laudin's answer was no answer at all; it was a conventional phrase. The ground under them began to shake. He himself had caused this to come about. Secretly, to be sure. A man does not realize the number of his own conventional attachments until others begin to throw theirs aside.

Lanz said that his greatest sin had been something like relying on a miracle. Toward the end he had balanced fate as on a knife's edge: benefactor of humanity and pillar of the scientific world, or else condemned counterfeiter and jailbird. He had had no time for long paths or slow decisions. He had been like a runner whose breath gives out just before the goal and who jumps into an automobile in the hope that he will not be observed. "Impatience is always foolish," he added. The fact was, however, that science had reached a point where hundreds of men were bound for the same goal. He who reached the goal first was not always the chosen of fate, but the most determined and the coolest. His words had the dryness of a chronicle. He had been on the point of discovering the secret of the artificial production of sugar. He said this in a way that assumed Laudin's appreciation of the enormous importance of such a possibility. He indicated briefly: it would cause a complete transformation in man's economic life. But now he lay, hurt to death, upon that field of battle. This, too, shone through his words. All that he said was tinged with the spontaneous pride of something absolute. Like many scientists, he nursed an unconditioned adoration of science, a complete faith in its processes. When Laudin shyly suggested that the very importance of his end should have made him doubly careful in his choice of means, a sudden flash spread over his cadaverous face and he began, in curiously disjointed sentences, to speak of his life, the very foundation of which had had, to use his own expression, something macabre about it. It wasn't so much a question of hunger nor of uninterrupted humiliation. There was always the feeling of squeezing by night through the fence into some one else's yard. Always crushed against the wall—at college, at the university, in the laboratory. Always dependent on chance favors. Every book a favor, every retort a favor. Each semester had started with petitions—written petitions, personal petitions. You had to assure others that you were humble and worthy and, at the same time swear that you were decently average and under no circumstances had ambitions that did not become your station. For all society is stricken with the fear that some one might leave the trodden road and strike out upon a new path. The worst had been the actual earning of bread as copyist, tutor, coach. Every hour lost in this wretched fashion had finally hurt him like a wound. The feeling that time was running away from you was worse than actual want. The conquests of science into unchartered territory were growing with each day; each day knowledge expanded and interpretations shifted; great minds were continually at work; the neglect of an apparently unimportant fact could leave you far behind and reduce you to the position of a man discovering again the thrice-discovered. There stands nature, pregnant with her secrets; to decipher a single one often takes all the years of a man's life. But nature, stubborn and miserly, will not give up a secret if you do not woo her without ceasing, and pledge her the blood of your heart. He had done that. So much he could assert with a calm conscience.

The question might be raised, Konrad Lanz continued monotonously, what was the value of a man's heart's blood; it was no article of merchandise and society tagged it with no price. Nevertheless, he had undertaken, at the command of an inner decision, to transform into glittering coin a performance without exchange value upon the marketplace. He had anticipated an exchange value for it. He had borrowed against it, so to speak. He had, as it were, taken out a mortgage on a house of which only the foundations were laid. Had he been able to finish building it, there would have been no doubt of his solvency. He had borrowed from society; to be sure, he had had no visible security. The state was obviously the biggest and most unscrupulous of all counterfeiting concerns. Behind the notes it issued there was a promise, and this promise was generally a lie. Well, he had driven that same trade for a little and had increased the millions of lying paper rags by exactly fifteen. Imagination was paralyzed by the monstrousness of the comparison. An analogy: A man bombards Mt. Everest with fifteen pebbles. He is dragged to prison for trying to cause an earthquake. Oh, yes, of course, he knew exactly what Dr. Laudin would answer and would have to answer. If all the citizens of a state were to do the same thing, all society would fall into its component atoms. Each man would be a Morgan and a beggar at once; the cow would be feeding upon itself instead of on the grass. The present order of the world was such, that in a case like his own, the law was bound to become a very fury and tear the transgressor pitilessly limb from limb. For to show him any mercy was equivalent to a *reductio ad absurdum* of the entire system. In brief, society had either to condemn him wholly or, since his particular crime would not be acknowledged as such by any eternal tribunal, let him go wholly free. Since the law chooses not only to ignore but to protect, on the one hand that which, on the other hand, it seems to persecute in its most cruel manner, the individual's feeling of justice was bound to wither and die. "In the outer world you are condemned. In the inner world of the soul you are pardoned, you are somehow, and by some voice, freed of guilt. What a condition! The written law outlaws me forever, robs me of work, honor and reward. The living spirit within me cries. A wrong is being perpetrated, a wrong against life and against the spirit of man itself!"

Yet he was resigned. He recognized that he had wronged the community, somehow. He was conscious of it. Only he found it hard to determine the boundary line between inner justice and outer injustice. He sat there, tormenting his brain. "Where lies the truth? Does it lie in my despair and my desperate defense, in the fear for my mission and the relief that I sought, or does it lie in the implacable letter of the law, in this petrified concept which crushes my whole existence by merely stretching out its arm toward me, and annihilates me completely whether it visits me with its severest measures or permits some shadow of mercy to be wrung from it." That was why he was not interested in shadings. They could do him no good.

The man's soul was torn and tormented in an unheard-of fashion. A broken man, he sat before Laudin and, retracing the path that he had gone, sought with a disturbed and most unquiet conscience to gather the fragments of himself. He seemed to be talking for the sake of his own mental clarification. Hesitatingly he started again. "Now you're here with me, Doctor; you've been good enough to come . . . it's very queer . . . but when you entered it seemed to me as though you had never been away from me for long. It was like this . . . this very night . . . you seemed really to be here. No, I'm not fantastic; I don't see ghosts. On the contrary, my mind has always been hard and rationalistic and has had no place for dreams. To be sure, quite recently . . . to save as much as possible, you see, to use the counterfeited money only for the most indispensable things, I have been living almost entirely on bread and potatoes. I often felt as though I didn't have proper blood in my veins. Last night, after the preliminary examination, I dropped on this bed here and everything went black before my eyes. I thought I was going to faint. But it wasn't that. Out of the blackness there rose a radiant circle. Suddenly I found myself in an immeasurably lofty chamber vaulted by an equally high cupola. On the sides toward the south, the west and the north, there opened three mighty, arched doors. On the east wall of this temple there stood a throne. Upon the throne sat a majestic figure, wrapped in purple. Instead of a face it had a mask of gold. I knew it was the Judge. Through each of the three great doors endless streams of human beings entered into the temple. I was in the midst of them. They were people of all stations and classes, of all races and zones of the earth, men, women, children, the aged, youths and girls. They uttered no sound nor even a murmur, but all, like myself, were penetrated by a single emotion. What that emotion was I cannot describe. It was, at all events, an emotion of great power, and it seemed to be half one of reverence and half one of beseeching. We all believed in that figure wrapped in purple; our whole fate depended upon it; it inspired us with a trustfulness of religious depth. I was among the first and, as we came near to the throne, we threw ourselves upon our knees and the many, many thousands behind us followed our example. And now from those many, many thousands of throats there rose a single great cry: Justice! And in that cry there was a dread of yearning and desire, a longing and a certain expectation which shook one to the very depth of one's soul. The figure remained silent. No fold of its purple garments stirred. And again, after a heart-breaking pause, that unbelievably heart-breaking cry: Justice! No answer from that one above. And I, I could endure it no longer. I knew that all these men had been driven hither by a great terror, the terror of something horrible, from which they had fled and which would assuredly overtake them if they were not granted that which they besought. And so a bitterness came over me against that dumb form wrapped in purple; I grasped the mantle and tore it off; the mask of gold toppled and fell, and what we saw was a skeleton. Then a voice began to speak and this is the strangest thing, Dr. Laudin. It was your voice. But I was no longer in that enormous temple with its cupola, but in a common lecture hall. I sat with other students hearing you lecture. You were pointing to the skeleton and to the purple mantle that was lying at your feet, and you were saying: The time is past when this dead skeleton was a god and a judge. This god, as you see, has decayed and his living law has moldered into dust. We have forgotten to feed that god with the living substance of our soul. For that reason he has become a thing of bones. We have neglected to breathe new breath into his icy body. Thence our sufferings and doubts and our despair. You said that in your ordinary, everyday voice. I can hear that voice this minute. I knew, then, that there was no way of helping me."

He fell silent. His expression had something visionary and at the same time extinguished. Since Laudin looked down embarrassed and also silent, he murmured: "It was no dream. It was as real as the fact that you are sitting here now."

Laudin said: "I am willing to assume that it was no dream. Dreams are not apt to be so symbolical. Let us assume it to have been a vision of truth. In the end I could say similar things . . . or think them. In any event, it seems to point the way. Provided, of course, that one can summon a faith in the resurrection of this god. These are possibilities which, in my opinion, are excluded from the lives of any one now living, unless he were to break with everything that lies behind him. It is a very inclusive thing, justice. An idea. Right, that is something else. Right is a tool. A very earthly thing. Very accessible and very plastic. But to establish a proper relation between right and law is as difficult as to establish such a relation between punishment and guilt. That relation should be wholly valid and is full of contradictions. It should be wholly pure and is full of impurities. Demands for penalties that are too rigorous destroy humanity just as surely as neglect or venality or the custom of bribery. Rigidity is hostile to progress. I can imagine a time, a very distant one, to be sure, in which the concept, punishment, will sound as remote and barbaric as the notion of legal torture seems to us to-day. Many have come to me to find justice—far, far too many. I had to console them and put them off as best I could and dared not to lay hands of violence upon that purple robe. I had to feed them on formulas, on stop-gaps, on equivocations. Man becomes inured to nothing as quickly as to the inadequate. But that vision of yours, or whatever you choose to call it, may help to point the way. Whether it can help me is another question. As far as I am concerned it is probably far too late."

He arose, and breathing deeply, he added: "Every time that right is executed or comes to pass, it is probably only the compassion of some higher being which, contrary to our mortal intention, has penetrated into our minds and works in them."

"A hopeless enough saying," Konrad Lanz said sadly.

"Yet I know none that contains more of hope," Laudin replied with an unintentional double meaning.

Therewith he went, silently determined to include the unhappy man, even though against the latter's will, in that small circle of entrusted business that still remained to him.

59

Fifteen minutes later he arrived at the house in which Brigitte Hartmann lived. He had forgotten the address and had been forced to call up his office for it.

A dirty-looking charwoman ushered him into a large, desolate room, which seemed to be at once a parlor and a children's playroom. All kinds of toys were to be seen about; slack, gasless balloons, picture books and paper helmets. These things lay about on the green rep chairs and on the cheap carpet.

The door opened. Brigitte Hartmann appeared. Scarcely had she recognized the visitor than she uttered a cry and disappeared once more. Not until several minutes later did she return, this time with a many-colored shawl about her shoulders, and a snood of silver ribbon, which gave her a most comical appearance, holding her hair together above the forehead. After ten years' exile at Hartmannshof she had, in her own special way, to be sure, readopted the customs and the fashions of the city. Astonishment, shy joy, restless surprise, and the traces of an evil conscience flickered over her coarse features. All she could do was stammer. She put a chair in the middle of the room and eagerly brushed the seat. She went to the window, pulled at the curtain, came back, moved the chair to another place, said something about illness, the unexpectedness of the visit, the earliness of the hour, and all the time anxiously avoided looking at her caller. Her excitement grew. Finally she asked in an unnaturally loud tone of voice whether she could not offer the doctor a trifle—some bread and butter, a little glass of slivovitz; it could be gotten at once; it was no trouble at all; it would give her the greatest pleasure.

Laudin said: "Let us waste no time in trivialities, Mrs. Hartmann. I can easily explain the reason for my visit. I don't even know whether an explanation is necessary. You have probably heard or read yourself what has happened to Konrad Lanz."

An understanding gleam came into Brigitte Hartmann's face. Certainly, Doctor. Of course, Doctor. Naturally, she had read the accounts. She and her cousin had discussed it all evening yesterday. She seemed suddenly liberated as from a nightmare. The evil conscience was forgotten and she looked at Laudin with radiant triumph. Well, now what did the doctor think of that? Forging banknotes! That was roguery for you; that was scoundrelism. Hadn't she always prophesied that those people would come to an evil end? She had a good scent for such things; she knew their kind; no one was going to take her in. It was all sun-clear now. Now the doctor could see how pure her intentions had been. Now he would admit the bitter injustice that had been done her. She was happy, now. More happy than she could say. She could weep for happiness. It might sound a little heartless, to be sure; the misfortune of others should be revered. But since now—she thanked God and all his saints, and she was going to light a votive candle at the altar in the church, although she wasn't any of the extra-pious, not to speak of bigotry, of course—but since now her innocence had come to the light of day, no one could grudge her the bit of joy that it brought her. Didn't the doctor think so, too? If you please. . . .

The torrent of words died. The arms akimbo dropped. Her glance wandered into the corners of the room, came back, fled again, found no object and finally returned, full of fear and dread, to the commanding glance of the man before her.

Laudin had put both hands upon her shoulders. Nothing else. He gazed at her. Nothing else. His face had the expression of a profound and sacred and pain-touched earnestness. The pressure and the burden of this man's hands resting upon her shoulders was so great to Brigitte Hartmann that it seemed to be about to break her. It is perhaps not too much to say that her soul embodying itself in her physical being caused this pressure to tame and to disarm her wholly.

"On the day when you stole that will from your husband's desk," said Laudin, in a whisper, yet with a sharp and clear emphasis upon each word, "was it not clear to you, Brigitte Hartmann, that by that deed you destroyed the existence of two human beings, a mother and a child?"

Brigitte Hartmann's face turned as yellow as straw. "I . . . I . . . I . . .," she stammered, also in a whisper, but got no further.

"And though you may have been strong enough or insensitive enough not to feel the effect of this death sentence of which you were guilty," Laudin continued in the same whisper, "whence did you summon the courage to appear before me and to appeal to me for protection?"

"I . . . I . . . I . . .," the woman stammered, and now that yellowish pallor had reached her very eyes.

"The crime cannot be repaired, but it can be expiated," said Laudin, and his two hands weighed like heavy stones upon the shoulders of the woman. "I am convinced that you really desire me to consider you and to respect you as a fellow-creature, Brigitte Hartmann. At least, I have that impression. I am willing to show you the way that you must take in order to appear in my eyes and in your own as a woman who has a right to a share in the respect of her fellow-men."

Brigitte Hartmann had probably never heard such words in her life. It is to be assumed that the silent confession in her face, that the confused obedience which her demeanor expressed, were far less the issue of a moral collapse, or of submission to an overwhelming moral influence, than of a typical hysterical state. This condition, however, was in itself the result of that poverty of the heart, that frost of the spirit, that alienation from all tenderness, reverence and human kindness, which has become too common a phenomenon among women of her kind and class for them ever to reflect upon it, to be troubled by it, or to complain to fate concerning it.

"What must I do, Doctor?" she barely breathed; "what do you demand of me? I'll do anything. . . ."

"I demand that the estate of your husband be equally divided between yourself and Caroline Lanz. That is, I think, a very fair demand. In my presence you will write to the bank and direct it to transfer the sum in question to my office. So soon as you have done that, I shall have the account released. I'll dictate the letter to you now."

From the brief-case which he had laid on the table he took out a fountain pen and a sheet of paper. With the obedience of a marionette, Brigitte Hartmann sat down at the table, took up the pen, and with trembling hand wrote what he slowly dictated. When she had signed her name, he folded the letter, put it in his pocket, and said, with a bow as though he were taking leave of a great lady: "This is the last episode of our acquaintanceship, Mrs. Hartmann. We both have reason to congratulate ourselves that our relations have found so excellent a close. Good-bye."

These poor and pedantic phrases fulfilled the same function in his case that, let us say, a stout cane fulfills in the case of an utterly exhausted man who is forced to a last activity.

Brigitte Hartmann gazed after him with glassy and astonished eyes. She listened to the dying fall of his steps. Then she uttered a short, slightly mad laugh, which sounded like the clucking of a hen, and dropped into a chair.

60

In spite of his exhaustion, Laudin still found the strength to do the one thing that remained for him to do upon this day and which, undoubtedly, seemed to himself the most indispensable of his actions.

Doubtless, he could have taken another way of attaining the purpose which he had in mind and concerning which, for some reason, he did not give an exact accounting even to himself. He could have chosen a way that was less public, less provocative, less exposed to the misinterpretation of evil tongues. Had he been in a more equable mood, let us say, in a more trivial and perhaps more worldly frame of mind, he would himself have summoned the doubts which, later on, even the best inclined of his friends did not feel it possible to dismiss.

There was a great deal of talk and a great deal of newspaper discussion concerning the case at that time. It was certainly most unusual for a lawyer of the highest reputation and of the greatest influence to refuse to continue to represent his client in the very courtroom and on the very day of the trial. Yet a curious actuality of interest clung to his procedure. A few weeks before, the very same thing had happened at a notorious trial for fraud in Rome. There, too, an advocate of high rank and repute had declared himself unable, at the last moment, to represent the interests of his client properly, since a renewed and careful study of the documents as well as an examination of his own conscience had convinced him that he could not plead the cause with that conviction which both he and his client had the right to demand. At the same time and quite independently of these real events, a play appeared upon many stages in many countries and was widely discussed, in which the same conflict appeared.

The point that was especially debated was, whether from a human or a professional point of view, a lawyer had the right to act so, especially at so dangerous, not to say fatal, a moment for all concerned, as the beginning of the trial. Although the litigation from which Laudin withdrew at the last moment was, on the face of it, not sensational in character, but a mere civil process concerning money and inheritances, yet his theatrical throwing over of it stirred up a surprising amount of dust. Public opinion was divided between indignation and half-suspicious amazement. The matter was connected with the not very honorable rumors which were beginning to be current about Laudin, and which now came into the open, as vermin will scurry forth from an abandoned house. Later the chamber of advocates took up the matter and produced a whole series of expert reports and learned pronunciamentos.

Laudin himself didn't think of the consequences of his act. On the day and at the hour of the event he had, in fact, no power to think or reflect. Never before, perhaps, had he acted to such an extent under the influence of an imaginative compulsion. It was like the inevitable running down of a mechanism. When the machinery has done its appointed work, it simply stops. His conflict had little to do with the case that was to come into court on that day. The case of Altacher versus Ernevoldt had become indifferent. What he cared about was the scene, or even more, the image of it, graven into his brain. Trivialities were more decisive than the nature of the case which was about to be judged. The offices and the courthouse flooded his mind with joyless memories. This air so pregnant with dust and mold, had it not on innumerable occasions paralyzed aspiration and throttled the purity of the will? These numbers and names on the doors, these printed notices on the walls of the corridors —the eye had glided over them numberless times and had the impression of the hoary and the outworn, and of the hopelessness of endless repetition. There is a No. 17. It looks and has always looked like a man who has been beaten till he is crooked and grasps a pole for support. Eternities have gone by (so it seems; the actual time may have been a year) since the announcement of the magistracy shows a repulsive brown splotch in the midst of the printed text. The fourth flight of stairs on the second story is more hollowed out by footsteps than any other. It has been a source of annoyance a thousand times that, at one place, the banister is full of splinters and scratches one's hand. There are the faces of the court attendants, which never change. There are the secretaries and clerks, who have a self-important way of being confidential. There is the window of the house opposite where, for years and years, a bearded man in a little cap has been standing and filling his pipe, as though he had never, at any time in his life, done anything else and had looked that way since the day of his birth.

In the twilit corridors the litigants are sitting, silent, patient, modest, resigned. You had the impression that, for years and years, the same people had taken up their dwelling here in order to wait, just in order to wait. It is like an anteroom to hell, the hell of waiting. The act of waiting lends them a specific expression of wretchedness which is the same on all these faces. Waiting has made them weary and indifferent and soulless. Waiting is their fate. They look at the numbers. No. 17, or No. 46 (the latter looks like a rheumatic old woman trying to sit down), or at the names of referees or secretaries or judges, and at announcements and notices; and their imagination and their desire to live have slowly withered.

It seemed to Laudin as though he were walking down between two rows of his clients, men and women. There was no end to those rows. They had gathered as on a day of memorial. They stood there like shades and he, equally a shade, passed on between them. All looked at him expectantly; all demanded of him order in their lives and measured justice and their due. But he was no judge; he had no power over the law. He never concealed from them his powerlessness, the inadequacy of the intermediary or middleman. But they shook their heads and were of the opinion that for their sakes, that is to say, for the sake of each individual, he could play some little trick on the law and hasten the decision that was to redeem them. Their impudent delusion wounded him; their demand, repeated a thousand times, bored him to the point of pain; nevertheless, he was courteous and helpful and thought of ways out, because he knew that they were waiting, waiting, waiting. What were they waiting for? For a slothful mass to be set into slow motion over there in Room 20; for innumerable documents to be passed in review and unspeakable human suffering to be registered letter by letter. He was driven to the belief that the angels in heaven and the devils in hell also did nothing but wait, while here souls begged for admission and yonder the fiery kettles seethed.

Was that all that he had accomplished for more than twenty years—to wait with them that were waiting? And for this, his reward had been an unfailing income, securities in the bank, a house and a car, reputation and popularity.

One must not earn money with half justice, with justice that miscarries, with justice that fails, with justice that is its own contrary. Though he could say to himself that he had, to the best of his ability, defended the ignorant and the defenseless against the arbitrariness and false assumptions of those powers of stone, yet he had himself become too profoundly the victim of those powers to continue to draw self-respect from so poor a consolation.

The upshot of it all?

He suddenly remembered that in this particular section of the corridor between Rooms 62 and 24 (how singular that it's just this not very significant nor very important recollection that overtakes him now), that, about eight or nine years ago, an excited client had come up to him and had said: "Do impress the fact on the judge that it is this one thing and nothing else, which has destroyed my life and my happiness, this one thing alone: the way she let her stockings drag around her feet at home. Out in the world she was a fashion-plate; I had to pay for the latest things from Paris; at home she stumbled over her dirty stockings. I can't

stand it any longer; I shall go raving mad if I have to continue to see those stockings bunched around her ankles."
Of course, the man's suit for a divorce was dismissed; perhaps he had always been crazy, since he could not assign any
other reason for his morbid hatred. The fact remained that
he killed himself next day. On account of the stockings. But
those stockings do certainly symbolize the many trivial and
ridiculous things which destroy life and liberty just as surely
as an officially correct tragic action involving faithlessness
and murderous revenge.

He had nothing to show but facts like these, only the long
chain of his half defeats before the brutality of the real. He
had done much, and effected nothing; his will had been good,
his results had been ill. Everything had been partial, nothing
had been whole; he had brought proselytes to the purple
and helped to conceal the skeleton beneath. For he, if no
other, he should have known that there was nothing but a
skeleton beneath. (Confused by his own experiences, he
had made the symbol of another's vision his own.) Thus had
fate shown a logic hard as adamant, by causing him to crash
with head and heart against that very embodiment of the living lie by permitting an identical and pestilential poison to
bring bodily death to one on his radiant upward course, and
to corrode the mind and eternally darken the path of him who
was already on the downward slope.

The judgment had gone forth and had become law.

His sadness was as deep as a well; it penetrated deeper and
deeper into his being and reached the region where there
was nothing but the blackness of death.

When, standing in military erectness at the lawyer's table,
his face as white as plaster, he had announced his fateful
decision, it had seemed to every one as though he were not
addressing the court, but exclusively that Dr. David Kerkowetz who faced him in his weighty triumph, and as though
his separation from this cause was, in truth, nothing but an
ultimate separation from the other lawyer's person and do-

main. May Ernevoldt had not appeared. Bernt Ernevoldt could not even be found to be served with a summons.

Not far from Kerkowetz, Constance Altacher was sitting. She was dressed in mourning and had raised her black veil. She looked at Laudin with the great, pushing, restless, truthless eyes of a patient sufferer. That special phenomenon was vividly before him again. There was that conceit, that conceit of grief, of knowing better, of having higher sources of knowledge—that conceit which, in its self-indulgence, breeds hatred, stupefies the people, degrades the nations, that eyeless, imageless, rayless and invincible conceit, triumphant in the end, at least in this world of appearances, and here and now with Laudin's help and at his decision.

For here only the defeated could be victorious.

Then he drove home, that is to say to the apartment of Mrs. von Damrosch, and went to bed, with a high fever. He succeeded in concealing his condition from the old lady. But rather late that evening, when the leaden twilight in his brain had yielded to an empty dreaminess, he heard a careful knocking at his door.

It was Pia who came from Egyd Fraundorfer.

61

All afternoon she had walked about the house, restlessly, from room to room. She had had a kind of silent explanation with herself; it was a weighing and a viewing of issues that employed her. Perhaps she was considering how all these rooms and the complicated things that filled them had robbed her of life and freedom; perhaps she was trying to ascertain whether she had not given too much of herself to all this. Or perhaps she already knew that it had been too much, and measured and estimated and wondered and regretted. About her there was an air of leave-taking and of farewell, as though she were saying: Enough of this; we must now begin with something else. She visited the cellar and the attic and various storerooms and was amazed at the amount of dead things that were heaped up. She had the idea that every woman were carrying about on her own back just such a load of useless things, which had rusted or moldered in vain, waiting for some purpose. A woman might not notice this accumulation, because it took place with treacherous gradualness. But one fine day she might break down under the burden. Quite modestly and quietly, and to her own surprise, she might one day find herself throttled under such a mass of unworthy and thankless trash. There were boxes stuffed with old newspapers, broken toys, photograph frames, broken porcelain, and ink-wells with holes in them; there were little tables with only three legs, and dolls without a head; there were worn-out trunks, old calendars, torn boots, empty kegs, discarded clothes, moth-eaten rugs, twisted watering-cans, worm-eaten cupboards, and tarnished mirrors. Each of these objects had once had its living present, its justified claim and its speech; each had now become a sad, unworthy burden. Here was a graveyard which women kept out of a foolish sense of duty. As though to nurse skeletons were a task that they had contracted to do; as though rubbish could rearise and offer new delight and use; as though there were no stars in the sky above.

But other things, too, recede and fall away like empty trappings. There comes a new independence, and a condition of straight seeing arises from a brooding astonishment. Each thing within the circle of our vision withdraws to its natural distance from us. But this general rectification and proportioning of life does not take place without a singular pain, nor without gnawing remorse, nor without a care-worn consciousness of neglect that can never be repaired.

During all these hours, Relly followed her mother about. It was after school and she declared that her lessons for the next day were done. She busied herself here and there, but always remained close to her mother. Yet she was most careful to ask no questions and only now and then looked at Pia with a secretly testing glance. "You might do something much more sensible, Relly, than run about my legs like a little dog," said Pia, once. "Something more sensible?" Relly asked with doubtfully upturned nose. "There aren't so many sensible things to do, and the foolish things are sometimes not the least agreeable." That night, at table, she looked at her father's chair, got quite pale suddenly and, choking on a potato as if it had been too hot, she said: "For a whole week, whenever I've thought of him, I've had a feeling of distance and estrangement." She began to cough, and Marlene, who had looked at her plate in austere embarrassment, patted her back with an air both of reproof and superiority. Marlene was filled by a very clear perception of reality. But she would not give more attention to her perceptions and premonitions than inner experience and outer activity forced her to do.

The sisters said goodnight to their mother, but a few minutes later Relly slipped back into the room. For a moment she remained near the door, with her arms hanging down and her eyes blinking strangely. Then, bursting into tears, she fell upon Pia's neck. After drawing back, half in vexation and half in shy pride, Pia was about to soothe the excited girl. But Relly had already drawn herself up, hastily passed her hands over her wet face, hurried to the door and, turning around there, said in a brave and sincere tone and with a tenderly persuasive smile: "There is one thing that you must not forget, mother; you can count on me, whatever comes or goes."

Half an hour later, at about a quarter of nine, Pia dressed to go out. She left the house, went through the desolate suburban street to the tramway station and, wedged in among drunken men who came from the little wine rooms, she rode to a station from which she could reach Fraundorfer's house within a few minutes. Since this visit was the result of mature deliberation, there was not the least hesitation or any sign of nervousness about her gait, or in her expression.

She was ushered into the disorderly study and received by Fraundorfer with a mixture of emphatic ceremoniousness and growling taciturnity, and by Herr Schmidt as a personality whose scent was not familiar, but not utterly alien either, and who could therefore be endured. Fraundorfer had on a greasy dressing-gown, full of ink stains, which robbed his limbs of what contour they had, and made him look like a huge mattress. His face was deeply furrowed, ill humored, full of hostile twitchings and sardonic repressions. A white cloth was tied around his forehead. He said he was suffering from neuralgia. The two white ends of the kerchief projected from his hay-colored hair like two sails which had gotten tangled up in a thicket. Pia thought he looked inexpressibly old. At first she was frightened and it was difficult for her to tell him her simple and easily understandable business.

Fraundorfer did not wait to be asked twice. The complete frankness with which he revealed to her Laudin's condition of mind and soul and the so-called fascination resulting from the far-reaching division in his inner life, had something icily cruel and scornful. He seemed to be discussing the minute characteristics of an historical personage. He spared neither the absent man, nor her who heard him, nor himself. Several times he laughed resonantly and turned, as though waiting for applause, to Herr Schmidt. It was whenever he had used a particularly cutting or crushing turn of speech. Pia grew alternately hot and cold in the course of this pitiless and passionate analysis, which was, at bottom, an act of self-laceration, and a half-tamed outburst of despair over the unforgotten and unforgettable loss of his son. At the very end he changed his tone and recounted to her, coldly and precisely, the events of the previous night.

After a long silence, Pia whispered: "I'm afraid that's much worse than I feared."

"I should say so," Fraundorfer agreed dryly. "I take

it to be the kind of illness from which one does not recover."

Pia quivered. "No," she said, and her smile was both feeble and absent-minded. "I don't agree with you. I don't think the sickness is incurable."

"You may take it as you like," Fraundorfer said rudely. The contradiction of a woman always struck him as something thoroughly improper. "In consideration of the nature of our Dyskolos, I have my doubts. He is one of those people who sticks to the trail with the patience of a well-trained hunting dog. At least, to the idea of it. He has a grim sort of logic. That's clear again from the affair that is exploited in all the afternoon papers——"

"What affair? I know nothing and have read nothing." Pia was frightened.

Frundorfer picked up a paper from the table. "Here you are. Mrs. Blum considered it her business to offer me this latest stew while it was still warm." And while Pia read, not only with her eyes, but with her nerves, the plentifully exaggerated article which described to-day's scene in the courtroom, he rattled on: "I'll grant you, there's a certain style about it. Up to a certain point, I'm almost prepared to be impressed. To take the pot with the soup from the stove and fling it hot into people's faces—there's something about that. But to what purpose, after all? An empty demonstration. And naïve and quixotic, like that whole business with the actress. Yes, yes, Herr Schmidt, you're quite right. Better hold our tongues in that respect. We haven't used our tongue to the best advantage, either, and have ourselves wallowed in many a mire. The bellies of the dwellers in Olympus and Walhalla are shaking with laughter over our swinishness and asininity."

Pia did not hear these speeches. She had dropped the paper on her knees and her glance, glowing from within, penetrated into a new and alien world.

"Ah, most excellent Pia, it is a wretched business," Fraundorfer said, proceeding toward a peroration, "the author of the history of human stupidity has gone into the depths, among the most miserable and the most foolish of the subjects of his discourse. He suddenly started in to be a romantic and went forth, with his ill-digested mysticism, to act the part of Judgment Day. It was a sort of falsified mixture of ethics and literature and plain imbecility! An attempt to gain satisfaction through the imagination! To overwhelm people with the imagination! Oh! Oh! No sobriety! No humor! No realism!"

Undoubtedly his potations had already exceeded the ordinary. An empty, thick-bellied bottle stood on the table. Pia got up. He scarcely noted it, or heard the soft word with which she took leave. Herr Schmidt accompanied her to the threshold. For a while Fraundorfer sat with a dark stare in his eyes. Then he rose heavily. He snorted and shook himself, and lit one of his mighty cigars and sat down with a growl at the desk on which reposed his voluminous manuscript. Sarcastically he regarded the title, put the title page aside, took up a fresh sheet of paper and wrote:

Egyd Fraundorfer
Fellow-Citizen and Contemporary against his Will
Dedicates
This Unfinished and Never to be Finished Work
To his most dear friend
Friedrich Laudin
The Errant Guide and Pathfinder
The Helpless Helper
The Administrator of Men and Things and Selves

62

For two days and two nights, Pia nursed Laudin uninterruptedly. She called in no physician, not only because Laudin had begged her not to do so, but because it was clear to her that his condition was one of depression and exhaustion for which rest was the only suitable cure. She had gotten in touch with the house by telephone. The chambermaid brought her the few things that she needed most. She informed the office by telephone, too. Mrs. von Damrosch offered to help several times, but Pia declined with thanks. Twice a day came Marlene and Relly. They arrived on their way home after school. Pia did not admit them to their father's room. She exchanged a few words with them outside; she soothed them in her serene and superior fashion.

All her helpfulness was inspired by the same serenity toward Laudin; the short questions which she asked him, the answers she made to his questions. She would sit beside the open window with a piece of embroidery or, occasionally, with a book. When she raised her eyes, she let her glance pass thoughtfully over the early green of the tree-tops in the park opposite. At meal times she went into the kitchen and brought the dishes which she had ordered, and which had been prepared according to her directions, to Laudin's bedside. Later, she herself ate, alone in the next room.

Laudin silently followed her with his eyes as she went to and fro, or while she sat by the window or, in the evening, under the shaded lamp. He observed the lovely curve of her forehead, the clearly cut features, the smooth golden hair, the still youthful and flexible figure, and he seemed to be seeking, to be seeking something. At no time did the singular silence between them have a painful or an oppressive effect. But it had an element of expectancy in it and something that pointed to a gradual convergence of significant thoughts.

Finally, rather late on the evening of the second day, when Pia was just about to make some final preparations for the night, Laudin sat up a little in his pillows, supported his head upon his arm and said: "We must make our decisions, Pia. We can't put off any longer doing the things that must be done."

"Haven't you come to your decision, yet?" asked Pia in surprise, or in apparent surprise, and passed the finger-tips of her left hand over her left temple, a frequent gesture of hers, especially when she sat down to converse. "I thought that you had long ago arrived at a conclusion. It doesn't seem to me that there is much to talk about. I suspect that you have really mapped out your road, Friedrich. As far as I am concerned, I have but to agree and submit. I told you that, and I haven't changed my mind. Pretend that you have a client before you. You're accustomed to that situation. You're accustomed to saying: Such and such things must be done. So let me be like a client. I shall obey you as completely."

Laudin looked at her searchingly. "That sounds very sensible, Pia," he answered, "and very considerate and, at bottom, intensely proud. There is more than a little pride in it when one says: dispose of me; I shall do quite as you wish. It is the obverse side of pride, the pride of renunciation, of giving in, by means of which the adversary—forgive me the word, but every explanation creates adversaries—is disarmed and put to shame. But I should not like to be disarmed and put to shame by you. I should like to come to an understanding with you, to a sincere and frank understanding, such as is suitable between two good old friends and companions. I do not know the exact state of your feelings. I do not know the precise attitude with which you are confronting me, nor with what reservations, although you are apparently so trustful, you are placing yourself in my hands."

"Reservations? I really haven't any, Friedrich; I give you my word of honor," Pia assured him.

Laudin continued in his warm, insistent voice: "After all that has happened, I don't want you to believe that I am merely trying to attain to that comfortable male luxury of having you help me toward a clean conscience and to have you erect some blue heaven of friendship over our heads.

I have too much experience in such things, Pia—the most horrible, the most implacable experience—too much, at all events, not to know what lies of consolation and of evasion and of procrastination may not be hidden by the word friendship at such moments of decision as we have reached. If we were friends, what would there be to decide? Friendship needs no decisions. You have nothing like that to fear from me, none of these painful retardations through a dwelling on ideas that are full of misunderstanding and even treachery. I want only to see clearly. I want to know your motives and your judgment and something of your emotional condition, in order that I may adjust both my inner man and my life, accordingly."

Pia made a helpless gesture. "What am I to answer you?" she asked. "You must know how it is; surely you do know it. I don't want to be an obstacle. If you desire to change your life and to rebuild your fate, I simply don't want to interpose myself between you and your determination. I could never forgive myself for that. I could never look you honestly in the eye again. Pride? Oh, yes, perhaps there is an element of pride in that. Do you grudge me the pride that is to protect me from the self-contempt which I should feel, were I to be an obstacle in your path?"

Her eyes had the luster of their own inner depth. Laudin could not take his glance from her. A growing suspense and curiosity took possession of him. It was not her words that shook him out of his disconsolate and fatalistic quietude, but her tone, a certain echo in her tone, a brimmingness which permitted him to suspect the unsaid beneath the said, which thus, but in a beautiful sense, was somewhat less than wholly frank. He wanted to question her. Since she had not the talent of giving herself quite freely and of her own accord, he wanted to help to liberate her from that lack of freedom. It seemed important to him, important above all things. He asked: "May I ask you a few things?" Of course she had no objection. It seemed to her the simplest solution that he should ask and that she should answer. All the while she observed with astonishment his curiosity, his suspense, his sudden vivacity and restlessness. She looked down at herself as if she had become different and strange. Women sometimes have the mysterious sensation of changing wholly within a few minutes, under the watchful eyes of a man; or else they receive from such eyes the certainty and confirmation of a change that has already taken place.

At first he thought that he would have to ask only two or three questions. As a matter of fact he asked a great many. He asked so many that it began to seem as though he had not seen Pia for years, and had heard nothing from her. One question gave place to another, and Pia tried to answer each as well as possible, careful of accuracy and gaining more and more courage from Laudin's glance and demeanor. First he asked her whether she had known the whole extent of his unblessed adventures, when she had persuaded him to move away from home. No, not entirely, she said; only what people had told her, what she had learned from Brigitte Hartmann's malevolent distortions, and more especially what his own behavior and mood had betrayed. With that she had had to be satisfied. The essential things she had learned from Fraundorfer. Strangely enough, it had neither surprised her so much nor stricken her so profoundly as one might think. He wanted to know why this was so. She said that she could not explain it. Somehow or other the revelation had been in her long ago.

He asked her whether she realized how great, how immeasurably great his misfortune was? Almost modestly she replied that she thought she did, that it had rolled upon her like a mountain. He wanted to know whether she realized that it was not a misfortune of definite outline, or an accidental one, not one that had depended upon a meeting with anyone or upon sensual impulses, but one that arose according to the laws of his very mind and was precipitated by life itself? Yes, of that, too, she had had her forebodings;

now she knew it, of course; she was afraid she did not understand it wholly. She lowered her eyes in order to raise them again, attentively and willingly, to his own. He asked her whether, if she had been enlightened by Fraundorfer on the morning of that decisive day she would have spoken quite as she had done, in the same moderate and thoughtfully friendly fashion. Undoubtedly, quite so. And would she, too, he continued, have left him in uncertainty concerning how much she knew, what she suspected and supposed, and not told him even if a dark certainty had tarnished his image in her bosom? She hesitated for a moment and then said that his image had not been darkened for her and could not very well be darkened. But since, by her own confession, she had been full of restlessness and of half knowledge, he inquired why she had not come to him, and why she had not asked for an explanation? To that she could only answer that such was not her way; it was not in her nature. He urged that she might have given him so much of her confidence. Since he did not speak out she would have considered it an unjust attack upon his personality to persuade him to do so. How did she know, he asked, that he was not waiting for her to persuade him. She was sure that he had not been waiting. Perhaps it would have saved him or at least helped him. She replied that their lives had never been carried on after any such fashion. It had never been a question of mutual explanation between them. She knew and had long adjusted herself to the fact that his whole being and activity were endangered by people's many and vain explanations among themselves. Hence, she had long ago attuned herself to stillness and to the absence of disturbance.

He was more and more astonished. There was an expression on his countenance as though he could not grasp the fact that it was really she, Pia, who sat beside him there, the same Pia who for seventeen years had walked the paths of earth with him, smiling, creating order, adjusting and sparing all things, almost wordless and, as was now clear, almost unknown. So that is Pia, he seemed to say to himself, with the same consternation which had overtaken him when he had stared at the trunk. But this time it had the power of a more living revelation. He leaned back among the pillows and pressed his hand against his forehead and reflected. In the meantime Pia moved her chair a little nearer to the bed. After a while he sat up again.

He wanted to know whether she hadn't felt that he had betrayed her. No, she had never considered him capable of betraying either a human being or a cause. If what he had done or, rather, what he had suffered, had seemed to her a betrayal, that is to say, if she had had occasion to doubt his honor and veracity, she would not have asked him to leave the house; she would have left the house herself. She accompanied these words by a strange smile and moved still a little nearer. Laudin was startled. His robust male psychology had not been aware of this distinction; it gave him an insight into the delicacy and strength of her perceptions. But, he objected, as though to test her more profoundly and thus to raise his assurance of her to a still higher point, such a doubt would have been perfectly legitimate under the given circumstances. Why, she asked in astonishment, was he trying to shake the foundations as she had never dared to do? Because he could not acquit himself of all guilt, because it had been his confounded obligation to be frank with her. She shook her head. If he were to begin to talk about guilt, they would slip into gray and pathless regions, she said very seriously, and moved nearer to the very edge of his bed. He had accustomed her and trained her through all the years that each of them was to settle his inner problems alone. If that had not been so, nor continued to be so, neither one of them could have adjusted themselves to the exigencies of life. "But we have exaggerated this silent agreement to a fatal extremity" Laudin cried. "What did you think? What did you imagine? How did you finally adjust your soul?" "I didn't adjust myself in the end," she said. "But since we weren't born as a pair of Siamese twins, I had to reconcile myself to a parting; and since such a thing as fidelity exists and has a meaning only so long as the temptations which beset it are ineffectual, I naturally thought that my time was over and that it was only courtesy and considerateness, and perhaps also a tiny bit of cowardice, that prevented you from telling me the truth. And, above all, I had the feeling that somewhere or sometime along your path you had lost me and had not noticed it, or noticed it too late, and had utterly forgotten that I was there. But that was a little my fault, too. Because I have always taken pains intentionally to get out of the way and to hide in a corner behind mere things, behind stupid, dumb things, you know, and in the end I could hardly expect you to look for me and find me and drag me forth." She smiled, but this smile was touched with pain. "Above all, I said to myself: there must be no noise." She ended with a gesture as though she were spreading a snowy cloth over something that was not quite spotless. "Only no noise, only no presumptuous self-importance. I know how that is and how people will stand around you with their empty lamentations." She was silent and looked at him.

"Well, and now? And to-day?" he asked in a hushed voice and stretched out a tentative hand toward her.

She looked at him. He did not dare to repeat the question. She seemed surprised. Perhaps, at this moment, the question seemed indelicate to her, almost an attack that frightened and confused her. Laudin felt that, felt it remorsefully, as could be seen from his expression. But it could hardly have been this alone which seemed to draw the mists from his countenance and make it appear to shine in the ever more powerful radiance of some unseen source of light. While he was tensely watching Pia, the unknown element in and about her, appeared to him with sudden precision. It was not what she had gradually withdrawn from him in the comfortable customs and daily recurrences of every day;

nor was it what she had possessed of youthful sweetness and early delicacy and springtime bloom and which was now forever gone, so that he would have been but the victim of a delusion of the senses had he tried to grasp it; flattered by a brief dream; no, it was not that either; it was something different and wholly new, a new form, a new eye, a new face, a new mind, which had grown up without his knowledge or his intervention and which now came to companion him, between one moment and the next on the decisive crossroads between his old life and his new.

In spite of the infinite intricacy of the problems that had been brought him and the excessively subtle interlacement of difficult and even tragic characters, he had seen in the last analysis, both as occasion and as outcome, only what was coarse, brutal, hysterical, untamed, morbidly passionate and abnormal. Although he had perceived it at certain times, he had not sufficiently guarded nor kept before his eyes the perception of what an enormous rôle, in any permanent and really inward union, between a man and a woman, is played by their being initially and instinctively upon the same plane and level of spiritual life. In the beginning the union is sensuous; all unions are—always. They wander on and on and believe that they hold each other, and actually it is long since they have been together. A shadow has slipped into the place of the companion. They are in a dream; they are like people who are not willing, at any price, to give up the illusion or their dream. And no spirit, human or divine, could search, and find any guilt in either. But this phenomenon was rare; it was the painful conflict of rare souls. So far, Laudin's vision had at times penetrated. But that the lost and forgotten member of the union, as Pia put it, chooses this shadowy existence only as a disguise, and in mysterious shame, in a deep feeling of its own worth, withdraws voluntarily in order, in the fullness of time, to return on a higher plane, in a more perfected state, riper for comradeships, sweeter in humanity, nobler in every relation to the world—

this was the thing that he had neither known nor experienced nor considered possible. But if this were possible, if such a thing had truly come to pass, then in the face of that, those dreadful phantom furies of his mind could melt away; then it was possible to believe—here his thoughts halted like birds that had flown high beyond their strength—to believe that that marvelous double being concerning whom he had speculated in so many dreary hours, that this being blended of two might in truth have become flesh in his own difficult and once so darkened life. . . .

Was it possible to believe that?

"You ask me what is to be done now," he heard Pia say. "I've thought about it. In the last few days I've done little else but think about it. I will tell you what my opinion is. I will answer your questions." And now at last she took his hand which he had stretched out toward her.

He heard her speaking and what she said had been drawn from the depths of his thinking and of his conflicts. With a kind of intellectual innocence she said bravely and simply the things that he had not dared to admit to himself:

"You must stop living as you have lived hitherto. Your way has not been the right way for you. You must not be a lawyer any more, nor carry on litigation any more, nor have conferences with clients, nor plead in court. You will give up the office or, for all I care, sell it if you like. That is necessary above all things. You must abandon this profession. It is not the right one for you. Or, at least, it has not been the right one for you for some time; I do not know exactly for how long a time. . . ."

"That, dear Pia, is a bold proposal," he replied with passionate surprise and yet with a secret breathing of relief, an enraptured breathing which did not yet wholly trust the possibility of his liberation. "It is a bold diagnosis and a rash plan. But can a man simply throw a calling overboard? A calling like that. Is not every true man born to his calling? And though he may not always feel the continuance of that call, does not life forge him into its chains? It is the pivot of existence; it is the inner spring. What else in the world am I to do? What am I good for?

He mustn't say that, Pia continued; he was good for other things. She was sure that he had higher qualities in him than those which he utilized in his daily slavery. She expressed it simply and trustfully. He had told her once, years ago, to be sure, that he had failed to find his true life's work and task. When, he asked in amazement, when had he said that and on what occasion? She couldn't tell him precisely; it was about the time when he had that notorious case in which one child had been substituted for another; surely, he must remember; he had been uncommonly depressed at that time. Yes, he interrupted her, he did remember. That legal knot had been so hard to undo, and the tangled threads had enmeshed even the judge and the lawyers. Exactly, she said, and it was then that he had said it might have been his mission to create the foundations for a new code of laws. How well she remembered that. It was never too late to change one's direction for a better one. On that now distant day, he had stood before her and had declared that only thus could he serve his country and his people. "But perhaps it is too late, now," he objected. "How can it be too late if you are profoundly determined and if it is the highest necessity of your nature?" "So you consider it a necessity, and the highest of all necessities?" he asked with a singularly watchful air. "I do, indeed."

"But I am chained by many chains, bound by a thousand duties, to business engagements, to the fate of many people; my word has been pledged and my personal credit is at stake. . . ." Oh, Pia knew very well what was at stake, more, perhaps, than he was willing to admit. But then the aim is a great one; it is worth fighting for; it must be won. She pressed the fist of her right hand into the palm of her left. "Must, Pia?" "Test yourself whether it is not as I say; be entirely honest with yourself, Friedrich, with yourself and

[343]

with me." What a power, as of magic, in her who was always so poor in words! Yes, he understands it and realizes it. But men will rise up against him and accuse him of disloyalty. "Let them arise; you must know best." "They will say that Laudin was unequal to his tasks and that he has gone the easiest way and lives merely to please himself." "Those who know you will not say that," Pia cried, "for they know that, unhappily, your mere pleasure in life is not very great, nor yet your talent for life." A smile quivered upon Laudin's weary features. "Whatever we do, the world is careful not to let us withdraw ourselves unstained," he said, "and you must consider, too, that we live according to a certain standard. There are the children; there is the house. . . ." "Very well, we have reached that dangerous point now," Pia answered, "but I will not have you mix up the consideration of mere bread-winning with those other considerations. It goes without saying that the basis of our household must be changed. We must use less money, a great deal less. We must sell or rent the house and take a modest apartment, or send Relly and Marlene to boarding school, and you must retire to the country, either alone or with me. Which it shall be we must wait to decide. You must find inner quietude. That is a task, as well as any other. It almost seems to me as though you must go a-hunting, a-hunting for yourself and you must try to trap yourself again and you will, surely you will."

"Pia!" Laudin cried, shaken to the soul.

"You are not yet forty-eight; you can begin all over again; you shall and you will. And if you desire to have me as your companion in that task, but in that task alone, then. . . ."

Suddenly, silently, she drooped forward. Her head rested on his bosom.

He laid both hands upon her hair.

THE END